BLOOD LUST

Simon spoke to Meghann. "Come feed, my pet."

When Meghann saw the blood trickling from Tommy's neck, all she could think of was how badly she wanted it.

Simon pointed to the bleeding mortal on the floor, and Meghann felt her blood teeth rip through her gums. "Finish him, little one."

Meghann needed no further invitation. She threw herself on top of the mortal and plunged her fangs into the wounds Simon had already made, sucking and tearing at her victim's flesh like a woman possessed. She felt an orgasmic rush go through her body when the blood started pouring down her throat.

No nausea attacked her while she devoured her host, hungrily sucking down all his nourishing, hot blood. She'd almost forgotten what it was like to feed from a mortal, the heady sensation of life force and vitality invigorating her soul while the blood infused her body with dazzling strength. . . .

Books by Trisha Baker

CRIMSON KISS

CRIMSON NIGHT

Published by Pinnacle Books

CRIMSON NIGHT

TRISHA BAKER

PINNACLE BOOKS
Kensington Publishing Corp.
http://www.kensingtonbooks.com

PINNACLE BOOKS are published by

Kensington Publishing Corp.
850 Third Avenue
New York, NY 10022

All Kensington Titles, Imprints, and Distributed Lines are
available at special quantity discounts for bulk purchases
for sales promotions, premiums, fund-raising, and educa-
tional or institutional use. Special book excerpts or custom-
ized printings can also be created to fit specific needs. For
details, write or phone the office of the Kensington special
sales manager: Kensington Publishing Corp., 850 Third
Avenue, New York, NY 10022, attn: Special Sales Depart-
ment, Phone: 1-800-221-2647.

Pinnacle and the P logo Reg. U.S. Pat. & TM Off.

First Printing: April 2002
10 9 8 7 6 5 4 3 2 1

Printed in the United States of America

PROLOGUE

December 17, 1957
New York City

The vampire lay flat on his back, impaled by an ornate, steel fireplace poker sticking out of his chest. It wasn't a mortal blow; the poker had missed the center of his heart but the wound was still enough to render him immobile. He could not move, couldn't even squirm as the nearly forgotten sensation of pain coursed through him.

His assailant's aim might have been off, but she'd been clever enough to drag him to the rooftop. The improvised stake might not destroy him but the sun certainly would if he couldn't get indoors before sunrise.

The vampire inhaled one breath through gritted teeth, hissing at the new agony that slammed through his body.

For long minutes, he forced more air into himself. *Concentrate on inhaling*, he told himself, *mustn't think about the pain*. If he couldn't block the pain, he would die here.

Through deep breaths, the vampire was able to put himself in a trance. Gradually, welcome darkness descended on his consciousness, taking away his pain and fear.

First, he focused on the void, allowed in no thoughts. When his concentration was total, he pushed his soul out of his body. In astral form, he stood on the rooftop and stared down at his helpless body.

The strength needed for astral projection pushed the vampire closer to death, but it was his only chance. He grasped the poker with his soul's hands, deeply thankful for the magic that gave his astral form the ability to move objects in the physical world.

The temptation was to try and yank the poker from his heart but that would be fatal. Everything must be done by slow degrees, allow his body to adapt to the change, not break his concentration.

Patient and beyond pain, the vampire pulled the poker out inch by inch. Finally, he was able to dislodge the poker and throw it off the rooftop. The thing had not even landed when the vampire was thrust back into his body, moaning at the intense pain and ferocious need for blood.

The gaping wound in his chest and blood pouring from his body horrified him. If he did not feed soon, he would bleed to death.

Blood was his only thought . . . everything else, even thoughts of hate and revenge, were shoved to the side. He must have blood to heal his body. The vampire forced himself to sit up.

He glanced at the body of Trevor, the mortal servant who'd been with him for nearly thirty years. He felt no grief at the man's passing, just frustration because the body had already been bled dry by the vampire who'd left him here to die.

The vampire tried to stand, but was overcome by dizziness and nausea. He had to crawl to the rooftop door, despising his weakened condition. How many would rejoice to see him this way, helpless and sick? At the thought of his enemies gloating, the vampire recovered some of his strength and managed to fling open the door, lurching down the steep stairs.

A quick glance at the sky told him dawn was only thirty minutes away. The vampire stood on the front steps of his town house, scanning the dark city street for prey. Damnation! Wasn't New York supposed to be the city that never slept? How could the street be so devoid of humans?

Central Park, he thought desperately. *Surely there'll be some lovers there or maybe a degenerate sleeping on a park bench.* Unable to walk upright, the vampire limped down the block to the great park.

He concentrated on nothing but his need for blood. Dimly he heard some vulgar driver curse him when he crossed the street against the light and the car nearly ran him over. A bitter laugh escaped him . . . what an anticlimax that would be for him, run down in the street like a mangy dog.

The vampire collapsed by a park bench, overcome by nausea. He vomited profusely, more precious blood leaving his body.

"Too much to drink, then?" a masculine voice with a strong New York accent inquired. "We can't have you dirtying the city, fella . . . into the paddy wagon with you."

Deo Gratias, the vampire thought in relief. *A cop!*

"What's wrong, can't get up?" The vampire pulled himself into the fetal position in an attempt to look more pathetic for his prey. He heard concern replace contempt in the cop's voice. "What in the hell happened to you?"

Gingerly, the cop turned the severely wounded man over and gasped at the bright gold eyes and vicious fangs protruding from his mouth.

"No," the cop whimpered, shock immobilizing him. Easily, the vampire stretched one arm up and dragged his prey down to the sidewalk with him. He attacked the jugular vein, greedily sucking down the blood.

He could not have asked for better sustenance than this strong, young man in the prime of his life. The vampire lapped up his prey's blood and strength, feeling them heal him. The monstrous wound in his heart closed, his clammy skin became warm. Pain vanished and power began to course through him once more.

Eyes blazing with triumph, the vampire raised his mouth and glanced dispassionately at the corpse. He'd bled the man dry. That was his custom, even when he was not ill. Why take a meager bit of blood when mortals offered so much more?

Had anyone seen him? It was dangerous to feed on an open street, but the vampire had had no choice. In full command of his senses again, he glanced at the park benches and up into the windows of the high-rises surrounding him. The devil had smiled on him . . . no witnesses.

With no effort, the vampire plucked up the dead weight of the brawny cop and slung him across his shoulder. He threw a cloak over his presence, rendering himself invisible to any mortals he might pass. Walking at his usual rapid speed, he was back in his town house within one minute. Three minutes later, he threw the cop's body, along with that of his unfortunate servant, into the furnace.

His prey already forgotten, the vampire stalked up the stairs to the dressing rooms he'd given his consort—the ungrateful shrew that'd tried to kill him tonight. He observed that she'd taken no jewels or furs when she fled his home. As far as he could see, she'd packed only a few essentials and her deceased father's mementos.

The vampire knew the significance behind the barely touched room. His consort wanted no reminder of him in her new life—she rejected his wealth and all the luxuries he'd bestowed upon her the same way she rejected him and all he stood for.

Their final argument flashed through the vampire's mind. He still couldn't reconcile the sunny-natured, vivacious beauty he'd spent the past thirteen years with to the screaming harpy that called him an evil monster and said he'd ruined her life when he transformed her and she was leaving him so she could learn a better way of life.

The vampire's face contorted into a twisted mask as he considered that last phrase—a better way of life. And why had the girl had such an abrupt change of heart? Who had put this notion of right and wrong in her head? It could only be Alcuin, the vampire's wretched uncle . . . the nemesis that had plagued him all his immortal life.

The vampire controlled an urge to spit as he thought of Alcuin, the medieval bishop turned sanctimonious ruler of vampires, and his pious decree that any who refused to live by his code that vampires not slaughter their mortal prey must be destroyed. But there was one vampire he hadn't been able to stop in four hundred years.

So Alcuin's new tactic lay in appealing to the vampire's consort and her unfortunately active conscience. The vampire had to admit it was a masterstroke . . . convincing his young consort that her only chance at salvation lay in slaughtering her master. For who expects to be betrayed by their lover?

Suddenly, the vampire's icy calm shattered and he turned his fury on the vanity table beside him, tearing it apart with his bare hands and wishing the inanimate furniture were the woman who'd betrayed him. How dare she, full of his uncle's piety, look down her nose and pronounce herself too good for him. How dare she leave him to die without so much as a backward glance!

But he hadn't died . . . the vampire stood up, his lips curving into a sinister grin that would have frightened anyone who witnessed it. Thanks to his consort, everybody was going to think he'd died when the sunlight hit his wounded body and turned him to dust. He'd disappear, the vampire decided. Go underground for a while and rebuild his strength until he was ready to have his revenge against the woman who'd betrayed him and the vile priest that convinced her to leave him.

I'll make you pay, the vampire vowed to his absent consort. *Maybe not tonight, maybe not a decade from tonight. But I promise you the night will come where you beg for death before I'm finished, Meghann O'Neill.*

Forty-one years later
May 3,1998, sunset

"Meghann!"

Lord Simon Baldevar came out of the miserable dream with his consort's name on his lips, his eyes wide and the Egyptian cotton sheets on his bed clutched tightly between clenched fists.

He sat up and leaned against the headboard of the immense tester bed, brushing his thick hair back from his face as he tried to banish the nightmare from his thoughts—no good would come of dwelling on that dark, bitter night when Meghann had left him to die. Instead, he reflected on the events of the past three nights.

Finally, he'd had the revenge he promised himself decades before. He'd found Meghann, and naturally Alcuin came to her rescue. But the smarmy prelate discovered he was no match for Lord Baldevar's new power. Even now, Simon was a bit surprised by the ease with which he'd slaughtered Alcuin.

Of course, with Alcuin dead, it would have been a simple matter to destroy Meghann. Simon smiled, remembering how shocked the girl had been when he threw his ax to the side and told her he had no intention of killing her. Murder had been the furthest thing from his mind when he looked at the beautiful creature lying battle-weary and helpless at his feet.

He felt himself harden slightly as he remembered

how she had looked that one night they were together, emerald eyes awash with tears of shame even as she had returned his kisses and begged for his touch, begged him to take her and make her his. And he had . . . taking her body as well as her blood when he pierced her ivory neck with his blood teeth and allowed the fresh, sweet blood to pour down his throat while Meghann threw her arms around him and writhed in ecstasy.

Unfortunately, their reunion had merely been temporary. Simon had allowed the girl to escape him. A few nights' separation was unimportant. Meghann would, despite all her protests and foolish attempts to avenge Alcuin with the help of her boy-lover friend Charles Tarleton, be back at his side soon enough. If everything had gone to plan, he and Meghann (though he doubted she knew it yet) now had an unbreakable link between them, something that would keep her by his side forever.

In the meanwhile, Simon thought while he dressed quickly in a pair of ancient black trousers and a tan riding shirt, he would take advantage of Meghann's absence and deal with the last obstacle blocking the path to his consort's stubborn heart.

The trapdoor opened and Jimmy Delacroix felt a rough hand grab his hair and yank him out of the pit where he'd been imprisoned all day.

Dizzy as he was from the lack of oxygen in the small, almost airless hole, Jimmy's only consideration was drawing air into his starved lungs, gulping greedily at the blessed air. Thank God he was out of that miserable space where he couldn't sit or stand but had to squat and was wedged in so tight he couldn't even move his fingers without scraping the walls of his narrow prison.

Then Jimmy heard the malignant voice order him to wake up, and his relief changed to horror as he remembered who'd flung him into the pit right before dawn. His terror did more to bring him to full consciousness than the amyl nitrate popper snapped under his nose.

"Bastard," Jimmy gasped, trying without success to pull himself up off the polished wood floor—damned if he would lie at the vampire's feet like a dead fish. He glared, keeping his eyes fierce and hard. He knew better than to let this thing that thrived on pain see how sick he was, how his bones ached from being stretched on a rack the night before, how the burning pain from having his fingernails ripped out with a hot pincer made him want to lean over and vomit. If the vampire sensed his misery, it would lean down to drink his blood like it had done the night before, growing strong not just from his blood but his agony.

Damn you, Jimmy thought, glowering at Lord Baldevar—the vampire Maggie had run from forty years ago, the rotten son of a bitch who'd snatched her from her family, transformed her against her will, and forced her to live with him until the night she managed to escape him.

Jimmy shivered as he remembered Maggie's reaction when she found out the thing was still alive. It was the first time in the six years they'd been together that he'd seen Maggie show fear. Not that she'd behaved scared around Jimmy . . . she always put on a brave face for him, so he wouldn't be frightened. But Jimmy had heard her whimper and scream during the day while she slept; heard her piteous cries when she screamed out, *"Don't! Don't! Simon, please don't hurt me!"*

But Lord Baldevar had hurt her and that was Jimmy's fault. What a fool he'd been to storm out of the house because he and Maggie had some stupid fight. The vampire had been waiting for him and it used Jimmy as bait to trap Maggie. It tortured Jimmy because it knew Maggie would come to his rescue.

Why hadn't it killed him last night, after it snatched

him out of Maggie's grasp? Did it want to torture him some more? Jimmy shivered, remembering all the sadistic punishments he suffered before Maggie found him and the thing stopped hurting him in favor of toying with her.

Lord Baldevar gave him an icy smile and sprawled in the only chair in the room. "Mr. Delacroix, I'm glad to see you've regained your facilities. You'll need them for our discussion."

"I'm not discussing shit with you," Jimmy snarled. "Where's Maggie? What the hell did you do to her?" More than for his own fate, Jimmy was scared to death for Maggie—his vampire lover, the woman who'd rescued him from an alcoholic abyss after a vampire slaughtered his son. It had been Maggie who helped him pick up the pieces of his life, telling him he could have revenge for his little boy if she'd let him teach her the weaknesses of her kind. During the day, while vampires lay insenate and vulnerable, Jimmy could attack those sick creatures that murdered their mortal hosts.

He owed Maggie so much but instead of helping her fight Lord Baldevar, Jimmy had only managed to make himself the vampire's prisoner. Maggie, along with her best friend Charles, had tried to free him but they hadn't been able to stop Lord Baldevar. Jimmy's last memory of the night before was the monster telling Maggie that if she wanted to fight with the angels, it was time for her to learn what happened to those who stood against him. What had it done to her after that?

Lord Baldevar raised an eyebrow and his lip curled down in mocking derision. "Maggie? Is my consort still such a child that she clings to her mortality by having you address her with the insipid nickname of her youth?"

Jimmy's right hand curled into a fist that was immediately kicked. The steel tip of the vampire's boot caught the ruined tips of Jimmy's fingers and he howled in pain while his torturer spoke in a calm, almost bored manner.

"Perhaps you'd like another session on my rack— no? Then try and behave in a civilized manner while we converse. To answer your question, I have done nothing to Meghann except give her the freedom she claims to desire."

"Then where the hell is she?"

Lord Baldevar shrugged. "Her whereabouts are not my concern at the moment. No doubt wherever she is, Meghann is fretting over you—weeping over what I've done to her precious mortal lover."

As Jimmy struggled to bring himself into a sitting position, the vampire stood abruptly, knocking over his chair. He spread his hands in a wide arc, encompassing the spacious but empty room. "Look around, Mr. Delacroix. This is the room where I transformed Meghann. It was a thing of beauty before I had it destroyed because I could not bear to look upon any object that reminded of the woman who betrayed me. For many years, I dreamed of how I would destroy Meghann once our paths crossed again."

"You'll never hurt Maggie—I won't let you!"

"I know Meghann indulges your ego, but permit me to point out you cannot even tie your shoes in your present state—a condition I have reduced you to. But you are quite right . . . I will never hurt Meghann. Not because I fear reprisal from a mortal wretch like you but because I love her."

Jimmy watched uneasily while the vampire paced the long length of the room. Why was it speaking to him like this, almost as if he were its confessor? Then the answer came to Jimmy and he nearly soiled himself in terror. The vampire was confessing its secret thoughts because it had no intention of leaving Jimmy alive long enough to repeat what he'd said to anyone.

Lord Baldevar whirled around and his lips stretched

into a bitter grin. "For decades, I dreamed of slaughtering that wench—of breaking her heart as she broke mine by killing her loved ones before I allowed her to die. Then I realized rage was clouding my ability to reason. Was I really going to destroy the only woman I'd ever loved because of a trifling accident?"

"What the hell are you talking about?" Jimmy demanded. If he was going to die, he'd face this thing down bravely and not crouch in fear on the floor. "What accident?"

Again the raised eyebrow gesture that indicated condescension. "Meghann does not confide in you, boy? There was no intent in her actions the night she put that poker in my heart—it was an accident, no more."

"It was no fucking accident! Maggie wanted you dead!"

At that, Lord Baldevar laughed—a cutting, bleak sound that made Jimmy's skin break out in goose bumps.

"I am quite sure that is what she told you. It is the same lie she tells herself but the truth of the matter is that I'd made a very foolish mistake that night. My uncle had approached Meghann—may that wretched prelate's soul agonize for all eternity. He dangled certain promises under her nose . . . chief among them the chance to be independent of me. Instead of realizing her enthusiasm was nothing more than my child bride growing up and chaffing at my rule, I became enraged and punished her rather severely for even contemplating leaving me. I only meant to chastise her but unfortunately Meghann did not realize that . . . she became afraid for her life. In terror, she grabbed that poker and I managed to slip right onto it.

"It only took a few years to realize how foolish it was to hate Meghann when my quarrel should be with Alcuin for putting idiotic notions in her head. Without his interference, it would never have occurred to her to leave me. So I simply built up my strength and when

I was ready, I slaughtered him and reclaimed my consort."

"No!" Jimmy shouted. "She's not yours . . . she
hates you! Maggie loves me!"

Lord Baldevar lifted him off the floor and shoved
Jimmy against the wall, amber eyes glittering with malevolence and derision. "Idiot, Meghann does not love
you. She loves what you represent . . . redemption and
her lost humanity. You are nothing more than her hair
shirt . . . in some twisted way, the girl assuages her conscience by devoting herself to a mortal lover."

"Fuck you!" Jimmy howled. "If she doesn't love me,
why did she rescue me?" Lord Baldevar's eyes narrowed and Jimmy felt a small rush of triumph. "Why
did she put on that show last night? I remember her
sidling up to you and acting all sweet and hot so
Charles could sneak up on you and could kill you. She
did it for me—me! Maggie damn sure wouldn't lift a
finger to help you if you were hurt. Didn't she leave
you to die?"

"Mr. Delacroix," the vampire purred in a silky tone,
"perhaps your injuries blunted your perceptions last
night. Do you know why I stand before you, whole and
unharmed? Meghann may have attempted to harm me
but in the penultimate moment, when her sodomite
friend could have separated my head from my shoulders, the girl wanted more than anything to help me—
she could not stand the thought of my death. It was
her brief hesitation that allowed me to regain my
strength. It is also the reason I allowed her to live in
spite of her treachery—the realization that underneath
the spite and fear, Meghann is still in love with me."

"No! No! No! I'm the one she loves!"

"Meghann does delude herself into believing that,"
Lord Baldevar agreed. "Poor child—still Catholic
enough to fear damnation for giving in to her heart
and embracing me. But there is no way I'll step aside
and allow Meghann to reject me because she is too

fearful to toss aside that pious morality that makes her willing to settle for a mundane existence with you."

"So what are you gonna do?" Jimmy sneered, and the hand grasping his throat tightened, forcing him to gasp out his next words. "Killing me won't make Maggie stop loving me."

"Why, Mr. Delacroix," Lord Baldevar said in a level tone, "that is nearly intelligent. Could you actually know something of Meghann's nature, after all? If I slaughter you, you'll live on in her mind . . . she'll never see beyond her romanticized view of your life together. It is quite difficult to overcome the memories of a ghost when wooing a lover. So killing you would serve no purpose."

Lord Baldevar pulled Jimmy closer to him, smiling when Jimmy couldn't stop himself from flinching.

"Don't fear me," he said with such malice Jimmy could feel nothing but fear. "I will not harm you. Instead, I am going to grant you your heart's desire."

Lord Baldevar's blood teeth shot out of his mouth, making his prisoner gasp. Slowly, seeming to enjoy Jimmy's panic-stricken gaze, the vampire dropped him to the ground and raised his left hand to his mouth, biting down savagely on his own wrist.

"No!" Jimmy screamed when he saw the purple-red blood mar the surface of Lord Baldevar's parchment-white skin and realized the vampire's purpose.

Lord Baldevar hunched down next to him and brought his bleeding wrist to Jimmy's tightly clamped, resisting mouth. Easily, the vampire used his other hand to clamp down on Jimmy's jaw, prying it apart and making his teeth unclench so that his mouth opened and he tasted the foul blood on his tongue.

"Come now," Lord Baldevar chided as Jimmy made a futile effort to spit the poison out of his mouth. "Isn't this what you crave? Didn't you plead with Meghann to transform you? Since she is not here, it shall be my pleasure to welcome you to immortality.

What did you used to say to your little boy before that vampire murdered him? Open wide," he said in the singsong lilt parents used on fussy children.

Jimmy shook his head as furiously as a rabid dog, thrashing about with a strength that belied his broken, feverish body. All his struggles were no match for Lord Baldevar and soon more blood poured down his throat, sealing his fate.

Jimmy thought he heard himself scream but soon all thoughts were drowned in the vortex of pain and chaos that overtook him. What was happening to him? Every part of his body ached with an unbearable throb that made his torture the previous night seem a pale shadow compared to the torment he underwent now. Worse, he could actually feel his mind slipping away from him, unable to stand the suffering and hurtling toward a hazy world where nothing—not the agony, not Lord Baldevar—could touch him.

No, he thought. *Can't go there . . . never come back if I do.* But he couldn't seem to stop the process . . . it was like falling off a cliff into a bottomless pit. *Gotta hold on,* he thought hazily. *Gotta hold the ledge . . . find something to keep me here.*

"Maggie!" he managed to shout, his last sane thought of his lover. Jimmy never knew it, but he spent all the hours between his transformation and dawn screaming her name.

ONE

June 30, 1998
Las Vegas, Nevada

Dr. Lee Winslow watched his patient and her boyfriend walk down his azalea-lined driveway, pleased by the young man's tender concern for his girlfriend, manifested in the arm around her waist. He felt the young couple had made the right decision, a fifteen-minute D&C instead of a lifetime of regret and thwarted dreams.

Lee shut the PATIENTS ONLY door and staggered through the waiting room, opening the door to the residential section of his house. He collapsed on a tan leather sofa, relieved that his long day was finally over. First, he'd been woken at 3:00 A.M. for a delivery that kept him on his feet until eight. Then there was a full schedule of patients and finally the abortion. Christ—on his feet for nearly seventeen hours. Lee curled up on the plush sofa, thanking God that none of his other pregnant patients were near their due dates. So there was no reason he couldn't take a hot shower before settling into bed with a glass of that twelve-year-old scotch he'd won on the e-bay auction. . . .

The phone shrilled at him, seeming to mock his intentions for a quiet evening at home. But it was his private line, so Lee let the machine pick up—he didn't have the energy to talk to anybody, and nothing except a patient emergency was dragging him out of the house tonight.

"Lee? This is Charles Tarleton. I'm staying at the Riviera, Suite 1430. I'll be here all night if you get this message. I'd, uh, really like to see you."

Charles Tarleton! Lee felt his mouth go dry and he raced over to his answering machine, rewinding the tape so he could reassure himself the message wasn't a figment of his imagination.

Dr. Charles Tarleton . . . wunderkind of the NIH for five years, a senior fellow by the age of thirty. They'd met when Lee, then a lowly assistant, had been assigned to aid in Charles's research to harvest stem cells from umbilical-cord blood for bone-marrow transplants. Charles and Lee worked well together, and it wasn't long before they began seeing each other outside of their research.

Not that there was too much time for socializing—what with Charles insisting on working late into the night and then sleeping all day. Still, they'd had very good times on the few nights a month Charles did allow himself time off. Then one day Charles abruptly resigned his fellowship and vanished, without a word to Lee.

I'd really like to see you. Lee felt a flush of anger go through him. Charles wanted to see him now . . . after ten years of silence? After taking off without a word of explanation? After leaving him to cry for months on end and wonder what he'd done wrong?

A dreadful thought occurred to Lee, making cold tentacles of fear wrap around his heart. What if Charles needed to see him because he had to tell him he had . . .

Oh, stop that! Lee scolded himself. Even if Charles had tested positive for HIV, he was fine. First, it had been ten years since they'd been together and Lee, at his mother's worried insistence, had been tested many times since then—each test coming back negative.

Still, no matter how Charles had hurt him, Lee wouldn't wish such a horrible thing on him. If that was Charles's reason for contacting him, maybe the only thing his ex wanted was someone to comfort him, a shoulder to cry on. In that case, it would be selfish just to sit here and ignore the message.

Don't play Mother Teresa, a voice reprimanded in Lee's mind. *If you go over there, it's not going to be because you're Visiting the Sick. We both know you've still got a torch for him . . . even after ten years, after being dumped like a two-dollar whore.*

I do not still have a torch for him, Lee fired back at that despicable, unfortunately correct, voice.

Oh, yeah? It replied. *Then why the thump, thump, thumping heart? Why the clammy hands? Look at yourself,* the voice continued in disgust.

You be quiet, Lee ordered and snatched his car keys off the end table in the hallway. He wasn't going to call; he'd go to the suite instead and confront Charles. If for no other reason, he was going over there for the explanation Charles owed him for his shameful conduct. Somehow Lee managed to convince himself that an explanation was the only reason he was heading toward the Riviera at breakneck speed.

"Lee!" Charles gave him a quick, fumbled embrace and beckoned him to come in. "It's great to see you . . . just great. You look fantastic."

"I look like a bum," Lee replied, stepping into the opulent suite. He hadn't even bothered shaving before he came over here . . . he knew the blond and gray (his mind refused to acknowledge how much gray) stubble looked horrid. And the sweat-stained Izod shirt and wrinkled khakis didn't lend much to his appeal either. But what did he care? He didn't have to dress up for a lover that couldn't be bothered to leave a forwarding address ten years ago . . . no matter how handsome he was, or how much Lee's heart had pounded when he saw Charles again. "You're the one who looks great. My God, don't you age?"

Lee meant the remark to be a joke, but Charles blanched as though Lee had accused him of performing unspeakable acts with small children.

Still, Lee thought, inspecting his ex, it was true—the man had not aged one bit in the past ten years. The jet-black hair was free of gray, and that did not appear to be the result of dye. There were no wrinkles on Charles's face, not even laugh lines. God, he was forty years old but he looked like a boy in his early twenties.

But even if Charles had somehow managed to elude middle age, he did not appear young or carefree. His skin was far too pale, but Charles had always looked pale, ignoring Lee's blandishment that he put his work aside for once and get some sun.

Charles walked toward the wet bar in the living room. "What would you like to drink?"

"I brought something." He held out the scotch he'd decided to bring, though he wasn't sure if it was a peace offering or something to whack Charles over the head with.

"Glenfiddich." Charles gave him a wan smile and carried the bottle toward the bar. "Please, make yourself at home."

Lee perched on a leopard-print sofa, watching Charles prepare the drinks. Something was wrong with his old flame . . . his hands trembled slightly and the drinks he prepared were ludicrously oversize. This wasn't the laid-back, cool man Lee remembered. What was going on?

Then Lee's eyes fell on the black leather easy chair a few feet from him and the long gold skirt draped carelessly across it. "Have you turned cross-dresser or brought your wife with you?" Lee inquired caustically.

Charles didn't look up while he poured a greenish liquid Lee assumed was a liqueur into a tumbler. "That belongs to Meghann. She's a friend."

"Does your wife approve of you traveling to Sin City with this friend?" Lee inquired sarcastically.

Charles met Lee's eyes, flushing guiltily. "Lee, I . . . I was never married. It was just an excuse for not seeing you during the day."

"You lied to me?" Oddly, Lee wasn't very surprised by the confession. Charles had never told him anything about his wife—not even her name, only that he could never see Lee during the day because the sunlight hours he didn't sleep through supposedly belonged to his family. At the time, Lee assumed Charles's reticence stemmed from guilt; now he found out it was because the wife never existed.

"It was necessary." Charles handed him the triple shot of scotch and sat next to him on the couch, swallowing two-thirds of his drink in one gulp.

"Necessary?" Lee echoed and felt the beginnings of anger. "What possible excuse can you give me for a relationship based on lies?" He put the scotch down on a blackjack coaster and glared at his former lover. "Why are you here? Why did you call me? To tell me you're not only a coldhearted bastard for the way you left me but a liar too?"

Charles sighed. "I'm here because I need your help."

"You need my . . . how dare you! Where do you get your gall? Reappearing in my life after ten years because you want something?"

"Lee, please." Charles put his hand over Lee's. "I deserve your anger, I know. I'm not proud of the lies I told you, but if you just let me explain I think you'll understand. After the way I hurt you, I shouldn't even ask for that much but . . . it's a matter of life and death. Please. I need you."

Lee took a closer look at Charles, his pale skin and

his sunken dark brown eyes that kept darting toward the door as though he expected someone to break it down any second, and felt some of his anger subside in the face of Charles's obvious anxiety.

"What is it?" Lee asked. "Are you in some kind of trouble?"

"I'm in a great deal of trouble," Charles said grimly. "And I'll warn you right now . . . if you help me, you'll be putting your own life at risk."

Lee thought he might have guessed the truth. "Did you do some kind of government project, Charles? Is that why you had to give me a cover story about what you were doing during the day?"

Charles gave a shaky laugh and drained his glass. "Nothing that mundane, I'm afraid. You see, I'm . . . I'm not . . . human."

Charles saw Lee's skeptical look and continued. "I have not been human since 1920. That's the year I became a vampire."

Vampire? Lee would have laughed at such a ridiculous statement if not for the calm, almost matter-of-fact delivery.

"Why do you think you're a vampire?" Lee asked, employing the soothing but not patronizing voice he'd used on paranoid schizophrenics during his psychiatric rotation in medical school. Remembering his earlier worry, Lee began to wonder if his former lover, despite looking quite healthy, was suffering from AIDS dementia.

"Because I have fangs, I must drink blood to survive, and direct exposure to sunlight will kill me," Charles said dryly. "I'm not delusional, Lee."

"I never said—" Lee began but Charles bolted off the couch, dashing toward the door so fast he was almost a blur to Lee.

"Meghann!" Charles flung open the door, and Lee saw a small girl fall into his arms.

"It's worse," the girl cried, and Lee knew she was

shivering by the way her teeth chattered as she spoke. "I tried to feed and . . . oh, God. I got so sick . . . I barely made it back here. . . ."

Lee forgot about Charles's insane ravings—his only concern was for the sick woman in his arms. He ran into one of the bedrooms and grabbed a zebra-print quilt off the king-size bed. The woman was obviously in shock. She had to be kept warm until an ambulance arrived.

"Here," Lee said and wrapped the quilt around the woman's shoulders. With her face pressed against Charles's shoulder, Lee could see nothing of her features but her bright red hair. For some reason, that flaming hair made Lee uneasy. Where had he seen hair like that before?

Charles bundled his friend up and picked her up, carrying her toward the sofa.

"You want me to call the ambulance?" Lee asked.

Charles shook his head, and the woman looked up from his shoulder, allowing Lee to see her features clearly . . . especially the lambent green eyes that made Lee fall to his knees, uttering a high-pitched cry of shock.

"Lee?" Charles questioned, holding Meghann's shuddering frame against him.

Lee looked up—not at him, but at Meghann. "Why did you leave me?" he cried. "Didn't you want me? How . . . what the hell are you? You look the same . . . you haven't changed at all!"

"Shut the door," Meghann whispered. Charles waved his hand, and the door swung shut. As Lee stared at Meghann in astonishment, it registered dimly on his consciousness that his ex-lover had just displayed authentic telekinetic powers with seemingly little effort.

"Meghann, what is going on?" Charles asked.

"I have no idea," she replied, looking at the mortal

on the floor in astonishment. "I've never seen him before in my life."

"Yes, you have!" Lee shouted. "You were my pretty lady and you left me on those church steps!"

"No," Meghann whispered, her voice thick with shock. "It can't be."

"What?" Charles asked. "Meghann, what the hell is going on?"

"Read his thoughts," she said. "You'll see."

Neither Charles nor Meghann was in the habit of using their power to read mortal's thoughts. There was no need to invade the privacy of their minds, except in emergency situations—which this surely was.

Charles put Meghann on the sofa, and then concentrated on Lee.

It's so cold, *the little boy thinks, and wraps his arms around himself to keep warm. Why doesn't he have a coat?*

There's a lady leaning over him, a very pretty lady with long red hair that the wind whips around her face. "Your name is Mike," she tells him, and her soft voice makes him forget the cold. "You don't remember your mommy's name or where you live. You're going to go into that nice church and tell the priest your name. But you're not going to mention me. Just your name, okay?"

He doesn't want to leave the pretty lady. He knows she just did something to help him even if he can't remember what. But she just stares down and smiles at him and he knows he has to do what she says. So he kisses her cheek and runs up the church steps. He turns around to look at her one more time but she's gone.

"He's the child you saved from Simon?" Charles gasped.

"Who is Simon?" Lee burst out. "For God's sake, who are you?" he asked Meghann again, looking at her with a mixture of awe, fear, and love. "I've dreamed of you for forty years! Every Christmas, I think of the pretty lady that sent me into a church with nothing but a first name." He turned around to face Charles, looking dumfounded. "It's all true, isn't it? You're vampires. That's the only way to explain how she can look exactly the way she did forty years ago."

"It's all true," Charles told him.

Lee drew in a shaky breath—vampires! Not a myth or fantasy, but real as he was, sitting in front of him. They both looked normal . . . no vicious fangs dripping from their mouths. No, Meghann and Charles looked quite human—scared, tense humans but human all the same.

A thousand different thoughts whirled through his mind, but the overriding one was that the pale, sickly woman on the sofa had saved his life forty years ago. Lee leaned over to kiss Meghann's cheek and hug her tightly. "I owe you my life," he said simply. "I wandered into that church, and within an hour I was the Christmas Miracle. The monsignor, he had a sister that couldn't have children. She and her husband were such good people, and they wanted a child so badly. But adoption took forever, and they were beginning to lose hope . . . and there I was, an orphan who didn't even know his last name. Oh, social services went through the motions of finding my family but within two weeks I was on my way to Raleigh with my new family. Thank you so much for leading me to the best parents in the world. I swear I'll do everything I can to help you . . . Meghann," he finished, remembering what Charles had called her when she came in.

"Meghann," he repeated, finally having a name for the pretty lady he'd never forgotten. "Can you tell me who I am? How our paths crossed? I always thought maybe you were my birth mother and you gave me up because you were too young or poor to keep me. But I guess that's not true."

A shadow crossed Meghann's face, and her brow creased. "It's not a very pleasant story, Lee. It sounds like you love your adoptive parents. Isn't that enough? Why do you need to hear about the past?"

"I do want to know," he insisted. "I want to know why I can't remember anything but a woman with red hair leaning over me. I don't even know my birthday or how old I was the night you left me. Please, Meghann. Tell me who I am."

"I can't tell you your birthday because I don't know it but I do know you were five that night. You can't remember anything because I wiped your memory clean. It was my gift to you."

"What was so terrible you'd take my entire life from me?" Lee asked.

"Charles, give me some brandy, it might help with the chills. And give Lee another drink—he's going to need something strong in front of him when I tell this story."

Lee watched anxiously while Charles prepared fresh drinks, the doctor in him taking over when he saw Meghann's blue eyelids and the shivers that racked her body. Privately, he thought Meghann resembled his conception of what a vampire should look like with that chalk-white skin and her bloodless lips.

He wrapped the quilt tightly around her shoulders. "Keep warm."

Meghann gave him a lopsided smile. "It's shock, I know. I'm suffering from . . . I guess starvation because I can't seem to feed without getting sick. But we'll talk about all that a little later. For now, I'll try and tell you what you think you need to know."

Charles came back to the sofa with Lee's scotch, and explained the green liquid he was drinking was absinthe—the only alcohol that could intoxicate a vampire. Meghann sipped at her snifter glass, and clutched the quilt while she talked.

"You have to know a little about us," she began, and pointed to Charles. "First, to understand what's going on now and the danger you could be in if you decide to help me. Also, if you're going to understand what happened to you when you were a child."

"I'm helping you," Lee said firmly. "No ifs, ands, or buts about it. I owe you my life."

"It could come to that," Meghann told him. "As it nearly did on December 17, 1957. That was the night after I tried to leave the man . . . no, the *thing* that transformed me into a vampire."

Lee was surprised by the harsh glare and ugly grimace that crossed Meghann's face. "Why did you want to leave the, um, thing?"

"Because he was evil incarnate," Meghann said simply, and Charles nodded at her words. "He loved to cause pain, thrived on the agony of his victims when he bled them. He tried to make me as vile as he was, taught me to kill my hosts. But it made me miserable, and then along came a vampire that told me I didn't have to kill if I didn't want to." She smiled and took Charles's hand. "I wanted to go live with my new friend and learn his way of life. But Simon"—she spat the name out as though it had a vile taste—"wouldn't let me go. He bled me, made me so weak I couldn't even move a finger, and left me on a rooftop to die when the sun hit my body if I didn't beg his forgiveness.

"Of course I gave in and he saved me before the sunrise could kill me. The next night, he laughed when I told him I wanted to leave him because I couldn't bear to kill. He said mortals were low and petty . . . not worthy of my pity or respect. He wanted to make me feel disgust with humankind, so much disgust I'd forget my guilt and kill with as much pleasure as he did. So he went and brought into our house a cheap, junkie whore who had her small son with her."

Lee made a small whimper of distress and Charles wrapped an arm around his shoulder.

Meghann's eyes, compassionate and sad, held Lee's. "Shall I continue? I warn you what you've heard is merely the tip of the iceberg."

Lee nodded and gulped down the rest of his drink, not even gasping when the fiery liquid poured down his throat.

"Your mother"—Meghann pronounced the word with contempt—"believed Lord Baldevar was a pervert that wanted to have sex with a small boy. Since he was paying enough to keep her in drugs for months to come, she made no objection."

"No!" Lee howled, looking sick.

"I'm sorry, Lee, but it's the truth. Your mother had never involved you in anything before," she lied. "That night was the first time she was willing to let someone touch you . . . she was very far gone in her heroin addiction." Hell would freeze over before Meghann told this man his mother had let all manner of sick people violate his child's body. He did not need that knowledge; it could only hurt and humiliate him.

"Did this . . . this vampire touch me?" Lee asked, his face gone almost as pale as hers.

Meghann laughed bitterly. "Simon Baldevar is many things, but he is not a child molester . . . as far as I know. That was merely a ploy to get your mother in the house. He watched the rage build in me . . . knew I wanted to tear her apart limb from limb for being willing to let someone hurt her own child. Rage, as he well knew, leads to blood lust—an insane need to devour human blood," she explained at Lee's blank look. "When he tore into her, I leaped at them, dying for a bit of blood. But Simon held me back with one hand while, with all dignity gone, I begged for blood much as your mother would have begged for a fix. He

drained your mother until she was dead and told me
if I needed blood so badly to drink yours."

Lee put his face in his hands while Meghann continued, seeming oblivious to him and Charles, locked
in her own memories. "It took me years to figure out
what Simon was up to that night. He knew I hated
him for making me kill; why present such an awful
choice to me? How I underestimated him . . . God,
he's treacherous!"

"What do you mean?" Lee asked.

It was Charles who answered. "He was out to crush
Meghann's spirit that night. He'd hoped that most of
the fight would be out of her as a result of the hell
he put her through the night before, but he knew fear
wouldn't be enough to keep her at his side. He had
to break the rebellion inside her. If he could make her
kill a child, Simon knew she would remain with him
because she'd think she deserved her fate—she'd feel
she was as evil as he was."

"But his little scheme didn't work," Meghann re-
sumed, her eyes hard and stony. "I refused to hurt
you . . . if you could have seen his face when he realized he'd lost!" She shuddered in memory, but Lee
thought he saw some cold glee in her eyes at the
thought of foiling this madman she spoke of. "In a
rage, he tore you from my arms, Lee, and said he'd
drink from you himself if I wouldn't.

"I couldn't let him hurt you—that was my only
thought. You cried and wept; I think he made you
more scared . . . he loved the taste of fear in a mortal's
blood. I got hold of this fireplace poker and managed
to put it through his heart and we escaped his house.
I took you to the nearest church, and I wiped your
memory clean . . . clean of the miserable tenement
you and your mother lived in, your starvation, her
drugs, the nights you were left alone while she worked,
and finally I took away all your knowledge of me and
Simon." Meghann touched his face, unable to find in

this clear-eyed, middle-aged doctor the little ragamuffin she'd helped so long ago. "I can't give you back your memory, Lee . . . it's gone forever. And why are you called Lee? Your name used to be Mike."

"I was renamed for my maternal grandfather."

"That's sweet." Meghann smiled and Charles nodded. "I'm very happy to hear you had a good life with your adoptive parents. It's what I prayed for."

"Well, what happened to you?" Lee asked. "How did you go from the church steps to this hotel room? Meghann?" He shook her gently, but she didn't respond.

"She fades in and out of consciousness," Charles told him.

"How long has she been like this?" Lee asked, prying open her eyelid to see if the pupil was dilated.

Charles sighed. "She's been lethargic for about a month. I thought she was depressed. You see, she had a mortal lover but he was . . . well, I'll tell you that story another time. But she wasn't depressed . . . Meghann is pregnant."

"Pregnant?" Lee gasped. "You can reproduce?"

"It's quite rare . . . and inevitably ends in death for the mother."

"Then why would Meghann—"

"Meghann was raped," Charles explained and his eyes became narrow slits of fury. "You see, after our master was slaughtered—"

"Master?"

"An older, more experienced vampire that taught me and Meghann how to survive. His name was Alcuin." Charles's throat tightened when he thought of his mentor—thought of that saintly man and all the years they'd spent together.

"Why was he murdered?" Lee asked.

"Because of me," Meghann said tiredly, green eyes filled with tears.

"No!" Charles grabbed her close. "Don't you ever

think that. Alcuin loved you, Meghann. He loved us both, and he wanted to save us from Simon Baldevar. And you know their enmity started long before either of us was born. At some point, Simon would have come after him anyway."

"Simon?" Lee was bewildered. "I thought you said he was dead—that Meghann put a poker in his heart."

Meghann gave him a twisted grin. "That was my mistake too, Lee. I assumed Simon would die because of my improvised stake. I didn't know the only way to kill a vampire is by cutting out its heart or decapitating it."

"So Simon didn't die?" Lee felt the back of his neck prickle in horror. Did that mean this awful thing that had tried to kill him when he was a child was still alive?

"No, he didn't die," Charles answered. "He bided his time and waited until about three months ago to attack. He killed Alcuin when he tried to protect Meghann. With Alcuin dead, it was easy to abduct Meghann and rape her."

"And kidnap Jimmy," Meghann put in, and the sad look in her eyes made Lee sure that must be the mortal lover Charles spoke of. "Charles and I got away but he took Jimmy and left me this awful letter saying he was planning to transform Jimmy—make him into some horrible creature I could never love. That was my punishment for taking a lover."

Lee flinched and took Meghann's icy hand. "I'm so sorry. Does Simon know where you are?"

"No—thank God. But he's got to be looking for me. You see, he raped me on Beltane. That probably doesn't mean anything to you but May first, on the ancient pagan calendar, was supposed to be the night for fertility. Simon chose the night he took me very carefully and he also performed a magical ritual to make sure I conceived his precious philosophers' stone."

"The philosophers' stone," Charles explained at

Lee's baffled look, "was supposed to be a magic elixir that would provide freedom from disease, brilliance, and eternal life. Alchemists believed in it, and tried to create it, during the Middle Ages. Sounds like vampirism, doesn't it? A great many vampires—Lord Baldevar among them—believe that the philosophers' stone will be the blood of the offspring of two vampires _and_ that drinking it will give vampires the ability to walk in daylight."

"You mean he's going to drink his own child's blood?" Lee was outraged.

"We don't think he'd kill his child," Meghann responded, voice thick with exhaustion. "He's wanted a child for a very long time—since he was mortal. A legacy, I guess. I think he would drink the blood but leave the child alive, but I can't be sure. He never saw fit to discuss any of this with me."

"Besides," Charles went on, "vampire pregnancy is extremely rare. The last documented case dates to the twelfth century."

"Do these cases describe the mothers' symptoms?"

"Don't get your hopes up," Charles told him and brought some floppy disks from a suitcase. "Basically, it's a bunch of hocus-pocus nonsense that completely ignores symptoms that would indicate diseases like preeclampsia to us."

"They didn't have floppy disks in the twelfth century," Lee said. "Where are the primary sources?"

"Ballnamore—an estate in Ireland. It belonged to Alcuin but in his will he left it to Meghann and me. It's our stronghold, where all the vampires that stand against Lord Baldevar gather together. Some of them have fought against him for four hundred years."

"So why aren't you there?" Lee asked. "Why are you in some hotel in Vegas? Surely these other vampires might have some ideas—"

"No!" Meghann interrupted and Lee thought she looked ready to faint.

"They don't like us," Charles explained, clutching his friend's hand.

"Why not?"

Charles gave him a bitter smile. "For me, it's good old-fashioned homophobia . . . can't stand a queer vampire in their midst. Alcuin despised that narrow-mindedness but he's not here to keep them in check and they're all furious because his will makes me his successor . . . me and Meghann together, that is."

"If they hate you for being gay, what's their reason for disliking Meghann?"

"Jealousy," Charles answered. "They couldn't stand the way Alcuin favored her . . . how he taught her everything he knew, even relied on her advice on a few occasions. They thought he was a fool for listening to a novice—I suppose I should explain that in our world anyone under one hundred years of age is considered a novice vampire. You can imagine their rage when his will named two vampires created in the twentieth century as his successors."

Lee frowned. "Being young isn't a good enough reason to hate anybody."

Meghann gave a bitter laugh. "Charles left something out. If I were merely young, they'd content themselves with treating me with disdain and contempt. They despise me because Lord Baldevar transformed me. They think that automatically makes me as twisted and evil as he is . . . it doesn't even matter to them that I tried to kill him. They'll never think of me as anything but Baldevar's slut . . . which is what they called me whenever Alcuin wasn't around. And if they knew I was pregnant, they'd never believe I was raped. God only knows what they'd do. They might try and kill me or they might use me as some kind of bait to lure Lord Baldevar into a trap."

"So I went to Ballnamore by myself and told them of Alcuin's death," Charles said. "I said Meghann hadn't come with me because she was too grief-stricken after Lord Baldevar kill . . . kidnapped Jimmy. And I snuck into the archives and copied down the information. Then, Meghann and I came here. No one is going to have any reason to think we're in Las Vegas. It's a perfect hiding spot from our so-called allies and Lord Baldevar while we try to make Meghann well." Charles paused and met Lee's eyes. "And you're here. We need you."

Lee frowned. "I may be an obstetrician but I don't know anything about vampires. . . ."

"Somehow I didn't think you would," Charles said with a trace of a smile. "I can provide you with any information about a vampire's physiology that you need. We want you to perform an abortion. Not one mother has survived vampiric pregnancy, and the children that survived the birth were hideous monstrosities. Unfortunately, I can't bring myself to perform a D and C . . . put Meghann through that kind of pain even if I do know abortion is the only option—"

"What do you mean, put Meghann through pain?" Lee interrupted. "Wouldn't you anesthetize her first?"

"There isn't an anesthetic in the world to penetrate a vampire's bloodstream—it wouldn't take hold. But we sleep during the day. Actually, sleep is a mild word for our condition—it's closer to coma. Nothing disturbs us except an attack on our lives. Fledgling vampires might even sleep through that, but the stronger of us will wake up and some even manage to kill their stalkers. But I digress . . . Lee, we think Meghann will sleep through a D and C. You're not threatening her life—"

"I'm threatening the fetus."

"Maybe," Charles responded. "But this is our only chance. Please, you're the only mortal doctor I . . . we can trust. Will you do a D and C on Meghann during the day?"

Lee glanced uneasily at Meghann's paper-white skin and blue-tinged fingernails and saw she'd fainted

again. "She's in shock already, Charles. Invasive surgery . . . and keep in mind D and Cs carry a risk of
hemorrhage . . . could kill her."

"This pregnancy will kill her anyway. Please, Lee,"
Charles implored.

"Let's bring her to my house," Lee said. "I can give
her a thorough examination there. And you said sunlight will destroy you? Well, I think my house is just
the place for you two. You know as an ob-gyn my hours
aren't regular. So I fit the house with aluminum shutters to block out the sun so I could catch up on my
sleep during the day."

Lee directed Charles to lay Meghann, who hadn't
stirred during the brief journey from the hotel to his
house, on the examining table and put her legs in the
stirrups. A quick exam confirmed that she was eight
weeks pregnant.

"How did you know you were pregnant?" Lee asked
Meghann, who'd woken in time to yell in protest when
Lee inserted the steel speculum for the pelvic exam.
"Missed period?"

Meghann shook her head. "After I transformed, my
menstrual cycle became erratic—once or twice a year,
if that. No, about two weeks ago, I started waking up
tired all the time and then my breasts became very
tender. So I bought a home pregnancy test like any
mortal woman."

Lee listened to her heartbeat and glanced in consternation at her jutting ribs. "Are you always this thin
or did your weight loss coincide with your other symptoms?"

"I've lost about twenty pounds in the past week."

"Jesus!"

"Don't you see now why she needs an abortion?"
Charles said.

"I agree the pregnancy is affecting her health," Lee

replied. "But her malaise is precisely what's going to make an abortion so dangerous. I'd be much more comfortable with treating the worst of her symptoms, and letting her recover a little before having the abortion. An abortion can be performed safely up to twenty-four weeks into pregnancy—we have plenty of time. Have you any idea what's making her so sick?"

Charles shrugged helplessly. "All we know is she can't drink blood, and no vampire can survive without blood. It would be like starving a human."

Lee frowned. "What happens, Meghann, when you . . . er, drink blood? Has your appetite for it decreased since you got pregnant?"

Meghann gave him an admiring glance—she'd never seen a mortal accept vampires with such equanimity. Maybe it was because of what happened to him when he was a child or maybe he was simply in shock and hadn't fully absorbed the enormity of his discovery yet. "No, in fact I crave it constantly. It's all that's on my mind. But when I drink . . . a few minutes after I swallow, I become horribly nauseated. The first time it happened, I was just nauseated and a little dizzy. But now . . . now I throw up. What am I going to do if I can't digest blood?"

"Couldn't we give you transfusions?" Lee asked, and Charles shook his head.

"If we could accept transfusions, vampires would no longer be a threat to humans. Unfortunately, we must drink and digest."

"Why?" Lee asked, fascinated. "What happens when you digest blood?"

"It works much the same way absorption of B_{12} works in humans. We drink blood, and it travels through our stomach to our small intestines. Now, you know that in humans the B_{12} vitamin travels to the small intestine where it's absorbed by the ileum and transformed into proteins that are stored in the liver and kidneys before being transformed into enzymes that the human body needs to remain healthy. In vampires, after we transform, our ileum develops specialized tissues that transform antigens in the blood into an enzyme that doesn't exist in mortals. We discovered it about seventy years ago. That enzyme is responsible for our powers."

"What are your powers?" Lee asked. "Do you really live forever?"

"I'd have to answer yes in that I've only known vampires to die from unnatural causes—like decapitation and exposure to sunlight. No vampire, until Meghann, that is, has been struck down by illness. We are immune to all mortal diseases, we heal from blows like gunshot wounds in a matter of seconds . . ."

"How do you get this power?" Lee asked. "How do you become vampires?"

"You must be bled by a vampire to the point of death. Then, the vampire allows you to drink its blood. If you haven't been sufficiently drained of human blood, the vampire's blood poisons your system and you die quickly. But if you are drained, transformation begins. Your entire body, your whole genetic code, undergoes a radical change. Assuming you survive the process, you develop superhuman strength and the aging process stops. But if you don't have a steady diet of human blood to keep an acceptable level of the enzyme in your bloodstream, you die."

"So vampirism is purely biological," Lee mused. "After you transform, you drink blood to create this enzyme—"

"Not quite," Meghann interrupted. "We know the enzyme gives us our power, but we don't know why. We also don't know why an enzyme should make us cast partial reflections—"

"You really can't be seen in mirrors?"

"We present hazy outlines," Meghann said and gave him a slight smile. "Now, why would an enzyme do that? The answer is that it doesn't. There's more than pure science to us—there's the mystical side to vampirism and we have no way of explaining our mirror images or our ability to summon the dead, control and read mortal thoughts, our telekinetic power . . ."

"Meghann," Charles said at Lee's bemused, saucer-wide eyes, "we can go into all of this another time. Lee doesn't have to absorb it all tonight."

"No," Lee agreed, feeling much like Alice fallen down the rabbit hole—*summon the dead?* He shook off his horror and returned to the situation at hand. "Putting mysticism to the side, though, it sounds like Meghann has a simple vitamin deficiency. When . . . uh, humans become B_{12} deficient it leads to symptoms like hers . . . fatigue, weakness, weight loss. The pernicious anemia that occurs due to B_{12} deficiency isn't that uncommon in pregnancy."

"So if she expels the fetus, she should be able to digest blood again," Charles said.

Lee nodded. "But if I have any problems with the D and C tomorrow . . . if her blood pressure drops or she hemorrhages and I have to stop, we have to consider ways to help Meghann without terminating the pregnancy. In humans, we'd simply inject the patient with B_{12} since they aren't capable of extracting it from food. Is there any way to synthesize the enzyme you need . . . since Meghann can't extract it from blood?"

"Lee," Meghann said, "we've been trying for almost a century to synthesize that enzyme with no success. If we could make the enzyme, we wouldn't have to drink blood anymore. Right now, the only way to manufacture the enzyme is by drinking blood and I'm not able to do that anymore."

"So you see why abortion is the only option," Charles said but he was looking at Meghann instead of Lee.

Meghann nodded, but her eyes glistened. "You

know how much I wanted to be a mother—it didn't even matter that it was Simon's baby."

"I know, honey," Charles replied, kissing her cheek. "It was hard for me too . . . knowing transformation meant I'd lost all hope of becoming a parent. But you know what would happen if you did give birth. You heard the accounts of those poor, malformed babies. It's settled. Tomorrow, Lee will give you the D and C."

"Wait," Meghann said, seeming to struggle to stay awake. "Lee, I'm very grateful for your help. But you must understand . . . Simon Baldevar wanted to get me pregnant. The last time we saw each other, he left me a letter saying he'd leave me alone until I came to him of my own free will but I don't believe that for a second. I think he believed that once I found out I was pregnant, I'd seek him out because I wouldn't know what to do." Meghann laughed bitterly. "Even if I could carry this baby to term, he'd be the last person I'd want around. But when he doesn't hear from me, he'll seek me out . . . he'll want to know if he succeeded in making me pregnant. If he finds out I had an abortion . . ." Meghann paled, breaking out in tremors that Lee thought had nothing to do with her illness.

"He'll kill her . . . and anyone who helped her do it," Charles finished.

Lee swallowed nervously. He might not be able to remember the evil thing that tried to kill him when he was a child, but the terror in both Meghann's and Charles's eyes was enough to make his mouth dry and his hands turn clammy.

"I don't care," Lee said and took Meghann's hands. "You saved my life and now I'll do my best to save yours." He helped her off the examining table, and directed Charles to carry her to one of the guest bedrooms—a large, cheerful room painted white with plenty of plants and wicker furniture.

"Try and get some rest," Lee said when Meghann was settled under the flowered quilt. "Hopefully, when you wake up tomorrow night, this will all be behind you."

TWO

Lord Baldevar selected a lightweight navy blazer from his walk-in closet, thinking wryly that even a vampire was not immune to a New York City heat wave. The oppressive July humidity and mugginess made his usual suit and tie impossible, he thought as he plucked a pair of gold and onyx cufflinks off his dresser.

He was fastening the cufflinks to his cream silk shirt when a brutal pain ripped through his side, making him gasp and clutch the dresser for support.

It hurts! It hurts! Make it stop. . . .

Abruptly, the high-pitched, whimpering voice left his mind and the pain vanished as Simon said aloud, "Meghann?"

There was no reply—not that he'd expected one. The brief visitation was far too quick and unexpected for him to hold the presence long enough to identify it. Still, it had to be Meghann. He'd transformed many vampires over the centuries, but his link to them had diminished over time. Meghann (not counting the thing in the basement) was the only one young enough for him to still feel her pain and distress.

For a moment, Simon was tempted to abandon his plans for the evening and concentrate on his missing consort's whereabouts but it was not the right time.

For one thing, it was only twilight—the sun had not yet completely set. Although he was old enough to be awake and functioning during dusk, there was no way to employ his occult powers without a serious drain on his energy. Too, he hadn't fed last night. Better to go outside and feed, get his strength up before he attempted to find Meghann.

Leaving the protection of his shuttered town house, Lord Baldevar slipped a pair of Ray Ban sunglasses over eyes that needed protection even from the weak light of the slowly setting sun. It was a quarter to eight now—had he attempted to leave his home even fifteen minutes earlier, the wretched sun might have blinded him.

But why complain? Perhaps in a few years he'd be able to go outdoors at noon if he desired. That pain-wracked distress call—if it indeed belonged to Meghann—was a very good sign that his Beltane experiment had been successful.

Simon smiled, startling two young female tourists who gawked at him as they passed each other on Fifth Avenue. Briefly, he considered offering the young women a drink and making them his evening meal but he decided to get a bit more air before settling on a victim. After all, his company was not due until ten— he had plenty of time.

He kept smiling, finally admitting to himself how uneasy he'd been at Meghann's silence. He'd fully expected her to (willingly or unwillingly like the scream that had invaded his mind) contact him long before tonight. Beltane was two months ago . . . he'd started wondering if her silence meant he'd failed to impregnate her.

But he should have remembered how obstinate the girl could be, Simon thought, stopping to admire a stunning cabochon bracelet in the Cartier display window. Should he buy the hopefully expectant mother this pretty bauble studded with emeralds that matched her eyes?

No, no . . . he had a far better gift for her. As soon as he found out where she was hiding, Simon planned to present her with Jimmy Delacroix. Surely her lover's demise would teach Meghann a badly needed lesson in obeying her master.

Simon's mood darkened as he reflected on his last meeting with Meghann and he walked rapidly, the sights and sounds of the bustling city around him no longer registering on his senses.

That she'd been frightened and defensive when she first found out he was still alive, Simon fully understood. After leaving her master to die, she most certainly should have feared for her life. But after he'd told the girl he was willing to forgive her and make her his consort again, what did she do? Weep and whine because he'd slaughtered Alcuin, flaunt her mortal in front of him, and plot with her sodomite friend to kill him.

Ah, well, what was the point in brooding over Meghann's loathsome behavior like a jilted lover? He'd punished her severely for her transgressions. Good mood restored by the thought of how devastated Meghann would be when she saw what her defiance cost her no longer mortal lover, Lord Baldevar turned his attention to feeding.

He was glad to be in Manhattan; the city had always provided remarkable sustenance. Perhaps it was because the people who lived here inevitably took on the characteristics of the city they inhabited—brash, occasionally crude, brimming with an energy and intensity that people who occupied older, more sedate cities lacked. It had been years since he'd had time to fully savor the attractions of Manhattan. Over the past decade, he'd merely come for a few nights at a time to apprise himself of Meghann's activities. It did not surprise Simon at all that after her apprenticeship with

Alcuin she would choose to return to the city where she'd grown up, where they had met and fallen in love.

Feeling a bit sentimental, Simon decided to head downtown, toward the Time Square area. That was where he'd taken Meghann for her first hunt. He laughed aloud as he remembered Meghann, freshly transformed and indignant when he told her to dress like a streetwalker. It was only after he'd explained that being perceived as a hooker was the easiest ruse a female vampire could employ to lure prey that Meghann acquiesced, her eyes wide with apprehension and glee at all her new powers.

She'd learned so quickly, Simon mused. The girl had taken to vampirism with a speed that delighted him. Every new lesson she absorbed rapidly, showing her gratitude toward her teacher in lovemaking so passionate it nearly took his breath away.

What happened, Meghann? Simon asked his absent lover. *You had more promise and natural ability than any other fledgling. What happened to make you hate yourself . . . and me for transforming you?*

Simon shrugged and waved his hand, making a cab swerve abruptly when it came a bit too close to him. Meghann was young, and making mistakes was a privilege of youth. No doubt her Catholic upbringing made her vulnerable to Alcuin's mealymouthed view of immortality, and caused the guilt that made her reject her master. At any rate, that was all in the past. It was the present that mattered and Meghann was no longer in a position to reject him.

When Simon finally approached Broadway, the area turned out to be a disappointment, so changed he barely recognized it. When he'd first come to New York, in the forties, the Great White Way had offered stunning productions written by geniuses like Noel Coward and Cole Porter. Now he saw there was such a dearth of mortal imagination that many of those same shows had been revived but he doubted they could match the vigor and style of the originals. The few new plays offered did not interest him either—they seemed gaudy and dull.

Even worse than the tepid entertainment promised by glittering marquees, Simon missed the air of danger that used to pervade these streets. Decades, even a few years before, patrons of the theater district made sure to stay in well-lit areas for fear some derelict might rob their valuables or assault their person. Now Times Square was so sanitized and antiseptic he actually saw a Disney store doing a thriving business, and tourists walked the streets with impunity. What had happened to the shifty-eyed hustlers that lurked in dark alleys? Where were the dope fiends, the streetwalkers, the pickpockets? Where did a vampire go if he wanted a bit of depravity with his evening meal? It seemed the cops patrolling these streets had chased those unfortunates to darker corners of the city, and Simon did not have time to seek them out. What did that leave him with? Perhaps he could surprise some wholesome tourist or theater patron . . . show them there were still things to fear on the New York City streets after dark.

A booming, shrill voice interrupted his thoughts. "Repent!" a woman yelled at the passersby who ignored her existence. "Repent or be roasted over the fires of hell for eternity! You must repent now to be saved!"

Lord Baldevar smiled—so all the crazy characters had not been driven away after all. He walked toward the screeching howl, planning the charade he'd played out many times before with fanatics—the sober, earnest look he'd put on his face as he listened to the woman's spiel and allowed her to hand him some poorly spelled, cheaply made pamphlet that told him salvation hinged on turning over a considerable portion of his wealth to whatever organization she was affiliated with. Then, when he convinced his victim of his sincere desire to be saved, it would be a simple matter to lure her home with him to pray for his soul.

Unfortunately, Simon found his target was a fiftyish crone with permed gray hair, granny glasses, widely spaced teeth, and soft, wattled flesh. He'd sink his teeth into the garbage pail next to her before drinking from that age-diluted stream.

Resigning himself to a walk to the notorious meat-packing district and the debauched mortals that could be found there, Lord Baldevar found his spirits raised when a teenage couple approached the zealot and began haranguing her. He assumed the couple was a boy and girl, though it was difficult to tell at first since the deep-voiced one had long, greasy blond locks that trickled over a cheap black T-shirt. No, Simon decided, this was definitely a boy—no girl would appear in public with her hair in such unwashed disarray. Not that the girl with him was any prize. Unlike her skinny, small companion, the girl was tall but her obesity made her appear shorter than she was. She had frizzy, badly combed brown hair and a slight overbite.

These two weren't beauties, but they would serve his purpose. Besides, it was growing late. He wanted to feed and wash before his company arrived. It would be the height of rudeness to appear before guests in bloodstained, soiled clothing.

From the loud argument that drew amused stares from passersby and cheap silver-plated inverted penta-grams around their necks, Simon gathered that the youngsters were neo-pagans, which gave him the perfect opening gambit to win their trust. Interrupting the raving old fanatic with a slight clearing of his throat, Simon turned to his intended meal and said, "Why bother this lunatic? Let her worship as she pleases. After all, do what thou wilt shall be the whole of the law."

Of course, the zealot turned her abuse on him but Simon barely heard her . . . he was too busy clamping

his lips together to refrain from laughing at the eager,
shining expressions on the faces of his prey.

"You know of the Great Beast?" the boy questioned.

"I knew him," Simon answered gravely, refraining
from rolling his eyes at the alias for Aleister Crowley—a
drug addict and charlatan who'd tried to pass himself
off as an esteemed practioner of practical magick.

Simon had encountered the fake in Egypt around
the turn of the century, having gone there to supervise
Howard Carter's excavation of the Egyptian tombs, a
project he'd funded very generously in the hopes he
might discover a clue to the origins of vampirism. Con-
trary to popular fiction, he'd learned nothing of vampire history from the pyramids but he had been able
to amuse himself with Aleister Crowley.

He'd learned the pompous junkie used to belong
to the Order of the Golden Dawn, a mortal organization that the damned prelate Alcuin had chosen to
reveal the secrets of the cabala to.

Annoyed by Alcuin's attempt to spread his theology
to mortals and hand them divine knowledge they
should never have been privy to, Lord Baldevar had
attached himself to Aleister Crowley—expelled from
the order for his sadism and debauchery. For an
amusement, he'd appeared to Crowley and told him
he was Aiwass, an ancient Egyptian deity. The gullible
magician wrote down everything he told him, and
Lord Baldevar's words became the mainstay of Ordo
Templis Orelius, the religious order the egotistical
Crowley proclaimed himself head of.

Now Simon felt a malicious pleasure, seeing that the
nonsensical rituals he'd set down over seventy years
ago were still being slavishly adhered to by foolish mortals.

"You couldn't have known Mr. Crowley," the girl
said doubtfully, taking in Lord Baldevar's deceitfully
young appearance. Then her face cleared and she

smiled at him. "Of course! You mean you knew him in a past life."

"It was a different time," Simon agreed. "But why bother with this old hag? You don't think you're going to convert her? Surely you have better things to do with your time? As you may have guessed, I'm foreign to this city and a bit lonely for the company of adepts (he mentally recoiled from calling these simpletons adepts) like yourselves. Perhaps you could accompany me home and tell me how to set up a coven here?"

The couple agreed instantly, sparing Simon from having to use any form of persuasion on them.

"Don't follow the devil!" the fanatic he'd forgotten about screamed at the young couple after he'd flagged down a cab to take them back to the town house. "He's an abomination! Let God into your hearts and He shall save you from this unholy . . ."

The young couple simply got into the cab, although the girl did make a rude gesture with her middle finger at the woman.

Before getting into the cab, Simon placed his arm around the missionary's shoulder and whispered so only she could hear, "Madam, I shall leave you to a far worse fate than me . . . a long, long existence in your virginal twin bed and a painful death from the cancer that has once again lodged in your breast." He watched the woman's face cave in and gave her a mocking bow. "Good night."

Once home, Simon directed the young couple to what used to be his study when he lived in the town house with Meghann but nowadays had to be pressed into service as a magick temple.

The couple was, of course, enthralled with the room and the elaborate wooden and steel sigils that decorated the walls, the floor-to-ceiling bookcases teeming with ancient, well-preserved grimoires, and various magickal implements he'd collected over the centuries.

"Wow," the boy (who'd introduced himself as Osiris

in the cab) breathed reverently, picking up a Spanish steel sword Lord Baldevar had owned since the seventeenth century. "Is this your athame?"

Simon refrained from wincing at Osiris's hideous pronunciation and merely said, "I use it to open the circle."

He felt another flush of irritation at Meghann when he thought of the past forty years and all the trials he'd been through—trafficking with daemons and currying their favor so he could gain the power he'd need to wrest Meghann away from that smarmy cleric, Alcuin. If the little witch had stayed by her master's side as she promised to, he wouldn't have to devote so much time to sorcery . . . it was as bad as when he'd been a novice vampire and had to build his defenses to guard against Alcuin's constant attacks.

But as long as he was practicing, he'd have some fun. Simon grabbed a rowan wand he'd had since he was a mortal and pointed it at Osiris. "Demonstrate your powers."

"Huh?" The boy blinked.

"I've given you a room filled with objects imbued with power it took centuries to develop. Show me what you can do."

The girl, who'd given Simon the rather pretentious name of Lady Cerridwen when she introduced herself, told Lord Baldevar haughtily, "We can summon demons at will to do our bidding."

Since there was no way they could escape his house now, Simon threw his head back and howled, laughing harder at the identical angry flushes on the young couple's faces. "Dear child, you have no power but the capacity to delude yourselves. You've never summoned anything . . . nor will you. But, if you are fortunate, perhaps I will treat you to a display of real power and raise a daemon or two."

He was talking like a madman and it should have occurred to his young guests to leave his house but the couple stood their ground. Osiris raised his chin and said, "You're full of shit. Why should we believe you can do anything? Just because you've got a room filled with some old books?"

"They are called grimoires," Simon said calmly. "And you are quite right. I've given you no reason to believe my boasts are any more grounded in truth than yours. What say you to a wager?"

"Okay," Lady Cerridwen agreed before her boyfriend could speak. "What's the bet?"

Simon reached over her head, removing a wooden sigil to reveal a wall safe. Rapidly, he undid the combination (the date of his transformation) and removed several thick stacks of money.

He laid them on the black-clothed altar and turned to his gaping guests. "That is twelve thousand dollars. Raise a daemon and the money is yours. Fail and you walk out of here with nothing. However, if I summon, you will pay me with your souls."

Simon liked these modern times. In his day, someone would have protested mightily at the thought of handing over his immortal soul, but in this century mortals seemed to have little regard for it. No doubt because so few of them (no matter what they pretended) actually believed in an afterlife.

"You'll give us the money if we win?" Osiris asked, and Simon did not even need to read the boy's thoughts—all he had to do was look at the greedy eagerness in his eyes to see the boy thought him a rich lunatic. Simon noticed Osiris eyeing him, seeming to assess what kind of struggle he'd put up when Osiris and Lady Cerridwen tried to separate him from the money neither of the mortals could stop staring at.

"Of course I'll give you the money if you win," Simon responded truthfully. If these mortal nothings could raise the rug from the floor, let alone a monster, he'd go greet the sunrise. "And if I am successful, you agree to give the forfeit I demand?"

The couple looked at each other and then Osiris said, "Okay."

"Begin," Simon said, and leaned against the paneled wall of his study.

Lady Cerridwen grasped his sword, and spun around counterclockwise to form the magick circle that would protect her and her boyfriend from attack by any monster they summoned.

They made proper obeisance to the four elements of the circle—north, south, east, and west—though their flowery language must have come from one of those dreadful Hollywood movies.

Simon could see that the children were quite involved with their ritual, and seemed to sincerely believe they'd erected a magick circle since they were careful not to disturb its barrier. How crushed they would be when they discovered he was the only supernatural force in this room.

After the preliminary rituals were complete and all instruments had been blessed by being passed over a brazier filled with myrrh, Lady Cerridwen reached into her canvas backpack and fished out a worn, dog-eared paperback entitled *The Necronomicon*.

This was even more amusing than he'd expected! He knew of the cheap modern grimoire that claimed to be a faithful reproduction of ancient Sumerian spells. Of course, the writings were no more grounded in real magick than a stage magician's black hat, Simon thought as he watched the girl read carefully from the book.

"Don't you feel the monster's presence?" Osiris demanded, startling Simon from his mocking thoughts at Lady Cerridwen's fool words.

"Of course I don't." Simon yawned, not bothering to mask his boredom. "There's nothing in this room."

"You lie and stand outside the protection of the magick circle," Lady Cerridwen screamed, relishing her role as sorceress. "Apologize or we will destroy you!"

"Do it," Simon challenged and moved toward the fake circle.

"Don't break the circle!" Osiris ordered.

Simon put his foot over the imaginary circle and easily lifted Osiris off his feet with one hand under his chin. "You have failed to summon. There is nothing in this room and I will not indulge your silly fantasy one moment longer."

"Put him down!" Lady Cerridwen screeched.

Simon turned to her and said mildly, "Young lady, didn't your parents teach you what happens to undisciplined children who speak to their elders in such a way? Now, you and your paramour, with that inane ritual, have lost your wager. Let us see if I can do better."

Instead of the sword, Simon used Osiris to cast the circle though he didn't really need such protection. Immediately, a line of whitish blue light appeared, drawing gasps from Lady Cerridwen and Osiris.

Simon flung the boy against his girlfriend and watched the couple clutch each other, unable to take their eyes from the sphere of light. "That, children, is only the beginning." Filled with a sense of mischief, Simon threw back his head and screamed out one of his favorite conjurations from the *Key of Solomon,* speaking in Latin for added effect on his impressionable audience. "I conjure ye and most urgently command ye, Marduk, officer of hell, by the most mighty and powerful name of God El that ye in no way delay, but that ye come immediately hither before us!"

As he spoke, the temperature in the room dropped until his breath came out in frosty white puffs and the mortals cowering beside him shivered uncontrollably, their lips turning blue. Since Simon hadn't told the daemon to appear without noise or hideousness, it made a great production of appearing, the repugnant smell of sulfur and decay overpowering the small room as a vicious being came before him, awaiting his commands.

Simon heard the girl murmuring incoherently and saw his guests were both in shock. "What is this?" he asked, careful not to take his eyes off his infernal visitor. "I thought you adepts . . . this devil here is but a minor soldier in hell."

"No," Osiris choked. "No, no . . ."

"So now, children, you discover you had no true ability after all . . . your 'religion' was merely an outlet to defy your parents, an elaborate fantasy game. Perhaps you're also discovering you have no real faith? I can see from your bulging eyes and the pulses hammering in your necks that this is your first encounter with something otherworldly. You are like so many other mortals I've encountered . . . you give great lip service to the idea of being dedicated practioners of the black arts but the first time you are brought into the presence of evil, you want to run and hide."

Impatient because he was ignoring it, the daemon reached out one specter claw to scratch Simon's cheek and received a sharp reprimand. It bowed its head uneasily, understanding it could not intimidate him.

Simon had only called the monster to frighten his guests, and since that had succeeded wonderfully, he had no more need of it. He began the License to Depart and it sulked. Since nothing had been asked of it, Simon wasn't beholden to it.

It tried again to frighten him, making objects fly all about the room and howling with a great voice Simon had no doubt was going to temporarily deafen his mortal guests. But Simon had dealt with far worse imps than this and stood his ground, knowing the only way one could lose to a daemon was by showing or feeling any kind of fear.

"Be ye accursed, damned, and eternally reproved if ye do not immediately obey my command to depart!" Simon thundered, and the thing whined, but still refused to leave. Only after Simon tormented it by calling upon the power of devils greater than it did it finally go.

The magick circle disappeared and Simon waved his hand to make the overhead lights come on, shaking his head at the shambles the room was in.

Simon put his hand to his cheek and winced at the sharp pain and blood on his fingertips. No matter . . . the wound would heal once he fed. That in mind, he yanked Osiris away from his girlfriend and gave the boy a menacing smile.

"Please," Osiris whimpered, saying words Simon had heard a thousand times before. "Don't hurt me."

"Would you like to be like me?" Simon asked softly. "Have the power I just displayed?"

"Ye . . . ye . . . yes . . ."

Simon's grin broadened and he allowed his blood teeth to emerge.

"Vampire . . ." the boy choked when he saw the ivory fangs. "Undead . . ."

Simon didn't bother telling his victim that he was as alive as Osiris was. "Yes, a vampire . . . immortal and filled with powers you just witnessed. Do you want my power?"

"Yes," the boy said and his fear appeared to be subsiding.

"What would you do for it?"

"Anything!"

Simon raised an eyebrow. "Would you indeed?"

"Yes!" Osiris yelled, all his terror vanished. The boy threw himself at Simon's feet, kissing his black wing tip shoes frenziedly. "Please, please, please!"

"Would you kill?"

"I'll kill every night for the Dark Gift!"

Dark Gift . . . Simon rolled his eyes but continued with the charade. He reached into a small wooden cupboard and withdrew a scimitar blade that Meghann, of all people, had given him for their first anniversary.

As he brought the weapon to Osiris, Simon remembered how touched he'd been by the gift, an antique Meghann had obviously spent a great deal of the allowance he gave her on and devoted much thought to finding something he'd enjoy.

Perhaps he would send his servant to Cartier's, after all. For now, Simon put the knife in Osiris's slack hand and said, "Kill her."

"Huh?" The boy blinked and turned his horror-struck gaze to Lady Cerridwen, a silent witness until now.

"Show me you are willing to pay the price I exact for immortality. Sever your ties to humanity and kill this girl you claim to love."

"No!" Lady Cerridwen screamed and made a frantic run for the door. Lightning quick, Simon's arm lashed out and he caught the girl, throwing her toward Osiris.

He thought the boy might protest . . . maybe even try to turn the blade on Simon to save his girlfriend. But the boy, tantalized by immortality, raised the blade over his head and tried to stab Lady Cerridwen in the heart.

The girl, despite her weight, was quick and rolled out of harm's way. Simon moved against the door of the study and wished Meghann were here with him. Would she dare lecture him on mortals' innate goodness if she could see these two who claimed such love for each other fight like the baited bears he used to watch as a mortal?

"Hold still, you bitch!" Osiris panted and tried to pin his victim to the ground.

"Fuck you!" the foul-mouthed girl snarled and put her hands up to wrestle the scimitar from her puny boyfriend.

With a small cry, Osiris dropped the knife and Lady Cerridwen smothered his body with her bulk. Emitting a warrior's cry, she picked up the blade and stabbed Osiris repeatedly.

"Enough—he's quite dead." Simon moved toward her and snatched the scimitar from her, licking the unfortunate boy's blood off the blade.

"I killed him!" Lady Cerridwen panted, insanity shining in her eyes. "I earned your Dark Gift!"

"That is what you crave . . . eternal life?"

"Yes, yes, yes!"

"So be it," Simon said and drew the unresisting girl close to him. "But you really should ask questions when you strike a bargain with the devil. I shall give you eternal life . . . by draining your blood and allowing your soul to flee your dead body."

"No," Lady Cerridwen whimpered as Simon's fangs moved toward her jugular. "Please . . . my dad is rich . . . I can give you . . ."

Simon raised his eyes to the doomed girl. "Look around you, child. Do you think I have any need of more money? I only offer transformation when I receive something in return. Your plump body is of no interest to me and your banal intellect bores me. The only one way you can serve me is as food," he said over her hysterical sobs.

Simon glanced at the scimitar, and considered giving the girl a lesson in the proper way to use it. But his gold and ruby Rolex informed him that it was already nine o'clock . . . he simply didn't have the time for a long, drawn-out death. So he bent his head to her jugular and drank rapidly.

Youthful, he thought, tasting the blood like a connoisseur of fine wine. But not quite as potent as he'd hoped. Still, his cheek was healed and he now had the energy he needed to find Meghann and deal with the guests he expected in another hour.

Freshly showered and groomed, Simon peered at his reflection in the full-length mirror in his dressing room. See-through though it was, a vampire could make out enough of his features to ascertain that his tie was properly knotted, hair neatly in place.

Simon smoothed an unruly chestnut cowlick back into place, and reflected on the guests he was expecting momentarily. When he'd gone into hiding, he'd been forced to leave all his holdings vulnerable (minus the lockboxes stuffed with cash that he'd hidden all over the world) to maintain the illusion he was truly dead. Eager young vampires had seized his property, glorying in the thought that their master was dead.

Now that he'd emerged from hiding, prudent vampires had already returned his wealth to him; some had even doubled it. But others, perhaps thinking he was finally showing weakness by allowing Meghann to live, had not rendered onto Caesar what was Caesar's. The evening ahead should solve that problem.

Simon's sharp ears detected sounds downstairs—his human servant opening the front door and admitting two vampires to the drawing room. Simon decided to greet his guests with a small display of his new power. He narrowed his energy field down to the smallest pinprick, allowing no hint of his presence to escape the thick blackness he wrapped around himself. Thus disguised, he entered the drawing room of his town house, and observed his guests.

"Why has he summoned us here, do you know?" The question came from Isaac Spears, a male vampire. He was a pretty young man with carefully tousled blond curls and a full, pouting mouth. Simon had transformed the boy in the eighteenth century after he'd been useful in helping him obtain some ancient manuscripts from Alcuin.

"Lord Baldevar no longer shares his thoughts with me," the female vampire said shortly, and Simon grinned at the open jealousy in her voice. Gabrielle De Moiré, an exquisite beauty he'd transformed during the French Revolution. She'd been one of his favorites . . . until Meghann, that is. So Gabrielle still regretted losing his affections?

"Perhaps he wishes our aid in destroying that jade he's so besotted with," Gabrielle continued, and Simon's grin widened. She was indeed jealous. "I would love to help our master tear that drab to shreds. She has humiliated Lord Baldevar by leaving him, and then taking mortal lovers like a common harlot. Do you suppose our master knows of his consort's promiscuous ways?"

"I do know I consider it the height of hypocrisy for you to criticize my consort when you made your fortune as a mortal by selling your favors to the highest bidder." Lord Baldevar grasped Gabrielle's chin and smiled gently at her shock. "Come now. I transformed you nearly three centuries ago. Surely you have better things to do with your immortality than gossip like an old woman?"

"I merely consider your interests, master," Gabrielle said hastily and knelt before him, Isaac following suit.

Simon did not give them permission to rise, preferring to make them address him from their knees. "My thanks for your concern," he said wryly. "However, what is between me and my lady does not concern you."

"Master," Isaac said reverently, trying to control his fear. He had not been in the same room with his master in over forty years. The power Lord Baldevar always held loosely in check was now a thousand times stronger . . . you could almost see a dark light surrounding him. Lord Baldevar seemed nearly invincible, but then Isaac smiled to himself. He remembered there was one thing that made his master vulnerable . . . a pretty young vampire with bright red hair and green eyes.

Lord Baldevar raised an eyebrow at his still kneeling protégé, and Isaac paled. It was impossible; Lord Baldevar could not have heard his thoughts. Vampires could read mortals; sometimes they could read the thoughts of vampires in their own bloodline, but Isaac was too strong for his master to penetrate his shields . . . he hoped.

"You cannot imagine my thoughts when I found out you were alive, master," Isaac finally blurted out, unable to take his master's piercing stare.

Actually, Simon thought he could imagine his feelings quite well—shock, resentment, and then dawning horror. He did not blame Isaac for trying to usurp his power; Simon would have done the same thing in Isaac's place. The difference was that he had had the strength to seize power from his enemies when he was a young vampire carving a place for himself, but Isaac was no match for him. He would crush the boy like a bug.

"Enlighten me, Isaac. But first, stand up . . . both of you. May I offer you a drink?" Simon held up a crystal decanter filled with a ruby liquid. "Perhaps the blood of a saint?"

"Master!" Gabrielle breathed. "That is Alcuin's blood?"

"All that remains of him on this earth," Simon said with a vicious smile and offered his guests one port glass each of the dead prelate's blood.

Isaac raised his glass high and offered a toast. "To your well-deserved victory, master."

"Did you ever doubt I'd triumph, Isaac?" Simon said softly before clinking his glass against Isaac's.

Isaac said nothing, and he and Gabrielle perched awkwardly on Charles VI chairs while Simon made himself comfortable on a green damask sofa. After a long silence, Isaac began to speak again.

"Master, I will not pry into matters that concern your . . . your lady." By Simon's referring to her that way, both vampires knew Meghann had not lost their master's favor. Now they had to see if they had. "But let me assure you right now that we came here tonight to offer you any aid we can provide."

Simon raised an eyebrow, pleased that Isaac managed to set a trap for himself. "Did you?"

"Oh, yes," Isaac said hurriedly. "We are, in all matters, your devoted servants."

"You will swear to that?" Simon asked, giving the boy one last chance to save himself. "That you are loyal to me and have never entertained notions of challenging my rightful position?"

Isaac knelt before him once more. "I greeted the news that you had not been destroyed with gladness, master."

"Is that why you hastened to return all my holdings?"

Isaac paled. "What holdings, master?"

Lord Baldevar opened a Chippendale desk in the corner of the room, holding several thick documents. "The minor matter of this town house. You cannot manage your property any better than a mortal, boy. You lost this exquisite house several years ago in a bad investment. I was the dummy corporation that picked it up at auction. Then, there was the IBM stock I bought in 1955, my pharmaceutical company, several Swiss accounts . . . in other words, Isaac, the lion's share of my wealth that vultures like yourself seized upon my 'death.' Understand, I am not angered by your actions of forty years ago; you saw an opportunity to profit from my misfortune. However, I am quite dismayed that you have not made any attempt to repay me. Were you hoping Alcuin would slay me before I got around to demanding my wealth be returned to me?"

"Of . . . of course not, master." The vampire was all but shaking on his knees.

In a pretense of boredom with the conversation, Simon inspected a solid-gold letter opener on the desk while Isaac continued to babble anything he thought might save his worthless hide. "Master, I was busy making plans to . . . to . . . to trap Meghann for you! I thought to find her and offer my aid in destroying you, then disable her and bring her to you . . ."

"If I want Meghann by my side, I do not require your assistance. Is this half-truth the best you can come up with?" Simon spun around and hurled the letter opener at Isaac. It spun through the air before landing in the center of his forehead. Isaac screamed in agony, trying to dislodge the thing from his brain.

Simon was at his side instantly, hand firm on the letter opener, watching blood and brain matter seep from the wound.

"Do you think it's possible to lobotomize a vampire?" Simon queried Gabrielle, who was staring at the vampire on the floor in mute horror, no doubt wondering what Lord Baldevar had in mind for her.

He held her eyes. "Are you loyal to your master?"

She nodded silently.

"Wonderful. But Isaac does not seem to recall the first tenet of transformation. Won't you help him remember?"

"Obedience, master." Gabrielle quavered.

"Good girl," he said, giving her an icy smile. "All my children are required to give me unconditional obedience. Perhaps you simply forgot how to obey, Isaac? You need what mortals now call a refresher course." Simon yanked the gold letter opener from Isaac's head and plunged it into his stomach, making a neat incision all the way up to his heart.

Gabrielle clamped down on her lips to keep from screaming when Simon pulled Isaac's entrails from his body, a small wrinkling of his nose at the gore piling at his expensive shoes the only change in his glacial expression.

"Good dog," Simon said, wrapping Isaac's large intestines around his neck like a leash. "Come on, little doggie, sit up for your master or I'll make your next few hours a living hell you cannot begin to imagine."

The pain was excruciating, but Isaac knew it wouldn't kill him. He'd continue to live in pain unless Lord Baldevar beheaded him or he managed to escape. Blood poured from his mouth and ears as he slowly, painfully pulled himself into a sitting position.

"Good boy," Simon said, looking down at the destroyed vampire with cold delight. "Now beg."

"Please, master," Isaac managed to croak.

"Let's see if my dog can walk." Simon yanked on the entrails leash, dragging Isaac out of the room by his own intestines and gesturing for Gabrielle to follow.

Gabrielle followed them to the cellar, and became rigid when they approached an oak door. From the other side, she heard the unmistakable sounds of a vampire (no mortal could produce the horrible keen) screaming.

"Why doesn't it open the door?" she said faintly.

"It can't," Simon explained. "Alcuin was ever a thorn in my side but I learned one useful trick from him. You know how the vampire must beg admission to a house in those penny-dreadful books and movies? There actually is an obscure rite that can bar a vampire from entering any premises. Of course, it is not within a mortal's power to set the spell—another vampire must do it. My guest cannot cross the threshold of the room without my permission."

"Mon Dieu," Gabrielle cried when Simon threw open the door and the filthy, mindless creature came running up to them. She took a step back in fear, but the thing approached the door and then put its hands to its face, whining as though someone had thrown battery acid in its eyes.

"Have you had the pleasure of meeting Jimmy Delacroix before tonight?"

Thunderstruck, Gabrielle stared at the howling, shrieking vampire. *Pauvre enfant,* she thought, the unfortunate man had not survived transformation. Now he was doomed to spend eternity mad, unable to think or reason or do anything but feed.

"He was Meghann's mortal lover," Gabrielle whispered.

Simon smiled at his youngest spawn; the boy had ventured back to the doorway, howling and frothing at the mouth. He smelled their blood, and wanted it. His rage came from not being able to get at them.

"Hungry?" Simon asked the uncomprehending vampire. The thing merely looked through him and continued to yowl.

"Step back," Simon commanded. It took a few moments but the new vampire finally obeyed his master and slunk into the farthest corner of the room.

Simon flung Isaac into the room. The wounded vampire couldn't defend himself when Jimmy Delacroix leaped on top of him. In minutes, Isaac was dead. Frustrated by death, the new vampire whined and tore the corpse apart in an attempt to find more blood. Soon however, the act of feeding forced him into an uneasy sleep.

"Why do you keep him alive, master?" Gabrielle asked. "Did you not say such creatures have no place in this world, that they could bring unwelcome attention from mortals since they do not have the wit to cover their crimes?"

"He will not be in the world long," Simon told her. "I keep him alive because he is a present for Meghann."

Gabrielle pouted at the mention of his consort and undid one hook in the back of her dress, standing before her master naked. "I loved you for hundreds of years before the wench was even born. She scorns you, and conspires with your enemies. Why not take a consort who will give you all you want?"

The kill excited her, Simon thought, observing her hard nipples and heavy breathing. It excited him too so he lifted the girl up and had her against the cement wall of the cellar.

"I am pleased to see Meghann no longer has a hold on your heart," Gabrielle said afterward, smiling.

Simon laughed, and tossed the vampire her dress. "Whether she does or not is no concern of yours." He laughed harder at the tears in Gabrielle's turquoise eyes. "You cannot be fool enough to think that quick, mundane coupling meant something?"

"What does Meghann have that I do not?" Gabrielle demanded angrily.

In response, Simon grabbed her long, silver-blond hair and pushed her into Jimmy Delacroix's prison.

"You do not use such a tone when you address me."

"I'm sorry!" Gabrielle yelled. "Please, master!"

Abruptly, he let her go. "I forgive you—it was your jealousy speaking. Have you lost your mind to think I would even contemplate making a baseborn whore my consort? All you offer me is well-used flesh but I can buy that from whores less vicious than you."

Gabrielle pursed her ruby-red lips but did not dare rebuke him. "I beg your pardon, master."

"Pay a forfeit and you shall be pardoned," Simon said and plunged his blood teeth into her neck.

At first, Gabrielle did not protest. But when he drained her to weakness, she tried vainly to push him off. Simon dropped her to the floor, where she glanced up. "Master, please . . ."

He smiled cruelly and kicked the prostrate vampire. "Do you wish to live?"

"Please don't kill me," she whimpered.

"Get up," Simon commanded, and Gabrielle pulled herself to her feet shakily. Being bled made her dizzy but she did not dare disobey.

When they were back in the drawing room, Lord Baldevar handed her a thick portfolio bound in black leather. "This lists all my seized holdings and the vampires who have them. Visit every one of them and tell them what you witnessed tonight. Inform your friends that if my wealth is not transferred into the hands of my mortal attorneys within a fortnight, what Isaac suffered shall be mild compared to what I do to them." Simon waved his hand. "Go . . . you are dismissed."

The vampire fled, and Simon went upstairs to pour himself a cognac. While he drank, Simon reflected on Gabrielle's jealous interrogation—*what does Meghann have that I do not?* A bemusing combination of wide-eyed, exuberant innocence and smoldering sensuality that enthralled him completely was the answer Simon would never give anyone, including the object of his affections. Only an utter fool would make himself vulnerable by telling a woman he desired his heart's secrets. . . .

Without warning, Simon was seized by a blinding pain that made him fall to the floor, the cognac snifter shattering as it fell from his hand. He gasped, but forced himself to seize the pain, to immerse himself in it so he could know where it came from.

Meghann?

For a moment, her face floated before his eyes—the green eyes bright with pain and fear, hair soaked in sweat. *Don't let me die!*

Her image faded, along with the pain. Simon leaped to his feet, his heart pounding at the thought that Meghann was actually . . .

Discipline, he reminded himself sternly. This was no time to celebrate; he must confirm that brief psychic flash with Meghann.

Simon took a deep breath, and prepared himself for a session of astral spying. In his last communication with Meghann, he'd assured her that she would not see him unless she wanted to. However, he said nothing about keeping an eye on her from time to time without her knowledge.

He hurried to the study, pleased to note that his human servant had already removed the bodies and tidied up, and withdrew a small stone filter from the wall safe. It contained Meghann's blood . . . a small bit he'd saved the night she had allowed him to feed from her. He lit a brazier, and threw the blood on the flames. Simon concentrated his attention on the smoke rising from the brazier. The flames took hold, swirling together into one image—a mass of cherry-red hair. He held on to the image of Meghann, commanding himself to follow her.

Small white room, bright light, antiseptic smell of cleanliness. Not a hospital, but a room a doctor had transformed into a makeshift hospital for his new patient. Easily, Simon picked up on the mortal in the room—a middle-aged man with a bandaged nose and black eyes leaning anxiously over a body; he stood up and took a shaky breath . . . .

No! *Simon nearly lost the vision when his heart contracted at the sight of Meghann. His beautiful young girl, transformed by pain into a whimpering, emaciated skeleton, brow creased and eyes blazing from hollow sockets as unbearable agony made her scream.*

"Don't," *the mortal pleaded, putting a hand over her mouth.* "Honey, save your strength. Don't scream like that."

"Ch . . . Charl . . ." *she tried to say, and Simon watched Charles Tarleton grab her hands.*

"What is it, Meghann?"

"I called him, Charles," *she cried.* "Simon . . . I saw his face when . . . when I convulsed . . . he knows . . . help me . . ."

"Okay," *Charles soothed.* "Meghann, it's all right. Maybe it's for the best . . . maybe he can help you. . . ."

I'm the only one who can help her, nitwit.

Meghann bolted upright, grabbing Charles with a strength that surprised Simon.

"No," *Meghann hissed.* "You listen to me . . . don't let him near me."

"But if he can—"

"No!" she yelled and fell against the pillows, the adrenaline abandoning her. "Promise me . . . he can't know about the baby . . . if it's his help or my death, you let me die. Promise."

"Meghann, I—"

"Promise!" she screamed and her eyes rolled into the back of her head as she started hemorrhaging from her nose.

"Jesus," the mortal murmured after he cauterized her. "How the hell is she still alive?"

"It takes a great deal to kill a vampire," Charles said shakily, staring down at his now unconscious friend.

The mortal frowned. "She needs blood."

"Of course she needs blood!" Charles screamed. "But anytime she drinks any, she vomits and now this! Now convulsions, seizures. My God, how can a vampire live if she can't drink blood?"

The mortal shrugged helplessly. "I don't understand . . . I was so sure that if she drank your blood, the enzyme would be back in her system and she'd recover. Instead—"

"Instead, it made her sicker," Charles said tiredly and used a cloth to wipe the blood from Meghann's upper lip. "Lee, what are we going to do? If only you could abort the fetus . . ."

The mortal pointed to his bandaged nose. "I told you, all I did was put her legs in the stirrups and she woke up. She did this in the two seconds before she realized who I was. Jesus, I could be dead by now! Anyway, we can't perform an abortion with her in this condition. It will kill her."

"She's going to die anyway if we don't figure out what's making her reject blood."

Simon felt an iron hand grab him and a cold voice intoned, "Leave my daughter alone, nephew."

He found himself back in the town house; Alcuin had used his spirit to forcibly remove Simon from the astral plane.

Goddamn that meddling preacher! Even dead, Alcuin was still a problem. He still had enough power to protect his young apprentices, but how long could that last?

Simon smiled grimly; he'd heard enough to find Meghann. But his smile faded when he thought of all he'd witnessed.

Pregnant! He had to find Meghann; she'd die if he didn't help her. He'd hoped, for her sake, she wouldn't have to suffer through the sickness. There was no question she was going to grow weaker; Simon doubted Meghann or that young wretch had any idea what was needed to keep a pregnant vampire well. No doubt they'd try medical science and some educated poking through Alcuin's archives. For all the good that would do, they might as well use leeches to heal Meghann.

Magic would not be necessary to locate Meghann. Charles Tarleton had called the physician Lee. Lord Baldevar had a complete dossier on Charles Tarleton and remembered the sodomite had carried on an affair with some mortal physician named Lee about ten years ago.

Little one, he thought while turning on his laptop so he could access the files concerning Charles Tarleton, *I know I told you that you would not see me again unless you wanted to. But you did just beg me not to let you die, did you not? I say that counts as an invitation.* His lips twitched when he thought of how indignant Meghann would be when she found out the only person who could save her now was her master.

THREE

Las Vegas
July 2, 1998

Lee opened sleep-encrusted eyes and glanced at the illuminated clock radio by Meghann's bedside—2:00 P.M. Unlike Charles, who'd been forced by the sunrise to crawl away from his friend and stretch out on the cot they'd set up by the foot of the bed, Lee had kept vigil until exhaustion finally set in around eight in the morning. Not that he'd been able to do much for his comatose patient besides hold her slack hand in his and pray some magic cure would occur to him.

"You can't die," Lee said out loud to the still white wraith on the bed, and clumsily wiped at the tears on his cheeks. He couldn't stand this, being forced to sit here and watch this wonderful woman that'd saved his life slip away from him.

Think, he told himself. *You're a doctor . . . there's got to be some reason Meghann is rejecting blood.*

The shrill buzz at the PATIENTS ONLY door startled him. The night after Charles and Meghann showed up, Lee had canceled all his appointments, having his receptionist tell his patients he was bedridden with the flu.

The buzzer jabbed again, and Lee walked out of the guest room, shutting the door behind him.

"Mrs. Hilliard?" Lee questioned, indifferent to his

patient's dismay at his sleep-rumpled clothing, tousled hair, and bandaged nose.

"Doctor," she said timidly. "It's the beginning of the month—time for my Depo-Provera shot. I have a two-thirty appointment."

"Didn't Jeannie call and . . ." Lee sighed and mentally cursed his flaky receptionist. He really should fire the girl, who hadn't shown up for work on time in God knows how long and screwed up appointments routinely, but Lee wasn't any good at confrontations.

"I'm sorry," Mrs. Hilliard said. "If I've made a mistake—'

"No, no," Lee said. "It's not your fault. Jeannie was supposed to call all my patients and tell them I wasn't seeing anyone for the rest of the week. You see, I have a . . . uh, family emergency." That was no lie.

"Well, I can just reschedule—"

"It's okay," Lee told her and stepped aside so his patient and her six-year-old daughter could enter. "I can give you the shot in five minutes—there's no need to make you come back."

He touched the rheostat on the wall, and the dark house (shuttered in deference to his guests) brightened.

In the examining room, Lee rolled up his sleeves and washed his hands quickly before reaching into the refrigerator for the small bottle of Depo-Provera.

"Needles are bad," the little girl pronounced solemnly while Lee prepared the shot. "I had one today and it really hurt."

"Well, I'm going to try my best not to hurt Mommy. What kind of medicine did the doctor give you?"

"It was a vampire shot," the little girl said, and Lee almost dropped the needle.

"She means the doctor took blood," Mrs. Hilliard explained. "He calls it his vampire shot to calm her down. Laurie's having her appendix taken out and he wanted to know her blood type."

"Oh," Lee replied and used a cotton swab to sterilize his patient's upper arm before giving her the intramuscular injection of birth control that would work for three months before she needed another shot. Pity no one gave Meghann some Depo-Provera, Lee thought and wondered idly if a vampire could practice contraception with anything but a condom.

"Good for you," Lee told the little girl and gave her a red lollipop from the collection he kept for his patients' children. Then he turned to Mrs. Hilliard, pulling her plaid sleeve down over the bandage he'd put on her arm. "You can pay me outside."

"What is blood type?" Laurie asked him.

Lee gave the girl a simple response, actually glad to be distracted from his worry over Meghann. "All blood type means is that there are different kinds of blood."

"You mean some blood isn't red?" Laurie asked, and Lee laughed.

"No, honey, all blood is red but there are tiny differences. Now, do you know what a transfusion is?"

The little girl thought for a minute and then said, "On Mommy's soap opera, someone got in a car accident once and they had to get a transfusion."

"Right," Lee said. "They were in an accident and they probably lost blood when they got hurt. Now, when they got to the hospital, the doctors and nurses would have new blood waiting for them. When doctors put blood into a patient, that's called a transfusion."

"Where do they get the blood?" Laurie asked.

"Nice people donate their blood to help people who get hurt. And sometimes, when people have an operation like you're going to have, they lose a little bit of blood and they need a transfusion. But doctors have to be real careful about the blood they give you. Thank you, Mrs. Hilliard." Lee accepted her payment and gave her a receipt before turning back to Laurie. "You could get very sick if the doctor gave you the wrong type of blood."

"Does everybody have different blood?"

"There are about four different types and everyone is one of them."

"How do you know who's who?" Laurie asked.

"We have a test that says which type you are and I bet your doctor is testing your blood right now. Have you ever heard of antibodies?" Lee asked.

The little girl shook her head, and Lee explained, "Antibodies are very, very important. They're what prevent you from getting sick. When you get a cold, it's your antibodies that fight the cold and make it go away. But everyone has different antibodies . . . they're also what decides which blood type you are." There was no need to confuse the child by explaining it was actually antigens that determined blood type, and that antibodies simply rejected any antigens they didn't recognize. "Now, my blood type is B. Understand?"

Laurie nodded, and Lee continued with his very simplified explanation. "That means my antibodies are Bs—great big Bs." Lee drew a huge *B* on a legal pad. "Now, antibodies aren't very friendly to strangers. Let's say someone gave me blood from somebody with blood type A. What do you think would happen?"

"The Bs would get mad at the As," Laurie answered, and Lee ruffled her hair.

"Very good! They'd get real mad and tell those A intruders to go away. A and B would have a fight and that would make me very sick. And that's why the doctor gave you that test—so he'd give you the right blood."

Lee held open the door and as Laurie walked through, she turned to him and said gravely, "Antijobies are important."

Lee and his patient laughed together and he shut the door.

Antibodies are important. Lee stopped cold and then an earsplitting grin appeared on his face.

"Antibodies, antibodies, antibodies!" he chanted

like a rabid cheerleader. Lee ran toward Meghann's room. Maybe, just maybe, that little girl had given Lee the answer to Meghann's sickness.

Charles came awake to a hand shaking him and Lee screaming, "Come on! Come on! Wake up . . . I think I found a way to save Meghann!"

Charles bolted upright, clutching at Lee. "What are you talking about?"

"Come on!" Lee yanked him out of the bed, and Charles followed him to the basement where Lee had a small lab set up.

"Look at that!" Lee gestured impatiently to his microscope, and Charles leaned down to examine the small tissue sample.

Charles frowned, not looking up when he spoke to Lee. "It's agglutinated blood. Wait a minute . . . those blood cells—my God, those are vampire cells!"

"Meghann's cells, to be precise. I did a biopsy today—a small scrape off her ileum. She didn't wake up. That means she's even sicker than she was yesterday. But don't you see? You said that once blood gets to the ileum, it's supposed to be broken down. The blood isn't breaking down; the red blood cells are clumping together and that happens when—"

"When antibodies cause you to reject donor's blood," Charles said slowly, looking up from the microscope. "But I don't understand. Vampires don't have antibodies, not like mortals . . ."

"Maybe pregnant vampires do," Lee said. "I think the blood is clumping and Meghann isn't digesting it because she's having a transfusion reaction—rejecting the blood because it contains antigens her body doesn't recognize. If we give her blood with antigens comparable to the ones in her body, she'll break it down and start producing the enzyme again."

"But we tried that last night," Charles argued. "I gave her my blood. We're both vampires . . ."

Charles trailed off, and then the confusion in his eyes cleared and his eyes took on a look of guarded hope. "But we were transformed by vampires who weren't of the same bloodline. Of course! My blood has antigens hers doesn't—subtle differences—but enough to cause that violent reaction she had last night. If we were of the same bloodline, I'm sure my blood would have healed her."

"So all we have to do is get someone in her bloodline to donate blood!" Despite the purple circles under his eyes, nothing could overpower the joy in Lee's expression.

For a moment, Charles felt nothing but deep relief—Meghann would live! But then his own blood froze in his veins when he thought of who would have to be Meghann's donor.

Charles dashed back to the bedroom, taking in Meghann's corpse-pale skin and comatose state that hadn't been broken by the sunset.

"Meghann needs blood from someone in her own bloodline," Charles repeated dully.

Lee saw his lover's trepidation and nodded. "We must get blood from the . . . from the person that transformed her or someone in that bloodline. And we better do it soon. Charles, how much longer can she live like this?"

Charles considered their options—go to Lord Baldevar or someone of his bloodline. Did that mean asking someone like Isaac Spears to help Meghann? Even if one of those opportunistic vampires would agree to be the donor, it would leave Meghann completely at their mercy. No, that was out of the question—they'd exploit Meghann and her child in the hopes they could use them against Lord Baldevar.

Charles looked down at Meghann's still, waxen face. She'd forbidden him to contact Lord Baldevar, but would she feel differently if she heard Lee's theory? *God help me, Meghann,* he thought and clutched her hand. *I can't let you die. But how can I tell Lord Baldevar your secret? How can I turn you over to that monster?*

"Jesus Christ!" Lee jumped back, slamming into the dresser behind him when a short scream escaped Charles's lips.

"What is it?" Lee started to ask and then he heard the footsteps in the hall. He whirled around to face the intruder and saw a tall, handsome man with unusual yellow eyes in the doorway.

Lee felt his knees clacking nervously together, and his mouth was suddenly dry. Something about this man inspired intense fear. Lee wished the stranger would speak, shout, do anything but stand so still with those evil eyes fixed unblinkingly on Charles.

"You can't come in here," Charles said, all the color gone from his face and his black eyes wide with fear. He clutched Meghann's unconscious form to him. "We barred the house to you."

The apparition laughed—a low, menacing sound that made Lee grasp the bureau to stay upright. "Your pathetic power cannot keep me at bay. And what have we here?" The man turned to him and Lee felt a hand grasp his chin. Dimly, Lee heard Charles yelling for the stranger to let him go.

The vampire ignored Charles, and scrutinized Lee with open curiosity. "Even after four hundred years, coincidence can still amaze me. I never expected our paths to cross again."

Lord Baldevar's eyes made Lee feel naked and powerless. No wonder Meghann was so frightened.

"Meghann does not need to fear me and neither do you. I will not kill you when you've attempted to help my consort."

Lee swallowed a crazy urge to laugh. What was he supposed to say—thank you? He stared into the golden eyes and didn't see a shred of remorse for nearly killing him forty years ago when he was a child. Did this creature have a conscience?

Lord Baldevar turned from Lee and gave Charles a freezing glare. "Finding this physician is the one intelligent thing I've ever known you to do. Now, back away from that bed."

"Hell will freeze over before I let you near Meghann."

Lord Baldevar moved his hand slightly and Charles crashed into the wall behind the bed. Lee rushed to him while Lord Baldevar gave Meghann a slight shake and said her name.

"She can't hear you," Lee told him. "She's comatose."

"She'll hear me," Lord Baldevar said flatly. He undid a ruby and gold cufflink, pushing his sleeve up to his elbow.

Lee gasped when he saw the fangs emerge from the vampire's mouth. He bit into his wrist and put it to Meghann's mouth. Then, he gently pried her lips apart and put her tongue on his bleeding wrist.

Meghann's response was immediate. For the first time since last night, her eyes flew open and she started to devour the blood. Charles and Lee both watched in amazement as the near death pallor faded from her face while she drank. Her system must have produced the enzyme in a matter of seconds, Lee thought, stunned by how quickly she recovered, actually sitting up and clutching the arm she fed from.

Lord Baldevar was nearly as white as Meghann had been a few minutes ago, but he didn't pull his arm away until Meghann raised her mouth from his wrist. Then he used the bedsheet to wipe the blood off her mouth and neck. The only sign of softness the vampire showed was when he stroked Meghann's limp, lusterless red hair and the cruel line of his mouth relaxed slightly.

Meghann put her hand up, to beckon or ward Lord

Baldevar away Lee couldn't tell. "Am I a vampire yet?" she asked in a hoarse, drowsy voice.

He took her hand and spoke softly. "You've been a vampire for quite some time but you're sick now." It was hard to believe the man who held her hand and spoke so gently was the same monster that just sent Charles crashing into a wall.

Meghann's eyes were still glazed, and Lee wasn't sure she'd registered Lord Baldevar's presence. She was probably delirious, if she was asking him whether she was a vampire yet.

"Rest now," Lord Baldevar told her, and she closed her eyes at once, falling back against the pillows.

"Will she be all right now?" Lee managed to ask. "What about the baby?"

Lord Baldevar didn't look up from Meghann when he replied, "Meghann will recover. As for the child, he was never in any danger. Meghann was nearly killed by starvation because she did not have any of my blood to replenish her."

"Wrong," Charles said coldly. "Impregnating her in the first place is what's killing her . . . and still might cause her death in a few months."

Lord Baldevar glared at Charles as though he'd just remembered he was there. Carefully, he pulled his hand from Meghann's and whipped around to grab Charles by the shoulders and shove him against the wall.

It felt like his spine was going to collapse and then Lord Baldevar let him fall to the floor. "Your incompetence nearly cost me my heir. Unfortunately, I cannot kill you . . . it would upset Meghann too much. I will settle with you for endangering the life of my consort and my son after she has the child."

Flicking his hand contemptuously, Lord Baldevar turned his attention back to Lee. "Will you continue as Meghann's physician?"

"Of course . . . I'd do anything to help her."

"You are already doing a great deal. Deducing that Meghann needs my blood . . . you are an exceptional doctor. I wonder what you'll be capable of after you transform?"

"Transform?" Lee asked. Becoming a vampire had never occurred to him—all he'd wanted to do was save Meghann's life. Had Charles planned to transform him or was he planning to leave again once Meghann was well?

"I would be honored to transform you if you decide you'd like to be immortal," Lord Baldevar said politely. "If you leave your life in the hands of this fool, you'll never survive. He'll kill you the same way he nearly killed Meghann."

Charles gave a bitter laugh. "You claim such love for Meghann but you're willing to let her die so you can have a chance to make your warped fantasy come true?"

Charles gasped and clutched his chest; it felt as if his heart were exploding inside his body.

"Massive coronary event," Lord Baldevar told him calmly. "Meghann won't die as long as she receives the proper care."

"What do we need to do?" Lee asked, trying to divert Lord Baldevar's attention. "Does she need to stay in bed until the baby is born? When will she wake up? What should she eat? Should the delivery be caesarian?"

Apparently satisfied that his point was made, Lord Baldevar released Charles and addressed Lee. "She shouldn't be kept idle. Make sure she's active. It's unnatural for a vampire to sleep at night . . . she should regain consciousness soon. Like any expectant mother, she should eat well and be kept happy. There is time yet to discuss the delivery."

Lord Baldevar reached into his suit jacket and produced a small, handsome leather-backed book, placing it in Lee's unresisting hands. "This will explain all you and Meghann need to know."

"Infans Noctis," Lee read aloud from the cover.

"Night's Child," Lord Baldevar translated. "It is an account of a vampiric pregnancy—written down by the father. It should settle all Meghann's fears. After you read, you'll understand why this child will not be born malformed and see that there is every reason for Meghann to survive delivery. Read it at your leisure, Doctor. It's written in Latin—the language of the father, a Roman senator. Of course, that is not the original text . . . I keep that safe in a steel box so air won't destroy it." Again Lee had to resist the urge to laugh when he thought that this creature could kill another vampire or a small child without turning a hair but he went out of his way to preserve ancient texts. "Should you have any trouble with translation, Meghann can assist you."

Lord Baldevar turned from Lee and returned to the bed, holding Meghann's hand.

"What the hell are you doing?" Charles growled.

"I do not explain myself to underlings. Go prepare something for Meghann to eat; she is dreadfully thin. She'll wake up quite hungry."

"I am not leaving her alone with you!"

Lee saw murder in those gold eyes and grabbed Charles's arm. "Come on, you can't stop him."

Lord Baldevar laughed—a sound that made Lee clamp down on Charles's forearm with a painful grip. "Your lover is not only a gifted physician, but a pragmatist. You cannot keep me from Meghann; do not humiliate yourself by trying."

"Please," Lee whispered when Charles took a step toward the bed. "You can't help her if he kills you. You know he won't hurt her. At least he hasn't taken her away."

Charles turned on his heel and stalked out of the room. *Meghann, was this what it was like for you the thir-*

*teen years you lived with him? An endless sense of futility
and hopelessness because you couldn't defend yourself against
his power?*

"Damn him," Charles snarled, stalking toward the
kitchen. "Goddamn that monstrous fiend to hell! Poor
Meghann—what's going to happen to her now?"

"She'll live?" Lee ventured.

"She'll live at his mercy," Charles said, smashing his
fist into the stucco wall at his right. "Sorry . . . I'm
just so damned angry . . . at myself, at him. You don't
think he saved Meghann because he loves her, do
you?"

Lee thought of the way the vampire softened when
he addressed Meghann, but decided this was not the
time to engage Charles in a debate. "He wanted to
save Meghann so the baby wouldn't die?"

"Yes, there's that." Charles sighed. "But the bastard
has another purpose. You see, we are forever linked
to our masters . . . to the vampire that transforms us.
That link is made through drinking the master's blood.
With Meghann drinking that fiend's blood continually,
he'll gain a hold over her mind . . . a way to try to
influence her, control her."

"Meghann doesn't seem easily controlled to me."

Charles gave Lee a tired smile. "No, she's not . . .
a fact that drives Lord Baldevar up a wall. But if he
doesn't want her to miscarry, he can't resort to his
usual measures and torture her into submission. So
he's going to use the blood link and her vulnerability
to try and worm his way back into her life. But I won't
let that happen. I might have had to stand back in
there so he could save her life, but I won't let him
destroy her. If sharing blood weakens her resolve
against him, I'll be here to remind Meghann of her
hate. Goddammit, I will not let that bastard hurt my
friend any more than he already has."

Simon could hear the boy making his melancholy
promises, and shook his head. *That is what you left me*

for, Meghann? Whimpering fools who do nothing but wring their hands and whine about their helplessness?

He shuddered to think of what would have happened if he'd allowed the sodomite to remain in the room with Meghann. She'd wake up, and immediately start to wallow in self-pity and melodrama—all encouraged by her good friend.

Simon stretched out on the bed, pulling Meghann close to him and inspecting her emaciated body. *Poor child,* he thought, *it feels like your bones will break if I even touch you.* He couldn't find the voluptuous beauty he loved in this starved vampire. Her cheekbones stood out in shocking prominence on her face; he could count all her ribs.

Simon felt a brief flash of rage when he looked at this skeleton with a bit of flesh stretched tightly over her bones. *Damn you,* he thought and his fingers clamped down on her forearms. *Why did you do this to yourself, Meghann? Why didn't you come to me and let me save you?* How could she risk the life of her child and put herself through this kind of agony rather than contact him?

Meghann whimpered in her sleep, and he forced himself to relax. Still she thrashed and kicked at the bedsheets until he put her head to his heart and stroked her hair, murmuring the old endearments. Only then did her body go slack while her lips curved in a contented smile.

What an inconsistent, fickle child she was! He knew she'd raise the roof with her lamentations the moment she opened her eyes and saw him but now she clung to him like a frightened child. From the night he'd transformed her, Meghann seemed to change her feelings about him as often as the wind changed direction. One night, there would be cool silence for some imagined slight and the next she'd crawl into his lap and her green eyes would plead eloquently for comfort, beg him to soothe away whatever had distressed her.

There were ways to help Meghann realize her true feelings, Simon thought with an evil smirk. But first he'd have to give her a bath, he thought, staring down in distaste at her oily, unwashed hair.

He gave her a quick sponge bath in the small, adjoining bathroom and washed her hair twice, pinning it to the top of her head. Then he took her back into the bedroom, scowling at the contents of the wooden drawers containing her clothes. The drawers were filled with T-shirts displaying scruffy minstrels (he believed they were called rock stars) and vulgar sayings—did the girl own nothing feminine? Finally, he found a pretty spring-green nightgown with a scooped neckline and slipped that over her head.

He brushed her long hair free of the tangles that indicated it had been at least a few nights since she'd last brushed it, and glanced down at her sleeping face with satisfaction. Meghann was getting more color in her face and her eyes were beginning to move beneath her closed lids. She'd be awake soon and he intended to make sure she did not forget this particular waking for a long time to come.

Arise, Sleeping Beauty. Simon bit down savagely on his index finger and put it to Meghann's lips, rubbing the crimson liquid all around like lipstick.

Without opening her eyes, Meghann reached out with her tongue to lap up the blood. Soon she was sucking on his finger, but she did not open her eyes because of the slight command Simon put in her mind.

Meghann tasted warm, unbearably delicious blood pouring down her throat. She lapped greedily at the nectar . . . where had she tasted this before? Not mortal blood, not this strong, dark substance that made her feel alive again, that the child inside her cried out for.

She felt a light hand at her thighs, playing with her. Eagerly she spread her legs, craving more. She heard a man's laugh, low and self-assured, as he started to finger the aching flesh between her legs.

The finger at her lips was withdrawn and she whimpered a protest . . . she wanted more blood. Then she felt hard, firm lips force her mouth open . . . allowing her to taste the blood on the tongue that teased in and out of her mouth. *Yes,* she thought, *take me, make me yours. Let me take more blood . . . let me see you. . . .*

"As you wish, my pet," the hateful voice whispered, and Meghann's eyes snapped open. She saw the chestnut hair, then the amused, gloating amber eyes, and bit down hard on his tongue with her blood teeth. Lord Baldevar pulled away without a sound, laughing even as blood poured from his wounded tongue.

"You son of a bitch!" she howled, slapping his face with a harsh crack that echoed through the small bedroom. "Take your filthy hands off me!"

"Will you take yours off me?"

With a start, Meghann looked down at the bulge she'd wrapped her hand around, and pulled her hand away as though she'd been burned.

Cheeks flaming, she was caught between such shame that she'd allowed this bastard to touch her that she wanted to die and an overwhelming rage that screamed out to kill him. Anger easily won out and she lunged at him, punching, kicking, and biting like a woman possessed.

"Careful, wildcat," Simon said, dodging a right cross to his jaw. He grabbed her wrists, forcing them behind her back. "Kill me and you destroy yourself."

"Shut up!" she howled, all her depression and fear turning to hate now that the source of all her misery was in front of her. "I hate you, I hate you, I hate you! You evil bastard . . . look what you've done to me! You ruined my life, and what the hell have you done to Jimmy?"

Wildly, she glanced around the room. Yes, this was Lee's house . . . what the hell had happened? "Where is Charles?" Her voice shook with rage and fear. "Charles! Where are you?"

Charles appeared instantaneously, face pale and tense as he approached the bed. "Has he harmed you?"

Meghann sagged against the pillows with relief. Thank God . . . at first, she'd thought Lord Baldevar must have killed Charles and Lee.

Careful to avoid Lord Baldevar by staying on the opposite side of the bed, Charles took her hand.

"Why is he here?" Meghann demanded, ignoring Lord Baldevar.

"Tell her why I'm here," the vampire said calmly, his lips stretched into an amused grin. "By all means, I think you should be the one to explain to Meghann why I'm going to remain here. But first, perhaps she'd like news of Mr. Delacroix?"

"Jimmy!" Meghann said, and Charles thought he saw something flicker in the monster's eyes at the love and concern in Meghann's voice. "What have you done to him? I want to see him!"

"Of course," Lord Baldevar said immediately, making Meghann glare suspiciously. "When?"

"Now!"

"You've waited two months to find out his fate . . . will another hour kill you?"

"Why another hour?"

"You're going to eat whatever that nice mortal physician has made you so you start to regain your strength. Then, I'm sure you'll want to dress. Too, you'll need time to throw one of your childish tantrums when your catamite explains to you that you need my blood. Be at my home within the hour, Meghann, and you may gaze upon your boy-toy to your heart's content." Lord Baldevar murmured his address and gave Meghann a curt bow before vanishing.

Lee returned to the bedroom, carrying a wooden dinner tray laden with food. "Hey! How did he disappear?"

"Didn't you tell Lee about astral projection?" Meghann asked Charles.

"No time yet," he replied and took the tray from Lee, placing it on Meghann's lap.

"Lord Baldevar didn't disappear," Charles explained while Meghann sniffed cautiously at the chicken noodle soup and then began to eat. "Have you heard of the astral plane?"

"Isn't that where Shirley MacLaine goes to find out about her past lives?"

That actually drew a small smile from Meghann. "Whether she does or not, I have no idea. The astral plane is a spiritual realm. Have you heard of people's souls traveling to warn loved ones of danger? That's astral projection too. Basically, your soul leaves your body and travels the astral plane for enlightenment. But vampires can travel the plane with body and soul intact and we don't just use it to contact spirits—it's our way of getting from place to place."

"Huh?"

"Show him," Meghann suggested to Charles, and he vanished, reappearing in the doorway.

"We can use the astral plane to travel distances of up to thirty miles," Charles said, grinning at his bemused lover. "It comes in handy—leave the scene if someone sneaks up on you while you're feeding, get away from your enemies."

"So Lord Baldevar just left my house and went to his by flying the astral plane?"

"Probably," Meghann said and her eyes darkened when she remembered the loathsome bastard had found her. A small crease appeared between her eyebrows and she turned to Charles. "What did he mean when he said I needed his blood?"

"Meghann," Lee said gently when Charles simply looked at her with frustrated pity. "Haven't you wondered why you feel well? What made you better?"

No, she hadn't—everything had happened too fast, waking up and finding Simon leering over her. But before she opened her eyes . . . the blood on her lips that made her feel such energy, banished that awful fatigue and nausea . . .

"Oh, God," Meghann whispered. "Simon's blood . . . I drank Simon's blood and I was fine. But why? I don't understand."

Quickly, Lee explained his theory and nearly crossed himself at the unnatural light that appeared in Meghann's eyes.

"Damn him!" she cried and flung the tray across the room, creating a wild mess of splattered food and shattered cutlery, then pounded her fists through the mahogany headboard behind her. "Damn him, damn him, damn him!"

Her voice had risen to a hysterical scream, but Charles restrained Lee when he went to grab Meghann.

"Let it all out," Charles told her.

"I hate him!" she yelled, splintered wood flying everywhere as she attacked the headboard. "I hate him, I hate him, I hate him! I can't have him in my life! What's wrong with me? I should have had an abortion! If only I'd let you scrape it out of me, Charles, before I got so sick and he found us. But no—no, I wanted the baby."

"You couldn't know you needed him through your pregnancy," Charles soothed.

"That doesn't matter," Meghann said, pounding what was left of the bed. "What hubris, thinking I could outwit him on this—his precious philosophers' stone. How could I be so stupid? Now what am I going to do? He knows about the baby and I have to drink his blood for the next seven months. Charles, don't you see? He'll take the baby after I give birth! My child in Lord Baldevar's hands."

Meghann shuddered, and Charles wrapped his arms around his friend. "We haven't lost all hope, Meghann."

"What do you mean?" she demanded. "Of course we have, or I have. I can't escape the bastard now."

"You need his blood while you're pregnant, right?" Meghann nodded.

"But you'll have no need of him once the baby is born. I propose to cut off his head while you're in labor—when he's utterly engrossed in you and his defenses drop."

Meghann considered that . . . it wasn't a bad idea at all but something was making her deeply uneasy.

"Charles!" Her voice shook with fear. "How do we know he's not still here? You know we can't feel his presence."

Charles jumped, scanning the small bedroom with wary eyes. Meghann was right—they couldn't know if Lord Baldevar was still here.

We'll talk in places where we're sure he can't follow us—far out in the desert, Charles told her telepathically. He did not think Lord Baldevar could camouflage his presence and read thoughts at the same time.

Meghann nodded. *Or very near the dawn—when he wouldn't have enough time to fly back to his resting place.*

"It's settled, Meghann," Charles said and sat down beside her. "We'll accept this temporary setback. But try to look on the bright side. You're going to see Jimmy soon. Perhaps we can help him. Okay?"

"Okay," Meghann said but she couldn't control the tremor in her voice.

"Meghann," Lee said and reached out to pat her hand. "I know it's difficult but you have to try and relax or you'll never recover."

Relax, Meghann thought and shook her head. How was she supposed to relax now that Lord Baldevar was back in her life?

FOUR

Charles glanced at Meghann, her face pale and lips compressed into a tight, grim line as she maneuvered her '58 Cadillac convertible through the winding streets of Spanish Hills, the exclusive enclave of houses set high above the Las Vegas valley and home to Lord Baldevar. Not able to think of any words that might comfort her, Charles simply sat beside her, ready to offer whatever solace she'd need when she saw Jimmy.

Meghann sighed and thought she'd give anything if she could light up a cigarette right now, inhale the rich aroma of nicotine and feel her anxiety dissolve with each puff. But she didn't need Lee to tell her what her beloved Camels could do to the baby so she pacified her oral fixation by chewing on the end of a pen.

"It's going to be bad," Meghann finally said, breaking the tense silence. "He'd never let me see Jimmy unless . . . unless he didn't get through transformation." Was Jimmy merely psychotic or had something worse happened? Meghann shivered as she remembered Alcuin—a saintly man but forced to hide his face from the world because of the hideous deformities he'd acquired as a result of transformation. In her mind's eye, Meghann could see her mentor's face—the translucent skin that exposed a network of blue and red veins, the viciously long blood teeth that permanently hung out of his mouth . . . She doubted Jimmy would have the fortitude to face immortality if he had to spend eternity looking like that. Come to think of it, she probably wouldn't have been able to stand it either. Not that Lord Baldevar would have kept her alive—he'd have no use for a deformed lover.

Charles spoke, interrupting her thoughts. "Meghann, are you sure you want to do this? I could go in there and—"

"And what? Put Jimmy down like some hurt animal?" Meghann gave a bitter snort. "That's my job. Haven't you figured that out yet? I'm supposed to go into whichever one of these architectural monstrosities belongs to Lord Baldevar, see my poor Jimmy reduced to some raving imbecile, and kill him to put him out of his misery. The only reason Jimmy's still alive is that wretched fiend wants the satisfaction of making me kill my own lover, of feeding on my pain when I see what he reduced Jimmy to. But he's going to get the shock of his life tonight."

Meghann spoke confidently, but she had no idea if her plan, the one that had been formulating in her mind since Lord Baldevar left her that vile letter where he told her what he was going to do to Jimmy, would work.

But I have to try, she told herself, and held in her mind an image of Jimmy—her Jimmy, not the poor creature she was about to see but the tough, swaggering, acerbic man she'd spent the past six years with. She wasn't about to give up on him, let him go under without a fight.

After driving through a neighborhood of sprawling mansions that combined Tudor, Greek revival, and anything else the builders chose to mash together in a nightmare to assault the senses, Meghann finally arrived at a fawn-colored Mediterranean-style mansion with a Spanish tiled red roof, which was quite tasteful in comparison to its gaudy neighbors.

Eclectic, Meghann thought, admiring the sprawling

wings that jutted over the valley, bay windows, and iron trelled balconies of the cul-de-sac, towering over its neighbors on a high, lonely hill that was Lord Baldevar's new home. The only thing wrong with this breathtaking house was its owner.

Meghann sighed, well aware that her sudden aesthetic appreciation for Lord Baldevar's home was simply a way to avoid thinking about what awaited her inside. Taking a deep breath, she turned to Charles and linked her arm through his as they walked up the stone and travertine path toward the front door.

Head regally high, Meghann marched to the door and jabbed the bell with one long nail.

Within a few seconds, the door swung open and a tall mortal scowled down at her. "This is private property, kid. Get your ass outta here—oh, wait. Are you Meghann? Shit! I'm sorry. Um, I'm Vinny, Lord Baldevar's assistant. He told me you were coming by. Please come inside. I'm really sorry . . . it's just you're uh . . . well, not what I expected."

"It's all right," Meghann said graciously. She was sure few people wearing skull-and-crossbones bandanas and Marilyn Manson T-shirts had contact with Lord Baldevar. With a scowl, Meghann remembered the demure clothes the fiend used to force her into, making her the vampiric version of a Stepford Wife.

The mortal servant wasn't what Meghann had expected either. Not that his existence surprised her; she remembered from her time with Lord Baldevar that he required a round-the-clock familiar to keep an eye on his home during the day and dispose of bodies at night.

But the last servant, Trevor, had been a grim, silent man Meghann despised for the eyes that roamed over her body whenever his boss wasn't watching. Vinny, on the other hand, seemed quite respectful and eager to please.

Not bad looking either, Meghann thought. A puzzle

though—the patrician features and blond hair were at odds with the coarse voice that boasted a strong Brooklyn accent.

Curious, Meghann scrutinized his face a bit more closely and saw she was right. Although they were invisible to mortal eyes, Meghann easily detected the lines of small, microscopic scars along his jaw and under his ears.

Plastic surgery to alter his features and dye to change his hair, Meghann thought, noticing the black roots at his scalp. There was a story behind this servant. . . .

Stop avoiding Jimmy, a voice hissed, and Meghann sighed. First the house and now Vinny . . . was she going to inspect Lord Baldevar's furniture next to avoid her lover?

"Did Lord Baldevar tell you why we're here?" Meghann asked and indicated Charles standing behind her.

"He didn't say you were bringing anyone—but I guess it's okay," the servant replied uncertainly. "He told me you're here to see . . . well, you know—the freak."

"He's not a freak," Meghann said sharply. "He's simply . . . sick and we're here to help him. Now, if you'll excuse us, we have a lot of work to do. Come on, Charles."

"Uh, wait a second. Lord Baldevar left this for you—said you were gonna need it."

The servant plainly cowered at the white-hot fury in Meghann's eyes as she stared at the fire ax he held outstretched toward her. "If you don't want it . . ."

"Oh, no." Meghann snatched it from him, liking the feel of the weapon in her hands. Not that she had any intention of using it on Jimmy. No, she was hoping that arrogant motherfucker would put in an appearance so she could whack his head off like she should have done forty years ago.

What about the blood you need? Charles asked, knowing from the speculative look in her eyes what she planned to do with the ax.

Isn't Jimmy of my bloodline now? Meghann replied. *I'll rescue him from this hellhole and drink from him while I work on healing him.* Not that she expected her evening's work to go so smoothly but the thought of decapitating Lord Baldevar was a pleasant fantasy that soothed away some of her anxiety.

Vinny relaxed at the soft smile on Meghann's face and gestured impatiently at Charles. "Are you coming in or not? I'm not holding the door open all night."

Meghann kept her expression calm, but she and Charles both felt on edge while he put one foot over the threshold.

But nothing happened . . . no invisible force field barred him from entering Lord Baldevar's home.

In a way, Charles's easy entry disturbed Meghann more than being repulsed would. She knew this was Lord Baldevar's way of telling them he considered their combined forces so insignificant that he didn't need to bother barring the mansion to Charles because there was no way the young vampire could harm him.

"He's upstairs—last room on the left," Vinny said and pointed to the marble staircase.

"We know." Meghann had known where to find Jimmy the minute she entered the house. Easily, she'd sensed the presence of another vampire even if the emanations were substantially different from any she'd ever felt before.

"Look," Vinny said, withering under her brusque tone. "I didn't mean anything before. It's just that he scares me. I'm sorry."

Meghann softened and gave the mortal a quick smile to show no offense had been taken. What had happened to Jimmy was not this man's fault.

"Call me if you need anything," Vinny told her, giving her a warm grin in return.

"He likes you," Charles remarked as they headed up the stairs.

"That could be a good thing," Meghann said thoughtfully.

"What do you mean?"

"He's Lord Baldevar's familiar—has complete access to this house during the day. If he likes me, I'd offer him my body in a heartbeat if he'd agree to cut off his boss's head."

"It's a thought," Charles agreed. "Of course, he'd probably want money too but we can arrange that."

Meghann stopped before the closed cherry-wood door and tried to summon up the courage to turn the brass doorknob and face what Jimmy Delacroix had become.

Charles grasped her shoulders and Meghann turned to give him a weak smile. She thought he looked as uncertain and nervous as she felt.

Do it, Meghann told herself and flung open the door.

At first, it was an anticlimax because Meghann didn't even see Jimmy though she felt the desperately unhappy, unthinking presence nearby.

Indeed, Meghann was almost relieved by what she saw. She'd fully expected Lord Baldevar to have shackled Jimmy up in some dank, dark cell—whatever modern-day version of a dungeon he could arrange.

But this room far exceeded her expectations. It was a small, padded room much like the kind found in any well-run mental institution. Of course, it was thoroughly soundproofed so Lord Baldevar's neighbors wouldn't hear his insane fledgling howling the night away.

No bed or furniture, Meghann noted, but that didn't surprise her. In his current state, Jimmy would only tear them apart.

Where was he? . . . Then Meghann's eyes fell on a white-haired creature hunched over in a corner of the room, by the boarded-up window.

"Jimmy?" she said softly and stepped into the room, Charles close behind her.

She got no response, and expected none. Jimmy's name meant nothing to him now but she was surprised he hadn't tried to attack. Then she noticed the feminine, shapely leg beneath him and realized Jimmy's docile behavior was the result of feeding.

"Jimmy," she repeated and put her hand on his shoulder, forcibly wrenching him from the woman beneath him. But what she saw when he turned around and growled like some animal made her drop her hand and gasp in shock.

Good God, what had happened to him? If she saw him on the street, she'd never recognize him, so changed was his body and aura. Jimmy was gaunt . . . he'd lost even more weight than she had. But Meghann was relieved to see that apart from the long, unwashed white hair, he'd suffered no permanent deformities as a result of transformation.

Not that what happened to him wasn't terrible, that she didn't long to kill Lord Baldevar for what he'd done to this innocent man that never harmed anyone. To be kept like this . . . Meghann recoiled at the sweaty, foul, dirt-encrusted body, the rags he wore for clothing. If he wasn't immortal, she knew his unhygienic condition would have led to all sorts of running sores and illnesses.

But his physical appearance, revolting and pitiful though it was, wasn't what made Meghann's eyes fill up with tears that spilled down her face and onto her lover's emaciated filthy form. No, it was those mad, sightless eyes that stared through her without a spark of recognition. There was no consciousness there, no spark of wit or intelligence.

"Good God!" Charles thundered.

Meghann followed his disgusted gaze and her breath caught in her throat. The woman Jimmy was feeding from . . .

The ax fell from her hands as Meghann dashed to the bathroom connected to Jimmy's room, barely reaching the toilet before she started retching.

"Uck," she choked helplessly and watched all Lee had given her to eat leave her body as she vomited in loud, jerky heaves that made her ribs hurt. Thankfully, though, no blood came up so Meghann wouldn't lose any of the strength she'd gained from feeding or have to seek out Lord Baldevar and beg for more of his blood.

Shakily, Meghann stood up and flushed the toilet. Then she went to the sink and washed her mouth out with cool water before splashing some on her face.

Jimmy, she thought, and leaned her hands on the porcelain counter to regain her equilibrium. *What has that monster done to you?*

Meghann had known that Jimmy would kill any prey he was given; in his current state all he knew was his need for blood. Of course, he'd drain dry anyone he was given. But the other . . .

Meghann put her hands over her face, but nothing could block the image in her mind . . . that poor woman beneath Jimmy, that lone eye gazing out from a face gnawed away to nothing but a few shards of bone and limp, stringy muscle framed by a mop of beautiful blond hair that only emphasized the horror of her face.

Lord Baldevar didn't feed him, Meghann realized. Not normal food at any rate. He gave him prey and expected him to cannibalize their flesh as well as drink their blood.

A loud crash from the bedroom made her flinch and then she heard Charles scream, "Meghann!"

She dashed back into the bedroom and saw Charles struggling with Jimmy. By the different position of the corpse, Meghann surmised that Charles must have yanked the body from Jimmy before he could dese-crate it further, and been attacked for his trouble. Charles might be older but Jimmy's insanity gave him the strength of ten vampires and he was using every bit of it to try and hold Charles down, desperate for the blood he sensed flowing through him.

Offering up a silent prayer that Jimmy would some-day forgive her for what she had to do, Meghann picked up the discarded ax and flew at him. She used the long handle to put Jimmy in a chokehold to re-strain the thrashing, howling vampire.

Jimmy let out a long, inarticulate howl of rage while Charles allowed his body to go completely slack. Too senseless and blood hungry to react swiftly, Jimmy wasn't able to stop Charles when he pulled his arms free and then chopped down on Jimmy's forearms with all his strength.

Meghann heard the dull snap of his arms breaking, and pulled the ax away from his neck, allowing Jimmy to crumple to the ground, screaming with pain and frustrated blood lust.

"Jimmy," Meghann sobbed, sinking to the ground and wrapping her arms around him, "my poor baby, please hear me. Simon can't have taken it all from you, remember me, please. It's Maggie; I can help you." His nonrecognition made her weep harder. "Come back, Jimmy, come back. Oh, God, please . . ."

While she cried, Charles ran to her bag and quickly withdrew a small transfusion pack of blood, which Jimmy immediately sensed. He kicked Meghann from him and howled like a small infant at Charles, trying to grab at the bag with his useless arms.

Charles dropped the pack on the floor and Jimmy crawled over to it.

Please, Meghann prayed, watching Jimmy tear at the plastic with his blood teeth and gulp greedily. *Please let this work.*

Meghann and Charles both held their breath while Jimmy fed. First, his forearms healed but then . . . yes, yes, it happened! The wild, rabid look left Jimmy's eyes. He became still and calm, gray-blue eyes half closed.

"You were right," Charles said in wonder. "What did you put in that blood?"

"Clozapine and Valium to calm him down." Of course, Meghann had spiked the blood with enough of both drugs to sedate an entire psychotic ward of mortals.

"You're going to treat him like an insane mortal."

"Like a mortal in the throes of a bad reaction to LSD," Meghann clarified. "LSD-induced psychosis and transformation-induced psychosis (a disease she unfortunately couldn't write up for any psychology journals) are caused by the same thing—overstimulation of serotonin receptors in the brain. Clozapine blocks the receptors—hence, Jimmy's psychotic symptoms are suppressed."

"Do you think he'll have to take Clozapine with his blood feedings for the rest of his life?"

Meghann shook her head. "I'm going to start him off with high-dose feedings and gradually decrease the dosage until there's none in his bloodstream."

"How do we restore his mind?"

"Jimmy's been badly traumatized. Hopefully, between the drugs and being in a safe, nonthreatening environment, surrounded by familiar objects, he'll start to come back to himself."

Meghann knelt by Jimmy and hugged him close, not minding that the dirt and gore were ruining her own clothes. "I believe you can hear me, Jimmy. I know some part of you understands what I'm saying; you're just a little lost right now. I'm going to help you, baby. You'll get well. It's no wonder you're sick though—the way Lord Baldevar has kept you. Well, his reign is over."

"Is it?"

Meghann whirled around, the ax poised for attack.

"You look just like a deer in headlights," Lord Baldevar commented and took a step toward her, his grin broadening when Meghann brandished the ax threateningly. "Come now. Surely the catamite that stands so valiantly by your side has explained that you need my blood to survive?"

"I'll . . . I'll use Jimmy's."

"Will you? And what kind of potion did you give him to produce his newfound tranquillity?" Lord Baldevar gazed at Jimmy as a research scientist might at an intriguing specimen—interested but dispassionate. "Will your concoction affect my child if it enters your bloodstream?"

Not willing to concede that she hadn't thought of that, Meghann tightened her grip on the ax and narrowed her eyes. "Don't you dare hurt Jimmy!"

"Give me that before you hurt yourself." Lord Baldevar raised his hand, and Meghann yelped when the ax flew from her hands. He twirled the weapon in his hands, taking an experimental swipe at Jimmy's neck.

Charles came to her side, grabbing her by the shoulders before she could run at Lord Baldevar. "He's just trying to antagonize you."

"Even a dumb animal can perceive a threat." Lord Baldevar gave Jimmy, who simply stared up apathetically, a contemptuous glance. Then he turned his attention to Meghann, keeping the sharp blade of the ax at Jimmy's neck while he talked. "I should have known my little psychiatrist would embrace this mindless creature as some kind of crusade. What do you think, girl? That you can feed him a drug cocktail with his blood and restore his broken mind? Why, pray tell, should I allow this creature to continue to live?"

"If you don't do precisely as I demand," Meghann said with a coldness Charles had never heard in her voice before, "I'll take a coat hanger to this miserable bastard inside me."

For the smallest instant, something flickered in Lord Baldevar's eyes before his face became a cool, inscrutable mask—shuttered gold eyes giving no clue as to his thoughts.

Charles gave silent thanks that the monster's entire attention was on Meghann; it gave him a chance to compose his face before Lord Baldevar could see the shock in his expression. Was Meghann actually going to try and bluff Simon Baldevar? One look at her stony face told him that was exactly what she had in mind.

Frightened by what the sadist might do to his friend, Charles shoved her behind him.

"Don't you hurt her," Charles warned, thinking he sounded like a puny weakling trying to stand up to the schoolyard bully.

"Meghann." The vampire spoke quite calmly, each syllable of her name drawn out.

"No!" Charles cried when Lord Baldevar moved toward them.

"Cease your protestations. Do you think, no matter what vile threat she makes, I will raise my hand to the girl when she carries my heir? Come here, Meghann. I wish to speak to you."

When Meghann didn't move, Lord Baldevar raised the ax again and Meghann flew out from behind Charles before he could stop her.

Gray clouds . . . surrounded by gray clouds. They cut everything off . . . she can't feel . . . no sensation at all . . . just floating in a gray numbness . . . can't make her mouth form words . . . can't really think . . . where am I? . . . where's my body? . . . everything's so fuzzy . . . can't think . . .

Abruptly, the mist cleared and Meghann found herself sprawled on the floor, Charles staring down anxiously.

"What the hell did you do to her?"

Lord Baldevar gave him one freezing glare before he swooped Meghann up off the floor with one hand under her chin so they were eye to eye, with Meghann's feet dangling almost a foot off the ground.

"Tell me, did you enjoy that netherworld I just sent you to? Was it a pleasurable experience—having your consciousness ripped from you? Answer me!"

"No," Meghann panted, squirming furiously to get away from him.

"Would you care to spend your entire pregnancy there?"

Meghann went slack, her struggles turning to paralyzed horror when the enormity of his threat hit her.

"That's right," Lord Baldevar purred at her. "If you continue with your tantrums and defiance, I shall make you my little zombie and stuff a tube down your throat to give you blood and nourishment until you are ready to deliver my son. But don't worry; once my son is born, I shall bestow awareness upon you again. I want you lucid when I show you the heads of your insane lover and catamite friend. Since you show my son nothing but resentment, I don't believe I'll allow you to see the child before I slice your head from your shoulders. Now, are you going to behave yourself?"

Terrified, Meghann could only nod.

"Smart girl," he approved and let her drop to the floor. "I knew you'd become more amenable once I explained your position to you."

"Now as to that imbecile on the floor, of course you may come to my home any time you wish and apply your witchcraft to him." Lord Baldevar grinned at the shock she wasn't able to hide. "At least this project will keep you busy and I can keep an eye on you, make sure you don't get up to any mischief that might harm my son."

"I'm not leaving him with you!"

"Would you care to try and get him past me? Mr.

Delacroix remains here, where I can make sure he does not harm you or my heir. Disobey my wishes and I'll have Vinny throw his worthless body to the sun. Good night, my sweet."

Meghann raised a trembling hand to her face and a green glint caught her eye . . . the sparkle came from the light above hitting the emerald signet ring on her left hand, the ring Lord Baldevar had put on her hand the night he transformed her.

Funny, she'd been wearing it so long she hardly even noticed the medieval ring, set in antique gold with an emerald on each shoulder and old french on the bezel. She'd never taken it off because Lord Baldevar had had it sized so she could only remove it by breaking the ring or her finger.

She twisted it experimentally; it was loose from all that weight she'd lost. She yanked for a few seconds and the ring slid off her finger.

"Hey!" she shouted and Lord Baldevar, already in the doorway, turned to give her a quizzical glance.

Meghann flung the ring at him, hitting him squarely in the chest. If there was any justice in the world, she hoped she'd hit the spot where her stake had scarred him permanently.

Lord Baldevar caught the ring before it could clatter to the floor and held it loosely, meeting Meghann's angry, defiant eyes. There was no need for her to speak; she knew Lord Baldevar understood all she said with this gesture . . . that she'd no longer wear his brand, that he meant nothing to her.

He held the ring up to the light for one moment before it disappeared into his trouser pocket. When he spoke, his voice was calm but his amber eyes watched her with the keen alertness of a hawk about to swoop down on its prey.

"Soon, my love, you will regret your hasty action this evening and beg me to put this ring back on your finger."

"Arrogant motherfucker!" Meghann shouted after he turned on his heel and left before she could respond. "I'd wrap a water bug around my finger before I wore his ring again!"

"I'm sure he's well aware of that, no matter what he says to save face," Charles said and took her hand. "Come on, honey. We're going home now."

Meghann said nothing as Charles escorted her out of the house and then settled her in the passenger seat.

It was only after he'd driven a block from Lord Baldevar's house that Meghann began to speak.

"I can't do this," she said, her voice tight and high. "I can't . . . God, it's just like it was before! That horrible beast, brutalizing me into following his every command—"

"Meghann," Charles interrupted. "Don't you see? You won tonight."

"Huh?"

"Meghann, you scared him to death when you said you'd have an abortion if he didn't go along with your plan."

"But he—"

"I know—that spell or whatever he did to you, I can only imagine how horrible it was. But I was alert throughout the whole thing. Meghann, that wasn't easy for him to do. How do you think I got so close to you? He couldn't control you and fight me at the same time. I think he'd have to stand over you every minute for the next seven months to make it work. Who knows what condition that would leave him in? Don't let him trick you into believing he holds all the cards . . . it was a scare tactic, that's all. What do you think . . . he's letting Jimmy live as some favor? He would have decapitated him right there if you didn't convince him you meant what you said." Charles took his eyes off the road long enough to hold her eyes; he had to be sure she absorbed the full impact of what had just happened. "He wasn't able to read your mind when you said you wanted an abortion."

"My God," Meghann whispered. "You're right . . . he didn't know I was lying! So he threatened me to make sure I'd think twice about doing it." She felt perfectly safe saying that aloud; in a moving car they had to be safe from Lord Baldevar's spying.

"Were you doing anything different when you threatened him?"

Meghann considered. "No . . . just, there was nothing on my mind except a need to save Jimmy."

"Maybe that's what you need to do," Charles said. "Not think if you're going to lie to him—he can't see what isn't there. Think of what we may have accomplished tonight . . . you're alive, we might have a chance to heal Jimmy, and best of all, we may be on the way to discovering a way to shield your thoughts from Lord Baldevar. Now, I know I saw a Friendly's on our way here. Why don't you let me treat you to a sundae to celebrate?"

Meghann smiled . . . a small smile but an improvement over the sorrow that had been in her expression since the night Lord Baldevar kidnapped Jimmy.

There was hope, Meghann thought. Not only the things Charles had mentioned but him—him and Lee on her side, helping her face down Lord Baldevar.

Time hadn't rolled back, after all. Those thirteen years had been awful because Meghann had been so alone . . . no one to turn to, no one to comfort her after one of Lord Baldevar's vicious tirades. But now . . . now she had her dear friend to support her. With Charles by her side, never letting her confidence deteriorate, maybe she could handle Lord Baldevar.

FIVE

"Does it make you feel better?"

Meghann smiled up at Charles as he settled beside her on the sofa. "Don't you look handsome tonight."

"Mmph," he muttered noncommittally but preened a bit at Meghann's compliment. "It's not too much?"

"For a romantic dinner out? Absolutely not—you look perfect." He did, wearing the dark Saville Row suit Meghann had bought him for Christmas, his normally flyaway black hair slicked back into rippling, shiny waves.

"I'm still not sure about you going there by yourself," Charles fretted.

"Lord Baldevar hasn't been at the house when we've been there since that first night," Meghann pointed out. She'd seen very little of the fiend over the past two weeks and hadn't spoken to him at all. Even when he came to Lee's to give her blood, Charles stood by her side while she fed. Meghann had never imagined feeding could be as antiseptic as the impersonal wrist held out to her while she wouldn't even look at her feeder. "And I have a lot of work to do with Jimmy tonight. I told you I'm going to lower the amount of medication in his blood pack tonight so I need to watch him all night to make sure he doesn't have an adverse reaction. You don't really want to sit with my

patient and me all night when you could be enjoying
yourself with Lee? Now you're going on that date if I
have to drag you to Fiore's bodily."

Charles grinned at her no-nonsense tone and gestured to the leather-backed diary Lord Baldevar had
given Lee. "It reassured you?"

"Somewhat." At the very least, reading *Infans Noctis*
made Meghann understand why Lord Baldevar was
willing to attempt vampiric conception. Basically, it told
the story of Lucian, a Roman senator before he was
transformed (how he was transformed he declined to
say) and Melina, the beautiful Greek concubine he fell
in love with and transformed so they could be together
forever.

Like Lord Baldevar, Lucian was obsessed with the
idea that a child with the blood of two vampires flowing
through its veins would have all their strengths and
none of their flaws, like the need to hide from the
sun. Frustrated when Melina failed to conceive after
one hundred years passed, Lucian took her to a small
island in the Aegean Sea dedicated to the worship of
Aphrodite, goddess of fertility. After spreading Aphrodite's altar with their blood as well as that of a human
sacrifice, he and Melina made love before the goddess's statue and conceived their child.

"At least now we know where Lord Baldevar got the
idea for the ritual he put you through on Beltane,"
Charles said, reading along with Meghann.

"And how he knew what was wrong with me,"
Meghann said, tapping her nail against the passage
where Melina became desperately ill whenever she
tried to feed. In desperation, Lucian fed her his blood,
thanking God effusively when she recovered.

"Do you think he'd have attempted conception
without Lucian's diary?" Charles asked.

"No way," Meghann answered. "He'd never chance
a deformed child . . . our perfect fiend can't have
some misbegotten offspring. No doubt he'd leave it on

a hillside to die like they used to do in ancient times. Isn't it funny, though, how vampires are the opposite of humans? All those vampiric pregnancies we read about resulted in deformity because the parents weren't of the same bloodline. Only Lucian transformed Melina. It never would have occurred to me—that vampires must be of the closest blood relation to produce healthy children." Meghann looked up. "Do you suppose that's why I got sick . . . that in some twisted way it's a good sign, since Melina had the same problem?"

"Maybe. After all, morning sickness . . . that's a sign the hormones are coursing through a woman's body normally. Maybe you're developing antibodies . . . perhaps they help the child's development in some way."

She turned back to the book, skipping through Melina's uneventful pregnancy until she came to the passage where the child, after a hideous labor of five nights, was born absolutely perfect, though Melina died of hemorrhaging a few minutes before the child was born. The classical Latin prose raved about his cherubic good looks . . . the blond hair with a tinge of red, dark lashes against snowy white skin, the infant boy's perfectly shaped limbs and fine weight. The only thing wrong with the child was that he was born dead. Unable to take the loss of his consort as well as his son, the grief-stricken father recorded the tragic events in *Infans Noctis* and then committed suicide by greeting the sunrise.

Oddly, Meghann wasn't overly upset when she read that Melina died. Lee could cauterize her easily, or give her a caesarian before she lost too much blood. But she felt sad when she read about that perfect, stillborn child. What would he have been like if he lived? Would he be able to tolerate daylight? Would he develop blood teeth . . . would he need to drink blood at all? Could he grow up and pass for a human child? Play with other children? Poor thing . . .

"Breech birth . . . hung on his own cord," Charles observed, reading over her shoulder. "At least we know now vampires . . . that you have a chance for healthy offspring."

Meghann took his hand. "Charles? You know Jimmy might not recover. If . . . if he doesn't make it, would you please raise this baby with me?"

"Meghann." Charles clenched her hand, tears threatening to spill out of his eyes. "Are you asking me to be a father to your baby?"

Meghann nodded. "You and me and Lee. How could this baby ask for better parents?"

Charles caught her in a fierce hug. "Thank you." Then he shoved her away and gave her a sardonic grin. "How do you think Lord Baldevar will react to the idea of two fags raising his son?"

"It's a girl," Meghann corrected. "And he's never going to know . . . unless he can see us from hell."

Meghann and Charles heard Lee bidding his last patient a pleasant good night.

"Wish I still had patients," Meghann grumbled. More than that, Meghann wished her life hadn't changed . . . that she were still counseling battered women from the home office she'd established in her ramshackle, comfortable beach house. She conjured up a pleasant scene—saying good night to her last patient and then diving into the ocean for a moonlight swim with Jimmy.

"I know you miss it," Charles said, patting her hand. "But you'll get it all back . . . you'll see."

Meghann kept silent, but she had her doubts about that. Aside from Jimmy's state (she still couldn't look into those blank eyes without wanting to cry), unless Charles managed to kill Lord Baldevar, there was no future for her . . . he'd kill her after she gave birth so she wouldn't interfere with whatever horrid plans he had for her child. And that would be the kind fate—he might just keep her alive and try to force her back into the role of his meek, brainless little plaything. No doubt if she resisted his wishes, the fiend would either beat her or threaten to kill all her friends, or maybe he'd be low enough to threaten the baby to get what he wanted. Meghann shuddered and tried to force her thoughts out of their miserable ruminations.

Lee came into the living room, all ready for his big date with Charles, and Meghann looked on in amusement as her normally glib friend stared speechless at Lee.

"What he'll say as soon as he gets his tongue back in his mouth is that you look wonderful, Lee." Meghann thought Lee, in his neatly tailored charcoal-gray suit, with his ash-blond hair that had a sprinkling of silver, was every inch the distinguished professional, certainly what people referred to as a "great catch."

"Thanks." Lee may have been speaking to her but his eyes were on Charles, who got up and took his lover's hand.

Meghann dropped her eyes, feeling more and more she shouldn't be here. Of course she was happy that Lee and Charles had found each other again . . . she knew how hurt Charles had been when he'd been forced to leave Lee because sooner or later the mortal would question his odd hours.

There had never been any question of him telling Lee what he was. Two centuries before they were born, Alcuin had decreed no new vampires should be created. As for telling mortals . . . while it might ease the vampire's loneliness, it put the mortal in an awful position. He or she had to carry around an explosive secret, shield it from other humans. And it was only a matter of time before the mortal became so poisoned with jealousy that his lover never aged while he withered away, that the relationship would fall apart.

The only reason Meghann had been allowed to confide in Jimmy was that he knew about vampires before they met . . . one had slaughtered his family and left him only able to face the dark blind drunk until he had met Meghann. Then they had six wonderful years together and Meghann's only sadness was that her best friend couldn't have a lover like she did . . . one who knew all his secrets and loved him anyway.

Yes, she was very happy Charles found someone, though she wished it hadn't been her own miserable circumstances that led to the reunion.

"I'm gonna get going," Meghann announced, knowing they'd be on top of each other the second she walked out the door. She wondered if they'd even make it to dinner.

"Are you sure?" Charles questioned, reluctantly pulling his eyes from Lee. "You've never gone over there alone. Meghann, please, Lee and I can go out . . . you just stay here in the house or maybe go to a movie."

Meghann gave a short laugh. "You think if Lord Baldevar really wants to find me he'll wait for me to show up at his house? I am not going to spend my life in fear of him. Look, I swear I'll call out to you if I need you . . . not that he'd harm a hair on the head of his pregnant brood mare anyway." She walked out the door before Charles could present her with another argument, and willed herself not to cry. Tears never helped anyone. The thing to do was just sublimate her misery, work on helping Jimmy, and not dwell on how much she missed having someone look at her like Charles had just looked at Lee.

As Meghann strolled up the now familiar path to Lord Baldevar's house, she noticed the mansion was shuttered and dark. Hardly a surprise, though she sometimes wondered where Lord Baldevar took himself on the four nights he allowed her to visit and work with Jimmy. No doubt he oozed around the strip, terrorizing young women (prostitutes barely past their adolescence being his favorite prey, if she remembered right), and drinking their blood.

Sometimes Vinny was around to welcome her, but the servant's schedule was erratic—what with having to dispose of corpses in the vast desert around them.

Meghann opened the front door with the key Vinny had given her. Out of habit, she waved her hand to light up the foyer and the living room beyond. No matter that vampires saw as well as cats in the dark, a well-lit house was a comfort to Meghann, who had never cared for the dark.

She strained her ears for activity upstairs but the house was silent—she'd been hoping Jimmy might be moving around but no such luck. With a sigh, Meghann mounted the marble staircase and headed toward Jimmy's room.

"Hey, sweetie," Meghann greeted when she opened the door to Jimmy's room. She plastered a huge grin on her face, ignoring how her heart lurched when the apathetic gray-blue eyes didn't even move toward her.

Jimmy, lying curled up on the foam bed Meghann had brought, didn't acknowledge her until she moved closer and he smelled the blood in her canvas bag.

"Towel," Meghann said sharply and pointed to the beige towel lying next to the bed. For the past several weeks, she'd been trying (without success) to reintroduce Jimmy to performing simple tasks for himself.

Whining with frustration, Jimmy made a lunge for her but Meghann shoved him back and then picked the towel up herself, tucking it under his chin like a bib so he wouldn't get any blood on his clothes.

"Now," she said and gave him the transfusion bag.

Jimmy began gulping thirstily, blood teeth shredding the plastic while he made feral growls deep in his throat.

"Jimmy," Meghann said patiently, "we're not savages. There's no need to behave like a wild dog protecting his meat from the rest of the pack. I'm not going to take the blood from you."

Jimmy ignored her and wrapped his hands protectively around the pint of blood.

While he drank, Meghann removed a few containers of takeout from her bag, placing it on two paper plates. Fried chicken, mashed potatoes, green beans, and apple pie—that used to be Jimmy's favorite meal. A few weeks ago, she'd informed that low-life snake (the kindest term she had for Lord Baldevar) she'd be responsible for Jimmy's meals as well as his blood—she wouldn't have him reduce Jimmy any further by making him cannibalize his prey.

Meghann brought the food to the bed, and Jimmy, blood lust sated, began shoveling it into his mouth.

"No!" Meghann took his right hand and wrapped it around a plastic fork. Then, still holding his hand in hers, she speared a few beans with the fork and brought the food to Jimmy's mouth.

Six times she repeated the motion of fork to mouth before Jimmy caught on and made a clumsy effort to use the utensil.

"Good!" Meghann praised and this time her smile was genuine. For two weeks, she'd been trying to reintroduce Jimmy to silverware and this was the first time she'd made any progress.

While he ate, Meghann began his therapy. She went over to the CD player and put on *So Alone* by Johnny Thunders, their favorite singer.

"Do you remember our first date . . . when you played this album for me?" she asked Jimmy brightly. Meghann believed that the key to reaching Jimmy lay in stimulation of his senses, in making him want to think again. That's why she'd brought over all his favorite clothes and CDs; she was sure he'd recover if objects he was familiar with surrounded him. Also, since she was certain fear would keep him locked in his catatonia forever, she never once spoke to him of

Lord Baldevar or what he'd gone through. Instead, she kept up a steady stream of light chatter, as though she expected that at any moment Jimmy would join in the conversation. On previous nights, she'd discussed music he liked or read to him from his favorite books.

Now she was bringing up the happiest times they'd had together, as much for herself as for him. She had no desire to dwell on the present . . . or even worse, what the future might hold.

While Johnny belted out his version of "Great Big Kiss," Meghann sat down next to Jimmy, pulling his unresisting head onto her shoulder. "Look," she said and pointed to the pictures she'd brought with her. "Remember you were so excited about going to New Orleans because you got to see St. Peter House—the hotel where Johnny Thunders OD'd or got killed, depending on who you believe?

"From the handsome facade outside, you'd never know the hotel was little more than a flophouse, would you? That's such a great shot you took, Jimmy—the way the sunlight reflects off the wrought-iron balcony. You have such a gift for photography," Meghann complimented, looking at one photo of herself and Charles.

Traditionally, vampires couldn't be captured on film; they tended to show up as blurry, ethereal images. But Jimmy had patiently superimposed two negatives together, then done a little airbrushing to present Meghann with a photo of her and Charles, arm in arm beside the crumbling tomb of voodoo queen Marie Laveau. It was the first time Meghann had a clear image of herself since she'd been transformed. She grinned at the photo—a young girl with long red hair covered in green, black, and gold beads from the Mardi Gras celebrations—and her dark-haired friend smiling into the camera. Meghann smiled even more at the next picture . . . the one that Jimmy had set the time delay on his Nikon for so he could rush over and kiss her before the flash clicked.

"Do you remember the legend I told you—that if you leave something by her tomb, she grants your wish?" Meghann's throat closed as she realized what she'd wish for right now. More than anything, she wanted to see awareness flash in Jimmy's eyes. She couldn't stand that damned vacant stare, the way he looked through her.

Patience, Meghann told herself. *It's only been two weeks.* She got off the bed and scrutinized Jimmy, forcing herself to look at him objectively, see if there was any improvement in his condition.

Certainly, his physical appearance had improved after Meghann took a razor to that awful white hair and bathed him for nearly an hour before she was satisfied that he was clean. She'd been relieved to see the white hair was merely temporary and his normal dark brown hair grew back in after she shaved his head. Thanks to a vampire's quick metabolism, he already had a full head of shoulder-length hair she kept in the ponytail style he used to favor.

She also made an effort to dress him in clothes he'd have chosen for himself. Tonight, he wore a Sex Pistols T-shirt with jeans. One of Meghann's short-term goals was to have Jimmy start dressing himself again, picking out his own clothes from the collection of T-shirts and jeans she'd brought over and stored in a small bureau.

But none of it . . . not the clothes, the posters she'd nailed all around the small room, the music and books . . . seemed to have the slightest affect on him. Though the Clozapine kept him from raving, nothing Meghann did reached him, made him respond to her.

Well, what did you expect? a voice demanded. *It's only been two weeks. Did you think you'd dress him in jeans and a cool shirt, play* Ramones Leave Home, *and he'd leap up screaming, "I'm cured"?*

No, she hadn't expected that but . . .

Meghann kneeled before him, taking his slack damp hands in hers. "Jimmy . . . I need you, baby. You see, I'm . . . I'm really lonely and scared and I need someone to hold me, to make me feel safe. Damn it, I need someone to look at me like Charles looked at Lee, and you . . . you don't even know I exist!"

Stop it, Meghann told herself. *You get the hell out of this room if you can't control yourself. Don't you carry on in front of Jimmy. If you make him uneasy, you could set him back for weeks.*

"I'm sorry," she whispered and took a deep breath.

But then her control over herself shattered . . . shattered when she heard Johnny Thunders's nasal, reedy voice mourn softly, "I'm so all alone . . ."

Blindly, she ran from the room, castigating herself for playing such sappy, sentimental music when her mood had been melancholy to begin with.

She ran for the stairs, thinking she'd just head home, but then she remembered she couldn't go home . . . Charles and Lee needed their privacy. Besides, who in their right mind would want some pregnant, weepy third wheel around?

"Damn it," she cried and sank down on one of the marble steps. Meghann put her head on her knees and bawled. She had to do something to loosen the lump in her throat that she sometimes thought would strangle her and at least she could carry on in this empty house without anyone being the wiser.

She cried noisily, letting out all her grief and frustration. She cried for Alcuin, feeling as lost as a small child abandoned by its parent now that she didn't have her kindly, wise mentor to guide her. How was she supposed to figure a way out of this horrible nightmare without his advice? If only he were alive, he'd be able to help Jimmy—she was sure he would. And she wouldn't feel so horribly alone if she could just talk to Alcuin one more time. If she could just lay this frightening mess in his more experienced hands, she wouldn't have to worry every minute about Jimmy and the broken mind she was starting to think she might never fix. And she wouldn't have to keep putting on a brave front for Charles's sake or spend all her time trying to thwart Lord Baldevar. Meghann sobbed louder, giving in to the fear she covered with a brittle, cold exterior whenever she saw him. God, she was exhausted—she had no energy anymore; she used it all up in trying to keep Lord Baldevar from reading her thoughts. Meghann shuddered—wondering what would happen if he knew of her constant, gnawing worry that he'd kill her after she gave birth and then her poor baby would be all alone with the monster.

"Yaahhh!" Meghann started at the icy touch to her cheek and looked up to see Lord Baldevar sitting beside her, holding out a dripping cloth.

"Little one," he whispered tenderly before she could say anything, "if you don't stop weeping, you'll break the heart you insist I don't have."

Meghann drew in a shaky, ragged breath. What a fool she was, carrying on like this in Lord Baldevar's house—why hadn't she gotten into her car and driven to some secluded spot where no one would overhear her, particularly this beast?

Meghann glared, not at all fooled by the soft, compassionate gaze or kind words. Simon Baldevar was an opportunist—he'd see her sorrow as a weakness he could exploit for his own gain.

"Leave me alone," Meghann cried, feeling humiliated by the tears that kept pouring out of her eyes. "Just . . . go away, would you? I'm tired is all. I'll be fine in a few minutes."

"Leave you to weep by yourself so you can pretend I'm the pitiless fiend you want to hate? I think not. Come here." Lord Baldevar pulled her onto his lap, cradling her head against his shoulder while he held the cold cloth over her eyes.

She wouldn't fight, Meghann told herself. It was bad

enough she'd given this monster the satisfaction of seeing her cry; she'd be damned if she'd engage in some physical struggle that she'd lose along with whatever dignity she had left. And she certainly wouldn't take any comfort from the cool cloth over her swollen eyes or the broad chest her cheek was pressed to and she'd die before admitting sitting on his lap was certainly an improvement over the hard marble staircase.

Against her will, Meghann found a drowsy peace descending over her . . . the choking, horrible grief growing weaker and weaker as Simon crooned the same comforting murmur he'd used to get her through transformation.

Help me, master, she could remember crying through that awful pain and chaos she thought would destroy her before the night was over.

I'm here, Meghann, he'd whispered over and over—just as he did now. *Nothing will ever hurt you as long as you remain with me . . . hold on to me, little one, give me your heart and I'll make the misery disappear.*

Lord Baldevar had made the hurt disappear but he hadn't told Meghann the price of his aid . . . he'd used her agony to bind her to him forever; now a part of her was always open to suggestion from him. Alcuin had explained to her that since Simon's was the voice that got her through transformation, a part of her would always be comforted by him—whether she wanted to be or not.

Finally, her tears abated but Meghann kept her face pressed to the oxford shirt she'd soaked through with her tears, not sure of what she should say or how to behave. This meant nothing, she told herself firmly. It wasn't her fault Simon Baldevar was her master but she wasn't going to let him use that damned blood link to manipulate her any further. She'd dry her eyes, get off his lap, say as little to him as possible, and hopefully walk out of this house without further incident.

Meghann raised her head and said, "Thank you" in a cool, formal way she was proud of though she was dismayed by the hoarse quality of her voice. How long had she been crying?

Lord Baldevar's lips twitched. "You are quite welcome. Do you realize that is the first pleasant thing you've said to me in months? Meghann, must you continue fighting me? I can't stand seeing you so miserable."

"You . . . you make . . ." It was on the tip of her tongue to inform him he was the source of all her misery but something made her hold her sharp words back.

Seeing her hesitation, Lord Baldevar took her hand. "The past cannot be changed, Meghann. Does your anger gain you anything but the despair that made you weep alone on my staircase? And why are you here by yourself?"

"I thought Charles and Lee should have some time alone together."

"No doubt you put a smile on your face and assured Doctor Tarleton you didn't need him so he could amuse himself. Well, you may be able to put him off but I am not so easily dissuaded. Please, Meghann. Let me help you. If you cannot love me, can you at least try and end this strife between us . . . make peace?"

"Peace?" Meghann repeated the word as though she'd never heard it before. Certainly in all this time she'd never considered making peace with Lord Baldevar.

"Simon."

"Huh?"

He gave her a quick grin, one dimple flickering in his left cheek. "If you're going to cry on my shoulder, I'd like it if you'd call me by my first name instead of my title . . . or any of the unmentionable oaths you've addressed me with lately."

"No!" Meghann shouted. She wouldn't let him back

in her life . . . wouldn't take that perilous first step of addressing him by name, of allowing herself to see him as anything but the vicious, brutal bastard he was. "Leave me alone!"

Meghann scrambled to her feet but her balance on the slippery marble was precarious. In her distress, the agility vampires usually enjoyed abandoned her completely. She lost her footing and would have flown down the staircase if Lord Baldevar didn't grab her.

"Enough of this," he muttered and threw her over his shoulder like a sack. Ignoring her furious protests, he stalked down the staircase, throwing Meghann down on a black divan in the living room.

"Your temper nearly cost you our child," he told her, holding her down when she tried to leap off the divan. "I'm sure you would have come away unscathed but it's very likely a fall like that would cause a miscarriage."

"Good!" she snapped. Irrationally, Meghann hated him more for trying to comfort her. It was so much easier to deal with Lord Baldevar when he was terrorizing her than when he had this pseudo-concern shining in his eyes. She hardened her eyes, intending to say something that would rip away the false mask of compassion he had on and turn him back into the menacing fiend he truly was. "I don't want this baby anyway!"

That statement earned her a look of utter disgust. "Do you think I'm a half-wit, Meghann? Why do you think I put you in that trance? Because I cannot see your thoughts? Don't flatter yourself. I did it because I was deeply insulted that you think I'd believe any woman who risked her life to save some nameless orphan forty years ago would be capable of the callous attitude you display toward your own flesh and blood. Stop wasting my time with these foolish games."

"It's not a game!" Meghann yelled. "I don't want your baby!"

"Is that so?" Lord Baldevar cupped his hand under her chin and gave her a penetrating gaze that missed nothing. "You threw abortion in my face but I have yet to hear you offer me this child to raise by myself after it's born."

Meghann blinked her eyes rapidly, praying he wouldn't see her reflexive horror at the thought of her child being reared by him. "Is that what you want?"

"Perhaps," he said. "Perhaps I'll make you an offer—I hand you your lover after the child is born and you give me my son. Of course, you understand such an agreement would mean you had no right to see the child. And I'll also swear to allow you and your friends to live in peace."

"That's . . . generous," Meghann managed.

"Isn't it?" He smiled. "So we are agreed?"

"Yes," she said, eyes locked on her hands.

"No, no," he reproved and grasped her chin again so she couldn't look away. "Look into my eyes and say, I don't want my child. You may have him for your own once he's born."

It was a myth that you couldn't lie because you looked someone in the eyes. So why did Meghann stammer and flush when she met his eyes and said haltingly, "I . . . I don't . . . want . . . I don't want . . . my . . . damn you!"

Spying a red vase on a black lacquered table beside her, Meghann flung it angrily, watching it bounce off the cream wall and shatter into a thousand pieces.

"That was a Ming vase," Lord Baldevar said mournfully. "Why do you look so downcast? If you want the child, why fight me?"

"Why fight you," Meghann began incredulously. "You idiot—forget it. I don't want a tube in my throat."

"I will not harm you for speaking the truth. Now continue, Meghann. Tell me why you've lied . . . why you wanted me to think you despised your own child,

why you won't come to me when I can see you're so
frightened and alone."

"*If* I were frightened and alone, you'd be the last
person on earth I'd turn to. Now, let me go," Meghann
hissed. "I'm not telling you anything."

"Someday you'll know I'm the only person you
should put your faith in," he answered coolly. "Now,
tell me why you're trying to deceive me before I reach
into your mind and find out for myself."

When Meghann kept stubbornly silent, Lord Baldevar gazed at her for a few minutes before his eyes
widened with shock and something that looked suspiciously like laughter. "Protection? What can you be
protecting the child from?"

"You!" she cried, exasperated and past caring what
he knew or didn't know.

"But I'm the father."

"No, you're not!" she yelled. "I don't care if you
did impregnate me—you will never ever be a father to
my baby! My God, do you think I'd let a domineering
psychopath like you within ten feet of an innocent
child? Have you play your vicious mind games and
crush its spirit? Maybe beat it whenever the great lord
and master is displeased? I won't have it! I will not
allow you to ruin this child's life like you ruined mine.
So I guess you better lobotomize me or kill me or do
whatever else you have up your vile sleeve, because if
you ever hurt my baby you'll answer to me, Simon Baldevar!"

"Meghann," he whispered and now he looked at
her, not with rage or derision but admiration . . . admiration and the beginnings of hope. "Do I understand you correctly? All of this—your vicious remarks
and plans to destroy me . . . of course I know about
that! You've done all of this because you think I won't
be a good father?"

"Well . . . yes."

"You delightful, wonderful girl!" Lord Baldevar

swung her off her feet, planting kisses all over her face, smiling down at her in pure joy.

"Put me down! Stop slobbering over me! What the hell are you so happy about?"

He didn't put her down. Instead, he reseated himself on the divan, cradling her resisting form against him.

"My Meghann . . . I always knew you'd be a wonderful mother, so protective of those you love. Stop that squirming . . . you'll tire yourself. How foolish of me not to see it. Your misconception of me makes you think I'd be an unsuitable parent, so of course you would try to deceive me. And you probably also fear that I'll take the child and never allow you near him or simply kill you once you give birth. What were you planning—give birth under my nose and then flee into hiding with the baby? No, that wouldn't be permanent enough . . . no doubt I meet with a nasty death once you don't need my blood."

Meghann refused to give him the satisfaction of an answer.

"All right," he said and petted her hair. "You don't trust me yet. I shall simply have to change that."

"How?"

Lord Baldevar raised an eyebrow. "By showing you I mean only the best for you and my son. How else? I'll court you and you'll see all the poison Alcuin filled your mind with is false."

"Court me?" she gasped. If he had said he was going to kill her, she couldn't have been more appalled. "I . . . I . . . no! I don't want some vile beast that goes around destroying innocent men in jealous fits of rage courting me. And don't you dare blame Alcuin for all your flaws! He didn't have to tell me anything about you that I didn't witness firsthand . . ."

"Stop," he said, holding his hands up in a gesture of surrender. "You are right."

"What?" she said dumbly.

Lord Baldevar laughed at her shock and gave her hair a not too gentle tug. "You are right, Meghann. Since I found you at Doctor Winslow's, I've done nothing to present my charms in an attractive light—it's no wonder you fear me. Well, enough of that. Come along, we're going out."

"What do you mean, 'out'?" Meghann demanded when he took her hand and started dragging her out of the living room.

"You may remember the word from the nights before you decided to bury yourself alive. I've had enough of this self-pitying melancholy you've wrapped yourself in."

"Self-pitying," Meghann seethed. "How dare you—"

"I dare, Meghann. I dare because I care far too much to allow the vital woman I adore to remain a hollow-eyed, weepy skeleton and pine away into the grave. If you could only see your reflection. You look more like a death camp survivor than an expectant mother."

"I do not!" she cried, stung.

"Oh, no?" Lord Baldevar raised his eyebrow again, ignoring the scowl Meghann shot him. "Tell me how much weight you've gained since you started drinking my blood, scarecrow."

"One pound," she mumbled.

"I did not hear that."

"One pound." Meghann sighed. She'd been worried about her inability to gain weight—just as Lee was worried. The mortal doctor pleaded with her to eat more but Meghann simply had no appetite, though she did force herself to drink large quantities of milk and eat fresh fruit. "I just haven't been that hungry."

"Of course you aren't hungry. I have no doubt the gloom you've shrouded yourself in makes food taste like straw. Well, enough of that. It's time I rescued you from your depression."

For a minute, Meghann could only splutter in fury

but she finally got the words out. "You . . . you damned fiend! You're the cause of my depression!"

"I am not. You're miserable because you've forgotten how to enjoy the night. I'm going to make you live again."

"Let go of me! I enjoy the night just fine—I don't need you!"

"Is that so? Then tell me what you do with your time besides weep over that thing I reluctantly shelter and mope around Doctor Winslow's house."

"Well, I . . . uh . . ."

"I knew it!" When Meghann grabbed at a massive breakfront in the hallway to stop their progress, Lord Baldevar turned and gave her a level stare.

"Can I interest you in a proposition, Meghann?"

"What kind?" she asked suspiciously.

"Not the kind you seem to have in mind," he teased. "All I want from you is the rest of tonight to prove we can exist together in peace. One night in which we see if I can make you laugh or smile again. If at the end of the night you feel as you do now, I shall leave you alone."

"I don't know . . ." Meghann hedged. How could she even contemplate making peace with Lord Baldevar after what he'd done to Jimmy?

"I thought you loved your child."

"Of course I do."

"Then have you given any thought to what you'll do to our child if you refuse to accept me? Are you going to raise your child to despise his own father or if you never say a word make him miserable when he's caught in an atmosphere of cold hate between us? What does that mind science you're so fond of have to say about that?"

The question threw her. "I . . . I hadn't thought about it."

"Of course you didn't. You were far too busy plotting for that catamite to sneak up on me and chop my head off while you're in labor." Lord Baldevar laughed at the guilty but defiant surprise on her face and chucked her under the chin. "Don't waste your time trying to defeat me. You'll never succeed."

There was no hint of boast in the quiet voice and Meghann knew he could very well be right. Vampires had tried for four hundred years to destroy Lord Baldevar without success. Why should she and Charles be any different? Would it be better for her child to reach some sort of truce with him?

But then . . . what he was, the awful things he did . . . he'd influence the baby. *And if you give him a hard time, he'll take the baby from you,* a voice reminded her. *At least if you make peace, you're in the child's life . . . you can counteract his suggestions, make sure the baby grows up with a moral center.*

"I'm not going back to being your consort," Meghann said flatly. "Will you take the baby away from me for spurning you?"

Lord Baldevar took her hands. "I can be a great many things to my son but I could never replace the care of a loving mother . . . nor would I wish to. I want to raise this child with you, Meghann—whether you seek my bed or not. Convince me I can trust you not to go running off and I shall give you physical custody of our son. On my honor as a knight, I promise you that."

"When were you knighted?"

Lord Baldevar rolled his eyes. "During the Armada crisis—but that is not important. What say you, Meghann? Can I have one night to prove myself? After that, if you still cannot stand my company but promise to be civil for the child's sake, I'll leave you in peace."

"All you want is tonight? After that, you'll leave me alone?"

"If you want me to leave you alone, I will."

Meghann could tell by his expression he thought that was as likely as her throwing herself to the sun the next morning, and it was his arrogance that decided her. Did this vain fiend actually think he could charm her out of all her hatred and resentment in one night?

Meghann gave him a deep, mocking curtsy and held out her hand. "Lead the way . . . Simon."

He grinned at the unspoken challenge in her eyes and kissed her outstretched hand lingeringly. "With pleasure, little one . . . with pleasure."

SIX

Nothing Simon could do would change her feelings toward him, Meghann told herself firmly. Even though she'd agreed to accompany him willingly tonight, that didn't mean she had any intention of being anything more than a passive, silent companion.

Her resolution for a grim evening wavered slightly when Simon brought his apple-red Ferrari F355 Spider convertible to the front door and Meghann gave an involuntary gasp of appreciation. Without thinking, she ran to the sleek sports car, running a reverent hand over the aluminum and steel panels.

"It's fantastic," she gushed, inspecting the trademark round rear lights and dancing horse symbol nestled between them. Normally, Meghann's taste in cars went to classic American cars, like her own '58 Cadillac convertible. But what car enthusiast could ignore a brand-new Ferrari?

Ever the gentleman, Simon came to the passenger-side and held the door open for her, where Meghann noticed that even the doorstop was upholstered in expensive leather.

"I'd love to have a Ferrari." She sighed.

Simon gave her a quizzical glance while he got comfortable behind the three-spoke Momo steering wheel. "Meghann, you are no mortal to weep and sigh for objects beyond your means. If you like Ferraris, get one . . . get ten if it makes you happy."

"Alcuin said I should live within the means of the mortal profession I chose."

"Damned ninny," Simon muttered, and Meghann stifled a giggle. He raised an eyebrow at her overcomposed expression and continued. "But explain one thing to me, sweetheart. I do not know of many struggling psychologists that charge ridiculously low fees who can afford an impeccably restored fifty-eight Cadillac."

"I'm not your sweetheart and I didn't buy that car restored," Meghann retorted. "I paid a junkie four hundred dollars for a rotted-out old wreck and then rebuilt the car."

"Do you mean to tell me you restored that car by yourself?"

"It wasn't that hard—the engine was actually in pretty good shape but the bodywork took forever. I can't tell you how many nights I scoured the junkyards for parts."

"So in our time apart you've become a grease monkey?"

"Better than a dandy mechanics can rob blind because he wouldn't dream of dirtying his delicate hands," Meghann said tartly, thinking she'd already given Simon more conversation than she'd intended for the entire evening.

"Have you forgotten vampires are telepathic? No one cheats me, I assure you."

Meghann rubbed her cheek against the plush Connolly leather seat and watched Simon take the winding turns at 60 mph . . . a fast speed, but a pale shadow of what she knew this car was capable of. "How does it ride at maximum speed?"

"I don't know." At her surprised glance, Simon explained, "I haven't had a chance to take it out on a flat, isolated stretch of road yet. Would you like to do that?"

"Do what?"

"We could go out to the desert and see how the Spider performs. Perhaps go into town and get a picnic dinner to take with us? I'll let you drive," Simon invited.

Meghann's eyes lit up—get behind the wheel of this glorious car and speed along the desert roads? The desert fascinated her but she hadn't been able to make time to go out there yet. Then she remembered what took up all her free time—healing Jimmy. How could she enjoy herself with the monster that'd destroyed Jimmy?

"Don't look like that," Simon said softly at her downturned mouth. "You cannot help him by shutting yourself off from all enjoyment."

"What do you care if I help him or not?" she snapped.

"I don't. But I care very much about your well-being, Meghann, so forget your deranged lover and anything else that puts shadows under those beautiful eyes of yours. Your time with me is devoted to enjoyment—nothing more."

After a few moments of uneasy silence, Simon pressed a button on the car stereo and the small cabin was soon filled with the strains of "Clair de lune."

"Ugh," Meghann exclaimed, wrinkling her nose in distaste. Without bothering to consult the owner of the car, she reached over and scanned the radio stations, leaning back with a satisfied smile when she found "Welcome to the Jungle."

"I think not," Simon said mildly and shut the radio off. At Meghann's scowl, he said, "My dear, in this car we do not listen to those awful jackals you're so fond of. But here's something both of us can enjoy, young philistine." Simon pushed another button and the CD changed to Muddy Waters, eliciting an enthusiastic if unwilling grin from Meghann. Blues and jazz were the only things she and Simon could agree on as far as music went. Meghann remembered how surprised she'd been to find that the elegant sophisticate that swept her off her feet took such pleasure in seeking out all sorts of back-alley taverns and dives where they'd listen to the sensual, earthy music all night.

"Long Distance Call" came on and Simon turned to Meghann. "Remember when we first heard him play at that club in Chicago? What was it . . . fifty-three?"

"Nineteen fifty-two," Meghann corrected and her grin widened as she remembered the small, smoke-filled club on the South Side. "We were the only white people there and . . . look at the strip! My God, there's nothing like it." Wide-eyed, Meghann took in the glittering, gaudy neon and truly panoramic sights of the Las Vegas Strip. Her eyes darted around, drinking in sights she'd been too sick to notice when she and Charles first came to town. There were the life-size pyramids of the Luxor, the gaudy medieval pageantry of Excalibur, the pirate ships engaged in battle in front of Treasure Island Hotel . . .

"You've been in Las Vegas nearly a month and you haven't been on the strip? Good Lord, girl, you may as well enter a convent for all the fun you have." Simon swung the car into the driveway of Caesar's Palace, casually tossing the keys to an amazed valet. With amusement, Meghann watched him jump behind the driver's seat, drawing envious stares from his fellow employees.

"What kind of picnic can we have here?"

"In the Forum, dear girl, is the Stage Deli, which makes what is possibly the best pastrami in the world, even rivals New York delicatessens."

"We'll see about that," Meghann sniffed and observed the garish spectacle of gladiator waiters, toga-wearing cocktail waitresses, and vast Roman-style temples filled with slot machines. It was irredeemably tacky, vulgar even, but Meghann found herself charmed by the sight. She'd always liked casinos, ever since Simon first transformed her and took her to a casino hotel he owned in pre-Castro Cuba, telling her a rich vacation spot was the perfect place to teach a novice vampire the ropes—telekinesis she learned by manipulating the dice on the craps tables, and blackjack and poker sharpened her ability to read minds and win considerable small fortunes.

Simon took her hand, grasping it firmly when she tried to pull away. "Doesn't it feel good to be out in the world again, sourpuss?"

"It's all right," she allowed grudgingly, conceding to herself that the bright lights, hectic ringing bells of slot machines, and busy chatter of mortal gamblers were making her feel more invigorated. "But I'd like it more if you weren't here."

"If it were not for me, you'd be keeping your guilt-stricken vigil for your lost lover as we speak. Now, tell me why you cannot enjoy yourself with me. What is it, sweetheart? Fear Alcuin might spin in his grave if you find pleasure in my company?"

While they spoke, Simon guided Meghann through the crowd of gamblers and tourists to Caesar's famous Forum shops, a gargantuan complex of stores that tried in vain to resemble a classical Italian streetscape.

"Enjoy myself with you?" Meghann's voice dripped scorn. "Your only interests in life are bloodletting, sex, and making money—in that order. We have nothing in common, nothing to talk about."

"Oh, no? As I recall, you used to show enthusiastic interest in at least two of my preferred activities. And there is plenty we can talk about."

"Like what?" she asked absently, her attention focused on the ceiling above them, cleverly painted to resemble a Mediterranean sunset.

"We could decide what to name our son."

Meghann's head swiveled in his direction. "We're not having a son," she informed him. "I dream of having a daughter and my dreams almost always come true."

"I've been dreaming for more centuries than you've been alive and it's always a son I see. But don't glare—a daughter is as welcome to me as a son."

"I'm going to name her Isabelle," Meghann said, making a wicked reference to the mortal wife he'd killed shortly after transforming.

"Impossible," Simon said flatly. "If we have a daughter, there is only one name for her—Elizabeth."

"Was that some lover of yours?" Meghann asked, disconcerted by the obvious affection in his voice when he pronounced the name.

"Hardly." Simon laughed. "I cannot claim the Virgin Queen as one of my mistresses. I'm afraid my explanation is not at all salacious—I simply swore to Elizabeth I would name my firstborn daughter after her and no matter what my enemies say of me, you will never find anyone to tell you I broke a vow."

"You told the Virgin Queen you'd name your daughter after her? When? Oh, God."

At Meghann's green-tinged complexion, Simon gathered her up and set her down at the edge of a large marble fountain.

"Crackers," she managed to mumble and he had the plastic bag of saltine crackers out of her satchel and at her mouth in an instant.

"Slow," Simon ordered and she simply nodded her head, nibbling cautiously at one cracker.

"There now," he murmured, resting her head against his shoulder while Meghann felt the nausea start to recede. "It's just morning sickness, little one— soon it will pass and you'll feel better."

Meghann did feel better, though she wasn't sure if it was the crackers or the way that Simon rocked her like a small child that accounted for her sudden sense of well-being. Unconsciously, she leaned against his shoulder, thinking of how nice it felt not to be worried or scared. How long had it been since she was able to relax?

Too long you've been fighting and struggling against me. Let it go, sweet, let it go.

Think it's going to be that easy to make me forget what you are? Meghann glowered and pushed herself away from Simon. What was the matter with her, clinging to him like that? She should feel repulsed when he touched her, not comforted.

Simon laughed and stretched one long arm out to pull her back against him. "Do you truly believe you can force your heart to follow your conscience? All right, stop scowling like that—I'll say no more about it, we'll simply continue our evening together. Why don't you eat a few of those crackers and I'll tell you all about my deathbed promise to Queen Bess, as well as how I eased her from life into death, while you regain your equilibrium?"

Meghann nearly forgot her inner turmoil at Simon's words. "You helped the queen of England die? Why?"

"Because I loved her," he said simply and began telling Meghann of his last encounter with the Virgin Queen . . . a tale he'd never shared with anyone else.

March 24, 1603
Richmond Palace, England

"Identify yourself," the dying queen ordered in a strong tone that belied her illness, sitting ramrod straight on her lavishly carved and curtained bed.

The masked, cloaked man smiled; he admired the queen's courage. A stranger boldly entered her chamber, laid hands on her ladies-in-waiting to make them fall into an enchanted slumber, and the tough old monarch showed not the slightest fear.

He grabbed a beeswax candle from the mantel and advanced to the queen's bedside. Only when he stood right above her did he throw back his hood and remove the gold Venetian mask while putting the candle under his chin so his features were illuminated.

At her first sight of the amber eyes glittering in the candlelight, the queen's stern expression softened and she gave her old favorite a broad, if toothless, smile of welcome. "Hawk!" Elizabeth cried, using the pet name she'd given him for the unusual color of his eyes.

Simon fell to one knee, kissing the still lovely delicate white hand extended before him. "Your Majesty," he said softly, head bowed.

"I thought life had dealt me all its surprises," Elizabeth said, her voice hoarse and cracked. "Your handsome face was one I expected to see in the next world. Our reports said you were dead."

"For all intents and purposes, I might as well be. Lord Simon Baldevar, Earl of Lecarrow, died when unknowns attacked his estate. Although I escaped, my enemies are still searching for me so I am not enough of a fool to use my true identity. Perhaps in time I shall resurrect Lord Baldevar."

The queen's eyes narrowed. "How much time is left to you, Hawk? Already you approach middle age yet you seem exactly as you were a decade ago. Perhaps in your adventures you discovered the fountain of youth hidden away in the Americas?"

Simon smiled at the queen's astute appraisal. "As you see me, so shall I remain forever."

"Forsooth?" the queen asked, and he nodded. "Have you appeared at my deathbed to offer your sovereign some of whatever magic you have discovered for yourself?"

Simon's smile became rueful. "I would give a great deal to be able to turn back the clock for you, but I can only freeze it. I can offer you eternal life but it will be in the form you have now. Is that your desire, Bess?" Years ago, he'd been given the rare permission to address the queen so familiarly.

Elizabeth gave a delicate shudder. "I have already

endured too many years in this aged useless body. To spend eternity as I am now is surely one of Dante's circles of hell. Hawk, if you cannot grant me freedom from death, what do you offer in its place? One reason I always liked you was you never appeared before your queen without some token—unlike the others who only wanted to take from me and never give."

Simon hesitated one moment before offering a final service to his queen. "If you allow me, I can assure you a swift, painless passage into the afterlife."

Tears came into the queen's gray-black eyes. "I have lingered many months like this—old, withered, those damned vultures praying every breath I draw will be my last so that cowardly catamite can come to the throne."

Simon laughed at the queen's sardonic description of King James VI of Scotland—who was no doubt counting the seconds until he was King James I of England.

Elizabeth smiled back and spoke with a hoarseness so unlike the musical voice Simon remembered that he gave silent thanks he'd never have to contend with the rigors of old age. "You came to give me a final boon, Hawk, and I shall repay your tribute with the one thing I have left to offer—advice. However, you must be truthful with me. Why were you driven from my realm? Have you made foes in your new existence?"

Simon nodded and stretched out by the bed while the queen patted his head as a mother might do to her small son while he described a harrowing event. "There is a surprising number of my kind in the world. One, a former bishop named Alcuin, seeks to rule us all. Those who resist—as I did—are destroyed." Simon's lips twisted into a harsh grimace. His face turned choleric when he remembered being chained up like a wild beast by Alcuin and his disciples; only the imminent sunrise had prevented that wretched priest from decapitating him.

"This Alcuin must have strong followers or you would have avenged yourself by now. You must build your own army to defeat him."

"I did. He slaughtered them." In his mind's eye, Simon could still see that hellish night—his beautiful estate littered with corpses, finding the severed heads of everyone he'd ever cared for or respected.

The queen slapped his hand, bringing him back to the present. "What army could you have amassed, Hawk? Followers as ignorant to the ways and strengths of your new existence as you are? It was a mistake to challenge this creature so early in your new life. Bide your time, for you have plenty of it. Surely this Alcuin has had centuries to develop his power, and you must also use the centuries to create your own place. Do not confront him again until you are sure you can win. Make him vulnerable the next time you battle. Hold the fate of someone he loves in your hands," Elizabeth suggested slyly.

"My thanks for your advice. I shall make use of it," Simon told her with complete sincerity. It was not every man that received the counsel of the greatest queen the world had ever known—only a complete fool would disdain her suggestions.

"One final bit of guidance," the queen replied. "Have you found a bride to share your long life with or are you still the same indiscriminate tomcat that prowled through my court?"

Simon laughed and had the good grace to flush. He'd thought Elizabeth was unaware of his flagrant promiscuity—he should have known nothing escaped that sharp-eyed queen's notice. "Why burden myself with another wife, Bess? Women only hold my interest a short time before they begin to bore me."

"If you seek another beautiful but witless creature like Lady Isabelle, you will indeed be bored. Since you are beyond death's reach, I shall assume you are also beyond the normal reasons for marrying—lands, wealth, prestige. If I were you, I would use my unlimited time to allow myself the rare luxury of marrying for love." The queen's eyes glistened and Simon wondered if she was thinking of Robert Dudley and the love she'd denied herself to remain England's queen. He respected Bess far too much to spy on her thoughts so he waited patiently for the queen to collect herself and go on speaking. "Seek a vigorous young girl of good but not impeccable breeding; an overbred wench will never match your vitality and make sure she has the wit to hold your attention. Wit and spirit—that is what you need in a bride, my ambitious, restless young hawk."

Who would not crave a bride such as the queen described—beautiful, intelligent, spirited, and filled with enough passion to match him? But Simon had had enough women to know a creature like that was as rare as a unicorn. If he found her, he'd transform her immediately but in the meanwhile he was content to fill his bed and satisfy his blood lust with the fluffy young things that always seemed to be in abundance.

"Can you sire children in your new state?"

Simon shrugged. "The archives I read and my own research seem to indicate it is possible if rare." There was no need to burden the dying queen with his hypothesis that the spawn of two vampires would realize the promise of the philosophers' stone and walk in daylight. But he'd learned his lesson with Isabelle . . . he couldn't have his son with just any woman. The ideal Elizabeth had described was all he'd accept now, and if she never came along—well, he didn't miss sunlight enough to settle for another hideous match.

Elizabeth smiled. "If you should decide to have a family, I do hope you'll name your firstborn daughter for me."

"Of course." Simon smiled back.

"Then we have concluded our business and I am ready for the swift death you've promised me." The queen lay back against her satin pillows and pulled her eiderdown coverlet about her shoulders, her eyes betraying no fear at imminent death.

What a woman this was! If he'd been younger and of nobler birth, Simon would have come to court to woo the young Elizabeth; she might have been a match for him with her regal bearing, courage, and brains. Too, in her youth, she would have satisfied his penchant for red-haired maidens. But Elizabeth would have been too ruthlessly ambitious for his taste—Simon had no desire to share his bed with any woman as cutthroat as he was. Spirit was fine, but his wife would have to accept him as her master.

Simon held the queen's eyes and reached into her mind, projecting over his own face an image that made Elizabeth smile and gasp with joy. "Robin!"

"It's our wedding night, Bess," Simon replied, hypnotizing the queen into believing she was young and beautiful again. He wrapped his arms around the old woman and kissed her dry, wrinkled lips, smothering the distaste that made him want to pull away. He was going to give Elizabeth what she'd denied herself to rule . . . a fantasy of physical intimacy with her heart mate, Robert Dudley.

"Robin," she breathed, stormy eyes glazed over.

"Yes, my love." Simon pushed the sleeve of her plain white nightgown up. If he bit her on the neck, the marks would attract too much attention. Here, the wounds would go unnoticed among the wrinkles and liver spots surrounding them. He bit into the flesh right beneath her elbow, blood teeth sinking into a prominent vein.

Oh, she was sick! The near-death blood made him ill but Simon kept drinking, draining the queen while she writhed in orgasmic ecstasy. Bloodletting, he'd discovered, could be either supreme pleasure for his victims or unimaginable hell . . . whatever he wished them to feel.

Finally, the arm he held went slack and Simon looked up, careful to wipe the excess blood away on his sleeve instead of the bed. It wouldn't do for some sharp-eyed lady-in-waiting to notice blood on Elizabeth's sheets.

"Rest in peace, my queen," Simon said softly and shut her staring eyes.

Wanting to get the foul taste of disease-ridden blood out of his mouth, Simon looked around the queen's chamber, and his eyes settled on one of her younger attendants. He walked over to the girl and stroked her raven-black hair while he whispered, "Rise, child."

Glazed blue eyes met his while Simon pushed her low neckline farther down so he could drink from her breast, taking only enough to restore his strength.

After rearranging his victim's clothing, he gathered his mask and cape and lifted the enchantment from the room. In a few moments, everyone would awaken and discover the queen's body. Simon gazed at the dead queen one last time before disappearing.

"That . . . that was a very nice thing you did for Elizabeth," Meghann said when he finished speaking.

Simon smiled and took her hand again. "Still so certain this 'domineering psychopath' is going to destroy your child's spirit?"

"Doing one good thing in four hundred years doesn't excuse the rest of your life," Meghann said primly, hoping Simon couldn't see how unsettled she felt. For the first time, she saw him as neither the vicious monster his enemies considered him nor her cruel yet darkly exciting master.

Could he have made the whole thing up to impress her? Meghann wondered, and discarded the thought instantly. No, she decided, remembering the look in his eyes when he talked about Alcuin slaughtering his friends . . . Simon hadn't lied. Of course, he'd exaggerated when he told Elizabeth that Alcuin was some power-mad zealot that wanted the vampiric world under his thumb. Still, Meghann had never thought Lord Baldevar grieved for his dead companions . . . or for anyone at all.

"Who were those people that died when Alcuin first tried to kill you?" she asked.

"Don't you know?" Simon asked. "I thought your prelate told you all about Lord Baldevar's decadent mortal existence."

"Well, at least someone did," Meghann retorted. "You couldn't be bothered to tell me anything about your life."

"Meghann." Simon wrapped an arm around her. "Stop that struggling or I'll dunk your head in this fountain. Why do you look so downcast? Are you bothered because I never discussed the past with you?"

"Why should I be bothered?" Meghann sniffed, trying to look nonchalant. Why should it bother her that any time she'd asked about the past he'd brushed off her inquiries with a brusque cold answer that amounted to "mind your own business"? Why should it still sting that he'd never thought enough of her to confide in her?

"I thought a great deal of you, little one, and I always planned to tell you anything you wished to know when I thought you were ready. But I knew any account of my mortal life would have to end by telling you about Alcuin and I was simply enjoying your company too much to bring up that dreary business. Certainly, I never imagined you'd run off on me and go have your head filled with a pack of lies."

"Are you trying to tell me you didn't slay your father and brother? Didn't make your brother's widow marry you and torture her when she miscarried your child? That you didn't get syphilis and suck up to a homosexual vampire to become immortal and then kill him when you got what you wanted?"

"All of that happened," Simon agreed. "But you've been allowed to think they were all innocent victims. Believe me, everyone you just mentioned got precisely what they deserved. You'll understand that when I'm done. Unless you're too narrow-minded to listen to my version of the past?"

"You want to tell me your side of the story?" Meghann asked.

"Indeed I do . . . over our picnic dinner in the desert. What say you, Meghann? We'll get some food so those damned hollows in your cheeks start to fill out and I'll tell you all about how Lord Simon Baldevar came to be a vampire."

At the mention of food, Meghann's stomach roared to life—the first time she'd really felt hungry in months.

"You'll tell me all about your mortal life?" Meghann asked, not sure why she was so eager for this story. If she hated Simon, why did she burn to know more about him?

Because she really didn't know him at all, Meghann realized. She knew nothing of his life before he transformed her, other than the sketchy accounts given to her by Alcuin. If there was any hope for her making peace with Simon Baldevar, raising her child with him, it was in understanding what had happened to make him both the amoral fiend that cut down anyone who got in his way and the compassionate friend that would ease an ailing queen into a gentle death.

Simon stood up, rising from the fountain with the grace of an unfolding cat, and offered Meghann his arm. "Come along, my little Freudian. I think I'll begin my tale with the night I carried out the aim of the Oedipus complex and killed my father." He laughed at Meghann's shocked stare and continued.

"Mind you, I didn't slaughter him so I could marry my mother. No, all I wanted was the money the old skinflint refused to part with. It was 1578, and I'd just learned of an opportunity to invest in a shipping expedition."

SEVEN

Yorkshire, England
January 20, 1578

"It is a fool's notion," Payton, Baron Baldevar, declared. He gave his youngest son a look of scorn. "Why are you such a malcontent? Has your brother not generously agreed to let you remain on these estates after he succeeds me as baron?"

"If either of you toss me off this crumbling manse, you'll have to part with some of your precious gold and hire a steward since I will no longer be here to labor for nothing," Simon responded coldly. "If I am gone, who will supervise the sheep shearing from dawn until dusk and make sure our tenants do not steal from us? Roger? That he manages to tie his own codpiece without assistance is a constant amazement to me."

"You arrogant young whelp!" Payton cuffed him a blow that would have sent a weaker man to the floor. Though Simon's head snapped to one side from the force of the blow, he did not wince or even bring his hand to his wounded cheek. A long time ago he'd learned to show no fear of his father.

"Apologize to your brother," Payton ordered but there was no heat behind his words. Indeed, he seemed uneasy as his eighteen-year-old son merely stared at him without speaking.

Simon turned to his elder brother, busy stuffing

sweetmeats into his open mouth until his cheeks puffed out grotesquely, and gave him a cool bow. "My pardon, brother."

Roger looked up, swallowing hastily. "Little brother, how can you even think to disgrace our good name by becoming a mere pirate?"

Simon swallowed a bitter laugh—good name? The Baldevars were minor barons, all but forgotten by the rest of England in their cold northern estate. Payton and Roger were decades behind the times . . . thinking the north and its nobles of vital importance when the true heart of England was the south and London.

Payton smiled at Roger as though the fat dolt had made some remarkable insight. "Excellent point, son," Payton complimented, drinking deeply from a tankard of ale set before him on the scarred oak table. Then he turned back to Simon. "A nobleman does not dirty his hands with trade."

But a nobleman could rot away in a drafty, moldering excuse for a manor house and slave on his brother's behalf, couldn't he?

Simon took a deep breath and tried again to impress his point. "Father, Sir John obtained a royal charter. If the Crown approves the voyage, I hardly believe my noble name will be besmirched. With letters of marque from the queen, we can sail the Barbary Coast without fear of being attacked. Sir John has three excellent ships, and a loyal, well-trained crew. Why do you not see what a winning proposition this is?"

"If this knight already has his ship and men, what need has he of you?" Roger asked nastily.

Simon ignored the gibe, thinking the dullard would know very well why Sir John had approached him if he had not been busy stuffing his face and ignoring the conversation around him. But Simon outlined their plan again, speaking as he might to a particularly slow-witted five-year-old. "My gold gives provisions for the long voyage as well as items to trade once we get to Algiers. In exchange, we receive sixty percent of the profit. Further, Sir John has been to Algiers. Look at this example of the Muslims' wool cloths." Simon held out a marvelous red cape, shiny and soft to the touch. Then he compared it to his own coarse, poorly dyed black cape. "All we have are our sheep. If we produce cloth like this, learn to dye and cut our wool as the Muslims do, our profits will triple within a year. England is desperate for good cloth."

"What if your ships fall victim to bad weather or mutiny?" Payton demanded, and Simon could only assume the old man had not heard him when he said Sir John was an experienced captain with a loyal crew. "We would lose what little we have. Have you thought of that? Leave adventuring to men with more means than you have, Simon. Now, the matter is dismissed. Tell Sir John he must find another investor."

"I do not believe you understand me, Father," Simon said evenly, struggling to keep his outrage at being dismissed like a child out of his voice. "I am not begging largesse from your table. I merely ask for what is mine."

"What are you talking about?" his father demanded.

"My wife's dowry," Simon explained. "I wish to use her gold to form a trade company with Sir John."

"Impossible," Payton said firmly. "That money we use to restore the estate to its former glory."

"You doddering old fool!" Simon spat. "Do you think I will accept marriage to that old crow and sit by while you use my money to buy wasteful tapestries and cushions for my brother's broad backside?"

Roger pushed himself up from his chair and stormed over to his younger brother. He raised his fist and snarled, "You will not speak to your father like that!"

In an instant, Simon drew his sword and aimed it at his brother's unprotected heart. "You dare to lecture me on the ways of nobility and then you raise your fist like the lowest villein? Lower your hand before I remove it permanently."

"Simon!" Payton thundered at his side. The old man was furious but Simon also heard fear in that deep voice and it pleased him . . . pleased him so much he almost forgot his own anger. "How dare you draw a sword on your own brother! Resheath it at once."

Simon kept the blade to his brother's green brocade doublet, allowing the tip to make a small rip in the cheap fabric. He met Roger's frightened gray eyes and gave him a cruel smile before returning his sword to its scabbard. *Someday, my brother,* Simon promised Roger silently. Of course he could not kill his brother in the great hall with servants milling about, but someday an opportunity would present itself.

Simon turned back to his father, noting that for the first time in his life, his father seemed uncertain when he looked at him. Gone was the towering bully that raised his hand at the slightest provocation. Now Payton seemed small, shrunken with indecision.

Finally, his father collapsed into his seat at the high board and drained his tankard of ale dry. Only after he signaled a serving wench to bring him more drink did he finally address Simon. "The sins of disobedience and vanity run deep within you. You must . . . you must go to church and ask God to forgive your heinous conduct this afternoon. Spend the entire night on your knees."

Church . . . Simon nearly laughed aloud but it would do no good to let the old fool know he was all but signing his own death warrant by sending Simon to church. Instead, he simply bowed and said, "As you wish, sire."

Without even glancing at Roger, Simon stalked out of the great hall, ignoring the curious stares of the servants.

"Husband, I wish a word with you."

Simon gave his wife a glance of withering contempt

and wrinkled his nose in distaste at the odor of her unwashed body, the reek not at all covered by her cloying lavender scent. "There is nothing between us worth discussing."

"Sir, please." Alice put an entreating hand on his forearm, hastily withdrawn at the black look in his eyes. "I . . . I must speak with you."

Simon wrapped his rabbit-lined cloak tightly around his body, cursing the vile January weather and drafty, poorly lit hallway. On the other hand, perhaps he should give thanks for the dim lighting. The last thing he needed to see well was his wife, a small pudding of a woman who reminded Simon of a pear—flat at the top and gradually spreading into a wealth of unattractive flesh.

Matching him to this repulsive creature was the worst thing Payton and Roger had ever done to him. As the youngest son, Simon had thought he might never marry. After all, he had no fortune or title to offer a bride.

Then, Alex Joyes had moved onto an estate near their lands. Master Joyes, a prosperous London merchant, received the small manor and rich lands after he was clever enough to cancel a large royal debt. In exchange, the queen gave him an estate and the ambitious merchant immediately set about ennobling his family through marriage.

He had three daughters and enough gold to dower each one quite generously. Two of his daughters, at six and eight, were too young. Besides, they both showed promise of great beauty so Simon had no doubt his shrewd father-in-law would send the maidens to court where they might snare a great name.

That left only his eldest daughter—Alice. Originally, Alex tried to match her with Roger but he'd already been betrothed to a French girl; the marriage was due to take place in another five years. As for Simon's other brother, Michael, he was a priest—a career Simon might have wanted for himself fifty years ago. That left Simon—bought and sold between the two fathers after Alex made Payton an offer for more gold than the Baron had seen in ten years.

Simon had not fought the marriage because he realized how badly his family needed to rebuild their crumbling fortunes. What did it matter that his wife's appearance turned his stomach? There were serving wenches and peasants to serve his needs, and the gold would improve his life.

Now that Simon had discovered that he would not see so much as one farthing of his wife's dowry while his father lived, he did not even bother displaying to his wife the cold courtesy he'd given since their wedding six months ago.

"Say whatever you must so I may be about my business," Simon snapped, but Alice simply stood there, her lower lip trembling so hard each of her double chins quivered.

"Sir, our marriage," she finally said timidly. "We must . . . must . . . consummate it," she finally choked out, a red stain almost obliterating the dark moles on her cheeks.

For the first time that day, Simon threw back his head and laughed, feeling a mean pleasure when his wife's watery blue eyes filled with tears. "That is what you pester me for? Stud services? Go and speak with my father—I have not been paid yet. He has your gold—get him to lie with you."

"Please," Alice cried. "I want . . ."

Finally, a way to relieve the enormous frustration within him, Simon grabbed one flabby arm and pushed his wife into a dark alcove.

"What do you want—a man between your blubbery thighs?" Simon's speech was deliberately crude, to further upset this harridan he'd been matched to. "The stable is full of young lads willing to do anything for a gold crown. See if one of them can keep their cock hard at the sight of you. Or better still, wait until the blackest part of night when they'll see nothing at all."

"You are cruel," Alice sobbed.

"How am I cruel?" Simon demanded. "Did I not cut my own leg and smear our nuptial sheets with blood so your reputation would not suffer? You are lucky to have a husband at all. If my family were not so wretchedly poor, even my father would not have sold me into marriage with an elderly crone like you."

"I am not old!" Alice shouted and winced when Simon whacked her across the mouth.

"Lower your voice. Do you wish the entire household to know I am repulsed by the thought of bedding my wife?"

"I am not old," Alice repeated, apparently impervious to insult. "The midwife examined me and said I am still capable of bearing children though I be four and thirty. Don't you want a son?"

"What in the name of God would I do with a son?" Simon asked incredulously. "Rear him to accept his place beneath whatever spawn my idiot brother eventually produces? Tell him to put a brave face on it and pretend it does not matter his life is over before he draws his first breath? Do you think I would wish all that has happened to me on a son of mine? Shall we both sob into our beers when Roger and his sons live soft while we toil?"

Giving his wife one last slap, Simon turned from her and stormed out of the house, too engrossed in his dark, bitter thoughts to notice the frigid temperature on the long walk to the small village church.

God had played a marvelous jest on him, Simon thought—gave him brains and beauty and ambition, but had him born the youngest son to an impoverished family of barely passable lineage. What good was a sharp mind when his father wouldn't even send him to university? What did it matter that he had a handsome face and smooth tongue when there was no money to send him to court so he might advance himself?

Again he thought of his father and Roger . . . the two of them sitting in the great hall looking down on him, trying to convince Simon he should be grateful for the opportunity to spend the rest of his days shackled to that wretched lump of a woman they'd betrothed him to . . . should fall at Roger's knees and thank him for allowing Simon to do no more with his life than be his brother's steward.

It won't happen, Simon vowed. He'd had enough of this . . . enough of freezing winters on the moors that must be suffered through without adequate food or clothing, enough of slaving in behalf of a lack-wit brother . . . most of all, he had enough of other people controlling his life.

The key to everything was money. With gold, the estate could be rebuilt, he could go to court . . . maybe obtain a position in the queen's household. If he had money, he could make a better match for himself—once his current wife met with an unfortunate accident. Money would open all roads . . . give him prestige, a suitable wife, children.

Six months ago, his golden opportunity had arrived. Even now, Simon could smile at the thought that the day he dreaded mightily—his wedding day—might wind up being the most profitable of his life.

The only bright spot of the day was the friendship Simon struck up with his new father-in-law. Perhaps Master Joyes felt some sympathy at Simon's situation, because he made it a point to introduce him to Sir John Wolcott. The man was ten years Simon's senior and he'd been a captain under Thomas Windham for five years. From that wily explorer, Sir John learned all he needed to about raiding Spanish ships and navigation and saved his earnings until he was able to buy three ships of his own. Now all he needed was the gold to finance his first voyage.

And Simon could provide that gold if not for his father! Simon's eyes narrowed—did the old man think this was over? Oh, no. Simon was getting his gold—one way or another.

He threw open the double doors to the church and saw his old nursemaid, Adelaide, spreading a creamy lace cloth embroidered with looping vines and leaves across the stone altar.

"What happened to ye?" she demanded and rushed over to her former charge so she could examine the purple welt on his cheek.

"What do you think?" he asked bitterly. "Where is Father Bain? I am to keep vigil tonight so I may atone for the grievous sin of talking back to the pompous ass that sired me."

"And I'm sure ye talked to him in just that manner!" Adelaide snapped, her voice still full of the heather and burr of the Scottish lowlands she'd come from, along with his mother when she married Payton. She gave Simon an affectionate tug on his earlobe. "When will ye learn to keep that fresh mouth of yers shut?"

"Where is Father Bain?" Simon repeated patiently.

"Old Daisy Geedes lies dying and he went off to give her the last rites. Dinna fret, he'll be back soon. Now, what did ye and yer father quarrel over?"

Briefly, Simon told her of the argument, growing more agitated as he recounted the incident.

"Goddamn them both!" he snarled, completely unmindful that he was in the house of God. He pushed his hand through his thick chestnut hair, pacing back and forth like a caged lion. "Shortsighted fools . . . they are incapable of seeing past the next month, the next meal even. If they spend the gold on refurbishing that overgrown barn, what happens next year when we need new livestock? If we invest the money, it returns to us in the form of more profit."

"Yer father is a man for doing things as they were

always done—what his father did is what he shall do
and he expects Master Roger to do the same. He
doesna like change, dearie. As for yer brother, 'twill
be a cold day in hell before he respects an idea from
yer mouth. Jealous of ye from the day ye were born,
he was."

Simon nodded and let his old nurse ramble, repeat-
ing a story he'd heard hundreds of times before—how
his mother had loved him from the moment he was
pulled out of her. Since his mother died when he was
three after she miscarried her fourth child, Simon had
no memory of her and could only take Adelaide's word
that she'd favored her handsome little boy with his
chestnut curls and gold eyes like hers over his plain,
ill-favored brothers that resembled their father.

After she died, it was Adelaide that took over his
care, insisting Payton hire tutors for her young charge
and then standing guard over him when he might have
evaded his studies in favor of hunting or riding. If it
had not been for Adelaide, Simon might have grown
up as dull-witted as his brothers. Instead, he learned
history, philosophy, mathematics, astronomy, French,
and Italian. Always, she impressed upon him that the
only thing to free him from the bleak moors and a
life of sheep raising was his mind and his looks.

So here he was—as educated and handsome as
many men far better born than he was and sitting in
a small village church, trying to find some way out of
the hell his father was trying to condemn him to.

As Adelaide continued her work, Simon glanced
about the church, thinking that here was something
his father was willing to spend gold on. The pious old
man made every effort to buy his way into heaven and
had supplied the church with jeweled candlesticks, a
solid-gold crucifix with two large rubies on either side,
and a Jesus carved from ivory, but his true extrava-
gance was the stained-glass windows. The rare, priceless

glass, with its rich shades of blue, violet, rose, and green, had been shipped from Venice.

Simon scowled at the priceless objects, thinking them another example of his family's stupidity. To be an admitted, much less a fanatic, Catholic as his father and brother were was to ensure your decline and fall under suspicion. Why had they not adopted England's church? Simon did not see the pope helping them out of their desperate straits. Then again, if his father had abandoned the church, Simon might not have met Father Bain.

As though thinking of him were enough to summon him, the priest walked briskly into the church, smiling at Adelaide before he noticed Simon lounging on the altar step.

Like Adelaide's, his white brows furrowed in concern when he saw the bruise on Simon's cheek. "What was it this time, son?"

Father Bain laughed heartily when Simon told him he must spend the night in church. "So Payton sends you here? At least no one will remark about your absence when we set about our work. Adelaide, return to the cottage and start my meal."

Simon almost smiled when he thought of why the priest had retained Adelaide as his maid after he no longer needed a nurse. She might be as old as Simon's new bride but that in no way detracted from her buxom good looks . . . her hair was as black as Simon remembered from his childhood and her flashing green eyes and broad smile would make any man happy.

Adelaide departed, giving Simon a firm pat on the cheek.

Simon watched Father Bain remove a gold-and-jeweled candlestick from the altar and stick a fresh beeswax taper in it. Then he followed Father Bain into the confessional, where Simon pulled the plush Turkish carpet back to reveal a trapdoor.

Together, he and the priest traveled down the dark, narrow staircase, Simon making sure to pull the trap-door shut behind him in case anyone should wander into the church while they were downstairs.

Simon found himself remembering the first time Father Bain had taken him into this secret passage. Then he'd been a mere fourteen years old and sent to the church to ask forgiveness after a fight with Roger that nearly left his elder brother dead. It did not matter that the drunken fool had forced Simon's favorite horse over an overgrown hedge and killed the stallion with his foolishness. No, Payton had thrashed him a solid two hours and then directed the head groom to beat his youngest son when his arm grew tired.

He'd walked down to the church with his eyes all but slitted shut but his head was high and he was unrepentant. The priest had taken one look at him and asked if Simon was ready to beg God's forgiveness. It was at that point Simon had changed his life forever.

He had met the priest's eyes and snarled that God was no ally of his. God said his father was right to beat him and he must respect his elder brother even if he was a fool and a drunkard. Simon had wanted nothing to do with such a deity and renounced Him forever.

He had expected Father Bain to rail at him, perhaps run to his father, but the priest had simply held his eyes for a few moments. When he saw the young man was serious, Father Bain put his hand on his shoulder and said, "Follow me into my true temple, lad."

Even now, Simon could still remember how he had shivered at his first sight of that cellar room . . . the walls and floors completely covered in black silk, the few candles that cast long, frightening shadows about the room, the stone altar where a black cloth was draped in symbols Simon hadn't understood then. Most of all, Simon had been drawn to the marvelous manuscripts housed carefully in a sagging bookshelf in a corner of the room.

Father Bain had taken Simon's face between his hands and said, "Sometimes God does not grant us what we desire in life. But there are other forces that will give you everything you ever wanted if you but learn to control them."

Thus, Simon's apprenticeship had begun. He had deliberately misbehaved so he would be sent to church and had spent years learning to read the Latin manuscripts, the lunar phases, and the spells set down in the *Legementon* by assisting Father Bain in his rituals.

Now the priest turned to him and asked, "You are ready for tonight?"

Simon nodded. Both of them had known there was little chance Simon would convince his father to part with the money, so two weeks ago they'd started making preparations.

"You have abstained from women while the moon waxed?" Father Bain demanded, and Simon nodded.

"Only taken two meals during that time?" Another silent nod and Father Bain asked, "What did you do this morning?"

"I went to the river and when the sun cleared the horizon, I cut off the head of a virgin white cock. Then I threw the head in the river and drank the blood." Simon made a face of disgust at the memory. Sometimes he thought that, for all their sonorous ritual, he and Father Bain were no better than the midwives in the village that begged the devil for favors and offered him goat's blood. But the spells had produced positive results, so what did he care if he had to drink a little blood to achieve his desired end?

"Then you are ready." Father Bain sighed. "But, Simon, you must understand. The magick you undertake tonight is not easy. And you do not ask a minor favor . . . causing the death of another is a fearful undertaking. Son, the devils will take possession of your soul if you slip for an instant. Are you certain you wish to go through with this?"

Simon paled, remembering an incident from a few years earlier. A Jesuit had visited their estate . . . a good friend of Father Bain's, a renowned sorcerer. He and Father Bain, with Simon providing minor assistance, had summoned a spirit that first appeared as an extremely handsome man, speaking in a melodious voice. But the Jesuit hadn't properly consecrated his instruments and when his rod had touched the spirit, it changed into a hideous apparition—part goat, part man with great running sores and boils all over its body and it thundered at them, cursing in a language unknown to Simon.

He shuddered, remembering how it merely had touched the Jesuit and instantly the man's face wrinkled, became almost like crumpled parchment, while he danced about madly, a puppet controlled by a devil master.

Only Father Bain's quick thinking had saved him and his apprentice that evening. He had shouted for Simon to toss him the silver bowl filled with holy water. He had flung it at the devil and thundered out the License to Depart. Though the thing had vanished, none of Father Bain's best efforts could exorcise his friend of the devils within his body. In the end, Simon had taken his sword and cut the unfortunate man's head off. He and Father Bain had buried the body in a remote cove beneath one of the isolated cliffs nearby.

Simon would not allow himself to believe the same could happen to him tonight. In his bones, he felt what he was doing was right. No power in the physical world could thwart the power his father had over him, so he must appeal to the spirits. Otherwise, he would remain nothing all his life.

"I am ready," he said quietly, and Father Bain held his eyes a long time before finally nodding.

"Here," he said and thrust a hazel stick into Simon's hands. "Take it and consecrate it. Think of your hate

for your father as you do it and return to me after
moonrise."

Simon sat by a roaring stream, thinking the biting
wind and familiar fog settling over the moors suited
his bleak mood, and carved the long hazel branch into
a rod that would serve him later. He had no worry of
anyone coming upon him and disturbing his meditation. It was far too cold for anyone to be venturing
about.

Though his hands were red with cold, Simon no
longer felt the pain in them. He did as Father Bain
suggested and concentrated on his rage while his knife
shaped and carved.

He also thought of what would happen after he succeeded. Though Father Bain had never mentioned it,
Simon found it helped to imagine achieving the desired end. Perhaps the devils saw the images in his
mind and these helped them carry out his bidding. So
he imagined Payton dead and buried. He wondered
how long his father would lie in the great hall . . .
probably a few days as it was winter and there was no
urgency to getting him underground. Had Michael
taken final vows yet? Could he perform the eulogy for
his father?

Most of all, Simon imagined Roger. Without Payton,
Roger would be as lost as a dog without his master.
Simon had no worry he could manipulate Roger into
giving him what he wanted. Though he might bluster
a bit, it would take only a few hours to talk Roger out
of the gold. With luck, Simon could join Sir John in
Whitby by the end of the week and they'd sail by the
end of the month. Though the winter sea promised
to be choppy, both men were eager to set off for Algiers.

Simon looked up, startled, when a long dark shadow
fell across the hazel rod. A quick glance at the sky

showed his thoughts had so preoccupied him he missed sunset.

Simon reached into a silk bag at his waist and withdrew two pointed steel caps that he attached to both ends of the rod, and then magnetized it with a lodestone.

Rising, he held his rod outstretched to the moon and said the prayer to consecrate his rod. *"Nomine dei impero vobis ut meae voluntati pareretis et omnia quae destruere volo dilaceraretis ac ad Chaos redigeritis."*

He pulled his cape about him, holding it over his mouth and nose to ward off the stinging wind and snow that had started falling. Within a relatively short time, he was back in the church and descending the steep stairs to the temple.

Father Bain was already there and gave Simon a brief glance of acknowledgment before handing him a black robe. Without a word, both men removed their clothing and changed quickly into their magick robes, uttering the words that would charge the garments.

Next came what was perhaps the most important work of the evening—the drawing of the magick circle. An improperly drawn circle was the first thing a devil looked for when it answered a magician's summons. The smallest break in the circle and a daemon could enter, destroying the only protection a magician had against it. Father Bain had told Simon many tales of careless magicians putting one foot over the barrier of the circle and at the very best they simply received a strong shock that hurled them around the room. At worst, the devil might maim whichever parts of the body ventured into unprotected space . . . perhaps even kill the practitioner if the wound was grievous enough.

Simon dipped the tip of his ceremonial sword into a small alabaster pot filled with mandrake ground into a fine black powder. On a large space in the center of the room, he used the sword while he walked counterclockwise to draw a circle that was exactly nine feet in diameter. A few inches underneath he drew a second circle that was eight feet in diameter. In the rim between the two circles, he placed silver bowls filled with holy water that had Saint-John's-wort floating in it. The water and herb would repel any devil bold enough to try and enter the circle. Once again, he dipped the sword into the mandrake and wrote in the circle names of power for extra protection—*Adonai, El, Yah,* and *Eloa.*

Father Bain entered the circle through a small gap Simon made for him, bringing with him all the implements they would need for the evening's work, and quickly shut the hole once he was safely inside. Now Simon, as master of the ceremony for tonight, anointed the circle, swinging a brazier filled with the juice of laurel leaves, camphor, salt, white resin, and sulfur to purify the space.

Next, continuing in the Latin tongue as he'd done to consecrate his rod, he made proper obeisance to the elements of north, south, east, and west, ending the preliminary ritual by begging protection for his circle. "I beseech thee, O Lord God, that Thou wilt deign to bless this Circle, and all this place, and all those who are therein, and that Thou wilt remove from us every adverse power and preserve us from evil. Amen."

Simon couldn't be sure if the sulfuric fumes swirling around his head were addling his mind, but he thought he saw his mandrake outline take the form of a thin band of yellow light, transforming it into a true magick circle that would grant protection from the spirit he was now ready to summon.

First, however, the sacrifice must be made. Simon turned his attention to the goat Father Bain had brought into the circle and quickly cut its throat, offering it to the spirit he planned to beseech. Next, he lit a small gold brazier filled with coriander, hemlock, sandalwood, and henbane.

The foul fumes made Simon gag and splutter for a few moments before he was able to begin the conjuration. He turned to the east corner of the circle and shouted, "I conjure thee, O Spirit Flauros, appear forthwith and show thyself to me, here outside this circle, in fair and human shape, without horror or deformity and without delay."

Nothing happened except Simon had to swallow hard against the nausea building within him. Blinking his eyes to clear the stinging sensation from the smoke around him, Simon repeated the incantation, using a firm voice that belied the sickness that was getting worse with each moment. When the stubborn spirit again refused to show, Simon began a more potent conjuration. "By the Seal of Basdathea, answer all my demands and perform all that I desire. Come peaceably, visibly, and without delay."

The dark walls of the stone cellar blurred, swirling into a confusing mass, and Simon had the curious feeling of standing in space. He could not see or feel the floor beneath him but he knew this was a trick of the spirit. It wanted him to flounder about, and hopefully blunder out of the circle where it could destroy him.

Simon felt a cold touch of steel on his palm and looked down, seeing a steel sigil with the Second Pentacle of Saturn carved into it. Father Bain must have pressed it into his hand so he'd have some protection against the spirit he'd successfully conjured.

A fierce pain stabbed in Simon's abdomen and he knew he must give Flauros his commands quickly—before he collapsed on the floor.

"What would you have of me?" Simon saw nothing but the pitch-black around him, and the voice was a whisper that blew a cold wind on the back of Simon's neck.

He clutched the pentagram and turned himself

carefully, ordering the mischievous spirit to stay in front of him. When the spirit again changed position, Simon felt a piece of parchment put into his right hand, along with a feather quill and a steel box.

Quickly, he scrawled the name *Flauros* and dropped it into the box. The box was filled with sulfur and Simon shut it quickly, making the spirit wail in dismay. Simon didn't even have to hold the box over fire before the spirit moved in front of him, frightened by the thought of being cast into the lake of fire if Simon were to burn the box.

Simon gagged, but with a supreme effort kept from vomiting. He felt sweat running down his body freely and wanted more than anything to pitch himself into a river to cool his flaming body. He did not know how much longer he could remain on his feet.

Simon spoke quickly, though he was careful of his wording so the devious spirit could not deviate from his orders. "Hear me, Flauros, and hasten to obey. I order you to consume in your flames the body of Payton, Baron Baldevar. Do so without delay."

It seemed that the spirit departed but Simon knew this was an old trick of daemons. They would pretend to leave so a magician would not do the License to Depart and then be fair game once he stepped outside the circle.

Simon collapsed to the floor, his body convulsing and a vile black substance pouring from his mouth.

"The License to Depart, son!" he vaguely heard Father Bain scream.

Oh, God . . . he couldn't. He couldn't control his flailing limbs and it was getting so difficult to think. *Sleep,* he thought. *I want to sleep . . .*

A harsh slap obscured the cloud around his head. "The License to Depart or your soul is forfeit and your father will live!"

It was the mention of his father that gave Simon the strength to rise to his knees and speak between bouts of retching. Quickly, he spat out the License to Depart. "By the virtue of Adonai, depart ye unto your abode and retreat, be there peace between me and you, but be ye ever ready to come when ye shall be cited and called; may the blessing of God, as far as ye are capable of receiving it, be upon you, provided ye be obedient and prompt to come unto us."

With that, Simon collapsed in a fresh round of seizures and felt a dim sense of surprise when he realized the person screaming in agony and begging for death was himself.

EIGHT

Giving an ostentatious yawn, Simon stopped speaking and stretched out on the checkered picnic blanket they'd brought, staring up at the full moon with an expression that showed he was well aware of Meghann's consternation at the incomplete tale.

"So what happened after you fainted?" she finally asked impatiently and swatted his arm in annoyance. "Did your spell work or did you have to use earthly means like your sword to kill your father?"

Simon raised himself up on one elbow. "My sword? Have you forgotten the quarrel we had in the great hall? Why do you think I resorted to magick in the first place? The slightest hint that my father had been murdered and all suspicion would have fallen on me. Now, if you want to know what happened, hand over that slab of cake in your hands."

"But it's the last piece," Meghann said, looking down at the heavenly chocolate fudge cake with regret. She gave a poignant sigh, firmly dismissing the inner voice that had the nerve to claim her actions bordered on flirtation. "Would you really starve your own child?"

"Madam, you have had a side of ribs, three pieces of chicken, one pastrami sandwich on rye, and demol-

ished half that cake by yourself. You are in no danger
of malnutrition so you may spare me the sight of those
limpid, appealing eyes. Hand it over or I'm silent as
the grave."

"I wish you were in your grave," Meghann muttered
but she shoved the paper plate at him and Simon re-
sumed his tale.

"All of what I say next was told to me by others,
Meghann. For the next four days, I was oblivious to
the world around me. After I collapsed, Father Bain
completed the ceremony and put the room to rights
while I lay feverish and raving at his feet. There was
no question of him taking me back to the manor
house . . . a fierce blizzard had settled over the area
while we conducted our ritual. Somehow, Father Bain
dragged me up the stairs and laid me on the stone
floor, spending the rest of the night pouring snow and
ice over my body in an attempt to bring down the
fever.

"At first light, he planned to ride into the village
and bring Adelaide to the church. But before he could
leave, my brother Roger came blundering into the
church, babbling incoherently about Satan entering
the house and striking down my father. According to
Father Bain, my dear brother did not even spare a
glance for me thrashing about but demanded that the
priest come to the manor immediately and cast out
the devil."

"So they left you at the church?"

"No, no. Father Bain slung me into the coach and
they headed off. On the ride home, Roger told Father
Bain a rather extraordinary tale of being awoken in
the dead of night by a howl such as he'd never heard
before. He rushed to my father's room and said the
old man was writhing on his bed and screaming in an
unnatural voice. According to Roger, it took five strong
men-at-arms to restrain my father and keep him from

harming himself. That's when Roger set out for the church."

Simon paused to take a sip of iced coffee. "What happened next I shall regret missing to my dying day. No sooner had Father Bain dragged me into the house than my father appeared at the top of the stairs, his guards hot at his heels. My reputation as a sorcerer was permanently cemented when the old man came out of his madness long enough to point one trembling finger at me and shout 'why?' in a voice that shook dust from the rafters. Next, he charged down the stairs, no doubt intending to attack me. But halfway down the stairs, he burst into flames . . . Father Bain said one moment he was staring at a raving old man, the next he vanished into a giant ball of fire."

"You're making that up," Meghann accused. "Alcuin told me your father was found in bed by a maidservant—cause of death unknown."

"Was Alcuin there, madam? What the sham priest told you is the lie Father Bain recorded in the parish records so the whole world would not learn the bizarre circumstances behind my father's death. Roger went along so our family's reputation would not suffer—he did not even tell Isabelle the truth when they married. That was doubtless because he had no desire to frighten his new bride by informing her of her brother-in-law's penchant for the Dark Arts."

"So what happened after the demon made your father spontaneously combust?"

"Roger and the guards ran to my father and threw their capes on him to smother the flames but it was too late. All that remained of him when they removed their capes was a smoking, black cinder . . . not even recognizable as a man.

"Roger was the first to recover his wits, which surprises me mightily, as I never thought he had any to begin with. He had no weapon on him, as he'd run from the house with no thought but getting the priest to come exorcise my father. Apparently he grabbed a sword from the belt of one of the guards and launched himself toward me, screaming that I was an unholy monster and I'd somehow killed my father through sorcery. Fortunately for me, Father Bain was no soft indulged cleric but a man of good physical strength and he repelled my brother's attack, barely saving my head. While the guards restrained Roger, Father Bain denied my brother's charge in a voice that carried through the great hall. On his honor as a priest, he swore I had spent the evening in prayer with him by my side . . . which, when you think about it, was no lie." Simon gave a malicious smirk. "Of course, the good father never divulged the nature of my prayers. After that, he took charge. He ordered the guards to take my brother to his rooms and give him sleeping herbs so he could recover from his shock. Because of the condition of my father's body, there could be no question of him lying in state in the great hall. A coffin was ordered constructed and my father's body was removed from sight while the carpenter made the coffin. Father Bain gave my father the last rites, and prepared his soul to enter the kingdom of heaven. The next day, my father was buried."

"What happened to you?"

"I was put into Adelaide's care, bled by leeches to remove the bad humors from my blood, and given great quantities of violet tea to bring down my fever. Four days later, much to my brother's dismay, I recovered."

"Why didn't Roger accuse you of witchcraft and have you burned at the stake?"

"He wanted to but there was no way to bring formal charges with Father Bain's testimony. After all, how could he refute the sworn statement of a trusted, respected priest insisting I spent the whole night in Christian prayer?"

"Great cover," Meghann commented.

"Wasn't it? Of course, ever since the Dark Ages a great number of high church officials involved themselves in sorcery and necromancy, knowing no one would ever think to accuse them unless they became incredibly careless. Don't look so shocked—have you no knowledge of the cutthroat world of church politics? It would take more than a life of pious prayer to achieve the power and glory most of the clerics were after. At any rate, Roger not only had no legal way to kill off his little brother, he now lived his life in terror that he'd be my next victim unless he ceded to my wishes—a point I made very plain when he came to visit my sickbed the morning after my fever broke."

"You threatened him?"

Simon laughed, the deep, rich sound carrying throughout the still desert around them. "I did better than that, little girl. He thrust a cross at me . . . even as a mortal I had to bear with that dreary ritual . . . and I began thundering incantations at him. Fortunately for me, Roger was such a fool he visited me without a witness to corroborate anything I did. So I was able to fling curses at his head and within moments, he fell to his knees, begging me to spare his life. I said all he had to do was give me what was mine and I'd vanish from his life. Even in his terror, Roger could not bring himself to admit the gold was mine and said he would invest in Sir John's venture. I would go along on the trip and receive ten percent of Roger's share for overseeing the voyage. I told him I would not consider the arrangement for anything less than twenty-five percent and the fool agreed. Within a fortnight, I was on my way to Algiers."

Simon reached for her hand—making her jump when he ran one finger over her palm. "What think you, Meghann? When I began my tale, I promised you would see the foes I vanquished deserved their fate. Do you agree, or think as Alcuin did—that I was a

vicious mercenary destroying innocent lives without remorse?"

"Maybe you had some justification for your actions," Meghann said softly. She knew Alcuin would
never excuse any killing not committed in the name
of self-defense, but Meghann wondered if she would
have behaved differently in Simon's place. As long as
his father lived, Simon was trapped in the role that
awful old man had assigned him—youngest son in a
loveless marriage, spending his days doing no more
than keeping track of an unprofitable sheep farm. Simon was right to call his father a skinflint. He should
have taken advantage of his son's sharp mind and sent
him to court where he could have made a name for
himself or paid for him to continue his education.

"What was wrong with your father?" Meghann demanded.

Simon shrugged, moving a lock of hair that had
blown across her eyes, twirling the flame strands in his
fingers while he spoke.

"I have asked myself what was 'wrong' with my family many times and never arrived at a satisfactory answer. Perhaps the old man was merely cautious and
tightfisted. After all, you speak from hindsight of four
hundred years. You know England became a mighty
empire because of trade and exploration—my father,
an ignorant baron of the north, did not have your
knowledge. Nor did he have the kind of imagination
or foresight that is required to take risks."

"Why did he hit you?"

"Darling." Simon smiled. "You look so indignant.
Why aren't you glad I was on the receiving end of
blows at one time in my life? My father thrashed me
because . . . I suppose because I was expendable and
a bit of a nuisance. Remember my time, Meghann.
People did not love or coddle their children the way
they do now, perhaps because they died so easily and
there was no point getting attached to them. To my

father, I was born solely to advance his name. But with Roger alive and well, I was not even needed for that."

"So you were an understudy in case Roger died?"

Simon laughed. "That is one way to look at it. Also . . . Meghann, you look on my ambition and you're sympathetic. My little American girl was raised to admire self-made men but in my time ambition was all but a sin. Sympathy rested with my father . . . having to control a young hothead that dared to try and rise above his station. I was supposed to be content with my marriage and place in Roger's household."

"That's terrible." Meghann frowned. "And so is . . . was . . ."

"Yes?" Simon prompted at her twitching lips. "Either you've developed a nervous tic or you're refraining from laughing."

"No, no, no," Meghann said, her dancing eyes giving her away. "I would never laugh because you'd been married to . . . to a, um, unattractive woman. It wouldn't be nice to laugh because the image of some fat hag chasing you around and demanding you . . . con . . . consummate . . . ha, ha, ha . . ."

"Yes?" Simon said severely, giving her a dark scowl. "This amuses you?"

"Sure it does." Meghann giggled. "I know you—thinking you're God's gift to women and then getting saddled with some fat slob for your wife."

"You're not going to get away with cackling over my misfortune." Simon lunged for her, and started tickling her sides. Meghann yelped and tried to squirm away but he straddled her, tickling without mercy.

"Do you still think it's funny?" Simon demanded. "My being shackled to that pockmarked pudding of a woman?"

"Yes!" Meghann gasped out, unrepentant. "I hope . . . I hope she made you go down on her!"

"Now you're going to pay."

"Stop!" Meghann pleaded through her laughter,

red-faced and gasping for breath. "Please . . . the baby!"

"Using your pregnancy to worm out of your deserved punishment," Simon said reprovingly but he did stop tickling her. Instead of moving off her, though, he stayed on top of her and caressed her cheek, giving her a smile that made her heart thud uncomfortably in her chest. "What did I tell you, Meghann? You can enjoy my company. Shall I show you other forms of amusement?" Without waiting for a reply, Simon leaned down and began nuzzling a particularly sensitive spot behind her ear.

"Stop that," Meghann managed to gasp through the haze overtaking her as that knowing tongue on her neck sent little rippling waves throughout her body. Why did she always find it so hard to think when this satyr touched her?

"Have you ever made love in the desert, Meghann?" Simon murmured while he nipped her earlobe and ran his fingertips lightly over one leg, the sensations making her skin tingle pleasantly.

With a supreme effort of will, Meghann shoved him away from her, nervously backing to the farthest edge of the blanket. Always, no matter if he terrified her or made her so angry she wanted to kill him, lust remained an unbroken bond between them. How many nights had Meghann sworn she despised him only to wind up clutching his hair the moment he touched her, ripping his clothes off with abandon and urging him on with moans and sighs while at the same moment she wished she'd never met him?

She wasn't going to start up that old sick sadomasochistic cycle, Meghann promised herself. She'd come too far and learned too much to go back to being no more than Lord Baldevar's sex slave.

Simon eyed her silently for a few minutes before he stretched one long, elegant hand out to her. "There is no need to crouch like a virgin defending herself from marauding conquerors. I am not about to resort to rape—you may come closer without fear I'll molest you."

"I am not afraid of you," Meghann informed him and ignored the extended hand though she did move back to the center of the blanket. She was afraid of herself—afraid of the unthinking, unreasoning body that simply responded to pleasure and urged her to throw herself at Simon without any thought of consequence.

It's just sex, Meghann told herself. After all, she'd been celibate over two months now—two months too long, in her opinion. She only responded to Simon because she needed release. Well, Las Vegas had thousands of eligible men and any one of them could give her what she wanted without having to sell her soul to get laid.

"What makes you think I'll stand by and allow you to behave like some alley cat, lifting your pretty tail to any male that pleases you?"

"You wretched whoremonger, how dare you call me an alley cat!" Meghann screeched, her face bone-pale but for the twin slashes of crimson on her cheeks. She took a deep breath, preparing herself to use the astral plane and get back to town so she wouldn't have to spend another minute with this loathsome bastard.

"Pregnancy might hinder your ability to fly the plane," Simon commented with an amused smile when he saw the uneasy frustration appear on her face after she spent a full five minutes trying to fly without success.

"Go to hell!" she spat, and Simon laughed, grabbing her wrist to restrain her before she could get up and walk back to town to escape him.

"Why take such offense, little one? I never called you an alley cat—I simply said I would not allow you to behave like one. Have you forgotten my letter? You may scorn me and keep your chastity if that is your desire but I will not stand by and allow you other lovers over me." Simon gave her an appealing look, dropping his hands to loosely circle her waist. "Please don't leave, Meghann. I probably should not have shattered the fun we were having by touching you, but it would take a stronger man than I to resist such a sparkling, bright-eyed coquette beneath me. Please stay a while longer."

Was he mad? Stay with him after he'd proven he was as jealous and possessive as he'd ever been? As far as Meghann was concerned, that little speech proved Simon Baldevar was still the same evil, domineering fiend she'd been so right to run away from.

She glared up, ready to tell him so, ready to tell him to take his filthy hands off her, but he gave her a disarming grin that made time reel backward—made Meghann see the dashing stranger that had captured her heart almost sixty years ago.

It wasn't fair, Meghann thought when her heart lurched painfully. It wasn't fair that his face was so unmarked by time . . . that he could look just like he had that first night when he took her on the Staten Island Ferry and the wind from the river blew his chestnut hair about in a wild disarray just as the desert wind whipped his hair around now and softened his stern features. Too, that first night the moonlight had glinted off his sharp cheekbones and made her long to touch them just as she longed to reach up now . . .

Goddammit, what was wrong with her? The fiend had just told her he wouldn't allow her any lovers but him . . . as if she were his slave, as if he had any right to meddle in her life. And what did she do? Instead of putting him in his place, she stared up at him and fell for his handsome face when she knew all too well the black heart it concealed.

Meghann raised her head and gave him a level stare. No, she wouldn't leave . . . she'd stay around him until she learned to control the lust inside her. Pushing Simon away, she poured herself some milk, with a great show of nonchalance, from the carafe they'd bought at the deli, and groped about in her mind for a neutral topic of conversation.

"I shouldn't have laughed . . . it's terrible that your father made you marry her," Meghann finally said, daintily sipping her milk. "In fact, the whole idea of arranged marriage is horrible. I can't see anyone choosing who I should marry."

"I see merit in it," Simon told her. "It may have landed me a bloated hag when I was young and poor, but under arranged marriage I wouldn't have to entertain your tedious refusals of my suit. Instead, once you were pregnant, I could simply demand your father give me your hand in marriage."

"I am not," Meghann began icily, "some chattel to be sold or dispersed between the whims of two men. Anyway, even if you had knocked me up in your time, I doubt you'd have bothered to marry me. Earls, even pathetic younger sons of barons, didn't marry peasants."

"You wouldn't have been a peasant," Simon argued. "Your father . . . he owned a construction company, didn't he? That would make him a tradesman in my time, a prosperous member of the middle class. Maybe it would raise a few eyebrows if I married the daughter of such a man to legitimize my son, but by the time Elizabeth raised me to the title of earl, there were very few people that would dare tell me what to do."

"Well, my father wouldn't make me marry anyone that raped me!"

"My dear, if an earl offered marriage to a tradesman's daughter, it would not matter if I raped you at noon on London Bridge . . . not as long as I gave you the honor of becoming my countess. And you were not raped . . . unless my memories of a hot vixen begging for my touch are erroneous." Simon laughed, firmly grasping the hands that tried to maul his face.

"But I do not wish to shatter our new friendship so I shall offer you a compromise—I will not embarrass you with references to the night you conceived if you do not keep insisting you were raped. Is it a bargain?"

"Mmmn," Meghann muttered but she did drop her claws. "And who told you we were friends?"

"Do you still consider yourself my enemy, little one?"

Meghann shrugged, disturbed when the "yes" she wanted to shout out wouldn't come to her lips. "How do you know I won't pretend to accept you and still plot to kill you once I don't need your blood?"

Lightning quick, Simon's hand lashed out. For one dreadful moment, Meghann thought he planned to strike her but all he did was grasp her chin while staring into her eyes with an intensity that made her heart drop to her shoes. "My pet, you are simply too forthright to ever be an accomplished liar. You've never been able to dissemble or conceal your true feelings . . . that's why you have so many enemies at Ballnamore. Even if you never speak a word, they see your contempt for their old-fashioned ways and narrow view of the world."

"How do you know about all that?" Meghann demanded.

"Because I know you," Simon told her. "I can well imagine what those pious fools would think of my headstrong, prideful consort. Enough about those imbeciles—answer my question, Meghann O'Neill. Are you my enemy?"

"I . . . I don't know," Meghann said at last. She had to concede Simon had a point when he told her to make peace with him and she couldn't say she hadn't enjoyed herself tonight. The way they'd laughed and talked together—it was almost like being friends. She'd forgotten that sometimes she used to genuinely enjoy being with Simon, that as he'd pointed out earlier they never ran out of things to talk about or disagree over in a friendly, lighthearted way. But how could she forget all the atrocious things he'd done to her, to the people she cared about?

She thought her answer might anger him, but Simon only smiled. "A considered, uncertain response is certainly a vast improvement over what I would have gotten from you a few weeks ago. Somehow I do not think you are planning after tonight to go back to greeting me with scowls and spiteful words."

"Maybe not," Meghann answered. "But is that all you want—for me to be nice to you?"

"I want a great deal more but I have learned from our past encounters. I will force from you nothing that you are not willing to give freely. When you are ready to be a bit more than 'nice,' I shall be waiting."

You'll wait a long time, Meghann thought. What did he think—one dinner, some sob story about his dysfunctional family, a few gropes, and she'd leap into bed with him? Maybe it was to her benefit to be on his good side, but this was it . . . their relationship was going no further than it stood right now.

"Do you think your life would have been worse if you'd been born a girl?" she asked Simon to change the subject.

"Of course. It would have been easier for my father and Roger to use me."

Meghann winced at the bitterness in his voice. What must it have been like for him, to grow up in such a loveless atmosphere? Of course, his upbringing couldn't excuse what he'd become, she told herself firmly. Still, how different would her character be if she hadn't had her father's love and support when she was growing up? If her brothers had looked at her as a potential rival instead of the spoiled darling of the family they'd made their younger sister into? She remembered how Simon had always snapped at her whenever she spoke of her family, told her to stop speaking of people she'd never see again. At the time, she'd assumed he was jealous of her love for them but now she wondered if she'd caused him pain when she spoke of an upbringing so different from his own.

"Don't compare my life to yours, Meghann. We come from very different times. Too, your father was a far better man than mine. He had a large family, yet each of you were well provided for."

"Yes." Meghann nodded, remembering how every child, including her, went to college and one brother, Seamus, was sent to law school. She blinked rapidly, feeling the familiar tears that stung her eyes whenever she thought of the family she'd had to give up for immortality.

"Meghann." Simon pulled her against him, wrapping his arms around her and putting her back against his chest. "Don't become sad because the past is gone. Think of the future, of the beautiful child we're going to have. Experience the present . . . this wonderful, wild place we find ourselves in."

"It is beautiful here," Meghann agreed, drinking in the beauty of the desert. It wasn't just the stark outline of rock formations and the dark, fathomless lake nearby that captured her heart—the wild vastness of the place gave her a sense of exhilaration and freedom that she'd never felt before.

"Can you feel the power of this land, Meghann?"

She nodded, the wind buffeting her hair around her face as she gazed up at the star-studded sky. "It goes on forever . . . there's such energy here, such . . . such magic!"

"It is an enchanted spot," Simon agreed. "I fell in love with the Southwest desert the moment I saw it. Grand, impervious to time and mortals . . . this place does not call the heart of man, Meghann. It calls to us."

For a while, they sat together quietly, taking in the wild beauty of the desert. Meghann stared at the stark landscape, thinking how much the desert suited Simon. An untamed land, a harsh place that did not forgive or offer comfort, that would kill if you allowed it to but with a majestic beauty and power that had to be acknowledged.

No wonder he likes it here, Meghann thought and turned around, feeling a little bemused by the strength emanating from him. She'd be a fool to persist in angering this formidable creature instead of taking the olive branch he held out to her.

"Thank you for tonight," she said softly and smiled.

Simon smiled back and took her hand, kissing it lightly. "Anytime, little one—you have but to ask. Now, are you aware that it is past four? I best get you home before your chaperone starts tearing his hair out."

"My God!" Meghann cried. "Charles—I forgot all about him! And Jimmy . . . Simon, I lowered his medication and I was supposed to stay and watch him! What if he had a relapse? What if he got away?"

Simon waved her concerns away like an annoying fly. "You know he cannot cross the threshold of that room without my permission. And if he had become unruly, Vinny would have contacted me by now." Simon flicked open his blazer to show Meghann the small cellular phone he carried with him. "You may take his silence to mean that thing can handle a lower dose of your potion."

Meghann didn't bother telling Simon not to call Jimmy a thing, just promised herself she'd spend all of the next night with him to make up for her neglect.

"Here." Simon put the keys to the Ferrari in her hand. "I believe I promised you could drive."

Eagerly, Meghann got behind the wheel, familiarizing herself with all the buttons and paddles on the console while she adjusted the seat and steering wheel.

Used to her own simple Caddy, she struggled with the engine immobilizer for a few minutes before Simon leaned over and showed her how to put her foot on the brake and pull the right paddle behind the steering wheel.

"Now?" Meghann said, giving Simon a quick glance.

"Whenever you're ready."

Grinning widely, she selected first gear, hammered down on the go-faster aluminum pedal in the driver's footwell, and the Ferrari took off in a cloud of red dust. The car went to 183 mph in a mere eleven seconds, impervious to the rocky desert road, purring along at top speed in stealthy silence.

Expertly, Meghann navigated the winding curves and spared a glance for her passenger. Unlike Charles, who tightened his lips and clutched the dashboard when she got speed-happy, and Jimmy, who yelped and demanded she slow down before she killed him, Simon seemed to be enjoying the wild ride as much as she was.

Meghann watched the desert scenery race by and thought she had to get one of these cars for herself. It was more like flying than driving . . . she couldn't remember the last time she'd had so much fun as she was having right now, soaring through the desert night in this elegant machine.

Only when they approached town did Meghann reluctantly slow down in deference to the cars around her. Easily, she drove through Spanish Hills and parked the car in Simon's garage before heading over to her still beloved Caddy.

Simon walked her to her car and Meghann stood indecisively for a few moments, unsure of how to end this strange evening.

Simon lifted her hand and gave it a polite kiss good night, caressing the wrist for a moment before he turned and walked into the house.

On the drive home, Meghann considered the events of the night, still unsure of how she went from wishing Lord Baldevar dead to . . . to what? Liking him? No, well . . . maybe.

What was not to like? Even Alcuin had once conceded that Simon Baldevar could be very charming when he wished to be. But Meghann knew what lurked under that charm . . . didn't she?

She hadn't known of his lonely, brutalizing childhood. Maybe if he told her more, she'd understand him, and in understanding him . . .

Now you've lost it, a voice inside her head pronounced. *What—are you thinking you're going to change him? Make Lord Baldevar a good guy?*

Meghann laughed out loud at that thought, making a driver next to her wrinkle his brow in concern. No, Meghann had no illusions about Simon changing his stripes. But it was possible she could get him to make some concessions. Already she'd gotten him to leave Jimmy alive.

If she couldn't destroy him (and the zero-for-two record she and Charles had indicated she couldn't), then she had to find a way to have him in her life where she could tolerate him. Certainly tonight he'd been quite tolerable . . . except for when he started pawing her and giving orders for whom she could sleep with as if he were some king and she were his untouchable wife.

Meghann glanced at the strip—should she throw down the gauntlet and go pick up some gambler? No, not tonight . . . it was nearly five A.M.; she had to get home. Well, there was always tomorrow. Maybe she and Charles and Lee could go to some club. Meghann thought Charles would probably stand up and cheer if she found herself some transient stud to ease away her anxiety. Momentarily, she worried about being unfaithful to Jimmy but then she thought what he didn't know about what she did while he was ill couldn't possibly hurt him.

As for Charles, there was no reason to tell him how she spent her evening, Meghann decided, and pulled her car into Lee's driveway, careful not to block his

Jeep Cherokee. She'd work her way up to it, to gradually convince Charles that maybe they should make
peace with Lord Baldevar. If she hit him with it all at
once, he might decide it was she and not Jimmy that
needed to take antipsychotic medication, Meghann
thought, smiling at Charles when he came out of the
house. One glance at his shining eyes and rumpled
hair told Meghann his evening was all he'd wanted it
to be.

"Where's Lee?" Meghann asked, linking her arm
through his as they walked into the house.

"Sleeping," Charles said, the self-satisfied tone in
his voice making Meghann laugh.

"Hey," he said, looking her up and down. "You
seem . . . different, happy. Has Jimmy improved?"

Meghann shrugged and began making up the bed
for her daytime rest. "I just decided I have plenty to
be happy about—you and Lee are with me and the
baby is in all likelihood going to be born healthy."

Charles nodded and kissed her cheek good night.
"You're right, Meghann. Alcuin always told us to find
the good in a situation and focus on that. You have
every right to be happy over impending motherhood."

After Charles left, Meghann threw on an oversize
Mets T-shirt and crawled into bed, thinking she'd made
the right choice in not telling Charles just who was
responsible for her newfound equilibrium.

NINE

"Therapy's over for tonight, kid," Meghann said to Jimmy and closed *Please Kill Me*, a book about the birth of punk during the seventies. "I've gotta get ready for the big night out with Charles and Lee." Earlier that evening, her friends had surprised her with a slinky black sheath they'd bought at Versace and an invitation to go dancing, Charles insisting it was high time Meghann found herself somebody.

Of course, she reminded herself guiltily, Charles still didn't know that "somebody" had already volunteered his services as suitor or about the wild rides through the desert and occasional dinners she'd hardly discouraged. Meghann could not begin to imagine what Charles's reaction would be when he found out that it was becoming more and more of a temptation to give Simon a second chance.

Though Meghann hadn't been able to risk losing Charles's friendship by telling him of her changing feelings toward what he assumed was their mutual enemy, she had confided in Lee. Expecting a watered-down version of the incredulity and contempt she might see in Charles, Meghann was shocked when the mortal physician said a reconciliation between her and Lord Baldevar might not be such a terrible thing.

Lee's argument was simple. Yes, he knew of the

atrocities Lord Baldevar had committed—hadn't he almost suffered them himself as a child? But the situation had changed drastically in the forty years since Meghann had left him to die. Meghann was no longer a helpless young vampire living completely under her master's thumb. If Simon wanted her, he had to make some compromises—recognize her need for independence and treat her with the respect she deserved.

And he had, Lee said, pointing to Simon's impeccable behavior over the past six weeks. Hadn't he backed off when Meghann insisted their relationship remain chaste? Had he made any move to harm Charles or stop her from helping Jimmy out of his catatonia?

Meghann smiled grimly, thinking Simon of late used a more insidious method to thwart her efforts to heal Jimmy. Instead of brute force or threats, Simon had taken to lurking around the house on her nights of working with Jimmy and inquired whether Meghann would like to have dinner with him on the veranda overlooking his magnificent sculpture garden and listen while he told her more tales from his mortal youth. Or he offered a far greater temptation—Simon was finally explaining his magick to her, actually showing her how to perform a few simple rites. Just the other night, he'd taught her how to make herself invisible to other vampires by imagining a heavy cloak over her presence. Thus far, she hadn't completely mastered the trick; Simon could find her in two seconds, but she had been able to fool Charles about her whereabouts for a full five minutes the other night.

With lures like that, Simon certainly hadn't had to twist her arm to get her to spend time with him. But it was more than simply giving her a more amusing alternative to her grueling therapy sessions with Jimmy. Somehow, she wasn't sure exactly when, she'd started looking forward to seeing Simon, started feeling that funny stomach-plummeting, heart-thumping tension at the sight of him that meant . . .

No! She absolutely was not going to fall in love with Simon Baldevar! Lee spoke from ignorance when he encouraged Meghann to listen to her heart—he hadn't been there the night Simon ruthlessly slaughtered Alcuin before her eyes or watched him torture Jimmy to the point of death.

Meghann sighed and forced herself to meet Jimmy's blank eyes. Looking into his gray-blue eyes with those shots of indigo radiating from the pupils used to be like watching a storm over the ocean; now they resembled faded old marbles. How could she possibly reunite with the creature that did this to Jimmy? Wasn't Jimmy Delacroix the ultimate proof of what Simon Baldevar was capable of?

"I'm sorry, baby," Meghann said and patted Jimmy's cheek. "I know I've neglected you. I promise I'm not going to do that anymore. From now on, we work the way we did when I first started your therapy . . . ten hours a night, four nights a week. We'll have you up and around in no time."

In the shower, Meghann wondered whether her last words to Jimmy were true. Thanks to the Clozapine he was no longer a raving psychotic, but no further progress had been made. Meghann knew that the smart, funny, brave man she'd spent six years with would not thank her for keeping him alive as a catatonic vegetable. Was it time to admit defeat?

No! How could she even think that? There was no way she'd call her attempts to heal him a failure after a mere six weeks of work, three weeks of which had been sporadic at best. She'd never forgive herself if she gave up on Jimmy now.

Finished with her shower, Meghann turned the water off, pulled the shower curtain aside, and let out a short, sharp scream.

"Jimmy!" Meghann gasped. By himself, unaided,

he'd walked from the foam bed into the bathroom and stood by the curtain while Meghann showered.

Meghann stared back at him for a few minutes, praying he'd do something else; speak, touch her, anything. But he simply stood and stared, though there was something a little different in his gaze. He looked like he was listening to something . . . waiting.

"Jimmy," Meghann said again and her face lit up when she realized why he'd come into the room. "You remember my signal that I was awake for the night was I'd leave the bedroom door open and then you'd come in and talk to me while I showered. You remember, Jimmy! Something inside you woke up and made you walk into the bathroom. I knew you weren't beyond hope, Jimmy." Meghann helped him sit on the ledge of the tub and did what she always did—chatted over the whir of the blow-dryer while she dried her hair.

"You made fantastic progress tonight! From now on, I think we'll try and mimic our old routines. I'll take you back home to Rockaway. You love the beach, Jimmy. I bet the salty smell of the ocean breeze, the pound of the surf, sand beneath your bare feet will do more for you than all the Clozapine in the world!"

How are you planning to get your catatonic vampire patient on a commercial airline? a voice inquired. *For that matter, do you think Simon is going to simply allow you to go back to New York and take Jimmy with you?* Reconsidering, Meghann decided maybe it was too early to take Jimmy out of the house.

"Don't you worry," Meghann said to Jimmy while she shimmied into the form-fitting black dress. "We'll walk on the beach again—and you'll be aware when we do it." Meghann gave him a quick kiss good night on the temple.

Eager to meet her friends, Meghann hurried down the stairs, the heels on her gold pumps clicking noisily against the marble staircase. A glance at her wristwatch showed she was running almost twenty minutes late.

She should probably use the phone in Simon's study and leave a message on Lee's pager that she was on her way. Not being of the same bloodline, she couldn't communicate with Charles telepathically unless they were in the same room.

"Oh, my," Meghann said after she parted the sliding doors to the study and saw Vinny, comfortably perched in his boss's leather armchair, snorting one neat line of cocaine off the triangular black lacquered wood and nickel steel desk.

"Shit!" Vinny howled, frantically gathering up the white powder and trying to stuff it back into a thin glass vial.

"It's okay," Meghann said quickly. "I don't mind."

Vinny gave her a guarded glance. "You're not gonna tell him?"

"How long have you been doing it?"

"A few years."

"He knows," Meghann said dryly. "Hey, don't look like that! Obviously it doesn't bother him."

Vinny sat down again, seeming somewhat relieved by her words. He extended the gold snorter to her, indicating another line on the desk. "Want some?"

Meghann declined and headed for the cushioned alcove by the bay window that overlooked the front of the house—her sharp ears had detected the sound of a car approaching. "If you really want to try and hide your habit from your boss, you better put your nose candy away. He's home."

"What? Damn!" Vinny gathered up his drugs and wiped the desk clean of any residue with the shirttail hastily pulled out of his waist.

"Get your nose too," Meghann told him, indicating the area beneath his nostrils.

While Vinny made himself presentable, Meghann remained in the picture window, watching Simon emerge from a classic Bentley—how many cars did he have? Her idle speculation turned to shock when she watched him open the passenger-side door and a pair of curvaceous legs in tan stockings appeared on the pavement.

"Who is that?"

Vinny followed her outstretched finger to the chic brunette on Simon's arm and snorted contemptuously. "That's Louise—a skank. She lets the boss fuck her six ways to Sunday . . . even does it with other broads while he watches 'cause she thinks he's gonna help her get some promotion at the hotel."

"Is that right?" Meghann replied icily.

Vinny misunderstood her tight-lipped expression and the storm beginning to brew in her eyes. "Look, you don't got anything to be jealous over. She's just for—"

"I know precisely what she's for, Vinny, and I am not jealous." Meghann brushed past him and stalked into the foyer just as Lord Baldevar entered with his office slut in tow.

The woman didn't seem at all surprised by Meghann's presence—she just looked her over with a resigned air.

Why would she expect another woman here? Meghann wondered. Then she remembered Vinny's remark concerning "other broads" and took a step forward, intending to inform this chippie that she was not part of the floor show for the evening.

"Meghann!" Simon spoke before she could open her mouth, giving her a warm smile. "I was not expecting you until tomorrow evening. You should have called—I would have sent Vinny to the airport for you." Taking advantage of Meghann's momentary disconcertment, he turned to his soignée companion. "May I introduce you? This is Meghann O'Neill— daughter of a dear friend of mine in New York. She's just finished college and I told her father that I'd be delighted to help her find some position or another. Meghann, this is Louise Caraway—she came over to discuss a bit of hotel business with me."

Meghann reluctantly held her hand out, feeling disdain drip from the mortal woman's grip.

"Are you staying here with Lord Charlton?" Louise asked, speaking to Meghann as though she were ten instead of the twenty Simon was trying to pass her off as.

Lord Charlton—so that was the identity Simon used among mortals these days. "I prefer to stay with some friends closer to my own age," Meghann replied and she saw Simon's eyes glitter at her gibe.

"I love your outfit. It's so . . . grown-up for a girl your age," Louise said.

Meghann smiled as though she were oblivious to the mortal's condescension. "I'm just happy it's an original. I've never understood women who embarrass themselves by wearing knock-offs."

Louise, wearing a pinstripe business suit of dubious provenance, managed to keep the brittle, haughty little smile on her face though it wavered slightly. "Are you going out somewhere that you're all dressed up?"

"Clubbing," Meghann responded. "You know, hang out with some friends . . . maybe find a new boyfriend." She kept her gaze on Louise when she spoke, not even deigning to look at Lord Baldevar. What nerve he had, decreeing that she couldn't take a lover while he continued adding notches to his bedpost. If he was going to play the field, there was no reason she couldn't too.

There's a perfect reason—I won't let you.

Go to hell, Meghann replied while the mortal woman asked another inane question.

"I hope we're not keeping you, dear. What time are you supposed to meet your friends?"

"Oh, I have some time yet," Meghann responded airily. "I wouldn't dream of leaving without having a drink. After all, Simon and I haven't talked in . . . why, I can't even remember how long it's been." At the entrance to the living room, she turned around and widened her eyes in exaggerated innocence. "Unless you'd like me to leave, Simon?"

"Meghann," he said and dropped Louise's arm so he could come over to her. "You know you are always welcome in my house. Besides, we have so much to discuss."

"I love this room!" Meghann said brightly, ignoring the hand that dug painfully into her shoulder to repay her remark about finding a boyfriend. "I always thought art deco had an unsurpassable glamour. I feel like I'm on the set of some glitzy movie from the twenties."

Meghann's compliment was sincere. One thing she had to give Simon Baldevar credit for was his exquisite taste and flair for style. The walls were lacquered in cream with the moldings and ceiling painted in gold leaf. That provided a quiet backdrop for the dramatic living room with its baby grand piano, silver-dusted vases, art deco sculptures, and glossy black lacquer end tables. The floor-length torchiere lamps, with their reeded shafts and urn-shaped bowls, provided the room with a soft rosy light that reminded Meghann of the Stork Club in New York City, where Simon had taken her for their first and oh so memorable date.

"Thank you," Simon said and stepped behind the wet bar, a half oval of gleaming black Lucite with several high metal stools surrounding it. "Would either of you ladies care for a drink?"

Louise requested a martini while Meghann said she'd just have mineral water with lime.

After placing the drinks on a bronze and glass table that Meghann was certain was a Printz original, Simon settled down on a violet divan with Meghann, leaving Louise to loll by herself on a silver-and-black chaise longue, no doubt thinking the stark setting complemented her own severe beauty of sharply bobbed dark hair and angular cheekbones.

"You're wise to abstain from alcohol, Meghann," Si-

mon complimented, clinking his own water glass
against hers. "Too much liquor ages a woman dreadfully—causes all kinds of dreadful lines and crow's-feet
when you grow older."

Meghann almost felt sympathy for Louise—coloring
under the foundation she used to hide the wrinkles
Simon acidly mentioned. What kind of game was Simon playing with this woman? Meghann wondered,
watching them both glare at each other. This wasn't
just or even primarily about sex. No, Simon was—what?

Toying with her, Meghann realized. He was toying
with the mortal, like a cat with a butterfly—pick, pick,
picking at it until there was nothing left and the cat
moved in for the kill. Simon was toying with this mortal
mistress, both through the degrading sex Vinny mentioned and the cutting insults.

Meghann filed the information away, feeling little
sympathy for Louise. It wasn't as if this were some unwilling victim. No, Louise was using sex to get ahead
but she'd picked the wrong person to play that game
with. Meghann wondered when Simon would tear the
veil from her eyes . . . let her see that all the insults
she'd endured, all the depravity were for nothing.

"Have you any idea of what kind of position you're
looking for, dear?" Louise asked.

"Oh, I don't know." Meghann spoke in a bland
tone, though her eyes darkened to emerald with malice. "I kind of thought I'd spit on feminist ideals and
sleep my way to the top so I could be part of keeping
the glass ceiling firmly in place and perpetuate the
myth that a woman can't succeed on her brains—only
on her back."

Louise flushed an unflattering red and glanced at
Simon, seeming undecided as to what he'd do if she
retaliated. Simon met her eyes and lifted one corner
of his mouth in a half smirk before he turned to
Meghann. "Don't even joke that way, Meghann. You're

far too special to sell your body like a common harlot for the purpose of advancement."

"Maybe," Louise said coldly, her blue eyes becoming little chips of ice, "we should reschedule our business meeting since you have to entertain your little guest."

"Yes," Simon replied absently, still looking at Meghann while he waved his hand, dismissing Louise as he would a servant. "Vinny will escort you home. Good night."

"Good night, Louetta," Meghann called, and the mortal spun around on her heel, nearly slipping on the polished laminate floor.

"What did you call me?" she gasped, and Meghann didn't have to read the mortal's mind to see her consternation—it was reflected in her bulging eyes and the hammering pulse at the base of her throat. Louise/ Louetta wanted to know how the hell this young girl she'd never seen before knew her real name.

"Louise," Meghann replied ingenuously and shrugged her shoulders, thinking she should tell the woman she wasn't the only one in the room keeping her true identity hidden. She smiled, not at all kindly, at the mortal's ill-concealed relief and said, "What else could I have called you?"

"Minx," Simon murmured into her ear after Louise headed for the foyer, taking one quick lick at the pearly pink shell of her earlobe. "No doubt you just brought to mind every distressing memory of the bluegrass trailer park and scrounging existence she's tried so valiantly to escape. Nice work, little one."

It was Meghann's turn to flush while ostentatiously wiping her ear. Just because she didn't care for the woman didn't mean she should be a willing participant in one of Lord Baldevar's sadistic games. She'd just behaved like an absolute bitch—what was the matter with her?

Simon tilted her head toward him so she could see the soft smile on his lips, the gloating expression in his eyes, and too late she realized why he'd brought Louise here when he never brought mortal lovers to his home. He'd wanted to make her jealous!

Well, it didn't work, Meghann told herself firmly and scowled at Simon's self-congratulatory grin, stifling a childish impulse to stick her tongue out at him. She was not jealous—Lord Baldevar could sleep with ten sluts like Louise for all she cared. It was just that the mortal's patronizing attitude had annoyed Meghann and she put Louise in her place. *Who does Louise Caraway think she is,* Meghann thought, *daring to look down her plastic-surgery-enhanced nose at me?*

Vinny came back into the house, laden with expensively wrapped packages Simon had ordered him to retrieve from the Bentley's trunk, while Louise hurried past him and out of the house.

"Kindly take Ms. Caraway home," Simon instructed his servant. "Then you may spend the rest of the evening in town—perhaps procure some more of that white powder you're so fond of."

Vinny blanched, looking shamefaced while Meghann gave him an *I told you so* look.

"Of course your recreational activities are none of my concern—though as I recall, narcotics were at the root of all your woes when we met," Simon said to his pale, trembling employee.

The mortal flinched and Meghann saw a flurry of images whiz through his mind—Vinny sitting in a jail cell thinking there were only two choices left to him, testify against his friends in exchange for immunity on the kilos of cocaine he'd been caught red-handed with or keep his mouth shut and rot away in a federal prison for the rest of his life. Then a third choice presented itself when an anonymous benefactor paid his bail—thirty-five years of service to a vampire, at the end of which time he'd be transformed.

"Of course," Simon went on, "I am not at all concerned that you'll betray my secrets to evade a de-

served punishment but I will warn you that if the drug
impairs your ability to carry out your duties, I'll have
to dismiss you."

There were no pink slips in that fiend's service,
Meghann thought while Vinny slunk out of the house.
Vinny would be dismissed into a hole in the ground.

Meghann glared pointedly at the strong hand gripping her forearm, but Simon made no move to release
her.

"I wasn't kidding around before," Meghann finally
said after several minutes of tense staring. "I am meeting Charles and Lee at a club—they think it's high
time I found someone and so do I. Now, kindly release
me. I don't want to be late."

Meghann met his eyes and waited for the dire
threats against her or any man she'd take to her bed.
Let him say it, Meghann thought, spoiling for a fight.
*Let him make some hideous chauvinistic comment or try and
detain me* . . . Oh, how Meghann wanted him to do
just one of those things so she could yell out all the
fury she'd felt from the moment she saw Louise on
his arm.

But all Simon said was, "How can you leave yet? You
haven't opened any of your presents."

Meghann's shoulders actually sagged at the anticli-
mactic response but she rallied quickly and gave him
her own nonchalant reply. "Maybe I don't want any of
them. You should give them to that streetwalker instead."

The gifts were no surprise to Meghann. During their
stormy, thirteen-year romance, Simon used to love to
surprise her with presents—sometimes to make up for
reprehensible conduct but more often the gifts were
simply one of Simon's more tender gestures toward
her.

"I'd give them to a leper colony before I handed
her a tribute. At least look before you reject your gifts,"

Simon urged and put a sleek gold shopping bag filled with beautifully wrapped presents at her feet.

"Fine," Meghann said, resigned to the notion that she wasn't going to get past him until she opened the gifts. She held her hand out and said, "Give me my presents."

Simon used her hand to pull her against him and then placed his other hand at the small of her back, imprisoning her against him.

"Do you mind if I take a small token for myself first?" Simon bent his head, barely grazing her lips when he leaned down to kiss her.

"Honeyed fruit," Simon murmured, running his tongue over her lips. "When I first kissed you, I thought that was your taste—sweet with an unexpected tanginess underneath."

Meghann wasn't thinking of fruit when his lips came down on hers. *Push him away,* part of her mind urged, but the thought of protest was quickly drowned out by the tongue that teased at the corners of her mouth, the firm lips that made her own part slightly under their gentle onslaught.

Meghann's hands lifted of their own accord, quickly stripping Simon of the Brioni silk necktie and undoing most of the buttons on his pinstripe shirt while she wrapped her legs around his waist and ran her tongue over his blood teeth, making him moan and crush her against him so her breasts were flattened against his chest.

At last, Simon came up for air, smiling at her flushed cheeks and overbright eyes. "Now, what is all this foolishness about going to a club?"

"Club?" she repeated before his words and the triumphant smirk penetrated her pleasure-addled mind. "What do you think . . . that this is some corny romance movie and you can just kiss me into blindly following your will? I hate you!"

Simon laughed and kissed the tip of her nose. "I

merely wished to show you other uses for that sharp tongue of yours. Now, why don't you open your gifts or shall I resort to the maneuvers of cheap movies and see if another kiss doesn't make you more amenable?" At Meghann's stiff nod, Simon laughed again and reached into the shopping bag to hand her a small black jeweler's box.

Meghann felt shaken and horribly confused. Part of her wanted to tell him what he could do with both his kisses and his presents and another part wanted to rip off her dress and throw herself at him. Every time they met lately, she had such conflicting thoughts and left his company in a state of unsatisfied irritation, with an ache inside that never went away.

Was she being silly, thinking all integrity and conscience would be lost because of one romp in bed? Would it be so horrible to be with Simon just one night where right and wrong were merely words and she wasn't burdened by a code of ethics that never got her anything she wanted anyway?

"Meghann."

She looked up, and didn't pull away when Simon reached for her hand. *He makes my name sound like a caress,* she thought.

"Meghann," he repeated softly. "Don't look so downcast. You are quite right—what does your struggle to live up to my uncle's piety give you except an aching heart when you deny your true nature? Sweetheart, put the battle for good and evil out of your mind and enjoy the evening. Open your present."

Meghann popped open the small black jeweler's box she was sure contained a ring of some kind but her eager expression changed to one of horrified outrage when she saw its contents.

"Eeeck!" she yelled and flung the box through the French doors at the end of the room, putting a round, gaping hole in the tinted glass.

"Meghann," Simon said with a look of perplexed

confusion on his face. "Didn't you say you'd rather wear a water bug on your finger than the ring I gave you? I only wanted to please you."

"You know I hate bugs," she said, giving a quick shudder at the thought of the two-inch-long vile insect she'd just stared at. She stood up and gave Simon a freezing glare. "I'm leaving."

"You won't do anything of the kind." Simon laughed, pulling her back down. "You haven't finished opening your presents."

"What else is in there—snakes? No, thank you."

"Stop pouting," he said and handed her a flat, gray box with the Cartier insignia on it. "I simply wanted to repay your harsh words. Now, open your present."

"You open it."

"With pleasure." Simon undid the clasp, revealing a wide gold bracelet, amethysts, rubies, and emeralds interspersed through it in the cabochon style he knew she loved.

"Thank you," she said coolly and put the bracelet on. "It's very pretty."

"Not half as pretty as you," Simon told her and reached into the bag for a rectangular package wrapped in brown paper.

Meghann tore off the paper and gasped at the oil painting before her.

"It's wonderful," she said softly, running a cautious hand over the exquisite painting of herself. "Who did it?"

"Who else could know your expression at that precise moment?"

Meghann gaped at him. "You . . . but, Simon, this is a work of art! I never knew you could paint."

Simon smiled at the compliment. "After Alcuin chased me from England, I spent a few decades in Italy—it would be impossible to live there any length of time and not be inspired to pursue artistic endeavors. Too, immortality means we have all the time in the world to develop talents we might never discover in the short lifespan of a mortal. Do you remember the scene of the painting, little one?"

"Of course," Meghann told him, settling into the crook of his arm. "We'd been together—what? Five years? That night was the first time I woke up during sunset . . . the first time it wasn't pitch-black outside when I opened my eyes."

Meghann could still remember her excitement, how she had nearly cried with delight when she opened the shuttered windows and saw the rose sky fading to purple. To see natural light again, the world lit up by the slowly setting sun instead of streetlights. She'd thrown her clothes on in a frenzy, imploring Simon to hurry, hurry, hurry! She had to get outside before it was completely dark.

She remembered Simon's soft laugh as she had pulled him out of the hotel and onto the crowded Paris street. "Patience, little one. This is not your last sunrise. Your powers are evolving—that is why you're starting to wake up earlier."

Meghann had all but floated down the street, not even seeing the famous Arc de Triumphe—she was far too entranced by the dying sunlight on the sidewalk. "How come the sun can't kill us now?"

Simon had laughed again and pulled her against him, putting his finger to her lips. *Be discreet, little one. Dusk doesn't harm all vampires but you must be cautious. If you awaken when the sun first starts to set, don't rush outside—you could get second-degree burns all over your body.*

"Did that ever happen to you?" Meghann had asked him aloud.

Before he was able to reply, though, she'd noticed a hat vendor across the street and rushed across the boulevard, ignoring the annoyed horns. She had grabbed the hat she favored off a dummy and stroked it lovingly. It was a beautiful creation—a large, floppy picture hat reminiscent of the beach hats of the early twenties. The deep-crowned hat was made from moss-green linen, with a dark green hatband of watered silk and a wide brim Meghann pulled up at the front.

"*Perfectionnez pour rouges les cheveux,*" the vendeuse had approved, nodding at Meghann's bright red hair.

"*Non, non,*" Meghann had said hastily when the woman handed her a small silver mirror. "*Je sais qu'il est beau.*"

The vendeuse had brushed aside Meghann's protest that she knew the hat was beautiful. "*Mais vous devez vous voir, mademoiselle.*"

"*Non necessaire, Madame,*" Simon had said smoothly, waving the mirror away. "*Je suis son miroir. N'est-ce pas, ma belle?*"

Meghann had smiled up at him, thinking he was indeed her mirror. She knew she looked beautiful by the frank appreciation shining in his eyes. "I love you," she had told him and kissed him lightly.

And that's what Simon painted—that moment when she smiled at him. It was a masterful painting, Meghann thought. She couldn't detect any brushstrokes, and the way he'd fleshed out every detail was superb—the small shadow across her face, the wispy strands of red hair peeking from the brim of the hat—but the true genius of the portrait was the way Simon had captured her expression. How did he get that sparkle into her eyes, paint that dazzling smile that made her look so beautiful?

"You are beautiful, sweetheart. All I did was draw what I saw."

"No," Meghann said, awed by the beauty in the painting. "You painted what you made. I was pretty before you transformed me . . . nothing like that." She touched the vibrant, glowing face of the portrait.

"You were always beautiful," Simon told her. "It wasn't transformation that enhanced your beauty."

"It was love," Meghann said softly. Love was what made her smile like that . . . what made that painting so special. The artist's love for his subject shone through every line of the picture.

"Do you still insist there was never any love between us . . . any bond beyond animal lust?"

How could I have forgotten? Meghann asked herself. Yes, there were horrible times between her and Simon. But she had loved him . . . how could she have fooled herself about that? How could she have forgotten how many times she smiled and threw her arms around him, feeling like the luckiest woman in the world because she was the one Simon chose to spend eternity with?

"Why didn't you show me this painting?" *Why didn't you show me this side of yourself?* Why was it so often the tyrannical monster she'd come to hate that he showed her?

"I did not paint this until 1970."

"What?" Meghann looked up at him in shock. "You painted this *after* I left you?" He had labored on a painting of a woman who put a stake in his heart?

"I needed to remind myself who you were," Simon said and brushed his hand over the painting. "That is the girl I fell in love with . . . a vibrant, sweet beauty who could light up the night for me with one smile. I despised Alcuin for taking you from me, twisting your mind with his insipid notions of good and evil. Painting you was my way of remembering what you were underneath the conscience that convinced you to leave me. Alcuin may have gained a lock on your conscience, but when I remembered those shining eyes full of love I knew I would always have your heart."

"But I tried to kill you," Meghann said. "Didn't you hate me for that? I thought . . . didn't you want to destroy me for that?" She just couldn't see Simon Baldevar, the amoral, vicious killer, spending forty years pining for a woman who had left him to die.

"Hush," Simon told her. "It would be different if you cold-bloodedly plotted my death. But that is not what happened . . . I backed you into a corner and you came out fighting. Getting a stake in my heart was far more a result of carelessness on my part than any action of yours. I know why you left me there, Meghann. You were frightened that I would kill you."

Meghann nodded . . . she'd spent forty years praying Simon was dead because she thought he'd destroy her if he wasn't.

"I don't want to hurt you, Meghann." He tilted her chin up, amber eyes mesmerizing her. "The only thing I want to destroy is the half-dead, listless creature that has replaced my beautiful consort. Let me make you shine again . . . let me free you from your guilt and lay the world at your feet."

"I don't want the world," Meghann said, speaking as though she were in a trance. "I just want . . ."

"Tell me."

She had to bite down on her tongue to keep from crying out—*You, I want you!* But she did want Simon— wanted him so badly her body shook. A part of her wanted to be loyal to Jimmy's memory, but she couldn't take having a lover that stared through her. She needed someone to hold her close and push the awful loneliness away, someone to set her on fire with his touch . . .

Be my someone, Meghann silently implored Simon and lifted her hands to his face, shivering at the contact of his skin against her palm. Why did people think vampires were cold to the touch? There was nothing icy or dead about the strong, warm flesh beneath her hand.

Simon kept still, allowing her shaking hands to explore his face. At first, she was tentative but her hands grew bolder as she traced the strong line of his jaw, ran her fingers over his high cheekbones.

Meghann inched closer to him, her eyes on the hollow of his throat, the strong pulse beating there. She rubbed her lips over it, savoring the salty-sweet taste of his skin. The scent of hot, pungent blood flowing beneath his skin roused her blood lust but she pushed herself away from his neck, wanting to prolong the pleasure before feeding.

Silently, she blessed his marvelous patience, the way he let her explore his body at her own leisure. Any other man would have thrown her beneath him by now—or tried to. Simon remained immobile, only his gold eyes showing how much he wanted her as she peeled off his shirt, kissing each inch of skin as she exposed it.

Meghann made her way from his heart down to his navel with light butterfly kisses, offering him a wicked grin before she peeled off the beautifully cut dark gray trousers and bent her head to him, bracing her hands on his muscular, well-shaped legs. Meghann grinned, basking in a delightful surge of power when she felt Simon tremble at her touch. His need made desire shoot through her when she ran her lips over his leg before she sank her blood teeth into the femoral artery on the inside of his thigh. Clever Simon, that was where he'd first taken blood from her, so she wouldn't notice the wounds right away.

"Meghann," she heard him moan while she sucked at the wound. The femoral artery was a virtual fountain of blood; the dark, rich substance flowed into her mouth and the pleasure she received in feeding was so great Meghann almost forget her true intention.

But she didn't want to drain his strength away or make him ill so she reluctantly raised her bloodstained lips from the wound and turned her attention to his penis, thick and hard and waiting to be drawn into her mouth, still full of warm blood.

Meghann felt his hands tighten almost painfully in her hair, forcing her closer to him. A long time ago, he'd taught her how to do this . . . how to suck slowly like she'd do with a Popsicle, how to tease the head by using her tongue in a circular, unhurried rhythm.

And she knew from past delightful experience that soon he'd yank softly on her hair, his signal that it was time for her to lie back and . . .

"Meghann!" A strident knock at the front door was followed by the aggrieved voice of Charles Tarleton. "Are you all right? Answer me!"

With a small cry, Meghann wrenched herself away from Simon, her eyes filled with loathing and self-contempt. What in the name of God was she thinking?

"Meghann!"

"I'm fine," Meghann called out, knowing her voice sounded anything but fine but speaking aloud to keep Charles from charging into the house. What a charming picture this would make for Charles . . . seeing her with her head between the legs of the devil they were supposed to kill when she went into labor. Hastily, she wiped at the blood on her chin and chest. "I'll be right there."

Shakily, she got to her feet and met Simon's eyes, shuttered and enigmatic as always. Was he angry? For once, he had a right to be . . . a right to be annoyed with a woman that threw herself at him and then backed away like a scalded cat. Why couldn't she either hate him or throw herself at him completely? She couldn't keep playing games like this where she wound up doing neither. Either she was Lord Baldevar's enemy or she was his . . . his what?

"I'm sorry," she finally said and started for the door like a sleepwalker, but she felt a hand slowly spin her around.

"Meghann." Simon ran one fingertip over her cheek. "It's not an apology I want from you and that is not all you wished to give tonight. Isn't that right?"

Meghann made some small sound of assent and Simon leaned down to kiss her forehead. "Run along now, child, and come back when you can resist the urge to run from me when the voice of your conscience comes calling. Remember I will be here when you are ready to listen to your heart."

Meghann nodded and left him to go open the front door for Charles.

Charles grabbed her, anxious eyes roaming over her. "We waited over an hour for you. Are you all right? Has he kept you here?"

"If I said I didn't want to talk about it right now, would you respect my feelings?"

"Of course," Charles said after a long, bemused glance at the slash of color in her cheeks and the green eyes that blazed in her ghostly pale face.

"Hey." Lee took her hand. "What do you say I ride with you and we'll meet Charles at the club? You still want to go out, don't you?"

"Sure," Meghann said, forcing false cheer into her voice. "That's just what I need now—bright lights and dancing till I can't breathe."

Charles watched his best friend and lover drive off before he turned to glare at Lord Baldevar, lounging elegantly against the door frame. He'd seen the guilt in Meghann's eyes and now he knew where it came from—seeing the way the bastard's hair was ruffled and his shirt was unbuttoned.

"Damn you," Charles burst out. "Why can't you leave her alone?" He knew Meghann wouldn't initiate anything with this fiend on her own. The despicable snake was taking advantage of her, using her vulnerability and loneliness to worm his way into her heart, as Charles had feared he would.

"Don't meddle in my pleasures, boy."

"I am not some boy and I'm not scared of you. I will not allow you to ruin Meghann's life! She doesn't want you. If she responds to you, it's your blood inside her—no more. I've known Meghann for forty years, Lord Baldevar. The only time she spoke your name was to curse you."

"When you have lived as long as I have, you will

discover forty years is nothing. It is the present that counts, sodomite." Simon slammed the door, bored and uninterested in a battle of wits with a foolish novice.

Damn that troublesome creature! Meghann would be his by now if not for Charles Tarleton's constant interference.

The pain and confusion on Meghann's pretty face when that boy-lover showed up made Simon realize what an error he'd made when he opted to transform Jimmy Delacroix instead of destroying Charles.

That Meghann felt pain at her lover's fate, Simon didn't doubt. But his absence hadn't been the kind of crippling blow that would make her vulnerable to her master . . . not as long as she had Charles Tarleton to lean on. Now it was too late to kill him—Meghann could lose the child in her grief if the sodomite met with an untimely demise.

But he might not need to kill the boy, Simon reflected. Already Charles's involvement with that mortal doctor distracted him from his determination to keep Meghann from her master. And Meghann, with her actions this evening, was proving that she plainly did not want to be kept from him.

Good humor restored by the memory of the lust smoldering in his consort's eyes a few minutes earlier, Simon decided to summon Louise back. Lazily stretching his hands toward the phone, Simon thought he'd better enjoy making a mortal woman submit to whatever debauchery he craved while he could. Simon would never think of being unfaithful to Meghann once they were finally reunited, and tonight had proven it was only a matter of time before she came back to him.

TEN

August 17, 1998

They're hurting her, these awful, dark, faceless figures. "My baby," Meghann pleads but that only seems to make them angrier. Why do they hate her so much?

"No!" Meghann screams when she sees the glint of steel in the moonlight—a shiny, deadly blade poised at her stomach, ready to murder the innocent child inside her.

But the blade goes through her and Meghann feels blinding pain. Worse, she feels her child dying . . . she feels its confusion as the nurturing darkness of her womb is invaded by cold steel and the small spark of life inside her is brutally extinguished.

Meghann raises her eyes one more time and sees another cloaked figure far away. His back is turned to her but she knows who it is.

"Simon!" she shouts with the last of her strength. "Don't let us die! Help me!"

Doesn't he hear her? Why does he keep his back turned? Why is he going away?

"Come back!" Meghann yells but her voice is growing weak and her vision is fading. She's dying, along with her baby. "Why are you leaving us? Help me!"

"Simon!" Meghann jerked herself out of the night-mare with one last howl. Wild-eyed and shaking all over, she clutched a pillow to her chest, trying to force herself to breathe regularly.

Just a dream, Meghann told herself. So why did she feel such a sense of oppression and dread that she wanted to scream again?

"Charles?" she called. Hadn't he or Lee heard her scream? Then her eyes fell on the note propped neatly on her bedstead.

> *Meghann,*
> *Our flight leaves at 8:30. Got a little concerned when you were still sleeping but Lee says expectant mothers need more rest. You've got the cell phone number—call me!*
> *Love,*
> *Charles*

Belatedly, Meghann remembered Charles's and Lee's trip to San Francisco for the forty-sixth meeting of the American College of Obstetricians and Gynecologists where Lee was giving a lecture on management of high-risk pregnancy. They were only going to be gone three days and had asked Meghann to accompany them but she'd insisted they take the trip together. Though Charles had had reservations about leaving her alone, he'd agreed to go—at least until he arrived at Simon's last night and saw what was going on between Meghann and her master.

Charles hadn't said anything to blame her or make her feel ashamed of what she almost did with Simon. Charles's attitude was that Meghann was a victim of the blood link between her and Simon. He insisted she couldn't be held responsible for her actions while she was drinking her master's blood but it was obvious she couldn't be left alone with him. From now on, Charles would remain with her when she had to see Simon to ensure he couldn't take advantage of her.

He'd stay with her while Lee went to San Francisco by himself.

It had been nearly sunrise before Meghann was able to convince Charles that while he meant well, he'd be doing her no favor by treating her like a backward child that had to be supervised. Her feelings toward Lord Baldevar were complex and based on much more than a mere blood link.

"But, Meghann," Charles had shouted. "Can't you see those feelings are ones he's putting in your head? He's making you think you want him when you don't!"

"You don't know that," Meghann had screamed back. "I don't know that . . . but I want to! I want to understand myself. I want to come to terms with him. Lee's right. I have to examine my feelings—no matter how dismayed I am by my findings."

Charles had given his lover a scathing glance before turning back to Meghann, speaking with a slow, careful enunciation that showed he was on the verge of losing his temper. "Meghann, I'm not going to stand by and watch you give yourself to a monster! You deserve more. I'm sorry you're having such a hard time finding love. If only you were a man so we could fall in love and get married!"

That ridiculous statement had cut the tension in the room with everyone, Lee included, laughing at such an absurdity.

"I could do a hell of a lot worse," Meghann had said, hugging her friend close.

"That's the problem," Charles had replied. "Look, I may not be in love with you but I love you like a sister. Do you think I should stand by and let you ruin your life?"

"Don't you think I know better than to be with Simon?" Meghann had replied. "Look, I want you and Lee to go away together because I need some time by myself. If a part of me wants him—a masochistic, self-destructive part—I have to face it down and cut it out of me, the same way I'd cut a limb off if it got gangrene. I want the next four days to be a time of retreat and meditation. That way I can tell Simon no by myself instead of needing you to stand guard over me so I don't throw myself at him. Can't you see? I need to turn him away by myself."

Charles had examined her closely before he finally sighed and nodded. "I should have known better than to think you'd settle for anything less than rejecting him of your own will—even when it's seriously compromised by having to drink his blood. Okay, we'll go to San Francisco and give you time to yourself. But I saw the blood on you last night. You don't need to feed, so promise me you won't go near him while we're gone."

Meghann had given her promise and Charles had reluctantly agreed to go with Lee to San Francisco.

Now Meghann wished her friend were still here . . . wished anybody were here. That nightmare had left her with a pounding heart and a driving fear that put her on the edge of panic.

Silly, she told herself. *That dream is just a manifestation of your subconscious fears. Part of you wants Simon but another part knows you shouldn't put your faith in him . . . knows all it would bring you is the pain you felt in that dream. That's all—you're not in any real danger.*

So why did Meghann feel as if the walls of the small room were closing in on her? Why was every instinct screaming at her to get out of the house? *Run,* was the undercurrent in her thoughts. *Danger . . . Danger . . . Run away!*

Simon, Meghann thought and nearly reached for the phone. Not that she needed the mortal appliance—she could simply summon him with the power of her thoughts if she wanted to. Then she wouldn't be alone with this crippling fear. Unlike the dream, he'd never turn her away. She knew he'd meet her, hold her . . .

No! She'd made a promise to Charles—was she going to break it a scant hour after he left, behave like a frightened child and demand someone pet her fears away? She wouldn't call Simon, she'd do precisely what she was supposed to do while Charles and Lee were gone—use the time to get her head together.

The desert, Meghann thought, and she was pleased to feel the constricting band around her chest loosen a little. Maybe she just needed to get out of the house . . . needed air and space so she could think.

Meghann showered quickly and pulled her hair into a casual ponytail, throwing on baggy jeans and her Mets jersey. But something still nagged at her, whispered she needed protection.

On impulse, Meghann went to the cardboard boxes stacked by the closet. Spacious though Lee's house was, he didn't have room for all her things so she'd left most of them in storage. She rummaged through the box where she'd stored Jimmy's possessions and soon found what she was looking for—a .357 magnum revolver.

Meghann felt a ridiculous sense of protection at the heavy weight of the weapon in her hand. For God's sake, why would a vampire need a gun to feel safe? Maybe because this was Jimmy's talisman? A .357 had saved him the night that vampire found his family. Jimmy hadn't been able to save his wife or son but three shots from the magnum had paralyzed the vampire long enough for Jimmy to flee the house and get help. After that, even though the thing had disappeared long before Jimmy returned with the cops, he'd kept the gun by his side and never went out without his magnum when the sun went down.

For the first time that night, Meghann smiled—remembering how she and Jimmy had found each other at a dark time in both their lives and helped each other. She had helped him conquer his alcohol dependency by teaching him he was not helpless against the

thing that killed his family. Once he started killing
vampires during the day he no longer needed to
drown his fear with alcohol at night.

For his part, Jimmy helped her control the treacherous blood lust that constantly screamed at her to kill.
Whenever she felt angry or frustrated, the blood lust
was there, slyly whispering that one kill would make
her feel better. Jimmy suggested that perhaps Meghann
needed a way—besides sex, absinthe, and cartons of
Camels—to relieve tension, and invited her to come
along with him for target practice.

Reaching for a box of ammunition, Meghann
smiled, remembering that under Jimmy's tutelage
she'd become a crack shot within a few weeks. She
recalled his astonishment, watching her shoot the magnum with one hand, when a mortal woman of her size
and weight would have been knocked off her feet even
if she fired with both hands.

Target practice, Meghann decided, and inserted car-
tridges into the chambers, snapped the cylinder shut,
clicked on the safety, and stuffed the gun down the
waistband of her jeans. She'd go to the desert and take
a few rounds of target practice while she did her best
to resolve her feelings.

Meghann drove her Caddy to the spot Simon had
taken her to for their picnic. Here she'd made the
mistake of letting Simon back into her life so this was
the perfect to place to banish him from her heart.

Meghann rummaged through her CD collection,
looking for something to suit her angry, confused
mood. She stopped at *Ace of Spades*, thinking the loud,
harsh riffs of Motorhead were precisely what this night
called out for.

Jimmy had introduced her to Motorhead, Meghann
remembered while she set up the empty soda bottles
she'd brought along for target practice. Prior to him,

she'd had no real interest in British punk rockers, preferring New York–based bands like The Ramones and The Heartbreakers. But Jimmy kept playing their albums and dragging her to concerts until she was won over.

And that, Meghann thought as she shot the bottles in rhythm with the maniacally high-energy songs, was what a relationship was supposed to be . . . give and take, exchanging thoughts and interests. Jimmy Delacroix and the six years they'd lived together were the closest thing to a normal relationship she'd had since she transformed. No dark, hungry desire that turned you inside out and made it so nothing else in the world mattered . . . just a sweet, good-humored friendship that also happened to include the best sex she'd ever had aside from Simon Baldevar.

Simon Baldevar, Meghann thought and knocked down a bottle. She wished he'd never come back from the dead and so thoroughly disrupted her life—just when she'd finally found a way to live happily as an immortal.

Damn you, Simon, Meghann thought savagely and blasted a target. *Why couldn't you leave me alone?*

She reloaded and acknowledged ruefully that Simon Baldevar wouldn't be a problem at all if she could just refuse him and mean it. That fiend had too much pride to chase after a woman truly repulsed by him. So what kept drawing her toward him, making her look forward to seeing him when she should despise him for all he'd done?

Lust? If only it were that simple. If Meghann thought her only feeling toward Simon was physical need, she wouldn't be upset. It was the other feelings, the way he made her feel safe and content, in spite of everything she knew about him.

Meghann leaned against a towering mesa and considered her situation. A year ago, if someone had told her Simon Baldevar could reappear in her life, murder

Alcuin, shatter Jimmy's mind, impregnate her, and then make her almost like him in a month's time, Meghann wasn't sure if she'd have laughed at such absurdity or bashed the unfortunate seer's brains in.

So how had he done it? To a degree, Meghann knew the answer. The ruthless, amoral fiend that murdered and destroyed lives with such ease was only one side of his personality . . . the side Meghann had no trouble resisting. It was the other part of him . . . the romantic, the endlessly innovative lover and utterly gentle man that could calm her with one tender glance . . . that was the creature Meghann gave her heart to.

Are you falling in love with him? a voice asked anxiously.

I don't know, Meghann responded.

How can you not know? the voice fired back. *You've had forty years to think about it.*

Actually, that wasn't true. From the time she had impaled him to the time Alcuin had told her Simon was still alive, Meghann refused to speak or even think of him. Part of that was childish superstition—it seemed that thinking of him might invoke him, somehow bring him back to life.

The rare times she did think of Simon, Meghann soothed herself with one litany—Simon Baldevar was a brutal monster that tore her from her family, forced vampirism on her, and made her live in his gilded cage of sexual bondage and spiritual servitude until deliverance came in the form of Alcuin. With such thoughts running through her mind, it was easy to believe she'd never loved Simon, never felt anything for him but hate, fear, and perhaps the smallest touch of lust . . .

Danger! Meghann's heart dropped into her stomach and her mouth went dry. There were immortals near her and they meant serious harm to her.

That dream—she'd thought it was symbolic, her ambivalent feelings toward Simon. Now she knew it had been a warning.

Shit! What the hell was she going to do? Meghann took a deep breath, knowing she must keep calm or she was dead. What was her best option?

Astral projection, she decided swiftly. Get the hell away from the threat. Pregnant, Meghann was in no condition to engage in physical combat. Even though she was fifty miles out of town and astral projection would only take her thirty miles, that was all right. She'd just make two trips.

Meghann closed her eyes and concentrated on a lonely stretch of highway thirty miles away . . . by the railroad tracks . . . concentrated . . .

No! Meghann almost screamed the word aloud in her terror, but to do so would bring her attackers closer. What was the matter with her? She'd felt the physical world start to fall away, her body start to drift, and then she'd stopped cold, her body remaining firm and refusing to become incorporeal.

Why? With a sinking heart, Meghann remembered Simon telling her pregnancy might hinder her ability to fly the plane.

Goddammit, those footsteps were too fucking close for her to have any hope of getting to her car and speeding away. And if she'd lost the ability to fly . . . what the hell was she going to do? Wait—Simon's invisibility trick?

Meghann wrapped the imaginary black blanket around her aura, imagining it as a tight sheath that covered her from head to toe. Thus covered, she began walking toward her car, knowing if she could just get to her car she'd be safe. No vampire could outrun a Caddy.

"Where do you think you're going, bitch?"

Stunned, Meghann whirled around and saw her attackers but first she wondered if her eyes were deceiving her.

"I'm going to my car," Meghann said calmly to Guy Balmont, a dense mass of a vampire, nearly seven feet tall. He'd been Alcuin's right hand until she and Charles came along. She only had a nodding acquaintance with the two men by his side. All she knew of them was that they were both at least two hundred years old . . . very old and most likely quite powerful. "Why don't you move out of my way?"

"Did you learn arrogance at the knee of your master?" Guy thundered, and Meghann felt serious fright—both at the hatred in his eyes and the broadsword at his waist, a twin to the one both his partners wore. The broadsword—weapon of choice for decapitating an errant vampire. Dear God . . . the blade in her dream . . .

"You and your faggot friend," Guy went on, spittle flying from his mouth in his fury. "Thinking yourselves so clever . . . that you could evade us. But I found you . . . Charles isn't here to help you, is he, slut? He's in San Francisco, carrying out his own sins against nature with some mortal."

Damn—Charles must have paid for that airline ticket with a credit card. Why had she and Charles forgotten how much the Ballnamore vampires despised them? Why had they thought they needn't bother with safety precautions once Simon found them?

"So you found me," Meghann said coolly. "Tell me what you want and get the fuck away from me."

"Don't act so haughty with me, wench. Your lover is not here to save you from your deserved punishment."

"If you are referring to Lord Baldevar, he is not my lover."

"You carry his bastard," one of Guy's henchmen snarled at her.

How the hell could they know that? She and Charles had been so careful; they hadn't removed any of the archives from Ballnamore and Meghann hadn't allowed any vampires, with their too keen senses, near her. Unless . . . were some of the vampires at Ballnamore in Charles's bloodline? Maybe his worry for her lowered his shields and made it possible for them to read his thoughts.

Knowing a denial would be futile, Meghann thought she saw another way out of this trap. These vampires were older than she—an advantage but it could be their downfall too. They'd underestimate her because she was a woman. And they couldn't read her thoughts, so if she got them to drop their guard, she might have a chance to get out of this mess alive.

Meghann crouched over, looking as if she were about to cry but actually slipping Jimmy's gun from her waistband. Thank God she'd reloaded it. She spoke, proud of the piteous quiver in her voice. "Don't you call my baby an abomination. This is a child like any other . . . innocent of its father's sins."

"You dare to compare that thing inside you with an innocent babe? It is the spawn of a whore and a wretched fiend and it is my duty to rip it from your womb before it can destroy us all. The Council knew I was right about you when we learned of your pregnancy. I have their permission to slaughter you for your treachery."

There—she had her finger on the safety catch. Meghann let out a snarl, praying the sound would prevent any of the vampires from hearing her click the safety off. "Is that what all this is about? You fucking hypocrite, don't try and pretend you're saving the world by killing me. You're hoping that Charles will be too grief-stricken when I'm gone to stand in your way. You loathsome, vile bastard! You want the position Alcuin left to me and Charles? Come and take it if you can."

One of Guy's henchmen lunged at her. Meghann's hand lashed up and she put the .357 to his head. When she fired, the vampire flew off his feet, blood and brain matter drenching Guy and the other apprentice.

She felt a violent power yank the gun from her hand but that was fine—she'd expected Guy to do that. While he concentrated on pulling the weapon from her, Meghann turned her attention to the wounded vampire, and his sword flew into her outstretched hand.

Sidestepping the apprentice that tried to grab her, Meghann leaped the short distance to the shot vampire, already managing to sit up and look around in a dazed manner. He saw Meghann land by his side but before he could even bring up his hand, she decapitated him in one swift stroke.

"Grab her, you fool!" she heard Guy bellow, and whirled around to face her other attacker. The vampire raised his sword but Meghann had no intention of engaging in swordplay. Instead she drove her foot through his groin, feeling a grim satisfaction when he fell to his knees, whining from the pain of his crushed testicles.

There . . . two down, one to go. Meghann knew better than to try and take on Guy. Her plan was to jump to the top of the towering mesa behind her; she could repel attacks up there and maybe leap the distance to her car.

Meghann bent her knees and prepared to lunge but a massive boulder flew at her. She tried to duck but the thing caught the right side of her face, smashing her cheekbone to pulp.

Screaming in pain, she fell to the ground, terrified by the sudden nausea and cramping pain she felt in her abdomen. *No, don't let me lose the baby.*

Meghann had to concentrate her energy on stopping the miscarriage, healing herself. As Alcuin had taught her to do, she turned her concentration inward . . . saw the contracting uterus and focused all her power on holding it still. Only after several horri-

ble moments of waiting did the contractions ease and
Meghann knew she wouldn't lose her baby.

While Meghann lay curled up and gasping for
breath, her attackers pounced. Dimly, she felt rough
hands yank her up, tear her clothes off, and tie her
to the mesa. Her face had healed, but she still felt
nauseated.

Guy's fist smashed into her face, bringing her back
to full consciousness. "Still Lord Baldevar's proud,
high-stepping whore, aren't you? How fortunate that I
found you before he could save you and your devil's
spawn."

Dazed, Meghann looked up at him and then she
began giggling hysterically.

"Stop that," Guy snarled and twisted her nipples
viciously. "Stop that immediately! How can you laugh
now?"

"You're a fool!" Meghann yelled, her voice shattering the stillness of the desert. Guy and his apprentice
backed away, seeming a little frightened of the bound
woman in front of them. "Can't you feel your enemy?
He's here, you moron!"

Meghann thought she saw the giant's hands tremble
and his apprentice went ashen. "What do you mean,
here? He knows of . . . no!"

"Yes!" Meghann cried, her voice stuffy because Guy
had broken her nose and it hadn't healed yet. "He
knows I'm pregnant and he's here! Won't it be nice
to see your old enemy now that you don't have Alcuin's
robes to cower behind, you low-life piece of shit?"

Meghann took a deep breath and transformed her
terror into energy she used to send out an urgent message: *Help me, Simon!* She had no doubt Lord Baldevar
would come to her aid; she was pregnant. But she had
no idea where he was; he could be too far away to fly
here. What if he was too late? How long could she
hold Guy off?

Summoning made her sick again; she was dizzy and

having trouble breathing. But the other vampires were not a threat to her right now; their heads were ringing from the power behind Meghann's call.

Dazed, Guy pulled himself up and slapped her hard enough to make her head slam into the rock behind her. "You'll be dead before your master arrives, bitch."

She couldn't stand being naked in front of this monster; she felt his muddy eyes roaming over her body and gave him a sneer she hoped masked her fear. "Take a good long look, Guy. You'll never see a naked woman again. Even if you do kill me, we both know Lord Baldevar will slaughter you easily." Guy raised his hand again but Meghann continued taunting him. "Why don't you tell your idiot apprentice that you've never won a confrontation with Lord Baldevar?"

"Shut up!" Guy roared and wrapped his hands around her neck. "I'll kill you, you little whore!"

Her throat was like clay in his huge fingers. Meghann felt them digging into her skin. She saw stars . . . he was crushing her larynx; she couldn't breathe.

Abruptly, he let her go and Meghann's head fell on her chest as she tried to force air through her wounded throat.

Then she felt a hand wrap itself in her hair, and Guy pulled her up, making sure she saw the sword he held to the fiery mass of hair clenched in his fist. "Lord Baldevar might be strong but I know how to crush him. Tell me, do you think that cold monster might actually cry if he saw his precious whore scalped . . . her oh so beautiful hair and the top of her skull spread on the floor beside her while the blood of his bastard offspring flows down her legs? Prepare to meet your maker."

Meghann saw murder in his eyes, murder and no hope a plea might reach his hate-filled, enraged mind. And Simon wasn't here. Who was going to save her baby? She couldn't let this thing kill her.

Guy raised his sword and Meghann saw the sharp tip coming at her abdomen.

"Azazeal!" she screamed in her panic. Dimly, she remembered Simon's story of that demon he had summoned to kill his father. She couldn't remember the name of the devil he'd summoned but she had taken a look at that leather-bound copy of the *Lemegeton* he kept in his study. Heedless of the consequences, Meghann yelled out one of the most powerful conjurations of the Key of Solomon in the moment Guy's sword grazed her belly.

"I conjure you, evil and rebellious spirit, that abides in Abyss of Darkness! Come to me, come to me, Angel of Darkness, and stand ready to do as I command thee!"

The mesa she was tied to exploded into a thousand pieces of rock and Meghann flew a good twelve feet. Dazed, she pulled herself to her feet and recoiled at the foul odor permeating the air.

"My God," she whispered reverentially when she saw Guy's henchman torn apart by an unseen force. Arms and legs were torn away as if they were mere matchsticks and then the decapitated limbs attacked the vampire's torso. Over it all, Meghann heard the same maniacal cackling that had nearly driven her mad the night Simon summoned, when he'd been so infuriated because she tried to kill him and save Jimmy. In a moment of rage, he'd conjured monsters even he had trouble controlling.

No, Meghann thought in horror. *I couldn't have called those things—no!* If they'd been almost too powerful for Simon to control, she had no prayer of holding them in her thrall. A minor demon, that's what she'd tried for . . . not this unholy force that was moving toward her . . .

Meghann spun around, and cowered within the small circle that appeared. Please let the circle protect her, please . . .

She saw something hover at the edge of the circle and breathed a small sigh of relief that quickly became a scream when it plucked her off the ground and shook her like a rag doll.

She waited for it to tear out her limbs and then realized her fate was going to be far worse. The thing was trying to get inside her . . . she felt its freezing form try to crawl into her. It wanted her body whole . . . it panted at the chance to possess a vampire's body.

Meghann fought with every ounce of her being and her effort only wound up being a slight nudge. She almost felt the thing's amusement at her struggles. It knew she'd weaken before long and it would be able to stay on earth indefinitely; for her immortal form could withstand the shock of possession, she wouldn't erode and die like a possessed human . . .

"Aufuge a ea!" Meghann heard a voice roar and she was unceremoniously dropped to the ground.

"What . . . hey . . ." was all she got out before Simon Baldevar grabbed her up.

"The License to Depart," he said quickly. "Meghann, you called this thing . . . you must make it leave." He put his hands on both sides of her forehead. "Concentrate, Meghann. Take my strength within you and use it to cast this thing back to hell."

Meghann felt something dark and infinitely potent surge through her body, its impact that of a jolt of electricity. This was her master's power flowing through her, and it alone could save her now.

As Meghann glared at the thing before her, her voice held the coldness and lack of fear that would intimidate the thing into obeying her. "Disobedient spirit, I deprive you off all office and dignity if you do not immediately depart unto your abode!"

The change in the atmosphere was immediate. The indescribable stench vanished and the desert returned to its balmy temperature.

Meghann's eyes darted around, wondering if the demon had destroyed her enemies. She saw the dismembered carcass of one vampire and of course there was the one she had killed, but where was Guy?

"Here." Simon stripped his shirt off and put it on her, buttoning it when Meghann's hands shook too hard to do it herself. "That rabble won't look on you anymore. Now, have they harmed you?"

"I almost lost the baby," Meghann said. "That's when they tied me up . . . when I was trying to heal my body . . . they ripped my clothes and tied me up . . . naked. Oh, God, I can't stand the way he looked at me and I thought I was going to die. I thought I'd die here in the desert . . . tied up and powerless to keep them from hurting the baby . . ."

"Cry, Meghann," Simon said when she fell into his arms, sobbing as though she would never stop. "Cry and get that horrible fear out of you. Cry for all that wretch did to you in an attempt to hurt me. No one will ever harm you again, I promise."

"Guy . . ."

"That coward will show himself soon and this harrowing night will be over." Meghann noticed Simon was clutching the sword she'd stolen from one of the vampires.

"I dreamed of you tonight," she choked out. "They were . . . kill . . . killing me but you kept your back turned, you wouldn't help . . ."

"Hush," Simon said and his arms tightened around her until she thought he'd crush her but she didn't mind. She clung just as tightly to him. "Meghann, listen to me. Don't you ever, ever summon from the *Lemegeton* again. I know Guy terrified you but that magick is not for you. Do you know I barely got here in time to help you repulse that thing? Guy and his minions I could certainly dispatch but you cannot summon things you don't know how to control. It could destroy

your body if not render you as mindless as Jimmy Delacroix. Understand?"

Meghann started to nod, but Simon's expression
changed, eyes becoming fierce and hard as one arm
reached out and Meghann was shoved away from him.

"Don't interfere," Simon ordered and then addressed Guy, standing before him and holding his
sword in the classic attack position. "Father Balmont,
are you sure you wish to spar with me? I am not a
pregnant, defenseless female and you no longer have
two strong brutes at your side."

"I'm not afraid to face you," Guy snarled and
lunged at him but Simon easily deflected the blow
while getting in his own thrust at Guy's forearm.

Meghann watched the fight . . . she'd never seen
Simon Baldevar with a sword in his hand. He must
have been a deadly opponent in his time, Meghann
thought, watching him force the giant of a vampire
back with a series of whirling slashes and ripostes. He
moved so fast he was almost a blur to Meghann's
eyes . . . a blur that moved against his enemy with a
lethal, vicious speed and grace.

"I'll make you watch me kill your whore," Guy
panted, just managing to block Simon's sword before
it attacked his heart.

Simon's response was a sharp thrust at Guy's throat.
The other vampire deflected him and tried to push
his weight down on Simon's blade to make him drop
his sword.

If Guy thought his solid mass was a match for Lord
Baldevar, he was sadly mistaken. Small beads of per-
spiration appeared on his forehead as he pressed down
on the sword with all his weight and that's when Simon
allowed his sword to go completely lax. Unable to adjust himself to the abrupt release of tension, Guy felt
his momentum carry his arm down to the ground and
from there it was a simple matter for Simon to stab

the hunched-over vampire in the back to puncture his heart.

Simon glared down at his dying enemy for a moment before lifting his eyes to search for Meghann. He saw her hunched over a pile of rocks, frantically pawing through the stones.

"My father's ring!" she screamed up at him when he touched her shoulder. "That . . . that cocksucker, he must have ripped it off my neck!" Meghann clawed at the rubble, not seeming to notice her long nails breaking as she tore the ground apart.

"I can't lose my father's ring," Meghann sobbed. "His wedding ring . . . my brother Frankie gave it to me . . . after I left you, I visited my family before I went to Alcuin. And Frankie said Daddy wanted me to have the ring . . . I was supposed to give it to my husband. I wear it around my neck, to keep it near me. But now it's not here . . . I can't find it! I can't lose it, I can't!"

"Meghann." Simon spoke in a low, gentle voice, rocking her back and forth as though she were a small child. "It's all right . . . no, don't cry. We'll find the ring, I promise. Hush now, hush."

Meghann clung to him, feeling lulled by the steady beat of his heart and the broad, comforting chest that pillowed her head.

"Now," Simon said, the calmness of his voice pushing her panic back. "Where were you when Guy took your ring?"

"It was after they tied me to the mesa. I felt the chain come off my neck but the mesa doesn't exist now. It blew up when I . . . when I called that thing. So I was looking through the debris . . ."

"Do you remember where the mesa was?"

Meghann nodded and pointed to a large boulder a few feet from them.

"Let's start our search there." Simon helped her

up, and kept one arm around her waist as they walked to the spot where the mesa had stood.

Immediately, Simon spied a small gleam of gold under the largest piece of stone and plucked up the ring. "Here you are, sweetheart." He deposited the ring in the breast pocket of the shirt he'd put on Meghann.

Instead of smiling, she looked up at him with somber eyes. She felt the solid-gold band through the thin fabric of the linen shirt and thought of how excited she'd been the night Frankie gave her the ring, the night she thought she'd killed Simon and visited the family she hadn't been near since she had transformed.

The wedding ring was Meghann's talisman, something she'd gained by leaving Simon to die and making peace with the family he'd kept her from. The ring was proof she was the independent, fearless woman her father had raised her to be, not the simpering little creature that obeyed Lord Baldevar's every whim.

Now that wretched Guy Balmont had forced her into a position where she had to depend on Simon for her life. Damn him, Meghann thought, feeling almost strangled by the anger and frustration inside her. She'd sought sanctuary with Alcuin to be free of Simon, and now Guy had pushed her right back into his arms. . . .

"What crisis made you cling to me last night?" Simon asked softly though his gold eyes burned through the pitch-black surrounding them.

Meghann started to speak and he grabbed her close, gripping her forearms in an iron vise that made her cry out.

"You're mine," Simon said fiercely. "Why does that simple truth make you writhe in embarrassment? What will it take to make you realize you belong to me?"

Before she could respond, Simon kissed her—no gentle caress like he'd given her the night before but a hard, possessive touch that unleashed a wild, primal desire inside her.

I want you, Meghann—body and soul. Surrender to me!

"Yes," she heard herself pant, everything save the tempestuous, dominating force tearing through her forgotten. "Please take me!"

Whore!

"Guy," Meghann cried and sat up. "I thought he was dead!"

"If I did not have ample reason before to kill him, I most certainly do now," Simon growled and gave a mock scowl at Meghann's giggle. He smiled and pulled her close for one more kiss before getting up and giving her his hand. "Wait by the car, and I shall destroy him. Then, we shall pick up where we were before that knave interrupted us."

Meghann shook her head. "It's my place to kill him, not yours."

Simon laughed, and folded her arm through his. "More and more, you are proving yourself my consort. Certainly yours should be the hand to wield the executioner's ax. Come along, sweetheart."

The impaled vampire sprawled facedown on the rocky desert floor, gasping for breath and squirming miserably with the sword securely lodged through his chest.

Simon gave Guy a chilling grin and grabbed his arm, tearing into his carotid artery with his blood teeth.

Meghann had to turn away . . . watching Simon feed was making her own blood lust rise. She glanced up at the full moon, thinking that instead of her finding answers, this trip out to the desert had resulted in more questions.

Something was happening between her and Simon, had been since the night she conceived. She'd been so sure, when Alcuin first told her Lord Baldevar was still alive, that he'd want to kill her. Instead, he'd declared himself still in love with her and laughingly told her she reciprocated his feelings, even if she denied it.

Meghann had denied it—vehemently and often. Hadn't she spent forty years of her life reviling him, thanking God she was free of him? Then he reappeared and it was almost as if they'd never been apart. But why? It wasn't as if time had mellowed him—he was still the same amoral fiend that took what he wanted with no regard for anyone else

May God forgive you for embracing a monster.

"Shut up!" Meghann howled out loud, startling Simon out of feeding. She yanked the sword out of Guy's body and used it to castrate him with one swift stroke. "Don't you call him a monster, you . . . you baby killer!"

Meghann brandished the sword high above her head, about to bring it down on Guy's neck, when he whimpered, "I have failed my master."

"What the hell are you talking about?" she demanded. "Alcuin would despise you for what you tried to do tonight."

"It's . . ." he tried to gasp out, "it's you he would despise now . . . Baldevar's slut . . ." Hemorrhaging from his mouth and nose, Guy was unable to continue speaking.

"Weakling," Simon muttered and put his hand on Guy's lank hair, allowing a small spark of life to flow through the dying vampire . . . just enough so he could finish his last words.

Meghann felt her heart plummet into her stomach at the eager, interested look on Simon's face. If he gave Guy a reprieve, then she was sure she didn't want to hear what he was about to say.

Guy managed to smile at her . . . the grin a hideous contrast to the pain in his eyes. "He made you his favorite to trick you . . . make you trust him. Alcuin didn't love you . . . just wanted to keep you away from

your master. Told me . . . told me to deal with you . . .
kill you if you ever conceived Lord Baldevar's child."

"You lying motherfucker!" Meghann swung the
sword at Guy's neck, decapitating him in the blink of
an eye. After he was dead, she continued to hack at
his flesh, swinging blindly. "Die! Die! Die! Die!"

She howled and thrashed when Simon pinioned her
arms to her sides and took the sword from her. "Let
go of me!"

"Your hysteria could harm the child," he said
calmly.

"It's not true! It's not!" Meghann cried. "Alcuin
loved me, I know he did."

Simon turned her around and caressed her cheek.
"Perhaps he was fond of you as long as you remained
pious and frigid toward me. However, if he ever
thought you were falling in love with me again, he
would have sanctioned your death without a second
thought."

Meghann choked out the word "no" but it was a
desperate plea instead of a furious denial.

"Meghann, he knew the implications of you reunit-
ing with me, and I'd wager my immortality that he
never once discussed them with you. You are carrying
a child that might release us from darkness. If he lives,
someday his blood might give us the power to walk in
daylight. If I possess such power, what will stop me
from destroying everyone that stands in my way?"

Suddenly, Meghann saw it—a ruthless vampire who
didn't have to sleep during the day. The rest of the
vampires would be completely vulnerable to him; he'd
kill them while the sun was up.

"That's right, Meghann. Alcuin knew he'd have to
either keep us apart or destroy you."

"Stop saying that!" Meghann yelled. "Alcuin
wouldn't kill me, never!"

"Wouldn't he? I killed him before making you pregnant to keep you safe. After you conceived, if you had

managed to leave me again, do you know what he would have done?" Simon's bleak grin frightened Meghann more than Guy's surprise attack. "Nothing. He would have kept us separated so I could not nourish you with my blood—just stood over your deathbed and watched you starve to death."

Meghann put her hands to her ears; she could not bear to hear any more of this. It was making the past forty years of her life a lie. Simon took her hands in his, breaking her heart as well as her faith in Alcuin with his words.

"What do you think, Meghann? That Alcuin would tell you to seek me out so I could save you? He kept you in the dark because he never fully trusted you or your good friend, Doctor Tarleton." Simon's lips curled derisively at her shocked look. "Meghann, I'm not spinning this tale of betrayal to convince you that you have no friends and make you turn to me for solace; I have no desire to win you by default. I simply want you to face some hard truths. Do you think Charles Tarleton would still be alive if I thought he wanted to kill you? No, Alcuin could see that you and Charles gave your first loyalty to each other so he lied to you both."

"Maybe he didn't know I had to drink your blood," Meghann cried, finding a straw to grasp at.

Simon laughed nastily. "Dear girl, do you know how *Infans Noctis* came into my possession? Isaac Spears stole it from Alcuin. He knew that secret long before I ever did."

Meghann didn't know it was possible to hurt like this; there was a bitter lump in her throat and a tightness in her chest that made it difficult to breathe. She took air in short, shallow gasps, willing herself not to cry. She would not cry over this . . . she would not cry over being betrayed by Alcuin, over the idea that all his loving guidance that reminded her so much of her mortal father turned out to be no more than a means to an end for him, a way to keep her and Lord Baldevar apart.

Meghann looked at the hellish scene around her—Guy Balmont's head glaring up at her, the eyes open and accusing, the dismembered corpse of his apprentice, all the rocks from the shattered mesa—and thought she had to get away from this cursed spot. She had to get in her car and drive far, far from this place where she nearly lost her child. If she never saw the desert again, it would be too soon. She started to walk, idly wondering if Simon would make any move to detain her. Right now she couldn't even look at him. How he must be laughing at her, a silly fool that couldn't even see she was being manipulated, that Alcuin only took her in to keep her from him.

Feeling dizzy and sick, she sagged against the Caddy, utterly drained and incapable of taking another step, even the small one of opening the car door. The world spun away from her and she would have slumped to the ground if not for the strong arms that picked her up and tossed her onto the front seat of the car.

Feed and you'll feel better. A wrist appeared under her mouth, and her nose twitched at the inviting smell of strong, hot blood.

Hungrily, Meghann bit down, feeling nothing but relief when the sweet taste of blood filled her mouth and banished her sickness. She lapped up the blood greedily, devouring not just the liquid but the power and strength flowing into her body from Simon's blood, wanting all that vigor for herself and the baby.

"Enough," she heard an amused voice say and the wrist was yanked away from her blood teeth and grasping hands. She became aware that her head was resting on Simon's lap, and tried to move but he kept her in place. "You must wait until you can feed on mortals again to drain your prey completely, little predator."

"Simon?" she murmured drowsily. "Is there something wrong with me? Why am I so tired?"

"Nothing is wrong," he responded calmly. "Nothing but being pregnant and utterly exhausted from that wretched attack. Sleep now, little one, and I promise you'll feel better when you wake up tomorrow night."

"Why didn't you kill me?" she said and twisted around to make herself more comfortable. Meghann knew her questions had some sense of urgency behind them but it was getting so hard to think or speak.

"What?"

"When you came back." She yawned. "Why didn't you just kill me? . . . ran off and left you to die . . . ruined our life together for nothing just so one of your enemies could . . . could use me against . . . you. Why don't you hate me?"

"Hate you? For what? Being young and vulnerable to the machinations of a duplicitous priest? Don't upset yourself by dwelling on the past. Just shut your eyes and get the sleep you need to recover."

"Where are we going?" she managed to slur out when she heard the Caddy roar to life. "I . . . Don't take me back to Lee's . . . scared to be alone . . ."

"Hush," Simon told her and stroked her hair, lulling her into sleep. "I am taking you where you belong . . . home with me."

"Good," Meghann said and closed her eyes. She could sleep now, knowing that Simon Baldevar was standing guard over her and her baby.

ELEVEN

August 18, 1998

   *Meghann looked around the dark, dank chamber with
loathing. This was where Simon had tortured Jimmy. Bile
rose in her throat when her eyes settled on the iron maiden,
the door to the casket ajar but empty now.*
   *Against her will, Meghann remembered when that foul con-
traption had contained the body of her lover. Was it her imagination or did she see small drops of blood glistening on the
brutal spikes in the door of the iron maiden? Jimmy's
blood . . . how it must have hurt when those spikes settled
into his flesh as Simon slammed the door shut and how Jimmy
must have screamed. . . .*
   *"No, please, no. I don't want to see!" Meghann pleaded
with whatever force, be it her subconscious or something
stronger, used her dreams to drag her back to this awful place.*
   *"Look carefully at this room, Banrion," a somber voice
intoned behind her, and Meghann spun around to see Alcuin
standing in the center of the room, his gentle brown eyes filled
with sorrow and pity while he addressed her. "This chamber
is a perfect reflection of Simon Baldevar's soul—dark, bleak,
twisted, and capable of any cruelty to gain what he wants.
Is that the kind of man you want to raise your child with?"*
   *"Don't you lecture me on what kind of man Simon is,"
Meghann fired back, for the first time addressing Alcuin without the utmost respect and love. She wasn't won over by his
addressing her with the pet name of Banrion; she remembered*

all Simon had told her. "Even he doesn't prey on pregnant women."

"What Guy did to you last night was despicable," Alcuin said, and Meghann had never seen his gentle eyes look so sad. "I would never deny that and I will not allow him to go on thinking he did it for me. But he was not the one that caused this situation. Guy, like everyone else, is terrified of Lord Baldevar. That terror brought all the flaws in Guy's soul to the surface. I am not trying to excuse Guy—he will suffer for his behavior. But I do not believe he would have hurt you if Lord Baldevar hadn't made you conceive."

"Would you have hurt me because Simon made me conceive?" Meghann demanded angrily. "Was Simon right—were you going to stand by and let me die without telling me I needed his blood to survive?"

"Never," Alcuin said firmly. "Lord Baldevar achieving the philosophers' stone may present a grave threat to all that oppose him but I would never sanction your death to neutralize that threat. Meghann, you are an innocent in all of this. I know that wicked fiend forced himself upon you. . . ."

Meghann sagged against the iron maiden. "Alcuin, that's a lie. Simon . . . he didn't force himself on me that night. . . ."

"No!" Alcuin came to her side, clutching her arms with a grip that hurt even in a dream. "Banrion, brute strength isn't the only way to rape a woman. Never underestimate Lord Baldevar's cleverness. I know what he did to you that night . . . he found every vulnerable, soft corner in your mind and exploited them all ruthlessly. I know he took advantage of your fear and uncertainty and when you lay weeping before him, he took you."

Meghann shook her head. "I was crying because he made me see that part of me . . . part of me loves him." There— she'd said it. Part of her loved Simon Baldevar; always had, always would.

Alcuin took her hands in his. "Banrion, trust me when I tell you what you feel is not love. You're simply very vulnerable right now and your vulnerability makes you reach out for any kind of comfort. But I beg you, do not turn to Simon Baldevar for solace. Remember the monster that lurks beneath the soft facade he's adopted in an attempt to win your heart. All his sweet, tender words and gestures are false. He doesn't love you, because he's incapable of love. Once you have the child, he'll destroy you . . . if not by killing you outright, then by making your soul as bleak and shattered as his own. Lord Baldevar is a vampire in every sense of the word. He will take everything from you, suck you dry, and leave you with nothing. Please don't give him your heart."

Alcuin's words cut into her like a knife. She couldn't bear to think that Simon was lying to her, that he didn't love her as he claimed, that the wonderful sense of peace she had when he held her close and soothed her fears was nothing but a calculated ruse to make her trust him.

"Oh," Meghann gasped. The thought of Simon not loving her . . . why hadn't she seen it before? Seen what kind of pain she must have put him through when she screamed that she hated him? She must have ripped his heart out when she was ready to walk out after thirteen years of professing to love him with all her heart and soul. How would she have felt if he'd been the one to turn her away all those years before?

Horrible, Meghann realized. Hurt and furious, but like him, she'd have been too proud to let him see her pain. No, she too would have thought of nothing but revenge—of hurting him as badly as he hurt her.

"I'm a fool," Meghann said, her voice dull and toneless. "This room, all the pain and death . . . Jimmy Delacroix . . . it's all my fault. I shouldn't have left Simon, I should have stayed with him and then everyone would be safe. . . ."

"Where would you be?" Alcuin demanded, and she still saw no anger or disappointment in his gentle eyes. "Dead? Resigned to your fate?"

"In love," Meghann told him. "Don't you see, Alcuin? Maybe I do long for things Simon can't or won't give me but I do love him. I wish to God I didn't but I do."

"You don't love him—it's simply lust and his blood in you."

"No!" she howled. "No, no! I love him . . . I don't know why, but I do. Maybe there's something twisted and bent inside me, but I do love him and I'm tired of denying it."

"Banrion, no. You're in shock—you don't know what you're saying. I know you . . . you'll feel very differently when you no longer need his blood. Then you'll see him for what he is and when you do, Banrion, you can destroy him if you'll just let me work through you. After you have your child, allow my spirit to enter your body and you'll finally be able to live without the threat of Lord Baldevar hanging over your head."

Now Meghann understood—she knew why Alcuin had come to her. He needed someone living so he could possess their body with his own strength to behead Simon Baldevar. Who better for the position than the only person in the world Simon wanted to trust—Meghann O'Neill, the mother of his child? Besides, with Meghann's gift for summoning, it would be very easy for Alcuin's spirit to enter her body.

"You only came to me tonight because you want to use me," she accused, ignoring the pain in Alcuin's expression. "All you care about is killing Simon—you could give less of a damn if he makes my soul as bleak and shattered as his own. Go away! Find someone else to carry on your holy war against Simon Baldevar."

Alcuin tried to grab her, and she clawed at him furiously. "Let me go! Leave me the hell alone! Why can't all of you leave me alone? If you want Simon dead, do it yourself! Leave me alone. I want out of here. Simon! Simon, help me!"

She felt a harsh slap on her cheek. "Wake up!"

Meghann sat up with a start, green eyes darting about wildly. Simon was leaning over her, the fury in his expression making her shake until she realized it wasn't directed at her.

Meghann felt her own anger. How dare Alcuin presume to tell her Simon's love was false or that she shouldn't put her faith in him! Who answered her last night, saved her from a demon she couldn't control, and delivered her from a madman that wanted to destroy her and her innocent child? Why should she continue to deny Simon when the only time she truly felt secure and happy was when she was with him? Because Alcuin insisted Simon would destroy her? Ha! It was Alcuin's fanatic lapdog that had tried to kill her, not Simon Baldevar.

A small voice tried to remind her of the evil Simon did to mortals but Meghann suppressed it ruthlessly. Why should she worry about the fate of humans she didn't know when every vampire in the world wanted to hunt her down for conceiving the philosophers' stone and the one person that could protect her was looking down at her so lovingly? Her conscience stabbed her when she realized that she was not overly concerned with how Simon dealt with others, as long as he treated her well and protected the baby.

Meghann put her hand on the small, star-shaped scar above his heart, the permanent mark of the stake she'd impaled him with. "Simon, do you think we could start over?"

"I've waited forty years for you to come back to me." Simon caressed her cheek, amber eyes probing hers until she felt exposed to her soul. "But Alcuin told you one true thing. My love for you does not change what I am. If you want to be my consort, you must be willing to give me the same things I demanded the night I transformed you—your heart and soul. Are you willing to give me all I want?"

"Are you willing to treat me like a woman and not a toy?" Meghann asked back and Simon laughed, pushing her back into the silk and velvet cerise pillows on the bed.

"Lie back and let me show you how well I can treat you," he murmured, wrapping his strong hands in her hair.

Eagerly, Meghann wrapped her arms around his

neck and he kissed her hungrily, seeming to ask how much of herself she was willing to give.

Everything, she thought hazily. *Take me, make me yours again.* She arched her neck, smiling when Simon's lips left hers to seek out the creamy flesh of her neck.

"It won't hurt the baby?" she asked anxiously.

"I'll only taste you, Meghann . . . not take enough to weaken you."

"Oh, God," she breathed when his blood teeth pierced her so gently she hardly felt any pain. All she felt was exquisite pleasure pulsating through her body as he drank from her. Meghann leaned back, feeling a delicious lassitude build inside her along with a lust that screamed out for Simon to take more, drink all of her . . .

With a small groan, Simon pulled away from her. "I'm not done, little one," he promised when her hands reached out to guide him back to her neck. He pressed down on the punctures, allowing a small amount of blood to flow into a crystal wineglass he held to her neck.

Simon took a bit of the ruby liquid from the glass, and spread it on her nipples. Meghann howled in pleasure and felt her body on the brink of climax as he sucked the blood off her breasts with slow, lazy strokes of his tongue that made her cry out and push his head down on her body. It had been so long, too long. She'd missed having a vampire lover; no mortal man could combine sex and blood lust for this unbearable pleasure. . . .

"Hurry," she moaned.

Simon raised his head and gave her a sardonic grin. "Little girl, I have waited forty years to have you like this. Do you think I would ruin this moment with haste? Keep quiet and relearn the exquisite value of patience."

Her eyes widened as she watched him cover her body in blood, making a crimson path from her breasts past her navel. His tongue followed the blood path leisurely, lingering at her stomach, the changes in her body and the hard mound of his child beneath his hands, the tiny life growing inside her.

He used the blood to reacquaint himself with every inch of her . . . painting long scarlet strokes over her legs that the tip of his tongue removed, nibbling at the arches of her feet, toes . . .

"Please," Meghann begged.

Simon looked up, holding the glass over her with a challenging grin. "Tell me where to put the blood, sweetheart."

Meeting his smirk with a bold glance, Meghann took the crystal glass and splashed the blood between her legs. "Lick it up."

Simon pushed her into the bed and bowed his chestnut head to her.

"Yes," she whimpered, feeling pleasure wash over her as he teased her again, licking with wicked slowness at the soft, needy flesh between her legs. "Oh, God, yes!"

Simon gave her a triumphant smile and pulled her beneath him, plunging so deep into her she almost thought he'd touch the child in her womb.

Meghann clawed at him and spread her legs wide, meeting each wild thrust with one of her own. She'd forgotten how good it was between them . . . forgotten how Simon made her the object of his complete attention, seemed to devote himself to her pleasure while at the same time he took everything in her, made her give more of herself than anyone else ever had.

Afterward, Meghann sprawled on top of her lover, and he smiled up at her flushed cheeks, bruised lips, and languid green eyes. "Feeling bleak and shattered, my pet?"

Meghann laughed, feeling nothing but an idiotic grin on her face and an urge to spin round and round, like a top.

"I'm happy," she murmured against his chest, a little surprised by that simple truth. When had her hatred for Simon Baldevar evaporated into nothingness? Was it because of the daily feedings that increased the link between them, the fact that he'd saved her life? Or had she, in her secret heart, never stopped loving him?

Simon plucked her up off the bed. "You shall be even happier, I promise you. Now it is time to get up out of that bed, wench. We have a long evening ahead of us."

Meghann glanced down at the huge tester bed, the wildly strewn sheets liberally splashed with blood—someone would think there'd been a massacre in this bed instead of two vampires tearing into each other.

"Maybe I want a long evening here," she suggested lasciviously. It had been so long since she'd been able to enjoy blood and sex at the same time. She reached out to stroke his arm. "You're the only vampire I've ever—"

"I know," Simon said, kissing her lightly. "And you will have many chances to lie with this vampire again but not now, sweet. Come along, I have some surprises for you."

"Max!" Meghann squealed when Simon threw open the door to an adjoining dressing room and her Irish setter joyfully bounded toward her, putting both paws on her shoulders.

"What a good dog," Meghann praised and then gave Simon a questioning glance. "Why is he here?" When she left New York, Meghann had put Max in the care of a house sitter, bringing him to Las Vegas only after Lee assured her he'd welcome the dog.

Simon put his hand out to the dog, allowing him to sniff cautiously. "I may be an evil fiend, but I'm not a tyrant, Meghann. How could you live here without your pet? I told Vinny to bring this charming fellow along with all your other things while we slept."

Meghann raised her eyebrows. "Who gave you permission to do that?" Just because she'd wanted to stay with Simon last night when she was so frightened didn't mean she'd had any plans to live with him.

"My dear, did you think I'd be satisfied with—what is the phrase?—a one-night stand? From now on, you stay with me. If our renewed passion weren't reason enough, I would think Guy's attack demonstrated how vulnerable you are. Of course, I blame myself for that entirely . . . indulging your childish need for freedom."

"Childish need for freedom!" she screeched, and Max backed away from Simon's hand, whining uncertainly. "You archaic swine, I'll have you know it isn't 'childish' for a woman to want the freedom to—"

"Meghann, you are not unintelligent so I can only assume you are not thinking clearly. Guy Balmont may be dead, but there are plenty of others, some of my own spawn, that are jealous of the way I favor you, who would try to kill you if they discovered you're pregnant. The only way I can keep you safe is to keep you near me. Besides, I told you a long time ago that your home is with me. Now, are you going to behave yourself or do I have to tie you down to keep you here?"

"Why, Simon," Meghann purred, "since when have you needed safety as a reason to tie me up?"

Simon grinned and took her hand, escorting her to a spacious, plant-filled bathroom. "I'll take that sultry look as acquiescence. Wash quickly, darling, and see if you can find in all those rags Vinny stored in your closets an outfit suitable for an evening out."

"My clothes are not rags!" she protested heatedly. "Don't go thinking you can go back to telling me what I can and can't wear. I won't have some overdressed fop dictating my outfits to me."

"Denim and those garish T-shirts do nothing for you. My sweet, have you no idea how lovely you are? When we lived together, I did not insist that you dress elegantly simply to be arbitrary. You are a beautiful woman and I wish to see you in clothes that complement that beauty." Seeing Meghann's eyes soften at the compliment, Simon pinched her cheek playfully and issued one more directive. "Get dressed, little one, and meet me in the bedroom when you're done."

Meghann entered the bedroom a half-hour later. "Do you approve, my lord?" She spun around gracefully, holding her hands away from her body so he could see how the high-necked, sleeveless bronze jersey clung to her lush curves. She knew the dull gold color of the gown brought out the copper highlights in her hair, which she'd placed high on her head in an Edwardian upsweep she knew Simon liked. A pair of oversize gold hoop earrings and the cabochon bracelet he'd just given her completed the ensemble.

"You dazzle me," Simon said. "Now, will this overdressed fop complement you?"

"You'll do," Meghann teased as she inspected the superbly tailored navy suit. Privately, she thought Simon was the best-dressed man she'd ever seen, combining the urbane elegance of his formal wardrobe with that broad-shouldered, powerful form.

"My dear, if you keep looking at me like that, I doubt we'll ever leave this room. But you are too bare to go out."

"Too bare?" she asked in bafflement. "What are you talking about?"

"Your hands, my pet. They are utterly naked." Simon reached behind her ear. "Now what could this be?" He opened his fist.

"Oh!" Meghann gasped at the emerald signet ring.

Simon got down on one knee, holding the ring out to her. "Meghann O'Neill, will you marry me?"

"You . . . you never asked me to marry you before," was the only thing she could think of to say.

"You never carried my child before. I am old-fashioned enough to want legitimate issue. More important, you defied Alcuin. The only way I can think of to honor you for choosing me over him is by offering you my name. Be my bride, sweetheart."

Her eyes darkened as she stared at the ring, and the man kneeling before her. How much had her feelings changed if she would even consider marrying him? This was it . . . if she accepted, it made all their time apart and all the things she'd stood for meaningless.

No, Meghann decided. It didn't, it couldn't do that. Admitting she loved Simon Baldevar didn't mean turning her back on all she'd done, on all the people she'd come to love during the forty years they'd been apart . . . did it?

"Meghann," Simon said when she simply stood and stared at the ring. "Why do you hesitate? Are you frightened?"

"Of course I am. I'm scared of the way you can make me love you, make me forget everyone I ever cared about . . . make me forget how I promised to honor Alcuin's code. I don't want Alcuin to be right— you can't leave me with nothing."

"Of course I can't. I wouldn't want to. Listen to me. I think your morals are foolish, but I am not going to force anything upon you. All I want is your love and loyalty. Give me that and you may keep your ideals . . . the ones that nosy cleric said I'd steal away. Keep your friend Charles . . . you may even continue to work on healing Jimmy Delacroix if you feel you have some obligation to him." Simon smiled at her openmouthed shock. "Now, will you marry me?"

"Why are you letting Jimmy live?" she demanded suspiciously.

"Would you prefer I did not?" Under his soft tone, Meghann caught the edge to his voice and knew Jimmy might be dead in the next few minutes if she didn't drop the subject. He had said she could continue to work on healing Jimmy—his reasons for that would remain his own. Simon never allowed anyone, even her, to be privy to his thoughts or motives, never let anyone get too close to him. Maybe this marriage proposal was a small step toward changing that; maybe as her husband Simon would share more of himself with her.

"What happens after Jimmy recovers?" Meghann asked. Was Simon only offering her this sop because he thought Jimmy was beyond help?

"You will tell him all that has happened between us—or I will. I rather doubt he'll still wish to remain with you after that. Not that it should matter to you . . . if you love me."

"I do love you."

"Then why do you hesitate?" Simon held out the ring again.

Meghann reached out to stroke his thick, elegantly waved hair. "I'll marry you," she said softly, pushing from her mind the thought of what Charles would say. Would he hate her now? If the shoe were on the other foot, she wouldn't turn him away. *Please,* she prayed. *Please let me somehow keep Charles's friendship.*

"Come along, child," Simon said, distracting her from her worry. "If we are to be married, you must purchase a ring for me."

"No," she said and smiled, determining that if she was going to do this crazy thing, it wouldn't be a half-hearted gesture. "There's a perfectly good ring for you right here." She went over to the bureau, and plucked her father's ring from the ivory jewelry box where Simon had carefully set it down the night before.

She turned back to him, the plain gold wedding band extended toward him in her outstretched hand. "I wouldn't have this ring or my life or my child's life if it wasn't for you. I can't think of any better way to put the past behind us and show you how much I love you than by giving you my father's ring. I know it's not very expensive or elaborate but it would mean a lot to me if you wore it."

Simon blinked rapidly, and then pulled her to him in a bone-crushing embrace. His voice sounded husky when he told her, "I would be honored." She wondered if she heard tears in his voice, but then he pushed her away and his eyes were clear. He smiled and said, "Your father would approve, Meghann. He wanted me to marry you."

"How can you know that?" she asked. "You only met my father once."

"As you may recall, he asked you to leave the room so he could speak to me privately. Once he ascertained that my intentions were honorable, he told me he was quite relieved you'd met someone a bit older . . . of course, he didn't know how much older. At any rate, he said you were a 'great kid' but high-strung, stubborn, and impulsive. He thought you'd run roughshod over a husband your own age, and ultimately wind up being quite unhappy with a henpecked man. Your father said you needed someone who could love you but be firm when you needed it." Simon grinned and took her arm. "Now, isn't it fortunate we're in Las Vegas? The marriage license bureau is open until midnight— yes, we're having a legal ceremony."

"No justice of the peace or Elvis impersonators," Meghann protested, and Simon laughed, nodding his agreement. "Wait—I know the perfect place! That rustic little chapel next to the Sands? Do you know it?"

"The Church of the West—of course I know it," he replied. "It's a lovely choice, sweetheart."

Simon smiled and linked his arm through Meghann's. She smiled back, thinking Alcuin had to be wrong—it would be impossible to fake the soft happiness shining in those gold eyes. And no blood link or clever manipulation would be able to make her feel thrilled, nervous, cautious, bold, and utterly secure all at once. That feeling, Meghann knew, only came from being in love.

TWELVE

"Do we look like a pair of lovesick fools?" Meghann giggled after dinner when their waiter, with a soft smile and flourish, presented them with a chocolate torte that spelled out *congratulations* with crème anglaise.

"This city caters to lovesick fools. I've missed you, Meghann," Simon said, suddenly looking grave.

Meghann returned his stare, not wanting to lie and say she'd missed him too—anger and fear had prevented that. But now, seeing the way his amber eyes glowed in the candlelight as he smiled down at her, none of it—their estrangement, Alcuin, Jimmy— seemed real. It was as if they'd gone back in time; she felt as in love with him as she had the night he transformed her.

"It's so romantic here," she said instead, sliding closer to Simon on the tapestried banquette. Fiore's was everything Charles and Lee had promised, with its dark, charming interior and soft jazz playing in the background. Charles and Lee . . .

"Oh, no!" Meghann exclaimed and started pawing through her beaded evening bag. She shoved aside the marriage license that officially made her Lady Baldevar and fished out her cellular phone. "I was supposed to call Charles last night. He must be worried to death. I have to get in touch with him."

"No," Simon said flatly.

"What do you mean—no?" Meghann demanded, her eyes sending warning sparks at him.

"Sweetheart," Simon said pleasantly, "how did you surprise Guy last night?"

"Because he didn't know about you—Guy was shocked when I called out for you. But I don't understand . . . shouldn't the Council know that I'd be dead by now if I wasn't drinking your blood? I mean, if you stole Lucian's diary from Alcuin—"

"I believe Alcuin kept the secrets of *Infans Noctis* to himself. In the other accounts, the women didn't sicken as you did so they were able to continue feeding from mortals throughout their pregnancy. That's why Guy and the Council couldn't know you needed me to feed you—they still don't. They also don't know that I saved you last night, that I'm aware of your pregnancy, or even that you survived Guy's attack. They know nothing so when Guy fails to reappear at Ballnamore, the Council will have no choice but to come here and seek clues. I want to flush them out of their little sanctuary."

"Oh," Meghann said, understanding. Ballnamore was still protected ground . . . Simon couldn't set foot on the estate. But once those vampires left their stronghold, he could destroy them. "But what does all this have to do with me not contacting Charles?"

"Have you figured out yet that they learned of your pregnancy by reading his thoughts the few nights he was at Ballnamore?"

Meghann nodded and Simon smiled at her. "Good. You and your friend are both rather resourceful and stronger than one might expect, given your age. But the fact remains you are simply too young to shield your thoughts from a much older vampire in your bloodline if you're under enough duress. Doctor Tarleton's worry over you makes him vulnerable. That's why if you get in touch with him and the Council comes nosing around here, they will immediately know of my plans."

Meghann blanched, remembering what Guy tried to do to her the night before. "But I can't not warn Charles. Don't you think when they come here they might try and torture him—or Lee—to find out where I am?"

"Sweetheart, that is why you cannot tell him anything. If they find him and read his thoughts, a quick glance at his mind will show them he knows nothing—mortals call it plausible deniability. On the other hand, if they find some spot in his thoughts that indicates he's hiding something, they may very well put him or his lover through hell to make him confess. Trust me, Meghann. I have deflected attacks and planned battle strategies for longer than either of you has been alive. Isn't it better for your friend to feel some anxiety for a few nights rather than lose his life?"

"What if he comes over to your house?" Meghann could see the logic in Simon's arguments—the Council wouldn't harm Charles if he knew nothing. And without any knowledge of Guy's attack, she knew her friend well enough to guess he'd only fear that she'd fallen under Simon's spell and was avoiding him out of shame.

"We won't be here," Simon replied. "After all, I'd be a poor husband if I didn't give my lovely bride a honeymoon. We'll return in a few weeks and end all this distasteful business with Alcuin's lapdogs. Why did your faithful companion and his lover go to San Francisco, anyway?"

Meghann explained about the convention, a mischievous smile lighting up her face. "Charles didn't want to leave me alone with you but I said he should because I wanted to learn how to fend you off by myself."

Simon raised an eyebrow and allowed one finger to

trail behind her ear. "Do you still wish to fend me off, wife?"

Meghann giggled, feeling a ridiculous sense of shyness when Simon called her his wife. "Isn't that what all your wives did—fend you off?"

"It is in shockingly poor taste to refer to my other spouses on our wedding night," he reproved and tweaked her nose. "Alice did not fend me off. Rather, I spent all my time cowering from the horrors of performing my marital duties with that unappetizing mound of lard. Isabelle I married solely to protect my hard-earned fortune. Marrying for love—you are a refreshing change, my third and final bride." Simon leaned closer and gave Meghann a wicked grin. "Now, my love, I have a special treat for you. What say you we go to the Seraglio and make use of the honeymoon suite?"

"You mean you'll take me to your hotel . . . where all the rooms are designed like harems?" she said, her coy tone undermined by smoldering green eyes. "Do you want a slave girl . . . *master?*"

The open lust in his gaze made her shiver and wait in a state of delicious tension while he settled the bill.

At last, Simon turned to her and took her hand, licking the palm. "Little concubine, come with me and see if you can enslave your master."

"Did you really have a harem in Istanbul?" Meghann asked drowsily after three solid hours of lovemaking. She stretched, feeling an exquisite pain in every muscle, and rested her head against her lover's shoulder, lapping at some blood still dripping from the punctures she'd made in his neck.

"I had everything a wealthy merchant in sixteenth-century Istanbul could desire," Simon replied and gathered her up off the enormous square bed with its elaborately carved pillars and canopy that sat on a dais within the center of the room. He carried her to a pretty blue-and-white-tiled circular pool in a corner of the room, settling down in the cool water with her still cradled against his chest.

"Was the real Istanbul anything like this?" she asked, taking in the plush suite with its elegant walls of pale wood and tiles placed every few feet to make a thistle design. Idly, Meghann wondered how much it cost to stay in this suite with its silver hooded fireplace, brightly colored Turkish carpets soft enough to sleep on, ebony inlaid with mother-of-pearl furniture, and fresh floral arrangements in elegant copper bowls strewn throughout the rooms. As a majority shareholder, Simon hadn't paid for the room. Instead, he went behind the reservations desk and helped himself to the key card for the suite.

"A bit," Simon replied, seeming to take the room in through her eyes. "If anything, the real thing was more luxurious. I cannot tell you what it was like to go from a drafty, crumbling manor in northern England to owning a magnificent house that boasted exquisite marble fountains, a garden filled with almond and apricot trees, flowers of radiant colors I'd never seen before, and that was only the exterior!" Simon laughed. "Sweetheart, I had doors carved of gold, wide expanses of glass I'd never dreamed of back in my medieval home, furniture inlaid with precious gems, and with all that luxury, I was merely considered a prosperous merchant."

"Were you happy there?"

"At that point, I couldn't conceive of wanting anything else. In Istanbul, I had everything I'd been denied growing up . . . a palatial home filled with every luxury, beautiful women to serve me, and since religion meant nothing to me, I had no trouble abandoning Christianity and embracing Allah. As a Muslim, I could serve the Ottoman. In time, I'm sure I could have been one of his viziers and then I might have allowed myself to have sons, knowing I could provide them with wealth and prestige."

"You became a Muslim? So that's how an English nobleman born in the sixteenth century came to be circumcised . . . I always wondered about that. Did it hurt?"

"I do not count the experience as one of my more pleasant memories."

"But why would you go through all that pain if—"

"That must be our champagne," Simon said at the hard rap to the hotel door and threw on the black silk robe he'd informed Meghann came to all guests complementary of the hotel.

Meghann smiled at his retreating back, and leaned back in the pool. Her naughty thoughts at what she'd like to do when Simon returned were interrupted by a booming male voice at the door.

"How's this for room service? Get waited on by the chairman of the board himself. You gonna tell me what you've got in there?" a cheerful interrogator, possessed of a strong Texas twang, asked Simon. "I sure hope it ain't Louise you're romancing with a three-hundred-dollar bottle of champagne."

"Not what, Del, but who," she heard Simon reply. "My bride, Meghann."

"Bride! When in the hell did you get married? Don't answer, I know you've got better things to do on your wedding night than talk to an old coot like me so I'll meet your gal some other time. Congratulations, partner. Think I'll go hunt up that round heels of ours. I can barely wait to see the look on her face when she finds out a multimillionaire just slipped through her fingers."

"Who was that cowboy?" Meghann asked while Simon poured champagne into two elegant crystal flutes.

"Del Straker, my darling—chief shareholder of this fine establishment. That 'cowboy' also owns most of Texas and a substantial chunk of the fast-food industry.

A few years back, he persuaded me to invest in the 'new' Las Vegas after your government succeeded in running the organized crime chieftains out of town."

"Why did he call Louise your round heels?" Meghann inquired, slowly sipping the champagne. Delicious though it was, she didn't intend to have more than one glass. While her bloodstream might be immune to feeling the affects of alcohol, there was no way of determining whether it would affect the baby's development.

"Louise is a private joke between us. Our casino manager is retiring soon and his ambitious assistant is dividing her favors between Del because he is the chairman of our board of directors and myself because I control the largest share of stock in the hotel after him."

"So she thinks if she screws the two of you, she'll become the next casino manager?" At Simon's nod, Meghann said, "Will she?"

"Good Lord, no. She'd be merely competent while the woman we've lured from Bally's is among the best in town."

"Did that woman have to sleep with you too?"

"Don't be ridiculous. Only an imbecile allows sex to interfere with business. I hire my mortal employees based on merit—no other consideration. Have you any other questions before we may abandon this dull subject?"

Rather than reply, Meghann splashed the rest of her champagne over his chest, running her tongue over the glistening mass of water and Perrier Jouet.

"Oh, wait," she said innocently, abandoning the pleasant work the moment she felt his arms tighten around her. Lazily, Meghann pushed herself to the other end of the small pool and pretended great interest in the shooting jet of water behind her. "I do have another question but it's not about Louise. You constantly tell me that you loved Istanbul; the superior

medical care, certainly the hygiene was better than the
hideous state of affairs in England, you had the wealth
and position you'd always wanted, you were willing to
let someone cut off your foreskin to fit into Turkish
society—why on earth did you decide to come back to
England and usurp Roger after all that?"

Simon stretched and pulled her back toward him,
rubbing her sensitive breasts against his hard, muscled
chest. "Are you still presuming anything Alcuin told
you of my history is true? Wait, let me guess. He told
you I was greedy and power-mad, that I simply couldn't
live without snatching my brother's title and slaughtering him."

Meghann nodded, and Simon shook with laughter.
"Sweetheart, it was my foolish brother's greed that
made me return home. You remember my brother did
not know Father Bain was my ally? Well, the idiot spoke
freely to him. I should explain that my partner, Sir
John, died in 1586 and his heirs were eager to sell his
share of the trading company we'd founded together.
I'd made a reasonable offer and expected it would only
be a matter of time before we arrived at an agreement.
Then, Father Bain wrote to tell me Roger had doubled
my last offer. He intended to buy Sir John's shares and
then toss me out."

"But you built that business," Meghann argued,
though the strong hands fondling her body made
thinking not only difficult, but seem an unnecessary
waste of time. "He did nothing but sit in England and
collect money. You're the one that went to Algiers and
then Turkey and traded and bought new ships and
had them target the Spanish Main, seize wealth in the
New World . . ."

"Knowing all that, do you think I'd stand by and
allow Roger to rip everything I'd built from me?"

"Of course not," Meghann said and clasped his
waist with her legs.

"I made plans to return home and get that idiot

out of my life once and for all. But while I was making preparations, fate played into my hands. You know I returned to England in 1588? What else happened to England that year besides the monumental event of my homecoming?"

Meghann thought for a moment and then her eyes widened. "The Armada! The Spanish navy tried to invade England but the English fleet defeated them."

"Indeed we did."

"We?" Meghann asked and then she grinned. "That's right—you told me you were knighted during the Armada crisis. What did you do?"

"First, I donated six of my ten ships to the queen's service. I piloted my own ship in Drake's offensive off the Flemish coast and received my knighthood for initiating the attack against the *San Martin*—the flagship of the Armada battalion."

Simon impaled her on him, guiding her hips up and down while he continued to lecture like a history professor in a dry, almost bored tone. "Of course, that gave me instant entry to Elizabeth's court and I soon became a favored courtier. The queen intimated on more than one occasion that she would not mind if my still Catholic brother that clung to the old ways met with an early demise. You must understand, Meghann, that the north of England was still almost feudal . . . completely behind the times and likely to embrace any wild plot to overthrow Bess. The queen needed powerful men she could trust in the north so the death of a fanatically Catholic baron needn't be investigated too closely as long as his younger brother was discreet in disposing of him."

"Yes," Meghann cried out, the word having nothing to do with agreement. She arched her back, bouncing wildly for some minutes before she leaned in to attack his jugular vein. There was nothing like it, feeling the blood pour down her throat while her body rocked from the force of her climax.

"I haven't taken too much blood from you tonight?" Meghann asked afterward.

Simon laughed and pulled her out of the pool, sitting her on his knee while he dried her off. "You did not seem overly concerned a few moments ago. Rest easy, little one. I drained Guy almost to death last night . . . you cannot weaken me tonight."

Dry, Meghann plucked up a towel and ran it over him, allowing her hands to linger at the bulging muscles in his arms and chest. What was it about Simon Baldevar that made her so wild, so out of control whenever she looked him? Granted, he was divine to look at with his thick, wavy hair, mesmerizing eyes, and hard body but so were any number of men. Why did she burn for his touch and then when she received it only want him more? What was it about him that made her willing to forsake everything just to be with him?

"Meghann." Simon sat her between his legs, brushing out her long, wet hair with one of the tortoiseshell combs she'd used to put her hair up. "Stop letting my uncle's dire warnings upset you. You'll see, darling. You don't have to forsake anything to be my bride."

"Why did you force Isabelle to be your bride?" she asked, still disturbed by the notion that he'd forced his brother's widow to marry him for no better reason than unrequited lust. "I can see why you murdered Roger and I know people were a bit more cutthroat in your time, that your morals are probably more, uh, flexible than mine. But why were you so obsessed with Isabelle?"

"I know my uncle told you I was in love with my brother's wife and I only transformed you because you resemble her but that is not true."

"It's more than a resemblance," Meghann pouted, remembering the oil painting Alcuin showed her of Isabelle. She was still rankled by the thought that Simon might have transformed her merely because she reminded him of a woman that spurned him four centuries before.

"Meghann, you needn't envy my deceased wife. First, anyone with half an eye would see that what appears to be a great likeness between you both is not that strong at all. Isabelle may have had red hair and fine features but a woman's beauty tends to be determined by her character. Sweetheart, you shine and capture my heart because of that dazzling vibrancy of yours—that wonderful passion that makes you reach out to take all life can give you with both hands. It makes you glow, turns you from being merely pretty into a ravishing beauty. Isabelle not only lacked your vitality, she did not have one other characteristic that might have redeemed her in my eyes . . . no mind, no wit, no touch of humor to her. Not only wasn't I in love with her, I actively disliked the woman. Here, get dressed."

Meghann accepted her bronze jersey and started dressing while Simon continued to talk. "Even so, I was prepared to be fair in my dealings with her once Roger was deceased. I would never contest the two-thirds' share of the estate a widow traditionally received at her husband's death. She could take her money, the son she'd born Roger, and leave with my blessing."

"This zipper is stuck," Meghann complained. "You broke it when you tore my dress off."

Simon held up his light blue silk shirt for her inspection . . . pointing to the many torn-off buttons. He came behind her, and fixed the unruly zipper.

"So why did you wind up marrying her?" Meghann asked.

"I'll tell you in a moment. First, we must decide where to go for our honeymoon. All our talk of my past leaves me homesick. What say you to going to a hunting lodge I have in the Yorkshire Dales? I'd like to take you on horseback rides along the cliffs and rolling hills covered in mist and heather. We can take your dog along—he'll have a fine time running through the moors."

"I'd love it!" Meghann said but then she quieted. "But what about . . ."

"Thank you for not ruining this night by mentioning him by name. There's stationery in the living room, Meghann. Write down for Vinny the precise dosage of drug to blood and he'll see that your 'patient' continues to receive his treatment while we're away."

"When are we leaving?" Meghann asked. "How are we leaving? No, wait. I bet you own your own plane."

"Lear jet," Simon replied. "It will take us to London in an hour. There's no need to pack, we'll buy whatever we need in London and York. I'll call Vinny and have him bring Max to the airport."

"So why did you marry Isabelle if you hated her so much?" Meghann asked while Simon pulled the ragged remains of his shirt on and buttoned the navy blazer to hide the damage.

"When my brother lay slain before me, his wife took it upon herself to explain why Roger wanted to cut me out. Apparently he was dying and the leech told him he had only a few months to put his affairs in order. So Roger made out a will that left everything in Isabelle's control until his son, Michael, reached his majority and left me more penniless than a beggar in Whitechapel. It seems while I was off fighting for England, Roger got his hands on Sir John's share of the company. Of course, I had what gold I'd managed to save but everything I'd built up was now being torn from me."

Meghann saw his eyes darken to copper with remembered fury, and sympathized with him. Alcuin didn't mention any of this when he portrayed Simon as a power-mad, ruthless scoundrel that murdered his brother for the hell of it.

"Roger was an idiot!" she said firmly, and Simon's

eyes lightened when he grinned at her. "Well, I mean maybe if he'd at least left you the trading company . . ."

"Yes, I might have been content. But to have my livelihood placed in the hands of some ignorant woman that could barely add and subtract without assistance . . . I had to marry her to reclaim my property."

"How did you get Elizabeth to allow you to marry Isabelle?" Meghann asked. "I thought there were laws in place that said you couldn't go around marrying your dead brother's wife."

Simon smiled and made a shushing gesture when he started speaking to Vinny on his small cellular phone while they waited for the elevator. Meghann couldn't help but notice that he was far more detailed and concerned sounding when he spoke of Max's care than Jimmy's.

"What you were referring to, little one," Simon said after he finished the conversation with his servant, "were the laws of consanguinity . . . what King Henry the Eighth used to annul his marriage to Catherine of Aragon. When you have wealth and a powerful queen on your side, though, any law can be bent to your will. Any suspicions I had that Elizabeth wanted my brother and one last bastion of Catholic resistance in the north dead were confirmed when she did not even order an inquest into my brother's death. Instead, she matched me to Isabelle and decreed that her dowry would be the trading company my brother left her. Then, Elizabeth gave me her final boon—something I had not expected at all. She raised me from mere knight to the rank of earl. From that day on, I was Lord Simon Baldevar, Earl of Lecarrow." The parking valet returned with the Bentley and Simon handed him some cash before opening the door for Meghann.

At a stoplight, Simon took Meghann's hand, running one finger over the emerald signet ring. "That ring, little one, came from Elizabeth Tudor's hand. She told me I'd foster my dynasty on the body of the woman that wore it. She was right—four hundred years in the future—but right all the same."

Meghann's eyes darkened, remembering one final bit of Simon's mortal history that disturbed her, that made her question her decision to raise her child with him.

"Simon," she said haltingly, looking out the window instead of at him, "why did you have to murder Michael? Just because Isabelle miscarried, did you have to pay her back by killing her innocent child?"

"Meghann."

She looked over at him, shocked by the desolate, ragged sound of his voice.

"Meghann," he said again, and her breath caught at the sorrow reflected in his eyes—she'd never seen him look like that. "It's suited me these past four centuries to allow the world to believe I murdered my nephew because I wanted to break Isabelle. Understand that what I tell you tonight is for your ears only. I did not arrange that child's death because I hated him. Rather, I did it out of love."

Love? Meghann thought incredulously while he guided the car to the landing strip at McCarran Airport. She accepted that Simon Baldevar was different from her, that his code of ethics (if you could call it that) was something she might never understand, but telling her love made him kill a child?

Meghann allowed Simon to lead her to the private bedroom of his jet, a long room paneled in brightly polished oak with no windows. She sat down on the edge of the king-size bed, petting Max's head and wondering what kind of madness allowed her to accept this man in her life again.

"What would you do if Max contracted distemper and developed encephalitis?"

"You mean brain damage? Why, I . . . I'd put him down."

"That's what I had to do with my stepson."

Simon kept his back to her while he spoke. "You know Isabelle conceived my child quickly. I was quite pleased that I'd no longer have to visit her cold bed, watch her eyes glare up at me while she chanted the rosary. Alcuin told you my rage knew no bounds when she miscarried? What he omitted was that she lost the child because she would not stop wearing her damned steel corset so she might continue to fit into her gowns, or allow my expert Moor physician to examine her. Instead, she entrusted my son's care to some ignorant village midwife and if there was any justice in the world, she would have died too when she bled my son away in her sixth month of pregnancy. But Isabelle recovered, though the miscarriage so damaged her she'd never be able to conceive again, and there I was, stuck in a marriage with a woman I despised and no hope of a child of my own. I simply could not dispose of her so soon after the questionable circumstances of Roger's death."

Dispose of her, Meghann thought. *He speaks so casually of murder. When did human life come to mean so little to him?*

Simon turned and offered her an icy smile, sprawling on the large bed. "Isabelle loved Michael with all her heart so I decided if I must be deprived of children, she would be too. Don't look so horrified—I didn't kill him then, merely took him with me to London when I went to serve the queen at court. Isabelle protested mightily but a few nights of rather imaginative sexual torture that included making her perform with my mastiff hound soon quelled her tongue. At first, I had no interest in Michael . . . keeping him by my side was merely a way to make Isabelle miserable. But then, as he began to grow from senseless infant to young boy, I began to see my nephew was far more like me than either of his parents. He was a bright child, filled with mischievous energy. I taught him his letters, engaged tutors for him. By the time he was five, he spoke French as well as English, had the rudiments of mathematics; I'd just hired a sword master for him."

Meghann came closer, drawn by the grieving look in his eyes that reminded her of how Jimmy Delacroix had looked when he told her of his son's death. But Jimmy had cried against her breasts, and Simon . . . somehow she felt more pity and pain for him, for the clear eyes and tight voice that showed a strong man who'd never allow anyone to see his tears. Meghann felt a little overwhelmed as she realized that by speaking of his grief, Simon was giving her the rare opportunity to see beneath the cool, detached mask he presented to the rest of the world.

"Then, in June of 1591, an epidemic of plague spread through London. I sent the child back to Yorkshire, wanting him away from the city." Simon looked over and gave her a small smile. "The little imp refused to get in the carriage . . . crying 'No, Papa! I want to stay with you. I want my horse and my sword.' But I insisted he go. In a few months, he'd be starting his service as page to the Earl of Northumberland and I gave in to Isabelle's hysterical, ranting letters that demanded she have one more chance to see her son. In effect, by doing that, I signed the boy's death warrant. He got to the estate and contracted smallpox . . . Isabelle had not told me the disease was raging through our village."

"I don't understand," Meghann said and came closer, taking his hand. "Alcuin didn't tell me he died of smallpox."

"He didn't. I hurried home the moment I heard the news and was greeted by my physician, Doctor Ahmed. He'd been beaten to within an inch of his life but he begged me to kill him. He didn't think himself worthy of living because he hadn't been able to fight

Isabelle's boorish guards when they beat the infidel doctor because he tried to treat Michael. I burst into the child's room and found my nephew, the child I meant to make my heir, being treated by Isabelle and the village cunning woman with leeches and red curtains hung over his bed. I thrashed Isabelle until she fell at my feet in an unconscious heap. Then Doctor Ahmed and I went to work on the child. In the end, Michael recovered from the disease but his high fever . . . in the words of my doctor, it made his mind 'soft.' "

"Oh, my God."

"I did not believe there could be a God when I looked down at that wonderful little boy and realized his mind would never function again. I could not let him live that way. Once he convalesced, I took him to the stables and left him alone. Fate took over . . . my stallion, Sulieman, crushed him when he crawled into the horse's stall."

"You killed him so he wouldn't have to live as a . . ." What a lethal opponent Simon Baldevar was. When he transformed Jimmy and warped his mind, he'd known what kind of agony it was to watch someone you loved stare at the world with dull, unknowing eyes. How much did he hate her to hurt her like that? No, Meghann realized, it wasn't hate that made Simon transform Jimmy . . . it was love. It was the love she'd thrown back into his face the night she left him, love twisted into an ugly desire for revenge, a need to hurt her like she hurt him.

Meghann took his hand and pressed it to her cheek. He'd done horrible things, things she'd never be able to forgive or forget. But was it possible love could melt the ice around Simon's heart at least a small bit?

Gently, Simon tilted her head up toward him, giving her a soft smile that dispelled her anxiety immediately.

This can't be wrong, she thought, hearing a low roar in her ears when he kissed her with a strange intensity that seemed to thank her for her trust and devour her at the same time. *Nothing that feels this good can be wrong.*

"I'm sorry about Michael," she said quietly.

"So am I, Meghann. Four hundred years later I am still sorry for his death. But that was just the start of my problems."

"That's right . . . after he died, Alcuin told me you got syphilis."

"We called it French pox then. Did he tell you I got it from Isabelle?"

Simon laughed at her sharp gasp. "No, pet, she wasn't unfaithful. After Michael's funeral, Doctor Ahmed drew me to the side. He asked if I'd noted Isabelle's appearance . . . how thin she was, that her hair was falling out in clumps, her fits of raving. He examined her and decided she had the pox . . . must have contracted it from my brother, Roger, because she was too far along in the disease to have gotten it any later. Doctor Ahmed said I would not know if I had the illness until my hair fell out and I too needed sleeping herbs to keep me restrained. So I began my quest to develop the philosophers' stone and the freedom from death and disease it would deliver before the pox could claim my mind."

THIRTEEN

London, England
May 14, 1592

"God's foot, sir," Elizabeth Tudor greeted as she accepted Lord Baldevar's arm and stepped from her royal barge onto the river quay behind his handsome rose-brick mansion. "Who is this devilishly handsome Turk in place of my English hawk?"

Simon laughed, knowing the Turkish garb he'd chosen to wear for the masque suited him. In place of the gentleman's accepted doublet and hose, he wore white pantaloons with satin ankle strips embroidered in gold stripes. His shirt was ivory silk with a cloth of gold sash about his waist. The splendor of his white and gold outfit was topped off with a sleeveless cloth of gold robe and a gold turban that sported two white feathers and a large ruby aigrette.

"Madam," Simon said smoothly. "I pale next to your magnificence." The queen too was dressed in Turkish fashion, wearing a white gown designed to resemble the tunic dress of Turkish royal women. The overskirt was embroidered in sparkling pink and white diamonds, sapphires, and rubies while the underskirt was a dazzling mass of silver flounces embroidered with small diamonds and jets. On her head she wore a flame-red wig, the hair dressed in a coronet of braids with silver ribbons interspersed throughout the braids.

He turned to the dark, silent gentleman by her side and bowed deeply before greeting the sultan's ambassador to England in flawless Turkish. "Al-Caid Ahmed ben Adel, your presence does my home a great and undeserved honor. I can only pray my poor preparations do not displease you. Allow me to assure you that you may dine at my board knowing all the animals were slaughtered in accordance with Islamic tradition."

The imposing figure smiled. "I believe I remember you, Lord Baldevar. You are the English gentleman that gave my overlord a small token of appreciation before returning home. My lord Murad, shadow of Allah upon this earth, was most pleased."

Simon smiled broadly, not at all surprised to learn the sultan had been pleased with his gift—the harem of six delightful beauties Simon had amassed during his time in Istanbul.

"We appreciate your attempt to honor our new ambassador with this taste of his own home," the queen said, following Simon through the gardens to the ballroom that took up the entire second floor of his mansion. "We look forward to depending upon your aid in settling Master Adel at court."

"I am in all matters your loyal servant, madam," Simon replied, knowing he'd just been handed the duty of interpreting between the queen and her new ambassador. Before his troubles, such a position would have been a pleasing step forward in the hierarchy of the court. Now it was merely another imposition on his time, time he'd far prefer to spend developing the philosophers' stone before the pox could take him.

Displaying more vigor than some guests decades younger than she, the queen insisted on dancing the moment she arrived in the ballroom and Simon obliged her with a lively galliard. Pounding out the frenetic steps, Simon thought that, for all her age,

Elizabeth was as quick and graceful a partner as he'd ever had.

"Look at the dandy," the Earl of Essex muttered jealously to Simon when Sir Walter Raleigh took Elizabeth from Simon's arms to dance the second dance with her. "I am blinded by that ostentatious outfit of his."

Simon said nothing, though he found no fault with Raleigh's garb. The clever courtier reminded everyone of his successful voyages in the New World by wearing a black doublet that glittered with Colombian emeralds and Mexican turquoise, and was trimmed lavishly in red fox fur.

The earl gave Lord Baldevar a sidelong glance. "What say you to giving me a spell to vanquish my enemies?"

"I know of no spell to clear an entire court," Simon said easily, dismissing the young earl's clumsy inquiry as to whether he was truly a sorcerer. "Besides, you have no need of the Dark Arts—someone has already cast a potent love spell on Walter Raleigh. What other explanation could there be for his conduct?"

"What conduct?" the earl replied, his black eyes alight at this hint of some gossip that would damage the man he considered his worst rival for the queen's affections.

"Sir Walter has married secretly," Simon informed the earl.

"Forsooth?" the earl said and then shrugged. "Her Majesty may be annoyed with him a short time but no doubt she'll forgive him as she forgave me when I eloped with Frances."

"Frances Walsingham was not Bess Throckmorton."

"Bess?" The earl's eyes nearly bulged out of his head and he gave a whoop of delight. "You tell me Raleigh has gone and married the queen's favorite maid of honor? The fool, the fool! How can you be certain it's not a rumor?"

"Lynette overheard the newlyweds discussing the wedding." Lady Lynette Marline was one of the queen's ladies-in-waiting. She'd been Simon's mistress a few months before but he'd broken off relations with his highborn lovers since he found out he might have the pox. Now he confined his urges to low whores.

"This is wonderful!" the earl exulted. "I cannot wait to see Gloriana's expression when I tell her what that popinjay has done. She'll strip him of everything . . . banish him from court . . . oh, this is wonderful!"

Simon put a restraining hand on his friend's jewel-encrusted red doublet. "Don't be rash, Robin! Do not tell the queen yourself . . . she despises gossipmongers almost as much as couples that marry without her permission. Arrange for the information to come to her ears through other channels, and if I were you I'd wait until Raleigh's at sea on his latest piracy venture. Then, Elizabeth will be doubly angered—once for his wedding and once for going to sea without her permission."

"My lord." John Dee appeared in front of him, eyes grave as usual. "Might I speak with you privately?"

"Will you excuse me?" Simon said graciously to his friend.

The earl clasped Simon's hands in gratitude. "You are a good friend, my lord."

Simon guided the astrologist into a private salon, smirking over how easy it had been to use the rash young earl. Now Walter Raleigh's ships wouldn't pluck any of the galleons Simon's own fleet was targeting on the Spanish Main. Poor Robert Deveraux, unable to see when he was being used.

"My lord," Dr. Dee said without preamble once the door shut behind them. "We must continue the Great Work tonight."

"Why tonight?" Simon frowned. He had no desire to go down to his laboratory once all his guests were gone and begin the laborious machinations of alchemy. It would be three the next afternoon before he found his bed.

"The philosophers' stone is within your grasp. Your astrological chart has undergone a great change."

Simon bit his lip, not wanting to give in to the sudden joy that made him want to leap about the small room. They'd thought themselves near success before only to have their hopes brutally dashed at the last moment. This time he would remain calm until solid proof was before him. "What sort of change?"

"Your *soror mystica* has made an appearance."

Soror mystica? The heart mate of the alchemist, the woman so many of his texts insisted was necessary to achieve the philosophers' stone? "When do I encounter her?"

"Three hundred and fifty years hence," John Dee said calmly. "I cannot be certain of the precise date, but your meeting will fall under the sign of Taurus."

Simon sank into a cushioned chair, the gay party outside the closed doors all but forgotten. "Three hundred and fifty years, you say? Am I in another incarnation of my soul?"

"No," John Dee replied, a small glimmer of excitement in his eyes the only change in his serene demeanor. "There is great change in your chart, but you . . . your soul undergoes no rebirth. Everything else changes but you remain the same."

"So I must have discovered the secret to immortality," Simon mused.

"A discovery you may prefer not to make, my lord."

"How could I not want to vindicate our theories and labors of the past three years?" Simon demanded. "John, I know I was right when I told you the *materia prima* is not metal but blood. We must purify blood to achieve perfection of the soul."

"My lord, I think your discovery an important one but look at all our failed attempts. We've calcinated blood, sublimated it, and distilled it with all manner of herbs and metals, yet we've never created a potion that gave us immortality. Our quest to achieve the philosophers' stone does little else except bleed the whores and vagrants of London dry."

Simon smiled ruefully, thinking of the many destitutes he'd scoured the streets for, masked and caped so he couldn't be identified. Then he took them into his coach, blindfolded them, and led them into his house, where he cut them up and drew blood for his experiments.

John Dee was right though; he'd never been able to purify the blood, never come close to releasing from it all the vile humors that caused disease and death. But somehow Simon knew he was right, knew the secret to the philosophers' stone lay in transmutation not of gold but blood, the substance of life.

"You say I might wish to stop yet you wish me to continue the Great Work tonight. Forgive me, good friend, for saying you speak in riddles."

"Your chart shows a loss . . . a darkness I do not understand. I would offer you whatever protection I can from this threat not because you are my patron but my friend. You know my reputation was in tatters after I returned from the Prague. You and the queen alone stood behind me. In thanks for your support, I shall construct for you a powerful amulet and attempt to scry your future."

"Thank you, John," Simon said, holding this learned man in the same esteem he'd held his old mentor, Father Bain. He'd have felt the loss of the old priest when he passed away in his sleep over the past winter far more keenly if not for Dr. Dee. "Enter my lab now and begin the preparations, please. I shall join you later."

Simon strode back to the queen's side, offering her his arm. "Your Majesty? May I escort you to the gardens? I've planned a small musicale for your amusement."

"Hawk." The queen smiled. "I'd wondered where you vanished to." She left behind a glowering courtier to take Simon's arm.

Simon escorted her to the center of his gardens, a source of justifiable pride for him. He'd modified the traditional English garden with rare flowers from the East so deep blue Puschkinia flowers and yellow azaleas from the Bosporus mixed in with traditional long-stemmed roses to make his garden a riot of color and intoxicating perfume on this summer night.

For the masque, he'd had a small musicians' gallery painted with cavorting imps and fairies set up between two willow trees, and it was here that he seated the queen on a comfortable velvet-lined stool. "I thought a selection from the *Hortus Deliciarum* most appropriate for tonight. Minstrels, you may begin."

The queen listened to the music, stormy eyes glistening at a solo by the lute player, a handsome young man with inky jet curls and delicate, pale features. "He plays like an angel."

"Aye," Simon responded, feeling moved as always by the poignant music pouring forth from the musician's skillful fingers. "I am honored that he plays for me."

"Wherever did you discover him, Hawk?"

"He was Michael's music tutor," Simon said softly, and the queen gave his hand a brief squeeze.

"He has one eccentricity, Bess," Simon said to lighten the painful moment. "Though he charged a fair amount for lessons, Master Aermville insisted that he could only teach at night."

"Did you question him on this peculiarity?" the Earl of Essex asked.

"Question him yourself." Simon called the young minstrel over and he bowed before the queen but Simon noticed the boy's sapphire eyes never left him.

The intense stare made Simon uneasy, particularly when the lad caressed his wrist in the moment he extended his hand to thank him for performing that evening. *Catamite,* Simon thought in distaste and hastily removed his hand.

The queen gave the young man a small gold ring set with pearls and diamonds and he smiled shyly, speaking in a low, almost tremulous voice when he thanked her. Simon had never seen a man so obviously effeminate. Then he shrugged off his dislike, reminding himself that many minstrels had unnatural predilections.

"We would know what you do with your days," the earl said to Master Aermville.

"I sleep, my lord," the musician replied, and the assembled crowd tittered.

"All day?" the earl pressed, and Simon's eyes narrowed when he noticed the boy's creamy complexion go several shades paler. No doubt Master Aermville debauched himself all night and spent the days sleeping off his excesses. But why such embarrassed timidity? Such behavior was hardly unusual. Maybe the musician was made nervous because his betters were interrogating him.

"If it gives him the energy to play such superb music, let him have his rest," Simon said and gave the boy a grin, wishing he hadn't intervened when he saw blind adoration in the musician's gaze. Quickly, he dismissed the entertainer and spent the rest of the evening dancing with the queen and engaging in a raucous game of primero with the earl.

Simon gave Master Aermville no further thought so he was quite surprised when he stepped into the library after bidding good night to his last guest and found the musician standing by the windows, watching the impressive mass of barges roll by on the Thames.

"My majordomo has not given you your fee, Master Aermville?" Surely the boy was not foolish enough to make overtures to an earl? He'd have him horse-whipped.

"My lord, I beg but a moment of your time. Please, I must leave soon, for the dawn approaches."

"You should have left hours ago," Simon pointed out and moved to the sideboard, pouring himself a goblet of dark Gascony wine. He did not extend refreshments to the musician, finding himself more and more unnerved by the open longing in the boy's eyes. "I will thank you to leave now without another word."

"My lord," Master Aermville said in a rush, "I know you take the blood of beggars and attempt to transform it into a substance that will make you immortal."

Simon's hand went to his sword and he put his jeweled goblet down with a sharp thud. "If you wish to make accusations, go and file a complaint of witchcraft with the sheriff. Otherwise, leave my presence else the only blood I shall take is yours."

"My lord, no! I am not threatening you with exposure. I merely wish to say I can give you what you want. I am . . . immortal. I can prove myself, if you'll allow me to."

This could be amusing, Simon decided and relaxed his grip on the sword. "How will you prove yourself?"

Master Aermville disappeared. Simon blinked but before he could react, the musician was at Simon's side, grasping him with a strength he could not believe came from this slight boy. When Simon tried to bring his arm up to ward him away, the boy pinioned it to his side with a steel grip.

"I will not hurt you," Master Aermville said, and Simon could only gape at the gleaming ivory fangs that descended from his mouth. The boy closed his eyes and leaned forward. For one horrified moment, Simon thought the boy meant to kiss him but in the next moment he felt a ripping, vicious pain in his neck.

Simon gritted his teeth, not wanting to cry out in terror like some child, and thought he could only pray this creature kept its promise not to harm him. He heard a noise and felt a pulling at the wound. *He's drinking my blood,* Simon realized, *suckling at my neck as if I were a mother feeding some monstrous babe.*

Simon's vision blurred and he felt a not unwelcome lassitude go through his body as the creature bent his supine body into his arms but Simon came back to immediate, outraged life when he felt Master Aermville's hand on his codpiece.

"Sodomite!" he roared, not caring that the creature could destroy him. This time he got his arm up and shoved the degenerate musician from him.

Simon drew his sword, not certain if the weapon would provide any protection but feeling better at having it in his hand. "Master Aermville, you have proven yourself inhuman, possessed of powers such as I have never encountered, but I warn you I will fight to the death if you lay hands upon my person again."

The creature staggered to its feet, the strange teeth still dangling from its mouth, now covered in blood. "I offer you my deepest apologies, my lord. All I can say is you . . . tempt me. I love you."

Simon fell into a chair by the fireplace, his paralyzed wits beginning to work again. Master Aermville could break him in two yet the creature groveled before him, a curious mixture of evil and weakness. It was as Simon always thought—love, though he privately thought the boy's emotion mere lust, could make the greatest of men weak fools prey to exploitation.

"You are a hard man, my lord," Master Aermville said. "I offer you my heart and you seek ways to use it for your own gain."

Simon kept his face impassive. "You are also gifted in seeing the thoughts of others?"

"Aye."

"Please sit with me," Simon said and extended the chair on the other side of the ornate stone fireplace.

"I find myself in need of a restorative. Do you take food and drink?"

"I like whiskey, my lord."

Simon turned from the sideboard, curiosity reflected in his gold stare. "Why do you address me as though I were your superior? Surely my noble title is something a creature like you scoffs at."

"I do not scoff at humans, my lord. I respect the manners of your world and my place in it. I am merely a musician while you are an earl."

"What are you called?" Simon asked, handing his strange guest the peat whiskey while he drank a large portion from his own goblet.

"Vampire, my lord."

Simon frowned—where had he heard that strange but somehow compelling word before? He cudgeled his memory and recalled his lovely Caucasian slave girl, Katya. She once told him a story of such creatures— *vampyr*, they were called in her mountain village. Supposedly, they flew into homes after midnight and drank the blood of sleeping children, so frightened peasant mothers wrapped amulets of garlic and holy water around their infants' necks to keep them safe.

"I do not drink from children."

Simon reseated himself, ready to seize the upper hand in this bizarre encounter. "Master Aermville, you tell me that you respect my world but you seem to have little respect for me if you would glance at my mind so impudently. I cannot converse with anyone that does not respect my right to keep my own counsel."

The creature flushed and bowed its head. "My lord, you are entirely in the right. My master would be most disappointed if he knew I attempted to break the privacy of your thoughts. Henceforth, I shall not pry."

"This is a power you can extinguish at will, Master Aermville?"

"Please call me Nicholas." He gave Simon a wan

smile. "I must extinguish the power to hear thoughts else become unhinged. Tonight alone . . . would you wish to have a hundred thoughts rushing at you?"

Callow sodomite, Simon thought with all his will, and Nicholas did not even blink. Either he was keeping his vow not to look at Simon's mind or he was deceiving him by not reacting. Simon decided the prudent course was to think as little as possible in the presence of this creature.

"May I inquire as to how you came by this marvelous power, Nicholas?"

"It is not marvelous," Nicholas cried and once again his eyes glistened with tears. "It is horrible! I am an outcast . . . a wretched, lonely thing that must constantly observe the world yet never participate fully."

Simon had to work hard to suppress his disgust at seeing this man (or something that resembled a man) weep like a young maiden. "Why are you outcast? Are there not others of your kind you could align yourself with? You just mentioned a master."

"My master is in the New World," Nicholas explained and accepted the linen cloth Simon gave him to clean his face. "His kin, they are . . . kind but their life is one of piety and prayer. I still seek worldly delights like music and fetes and . . . love."

"Love?" Simon questioned, remembering the musician's adoring gaze at the party. "Is that why you come to me?"

"You are a comely man, my lord. I know you enjoy the attentions of many beautiful women and I know my suit repulses your natural inclinations. But I thought if I gave you that which you most desire—an escape from the miserable death of the pox—you might consider accepting me."

"I am aware that I am well favored," Simon said dryly. "But I cannot believe you would give me immortality on the basis of my handsome face."

"It is your character that fascinates me," Nicholas

said softly. Simon saw the musician looking at his hands, seeming to want to take one and hold it as a lover, but Nicholas wisely held back. "I've seen much of you . . . most no doubt things you'd never want anyone to know but I cannot help thoughts flowing to me. When I used to tutor your stepson, you'd come and listen to me play, remember? Many times, your thoughts would come to me. I know of your wife, that you forced her into marriage once your brother was dead. I know of what you do downstairs and I know nothing stands in the way of your ambition."

"And these are all things you admire?"

"No!" Nicholas cried, seeming horrified by the thought. "I feel that under the hard shell you've encased yourself in there is a man capable of great tenderness. I saw how you held young Michael on your lap and tonight your grief for him pierced me. The calm you felt as I played? That too is part of my gift . . . I can bring comfort to tormented minds. I know that although you play sordid games with whores and beat your wife frequently, you've displayed kindness to your noble mistresses. I think if you had my gift, in time you would let go of your hateful side and come to be a man of vast gentleness."

Only by a fierce effort was Simon able to keep his mind blank at the flowery, sentimental speech. "Allow me to see if I understand you. We shall become lovers and in return you will give me your gifts for my own?"

"Yes. It is called transformation, my lord."

Transformation—Simon reflected that the word wasn't far apart from *transmutation,* the alchemical process he'd been performing so diligently over the past few years.

Simon poured more whiskey, refilling Nicholas's cup also. "I would ask more questions before committing myself."

"Of course. Ask me anything, my lord."

"Explain this transformation to me. Tell me how

you came to these great gifts . . . I do not care that you see them as a curse. To me they are a great boon."

"You are a wise man, my lord. You were not wrong to focus on blood when you chased the philosophers' stone. Blood is the secret to us. We do not know how but at some point beings like us came into existence . . . creatures that carried a special humor to their blood. We make others of our kind by draining them of their mortal blood and infusing them with the blood from our veins."

"So I would drink your blood as you must have done to some creature?"

"I was transformed in 1410," Nicholas explained. "I encountered another minstrel in my travels and he made me as I appear before you. He drank of me for some nights and then, when I felt myself near death, he put his wrist to my mouth and I drank. I will not dissemble, my lord. It is . . . you have never known such suffering. I will say no more but if you decide to join me I shall do all I can to keep you comfortable during your transformation. Also, after you transform, you'll have a ferocious need to drink and I'll make sure mortals are available to you. Of course, you must not kill them."

Simon frowned. "I am to let them live so they tell everyone they meet of the evil earl with unnatural teeth? It can only be a matter of time before I'm dragged to the stake."

"God has endowed us with gifts to allow us to feed and not harm. You will find that you merely have to think a command and it is obeyed. You will tell anyone you drink from to forget the experience and before they turn from you it will be as you command." Nicholas glanced at the lightening sky. "My lord, I must depart."

"Yes," Simon ruminated. "I'd forgotten you avoid the day. Why is that?"

"For all you gain in return—life everlasting in the

beautiful body you have now, abilities to make the deadliest sorcerer tremble before you—there is one thing you must give up and that is the sun. You must make sure you are thoroughly shielded from the sun during the day as the smallest spark of sunlight can cause great damage to you. If your body were exposed to the sun at its zenith, you would be consumed in flames. Now, I must take leave. May I return after sunset this evening and ask if you are ready to receive my gift?"

From the lovesick expression in the creature's eyes, Simon had an idea the gift wouldn't be the only thing he received but he smiled and said, "I shall welcome you into my home. You say you must beat the sun home? Do you need my carriage to get you to your dark place?"

"You remember when I vanished? I may do that and reappear in any spot within thirty miles. Good day to you, my lord." Before Simon could say anything, Nicholas leaned over to kiss him full on the lips and then disappeared from sight.

FOURTEEN

The Swan Inn
May 16, 1592

Simon sat by the small, filthy window of Nicholas's bedroom, concentrating all his attention on the rushing stream outside. Strange but even with the window shut and a distance of nearly twenty feet he could hear the roar of the water as clearly as though he were sitting on the riverbanks.

He felt a mouth kiss his neck but by this time he'd become practiced in not shuddering, didn't even have to dig his nails into his palm to suppress his true emotions.

Nicholas, wearing naught but a cream silk shirt, moved to a small wood table by the fireplace and poured a goblet of light, golden wine, adding a small sprig of rosemary before he extended it to Simon.

"A loving cup," he said and leaned over to kiss Simon before they drank from the cup at the same time.

He accepted the embrace and drank deeply to suppress his desire to gag. Another glance out the window showed him the sky was beginning to lighten. It seemed that in that one moment between pitch-black night and the sky changing to violet, Nicholas's skin went from snow-white perfection to the dull, unhealthy look of an invalid in his last throes of illness. His eyes lost their spark and deep black circles appeared beneath them. Would the creature undergo any further metamorphosis, as the dawn grew closer?

"I must begin my rest," Nicholas said, his voice labored and uneven. "Please take me to the cabinet, lover."

Wondering what Nicholas meant to do, Simon grabbed him about the waist and took him to the small wooden cabinet where he stored his clothing.

"Remove some of the clothing," the creature whispered, feeling like dead weight in Simon's arms.

Simon opened the top of the cabinet and removed a half dozen lawn shirts before turning back to Nicholas.

"Put me in . . . inside . . . and co . . . cover . . . me . . ."

Simon could surmise the rest. He found himself straining when he lifted Nicholas's weight—the creature had drained him considerably throughout the night. Simon had deep gashes in his neck and both wrists, as well as wounds on the more intimate parts of his body that he'd rather not remember.

He placed Nicholas's body in the cabinet and concealed his presence with the shirts but before he could slam the top shut, a halting voice spoke from beneath the clothing. "I am . . . I can normally get myself hidden but . . . tarried too . . . late. Stay . . . use bed . . . talk, tonight . . . love you . . ."

Simon brought the top down with a bang that reverberated throughout the small room and ran to the fireplace, chamber pot in hand. He gobbled up the ash from the fireplace and then shoved his finger down his throat, emptying his stomach into the chamber pot.

Loving cup, Simon thought with a sneer. No doubt the wine was drugged so he'd spend the daylight hours in a stupor, waking up just in time to service that . . .

No! He would not think of what he'd done with Nicholas during the night . . . all he would do is give thanks that the sodomite had not violated him. It accepted his explanation that loving a man was new to him and seemed content with the kissing and cuddling young couples engaged in before they wed.

Still, even that left Simon cold and shaking, feeling acutely the loss Dr. Dee had foretold. To gain the gift of immortality, he'd had to prostitute his body to a sodomite. His flesh crawled at the thought of that . . . that thing touching him. It would pay dearly for all he'd had to do that long night once he no longer needed it.

Simon had much to do during the day if his plans were to succeed, but before he could do anything, he must find some equilibrium, restore some semblance of calm to his spirit.

He stalked to the door of the rooms Nicholas rented and grabbed the arm of a plump serving wench passing by. "You! Fetch me a bath."

"Ain't no one allowed in them rooms during the day, milord."

"Not even for five gold pieces?"

The girl's berry-brown eyes widened and she dashed down the stairs, returning several minutes later with three burly footmen carrying a large oak tub filled with steaming water.

Simon gave each man a silver piece and then turned to the little serving wench. "What is your name, girl?"

"Molly, milord."

"Will you wash me, Molly?"

"Aye, milord!" she said, and Simon was hard put not to laugh at her enthusiastic gap-toothed smile. He leaned back and allowed the girl to soap him down. He had to wash the scent of the sodomite off his skin before he could do anything else. The bath was soothing his spirit, as was his view of Molly's magnificent tits, temptingly displayed in her low-cut blouse.

"Are you a virgin, Molly?"

"No, milord. Shall I go to the bed, then?"

"No," Simon said sharply, remembering all that he'd suffered through on that devil-damned bed. He gave the wench a smile to take the rebuke from his voice and stood up, smiling at her awed stare.

He laid the girl beside the fireplace on his black silk cloak and laughed when she exclaimed, "I ain't never felt such fine material."

"Have you ever felt anything so fine as this?" he said with a roguish grin and guided her hand to his cock.

Simon took his time, savoring every inch of feminine skin with soft kisses and pets before he plunged into his willing partner. Molly may have been a mere peasant and not all that attractive with her freckles and coarse features but after the horror of last night, the girl's touch, her wonderful soft curves—all of it was like a benediction to him; the lovemaking made him feel whole again. Now he could consign the night and its filthy happenings to the most remote corner of his mind, never to think of it again.

After the girl left, Simon dressed quickly in an open-necked lawn shirt and dark hose. Rummaging about Nicholas's rooms, he found a quill and parchment and scrawled a message to John Dee, awaiting news at Simon's home, along with Dr. Ahmed. Nicholas did have some cleverness—he insisted Simon leave his home with no companions and no word of where he was going. Simon nearly laughed allowed—stupid creature, thinking it could defeat Lord Baldevar by draining his blood and pressing a sleeping potion upon him.

Downstairs, he found a young lad willing to take the message back to his house in London. The Swan was in the village of Cheswick, not a far distance. With luck, Dr. Dee and Dr. Ahmed should arrive well before noon.

Simon sprawled against a venerable oak tree to await the arrival of his friends, enjoying the warm sun on his face. If everything went according to plan today, this might well be the last time he saw the day so why should he shut himself up in Nicholas's dark rooms?

Nicholas—Simon's mouth turned down in contempt. If the creature was this foolish after two hundred years of life, what kind of soft-witted fool was he as a mortal boy? How could he trust Simon so blindly? No doubt the minstrel thought himself safe from harm because Simon couldn't transform without his blood. Well, that was the last mistake Nicholas would ever have the privilege of making.

Then, if his faith in a man he barely knew wasn't enough, look at the way the creature lived! Hiding away in a chest during the day—how utterly foolish. What if the inn caught on fire? What if a light-fingered maid decided to help herself to his clothes and left the cabinet open so he was exposed to the sun?

Simon would have far better defenses. He'd given the matter a great deal of thought and decided he'd return to Yorkshire and his isolated estate for this process of transformation. Remaining in London, a crowded city with no real privacy and Elizabeth's court aware of his every move, would be foolish.

Simon knew he could not remain in England indefinitely. He'd already written a letter to the queen, begging leave from the court due to illness; John Dee would deliver it into her keeping. He had to go where no one knew him or his habits. Perhaps he'd try Italy . . . he'd always wanted to see the magnificence of Florence. Of course, Simon didn't think it wise to stay in one place for any length of time.

Money wasn't a problem—he had gold enough to maintain a lavish lifestyle for decades. Too, he had no intention of allowing this new life to interfere in his business affairs. It should be a simple matter to hire employees to run his trade company during the day and then have them meet with him at night to report to him and receive instructions. As for his estates, he already had a competent steward in charge.

Simon thought it would be marvelously easy to hold on to his assets. If he stayed abroad, after a certain number of years, he'd simply declare himself dead and start writing letters in a new hand—that of the "son" who inherited his dead father's fortune. And by traveling from place to place, he'd have new opportunities to increase his wealth. Yes, this immortality was going to be a good thing. He'd have everything he'd ever wanted . . . unimaginable power and wealth, and never again could some disease make him quake in fear . . .

"My lord." A gentle hand on his shoulder made Simon's eyes fly open.

Dr. Ahmed stood over him. "My lord, I believe the suffering that Master Aermville mentioned has started. You are feverish and your skin is clammy to the touch. I have brought medication but are you sure you can handle the tasks before you?"

"I must handle them," Simon said and accepted his physician's help to rise off the ground. When he stood up, the world spun around him and he vomited again.

Dr. Ahmed guided him to the small stream and after tasting the water to assure himself it wasn't overly polluted, he spooned some into his patient's mouth.

After a few sips of cool water, Simon felt somewhat restored, though he needed to lean on his physician as they walked back to the inn. "Think you I need blood already?"

"We brought a small amount of chicken's blood." Once they got to Nicholas's suite, Dr. Ahmed handed him a small brown flask and Simon drank thirstily, surprised to find the pounding in his head abated when he finished drinking the blood.

Simon nodded to John Dee, standing in the center of the room, a heavy black trunk at his feet. "Where is the vampire?"

Simon went to the cabinet and asked Dr. Ahmed to stand with his back to the window so his body would block the sunlight from entering the room. Nicholas destroyed by the sun would be no bloody good to him.

Simon and John Dee peered down at the sleeping creature. "It does not look . . . it doesn't seem alive, my lord."

"No," Simon said thoughtfully. "It doesn't." Nicholas no longer had pasty skin and black circles to mar his complexion. Now he looked like a dead man lying in state, skin waxen and tense but somehow slack at the same time. Nicholas did not appear to be breathing and when Simon put his hand on the creature's chest, several moments passed before he felt a faint heartbeat beneath his hand.

Simon met Dr. Dee's eyes and the astrologist saw his uncertainty. "My lord, you worry it will pounce when you lay hands upon it?"

"Aye," Simon said. He gave the body a cautious poke, ready to leap away should the eyes in that deadly calm face open. But Nicholas went on in his unnatural slumber even when Simon jabbed him with the hilt of his sword.

"My lord, you must be careful and allow no ill wish to dwell in your thoughts concerning the vampire when you hold him. I cannot be sure but I believe the thing will only rise if it senses danger."

"My lord," Dr. Ahmed implored his patient, "the worst part of this day lies before you. Perhaps we should desist. We can put the vampire back in the cabinet and he'll arise none the wiser of your adventures today."

"And then what?" Simon demanded. "Did we not all agree Master Aermville could not be trusted—that he no doubt means to make me his catamite and take all my blood before leaving me a corpse? Who can guess how many times he's offered immortality to susceptible fools planning all along to take everything and give nothing in return? This time, though, he shall be fooled. Do not concern yourself over me. I shall nap on the ride home to restore myself."

"You are right, my lord." John Dee sighed. "We cannot chance what he might do to you should he rise this evening so let us see if we cannot wrest from this creature that which he has no intention of giving freely."

The nap helped, though Simon was still shaky on his feet when he and his two capable practitioners began their preparations.

They'd decided to use a solar on the third floor for the ritual, all three regretting the loss of the laboratory and the cedar-wood altar where they'd done so many works. Unfortunately, the laboratory was in the cellar so it would not provide the light they'd desperately need to complete their experiment.

Simon began the work by nailing a thick curtain over the window to protect Nicholas's sleeping form from the sun. Then all three kneeled down on the floor, saying the prayer John Dee had designed for daily protection from all harm.

Next, Simon cast a circle that encompassed John Dee, Dr. Ahmed, and the prone body of Nicholas Aermville, and that had the covered window as its northern point. In the space between the outer and inner circle, Simon placed lilies and mistletoe. Both provided powerful protection but in *The Occult Philosophy*, Dr. Agrippa hinted that mistletoe could be used to gain immortality. In between the flowers, he used a rowan wand dipped in balm of Gilead to write the names of *Aub* and *Vevaphel*. They were angels that protected from those that attack by night, so Simon thought they should provide protection against Master Aermville.

Simon consecrated the circle and then gave a plea for help in his extraordinary experiment. "O God

Who hast created all things, through Thy Holy Name, grant that this experiment may become true and veritable in my hands through Thy Holy Seal. Amen."

Next, using the blood of a virgin woman that John Dee had acquired the night before, Simon drew the Sixth Pentacle of Mars on the floor—it not only provided protection if the magician was wounded, but his enemies' own weapons would turn against them.

Nicholas was moved onto the pentacle and Simon removed a sword from beneath a crimson silk cloth— never before used and saved for an extraordinary occasion. John Dee handed him a silver brazier filled with holy water, rosemary, marjory, and mint. The sword was passed through the smoke and then Simon consecrated his instrument with a chant from the *Grimorium Verum.* "I conjure thee, sword, by God the Father Almighty, by the virtue of heaven, and by all the stars which rule, by the virtue of the four elements, to receive such virtue herein that we may obtain by thee the perfect issue of all our desires. Amen."

Now Simon put the virgin steel to his right wrist and slashed horizontally, bemused by the blood that poured from him. Then he turned to his left wrist and repeated the process before handing the blade to John Dee.

Dr. Dee accepted the sword while Dr. Ahmed moved to Simon's side, dragging his patient to the curtained window.

"Not yet," Simon whispered when he saw the physician pluck up the linen strips he'd use to bandage Simon's wrists. "Aermville said . . . must be drained to point . . . of death."

The slashing of Simon's wrists had a dual purpose. One was to drain him of his blood that he might be able to accept the vampire's substance into his body; the other was for Simon's blood to serve as sacrifice. Simon had bled into a gold chalice Dr. Dee held beneath him, and now the astrologist raised the chalice high, beseeching the spirits' aid before they attempted to steal Nicholas's blood. "Come hither, ye who love all kinds of mockeries and deceits. Come hither and remain, and consecrate this enchantment, seeing that God the Almighty Lord hath destined ye for such."

Dr. Ahmed restrained himself until the chant was complete and then held his hand up. "Enough! My lord, can you see?"

"Spots," Simon managed to whisper and thought he felt something on his arm.

"My lord, I just gave you a fierce blow to your upper arm you did not react to. You no longer have blood in your vital areas; I must staunch your wounds else you'll die."

"It's time, John," Simon rasped, forcing the words out. He managed to raise his hand and poked himself in the eyes so his vision might clear and he could see his friend bend over the prone body of Nicholas.

Sword in one hand, copper basin in the other, John Dee used the point of his boot to nudge Nicholas's head over, exposing his neck. He then put the sword to the vampire's flesh and cut him open.

In the next moment, he was kicked from the circle and the creature was on its feet, screaming in a terrible shriek that brought Simon back to semiconsciousness. He felt Dr. Ahmed grab him close and heard the physician say firmly, "No closer, foul creature! I can throw aside this curtain and expose the room to full day before you take one step toward me."

"Simon!" Nicholas cried out. "What has happened? Who are these men? How did they invade our sanctuary?"

"Our sanctuary?" Simon questioned and threw back his head to laugh—an awful sound that made even the vampire flinch. "These men are my dearest allies and we mean to have your blood or let the sun incinerate your worthless carcass."

The creature sank to its knees. Simon would never be certain whether it suddenly appeared drained of strength because Simon betrayed it or because it simply couldn't defend itself long during the day.

Tears came out of its eyes and it bowed its head. "I trusted you . . ."

"Fool," Simon said harshly. "What did you say to me? That you hoped to bring out my . . . tender side with your blood? There is no softness in my heart for perverted creatures that dangle immortality as long as I endure their unnatural embrace. But even knowing you probably meant to destroy me once you had your fill of my fine form and blood, I am prepared to offer mercy. Allow Doctor Dee to gather your blood and we shall take you to a dark corner when you've served your purpose. Tonight, when you arise, you leave London and never attempt to contact me again. Are we agreed?"

"Simon, no," Nicholas cried. "Love me please! You are breaking my heart. Though you'll transform once you drink my blood, you'll never survive the procedure without my guidance . . ."

"I'd rather find myself in hell than spend eternity beholden to a sodomite. Whether I survive is not your concern. Are we agreed?" Simon nodded to John Dee, standing warily a few paces from Nicholas.

Nicholas glanced at John Dee, holding the sword out, at Dr. Ahmed and his hand clutching a fistful of curtain, at the pure malice shining in Simon's gaze, and finally nodded. "Do with me as you will, Lord Baldevar."

John Dee picked up the hurled copper basin and cut Nicholas again, allowing a generous portion of blood to flow into the basin. Throughout the bleeding, quiet tears poured from the vampire's eyes and he shook from the force of his weeping. John seemed disturbed by the creature's sorrow but Simon felt no emotion save fierce triumph and utter disdain for Nicholas Aermville. To have such extraordinary power and allow yourself to be broken by love! Simon would guard his gift jealously—he'd never part with this magick for something as foolish and sentimental as love.

Dr. Dee brought the copper basin to Simon and he glanced at Nicholas Aermville—saw the creature had once again dropped into his strange daytime state.

"Raise the curtains, Doctor Ahmed," Simon ordered, wondering if Nicholas knew he had no intention of allowing him to live. Surely Master Aermville might seek him out and try to destroy him for his treachery.

Blinding sunlight filled the room and Simon felt something that had not entered him since the night he killed his father—fear. Nicholas Aermville did not die quickly—his body first smoked and then caught on fire and the creature screamed until the very end, when the flames finally reached his heart and ended his unnatural existence.

At last, there was only a small pile of ash where Nicholas had lain, and Dr. Ahmed pressed the basin to Simon's lips. "My lord, you must drink quickly else the blood shall lose its potency."

Simon shuddered, remembering how Nicholas howled out his torment. Could he end that way? If he took this blood, always he'd worry that such a fate would be his.

No! He was stronger than Nicholas Aermville, more clever and cunning. No one would ever get him near the sun. Simon clutched the basin and swallowed down the blood, grimacing at the fetid taste. He hoped to find blood more tolerable as he drank more of it— right now he had to force it down.

Simon heard a high-pitched screech of agony and realized he'd made the noise. Dear God . . . the pain, it consumed him. Never had he been in such torment.

Dimly, he heard Dr. Ahmed and Dr. Dee praying over him, beginning the prayers and conjurations that were his only hope to get through this hellish experience alive.

FIFTEEN

Charles Tarleton entered a large banquet hall in The Seraglio with Lee at his side, feeling an eerie sense of déjà vu as he glanced around the elaborate gold-and-gilt patterned hall. He'd first met Meghann in a hotel in Cuba—also owned by Lord Baldevar. That time he'd been there as Alcuin's spy, to observe Meghann and report back to his master about Lord Baldevar's consort.

Now, some forty years later, he attended another party, this time at the behest of the engraved invitation to a retirement party that had arrived at Lee's house two days ago. The invitation would have been thrown into the trash if not for the neat, Palmer-method script message at the bottom—*Please come to this party as guests of "Lord Charlton." You have every right to be angry but I can explain everything.*

Oh, Meghann, Charles thought sadly, *you think I can't guess what happened? I left you alone to pursue my own pleasure and you were left vulnerable to that bastard because of that damned blood link between you two. But don't you worry, friend. I'll help you fight whatever insanity pushed you back into his arms.*

Charles scanned the crowd anxiously, disappointed when he realized there were no vampires in the brightly chandeliered room or outside on the sweeping balcony. Lord Baldevar and Meghann hadn't arrived yet. Charles suppressed the anxious voice that whispered maybe they weren't planning to come at all, that Lord Baldevar might have had second thoughts about exposing Meghann to her best friend.

"I don't understand," Lee said in a low tone to Charles after they were seated at a table by the balcony that allowed Charles a view of the entire room. "That press release outside says Lord Charlton is on the board of directors here. How can a vampire hold a position like that?"

"It's not as hard as you'd imagine to be a vampire and pursue your mortal interests. I managed to work for the NIH. False documentation is easy to obtain, and as for keeping normal hours . . . I just confided to the director of the NIH that I had porphyria so I preferred working at night."

"Wouldn't Simon have to go to board meetings during the day?"

"He'd send his lawyers," Charles explained. "With specific instruction on how he wants to vote on certain issues. If during the day a board did make a decision he wasn't happy with, he'd just call them together at night."

"But why would they kowtow to him?"

Charles rolled his eyes. "Why do you think? Actually, he probably doesn't even need to use vampirism to persuade them . . . Simon Baldevar gets away with conducting business at night because he's a financial wizard; no one's going to disdain his suggestions just because they come at night. Alcuin once told me that in four hundred years, Lord Baldevar never put a foot wrong when it came to investing and he has an uncanny sense for what will take off. He sidestepped the Crash of twenty-nine . . . damn near tripled his fortune through cotton speculation during the Civil

War . . . and you're just trying to keep me from thinking about Meghann with that monster!"

Lee smiled sheepishly. "Guilty."

"Some of this is your fault, you know! Why the hell didn't you tell me Meghann's feelings toward that monster were changing?"

"Why?" Lee flared. "So you could badger her like you've done to me the past month? How many times do I have to tell you I'd never betray a patient's confidence or a friend's? And Meghann is both to me. And I didn't tell you because . . . well . . . I was scared you might cut her out of your life if she went back with him. Charles, I couldn't stay with you if you hurt Meghann!"

For the first time in weeks, Charles's jet eyes softened. "You really love her, don't you?"

"I owe her my life," Lee said simply. "But even if I didn't, I'd love her anyway. Meghann is special. I'm not going to stop being her friend simply on the basis of who she sleeps with, and you'd better not either."

"Don't you know that's what Simon Baldevar wants me to do?" Charles questioned caustically, lighting up a cigarette and ignoring Lee's censuring glare. "He's hoping I tear into her tonight and break her heart so he can convince her she doesn't have anyone in the world but him. Don't worry about me falling into that trap . . . I'm here to tell Meghann I love her and forgive her for what she's done with Lord Baldevar."

"You sound like an outraged father," Lee observed and rolled his eyes. "Somehow I can't see Meghann accepting you scolding her like a naughty child."

"What else can I do? Condone this lunacy? Has she completely lost her mind?"

"Ask her," Lee said and jerked his head to the front of the banquet hall where Meghann stood with Lord Baldevar, one arm linked through his, smiling at the crush of people that came up to them.

"My God, I had no idea she was that beautiful," Lee said softly.

Neither had Charles . . . he'd never seen his friend look that radiant. His breath caught in his throat at the sight of her and for a moment he only felt brotherly pride that his Meghann, with her glowing skin and sparkling eyes, was easily the most beautiful woman in a room filled with showgirls and models.

Charles smiled, thinking pregnancy rather becoming to Meghann. She wore an Empire-style voile gown, cut low and tied with velvet ribbons under her full breasts to show them to their best advantage, while the flowing material of her wide skirt masked the bulge of pregnancy. The dark green color of the gown emphasized her fiery hair, worn down her back in a simple plait held in place with jade combs. Charles's eyes were drawn to the magnificent emerald necklace and earrings she wore. The first night he'd met her, Meghann had those jewels on—Lord Baldevar must have saved her jewelry.

But that night her exquisite gems couldn't light up her pallid skin or lend any spark to her apathetic green eyes. It was that despairing air that gave Charles the courage to approach Lord Baldevar's consort, see if she might desire freedom from her master.

Tonight, though, the emeralds provided an exquisite backdrop to snowy-white skin that glowed with pearly luminescence and snapping green eyes that danced with merriment. Charles stared at Meghann, wondering if he'd ever have approached her had she looked the way she did tonight . . . all but humming with happiness as she clung to her master's arm, a blinding smile lighting her face when he looked down and caressed her cheek newly flushed from feeding.

No, Charles thought. He'd never think to ask this woman to leave her lover—it was plain that all he'd earn would be a firm rebuff at the least, possibly violence if he tried to point at any flaws in the man she was so enamored with.

Damn it, Meghann, Charles thought, lowering his shields and directing the thought at her. *After all he's done to you, how can you possibly be so happy with him?*

Meghann's eyes met his and a sweet voice entered his mind. *He's done things you don't know about.*

What things?

I'll explain if you allow me to. Gently, Meghann pried her arm from Lord Baldevar's and started toward her friends.

"Meghann!" Lee leaped up and put his arms around her, kissing her cheek before he gave her a reprimanding glance. "You shouldn't have taken off like that."

"I had to, Lee," Meghann said, and Charles heard no uncertainty in the pleasant but firm voice. "It was to protect you both. Charles?"

Charles stood up shakily, knowing his future friendship with Meghann was going to be decided by how he behaved now. Despite her radiance, he saw a shadow of uncertainty in the bottle-green eyes that never moved from his face.

A laugh almost escaped him . . . could Meghann actually think he'd reject her when all this month he'd worried she wanted nothing more to do with him?

Meghann came to his side at the tears in his eyes. "Charles, you don't have to cry over me."

Charles grabbed her in a bear hug, crushing the air out of her. "I'm crying because . . . Meghann, I thought you didn't want to be my friend anymore!"

"Oh, Charles." Meghann stood on tiptoe to kiss his cheek, clucking at the improperly knotted tuxedo tie. Expertly, she redid the bow. "I thought the same thing . . . I thought you'd never speak to me if I . . ."

"Meghann." Charles took her hands, forcing himself not to scowl at the signet ring that once again glittered on her index finger. "Please, honey. Explain all this to me. Why are you with him?"

Meghann's eyes met his again, burning with a disturbing intensity when she asked, "Do you trust me?"

"Always," Charles responded firmly. He knew Meghann wasn't asking if he trusted her to make the right choice regarding Simon Baldevar . . . no, Meghann wanted to know if he trusted her not to lead him into harm.

Meghann nodded and took his hand, stretching out her other hand to clasp Lee's. "I love you both; I've missed you terribly. I don't know what I would have done if you didn't show up tonight. Will you come with me now, so you can see all that's happened? This isn't something I can explain. You have to see it for yourself. Oh, wait—they're making their announcement." Meghann plopped down into an empty seat between her friends and made a shushing gesture to Charles.

Why do we have to sit through some mortal announcement before you tell me how you lost your mind?

Meghann's eyes took on a dangerous shine. *Do I appear crazy to you?*

No, she didn't. Charles wasn't sure what he'd expected tonight but it certainly wasn't the lively beauty beside him. He'd imagined Lord Baldevar must have broken her in some way to get her back at his side. Now Charles was forced to acknowledge that, far from harming her, his enemy had restored Meghann somehow, banished the depression that kept her uncertain and tense all these months.

But how? It was beyond Charles's comprehension how Meghann went from the tight-lipped hatred and never-discussed fear that were her only emotions toward Simon Baldevar for forty years to staring at him with adoring eyes that followed his every move as he stood on the dais in the center of the hall with a cluster of men and women Charles intuited was the board of directors.

Lord Baldevar intercepted one of Meghann's glances and gave her a smile that transformed his hawkish features from the predatory mask Charles was so familiar with to an almost . . .

Charles leaned back in his seat, clamping down on his jaw to keep his mouth from hanging open with astonishment. Meghann wasn't the only one who'd changed. Charles kept his gaze on Lord Baldevar and observed that, while the vampire wasn't any less imposing a presence, there was something a bit less glacial about him when he looked at Meghann. If Charles didn't know his enemy so well, the meltingly soft amber eyes locked on Meghann would almost charm him.

Suddenly a soft hand took his. *You see it too?*

Dumbfounded, Charles could only nod. *You have a lot of explaining to do.*

Meghann nodded but then sat a bit straighter in her chair. Charles was about to question what caused this sudden alertness when he felt what bothered her, a bitter, dark hatred directed at Lord Baldevar.

Charles followed Meghann's gaze, finally settling on a raven-haired mortal woman standing off to one side of the dais. The woman's mouth was pulled into a little snarl that made her appear almost ready to leap onto the dais and attack not only Lord Baldevar but a man introducing himself to the room as Del Straker.

Puzzled, Charles watched the chairman of the board and vampire shareholder shake the hand of an elderly man with a shock of long white hair, almost yellowed with age. They thanked him for his eighteen years of service and the old man made a quick speech before a fiftyish, matronly-looking woman was invited to the podium . . . the new casino manager for The Seraglio.

Charles didn't have to read the unhappy woman . . . the betrayal and rage simmering in her eyes told him what must have happened, and he turned back to Meghann. *One of your lover's victims?*

Meghann gave a nonchalant shrug. *I have no sympathy for women that exchange sex for promotion, and neither does Simon. Excuse me, I want to tell him we're leaving.*

Bemused, Charles watched Meghann approach her lover from behind and wrap her small arms about his waist. She picked a fortuitous moment to drag him off the podium, right as the photographers started snapping pictures of the new casino manager being welcomed to The Seraglio by the board of directors.

Frowning, Charles wished Meghann hadn't chosen to speak telepathically to Lord Baldevar—he couldn't follow the conversation and he wanted to know what made Meghann blanch and seem so anxious. The fiend hadn't threatened her, had he?

"What's going on?" Lee too was disturbed by Meghann's abrupt change of mood—going from dazzling happiness to darkened emerald eyes and hands that fidgeted with her long plait of hair.

"I don't know . . ." Charles started to say but Lord Baldevar's putting one large hand over Meghann's and gently pulling it from her hair caught his attention. He grasped her hands and Charles would never know what he said to her but the nervous expression left Meghann's eyes and she smiled again. What did Lord Baldevar do to reassure her?

He reached into his tuxedo jacket and handed Meghann a valet ticket, and she reached up to kiss him good-bye . . . no polite, social gesture but a full, lingering kiss that made Lord Baldevar wrap one long, tuxedo-clad arm about her waist and pull her against him before releasing her with a small groan that reached Charles's keen ears.

The vampire gazed down at Meghann, and Charles felt the air between them nearly smolder. Good God, he'd never felt such an undercurrent of passion and sensuality as he did right now, observing Meghann with her lover.

"I think I see how he enchanted her," Lee whispered dryly at his side. "Be honest, could you resist that?"

Resist the heat in those gold eyes, the implied promises that made Meghann gaze up at Lord Baldevar, her body all but vibrating with need and desire? No, Charles did not have that kind of puritanical denial running through him and he couldn't blame Meghann for lacking it either.

He understood Meghann seeking Lord Baldevar's bed. There wasn't a vampire in the world that didn't know his reputation for being a sensual, accomplished lover—all but an incubus in the way he could make women respond to him. But why did Meghann have to give him her heart as well as her body? Charles knew Meghann well—for forty years, she'd taken lovers and with the exception of Jimmy Delacroix she'd always separated her emotions from her physical needs. Of all the people in the world, why did she give her love to a creature that had none within him to give back to her?

Lord Baldevar smiled tenderly as Meghann left him but the moment her back was turned he locked eyes with Charles and a sharp pain entered Charles's temple as the vampire directed a message at him—*Guard her with your life.*

Charles rubbed his forehead, puzzled by the communication. He'd expected threats, expected his enemy to fill his head with all kinds of horrifying tortures to show what would happen if he dared try and tell Meghann to leave Lord Baldevar. But that simple directive and the unwavering gold eyes that held his with no hint of his former contempt or hatred . . .

Then Meghann came back to his side and Charles had no more time to ponder the unsettling contact between himself and Lord Baldevar.

* * *

Del Straker gave Simon a friendly poke in the ribs and extended a glass of scotch to him. "How are you planning to keep your wife if you let her go wandering around with two good-looking boys like that?"

Simon returned the mortal's leer with one of his own. "Can you think of better companionship for my young bride than two men with no interest in women?"

"No interest in . . ." Del's eyes widened and he let out a booming, good-natured chuckle. "Don't you think of everything! What better way to keep her out of trouble than sticking her with two gay boys? I shoulda tried that with some of my wives—instead, I let them go off with their girlfriends and damned if the whores didn't go out to pick up men. But now I make sure the prenup states they don't get a dime if I can prove they were cheating on me. You got that clause in your contract with Meghann?"

"I would not insult Meghann by asking her to sign some document that states I believe she won't stay married or faithful," Simon replied, enjoying Del's astonished gaze. He knew the much-married entrepreneur longed to point out the folly of a billionaire getting married without any attempt to protect his fortune from his wife's grasping hands, but Del feared offending a powerful shareholder with such blunt words. "Besides, I don't believe in entering into a marriage fully expecting it to dissolve at some indeterminate point."

"But she's pregnant," Del protested. "That means she'll be able to get child support along with alimony and when you think of what any sharp lawyer's gonna ask for—nanny payment, trust funds, monthly expenses, tuition . . ."

"Meghann will never leave me," Simon said with absolute certainty, for Meghann was no longer the quick-tempered, impulsive brat who'd abandoned him forty years ago; this time she'd honor her vows to him. He had to admit though, this discussion with Del was amusing—in the event of divorce, where could Meghann sue a four-hundred-year-old vampire for half his worldly goods?

"How can you be so sure of her that you'd risk your fortune?"

"Del, all you have to do is be certain of your wife's character before you marry her—make sure she's not some greedy, calculating, fortune hunter." Idly, Simon's eyes settled on Louise Caraway, guzzling down liquor at the open bar. Simon wondered if the alcohol was supposed to give her false courage so she could confront him or was she drinking to blot out her crushing disappointment at not being named casino manager?

"Damn barracuda," Del spat, following Simon's stare.

Simon raised an eyebrow at the rancor in Del's tone. "What has she done to you?"

The mortal hesitated but then began speaking after Simon slipped some reassurance into his thoughts. "You know I'm thinking of running for Congress back in Texas?"

Simon nodded and Del pulled him into a secluded corner of the hall, speaking in a low tone. "The damned bitch came up to me tonight," Del whispered, his voice shaking with rage. "Showed me a video she made of me with her and some little hooker. Now she's telling me the whore's underage! Simon, she told me she'd put the goddamned video in the hands of the Nevada D.A. if we don't make her casino manager . . ."

"I'll take care of it, Del," Simon said calmly.

"How?" the mortal whined, his mouth pulled into a pucker that reminded Simon of a small child denied something. "She could have made a dozen of them . . ."

"Del, on my word of honor, by this time tomorrow night you will have your video along with any duplicates, and Louise Caraway will never bother you again."

How delicious power was . . . always Simon enjoyed this moment when supposedly influential mortals stood before him in abject gratitude.

"If you're right . . . how can I thank you?" Del said, pumping Simon's hand up and down.

"What are friends for?" Simon said expansively. "After all, when Meghann said she adores the ocean did you not agree to give us that wonderful estate you bought in the Hamptons as a wedding gift?"

Del had said no such thing—he and Lord Baldevar had been negotiating the price of the multimillion-dollar property for weeks. But now the mortal stopped pumping his hand and gave Simon a long stare before he finally nodded. "That . . . that's what I said. Thanks for your help . . . friend."

A friend in need, Simon thought wickedly and bid Del a good night. He left the banquet hall and turned his thoughts to Meghann. She'd been worried about tonight, though she tried not to let him see her anxiety. What a sweet child she could be—not wanting him to think she lacked confidence in his plans. He understood Meghann's fear . . . battle was something she had little experience with, and after Guy's attack it was only natural that she'd dread the confrontation Simon knew would take place tonight. He didn't think Meghann feared for her own safety but rather for that of Charles Tarleton.

It'll be over soon, darling, Simon promised and prepared to join Meghann but Louise Caraway planted herself in front of him, weaving in a drunken manner.

"You double-crossing son of a bitch," she slurred, and everyone in hearing vicinity gasped in shock.

Simon reached into their minds and commanded them to forget what they heard before he grabbed

Louise by the scruff of her neck and forced her through a nearby fire exit so he could speak to her in the privacy of the empty stairwell.

Louise scowled when he blocked the door but her frown changed to fear when Simon gave her a sharp crack across the face. "Clear your desk before working hours begin tomorrow, madam. As of this moment, The Seraglio no longer employs you. You may contact the personnel office regarding your severance package."

"You can't fire me!" Louise howled but her outrage was replaced by uneasy apprehension when Simon raised his hand again. "You . . . you were supposed to make me casino manager. You promised!"

"Did I indeed? Produce the papers where I made this vow."

"You won't get away with this," Louise hissed. "You give me what I want or I'll tell that little teenybopper you knocked up everything you did to me!"

"If you value your life, you will never again mention Meghann in my presence. A whore has no right to speak of a lady so far above her," Simon said pleasantly, knowing his even tone terrorized Louise far more than a shout ever could. He grasped Louise by her shoulders and banged her head into the heavy steel door, knowing the blow would make her see stars. "It has come to my attention that you are making a pest of yourself with the board. I expect all videotapes of your activities with Del Straker to be delivered to my home at three tonight. If it is entering your devious little brain to try and deceive me, keep in mind the marvelous Mother's Day present I plan for next May, Louetta Caraway." Simon gave Louise a malicious wink and chucked her under the chin. "That's right—I know all about little Louetta Caraway and the seedy trailer park she grew up in. I admire your attempt to claw your way out of such a sordid background—did you develop your aversion to sex because of your father's overtures?"

"No one knows about that," Louise gasped.

"No one except myself and the mother you've stashed away in that nursing home under a false name," Simon agreed, his smirk widening as Louise slumped, glaring at him with the impotent hatred he reveled in.

"Your mother recovered rather nicely from her stroke," he went on, watching her alarm grow with each word. "But I rather doubt that devoutly Pentecostal dame could withstand the horror of watching her little girl perform all manner of foul acts with another little girl. It might bring—what do doctors call the penultimate stroke resulting in death? Ah, yes—the Big One. Try to betray me and I'll personally hold your mother's head in place while she watches a videotape you never want to come into her possession. Remember, Louise, I'll expect those tapes at three—no earlier, no later."

Simon shoved Louise through the door, happy to find himself in this isolated area of the hotel where he could disappear with no one the wiser. He dismissed the mortal from his thoughts and flew to Meghann.

SIXTEEN

"Guy Balmont attacked me," Meghann said abruptly, and two concerned, aghast voices immediately fired questions at her.

"When? How did he find you? Why didn't we feel his presence?"

"Are you all right? Meghann, let me examine you. Did you sustain any injuries to your abdomen?"

Meghann took her right hand off the steering wheel, holding it up for silence. "First, I feel fine but I agree, Lee. You should examine me—if for no other reason, a month's gone by since the last exam. Guy didn't strike my stomach but I felt contractions during the attack. I was able to stop them quickly but I don't know if anything was damaged."

"Was there any bleeding?"

Meghann shook her head and watched through the rearview mirror as Lee sagged against the backseat in relief.

"Guy attacked you?"

Meghann turned her head, and saw Charles's pale skin was mottled red with fury and his eyes mirrored the hatred she'd seen in Simon's expression when he killed Guy.

"He knew you went to San Francisco," Meghann explained. "He planned his attack so I'd be alone—"

"What about Lord Baldevar?" Charles demanded and then his eyes lit up with comprehension. "Now it

makes sense . . . Guy didn't know Simon was here?"
At Meghann's confirmatory nod, Charles went on. "So
Simon saved you? No wonder you turned to him but,
Meghann, I don't understand. Why didn't you tell me
before?"

"I wanted to," Meghann said. "But Simon made me
see the only way they could know I was pregnant was
by reading your thoughts while you were at Ballnamore."

Charles frowned. "Yes, that makes sense but who
read my thoughts? No one on the Council is in my
bloodline and I don't understand . . . wait! The Council doesn't know you survived! That's why Simon spirited you away—he wants them to come investigate so
he can do away with them."

"And if I told you any of this and they arrived—"

"They could read me and Lord Baldevar would lose
the element of surprise." Charles glanced around the
isolated desert surrounding them. "Is that why we're
driving out of town? To lure them into Simon's trap?"

Meghann nodded. "He wants me to take you to the
spot where Guy attacked me."

"So he can fly the astral plane and arrive in a matter
of seconds. How can he be so sure the Council will be
waiting?"

"Simon felt the presence of other vampires the moment we returned," Meghann said. "He's camouflaged
our presence from them and he says when they sense
the two of us out here by ourselves . . ."

"They won't be able to pass up the chance to attack," Charles finished grimly. "I assume you have
weapons in this car?"

"Two axes in the trunk," Meghann answered and
pulled the car over to the side of the road.

She killed the engine and Charles fetched the weapons out of the trunk.

Charles handed her one, and she came out of the

car, gripping his hand. "Charles, you do know what you're doing tonight? If you stay by my side . . ."

"I'll do what I damn well should have been here to do when that lowlife attacked you." Charles glared over at the debris from the mesa she'd destroyed as if the red boulders were something obscene. "I'm receiving images, Meghann. How dare they torture you like that in our dead master's name! You think I care that I'll be considered a turncoat after tonight? I will not align myself with anyone that would try to destroy a pregnant woman and her unborn child!"

Meghann smiled softly, feeling some measure of happiness in spite of her anxiety over the battle she knew could only be moments away. The only shadow over her joy in the past month was the thought that Charles would reject her now that she was Lord Baldevar's consort again. But now, seeing him at her side, she felt that last worry slip away. "You understand now why I'm with Simon?"

"Meghann." Charles sighed. "I can only guess at how frightened you were after they attacked you. Of course you turned to Simon for comfort. I know no matter what else he's done, he saved your life. For that, I owe him a huge debt of gratitude and I intend to tell him so the next time I see him. But has it occurred to you that you're mistaking gratitude for love?"

"I know what I feel," Meghann said quietly. "God knows I've tried my best to deny it but even when I despised Simon, I think some small part of me still loved him. But this is a discussion we should have at another time . . . we have to prepare for attack now."

Charles nodded and glanced at Lee, standing a few feet from them. "Was it wise to bring him out here?"

"How can we be certain they don't have someone at the house? It's better that we have Lee where we can see him and protect him."

Charles started to nod and then stood ramrod

straight. "You feel it? Lee, get between me and Meghann!"

Meghann and Charles turned their eyes to the five figures approaching them from the mountains. Strangely, Meghann felt her fear evaporate and then realized where her sudden sense of relief came from—Simon was nearby, shielding his presence until the right moment came to strike, but he'd given Meghann a brief moment of contact to bolster her spirits. Now she could raise her head high and glare at the remaining members of the Council with unconcealed scorn.

She was surprised that Sir Walter (the oldest member of the Council after Alcuin and Guy) was able to meet her eyes—more surprised when he offered her and Charles a congenial smile. "Children, you won't need those weapons this evening. We mean you no ill will."

"Where I come from, attacking a vulnerable woman is ill will," Charles snarled.

Sir Walter sighed. "We've come here tonight to offer our apologies. Guy Balmont was only supposed to bring Meghann to Ballnamore to make her see reason and have an abortion."

"Is attacking me, ripping my clothes off for the sole purpose of humiliating me, and attempting to ram a sword through my womb your idea of reason?" Meghann inquired icily.

Sir Walter flinched and his companions fidgeted uncomfortably. "We never sanctioned such actions. We merely wished to get you alone and make you see the wisdom of having an abortion before Lord Baldevar learns you carry the philosophers' stone."

"You think we trust you now?" Charles cried. "You wouldn't send Guy unless you meant for Meghann to die—you know how he hated her!"

"Charles, we did not and do not mean for Meghann to die but the pregnancy must stop. Now, your new friend performs abortions, doesn't he?"

"Not on unwilling women," Lee spoke up from his position behind Charles and Meghann.

"This is why we sent Guy," Sir William said. "There is no reasoning with any of you. Now, we don't want to harm you but we are prepared to use force if necessary." Sir William gave Meghann a patronizing glance. "I know you somehow eluded Guy and his apprentices but that was a month ago, dear. You're in no condition now to fend off five vampires. If you force battle, all that's going to happen is Charles will be hurt and I don't think you want that. Why don't you come along peacefully?"

"Stay away from her," Charles said when the older vampire took a step toward Meghann, rage choking him so the words came out in an almost unintelligible growl. "I'll slice the head off the first one of you bastards to try and take her. And I won't be alone."

Sir William laughed uneasily. "You cannot think this mortal will help you. Charles, how can you slay five vampires with no one to aid you but a pregnant woman? Meghann aborts or she dies—it's as simple as that."

"Meghann is protected by your worst enemy—it's as simple as that," Charles retorted. "Are you stupid or simply denying the truth? Just who do you think got a sword through Guy Balmont's chest? It wasn't Meghann."

"You're not telling us Lord Baldevar has discovered her pregnancy?" Sir William didn't wait for an answer but turned to the cloaked figure by his side. "How could you not see Lord Baldevar in Charles's thoughts?"

"Show yourself!" Charles roared at the mysterious vampire. "How dare you invade my mind . . . Paul!"

"This is Paul?" Meghann said, when her friend simply gaped at the attractive but somehow weak-looking vampire. "Your lover—the one that transformed you? I thought he was dead."

"Afraid not, Lady Baldevar," the vampire said coldly, though his voice was far friendlier than the rage-filled eyes that settled on Charles. "Did you even care when that bastard wounded me for revenge against you because you took this tramp to Alcuin?"

"I cared," Charles said, and Meghann saw nothing but pity in his dark eyes when he gazed at his master. "I came to you, Paul, and that action . . . Simon Baldevar hurt you so he could get me away from Meghann before I could take her to Alcuin. She was alone with him and he nearly destroyed her—"

"Shut up!" Paul howled. "I'm so tired of hearing about this little slut! Why is she so special to you? I gave you transformation and you'd only stay with me ten years but this . . . this woman . . . forty years you've been at her side! Why?"

"She's my friend," Charles said simply. "And you know that's something we were never able to be to each other."

"I suppose this mortal is also your friend?" Paul threw Lee a scornful look. "Are you going to transform him because he satisfies your lust and tolerates you giving your heart to Baldevar's whore?"

"Stop calling her that!" Charles flared. "I'm sorry I couldn't be the eternal lover you were seeking and I'm sorrier that you're so alone but I will not allow you to take your frustration out on a blameless woman. You condone what the Council plans to do to her?"

"Of course I do. Since she's entered your life, you live only for her . . . some girl you've never even desired—it makes no sense. What hold does she have over you? Keep the boy if you want him but I'm getting this witch out of your life once and for all."

"No!" In a surprise move, Charles shoved Meghann from him and lunged at his ex-lover, brandishing the ax. Two of the other vampires grabbed Charles while Paul wrenched the ax from him.

"All right," Sir Walter said. "He's disarmed—grab

Meghann. Just behead her before Lord Baldevar arrives."

"I think not." Simon Baldevar appeared, standing behind Meghann. "See to Doctor Winslow, sweetheart."

Meghann moved to Lee, wide-eyed with shock at the encounter he was witnessing while Simon raised the broadsword in his right hand so the moonlight reflected off the steel blade. "Look familiar, Sir Walter? If your recollection is faulty, here is something to aid your memory." Simon tossed the object in his left hand high in the air and then used his power to make the jar containing Guy Balmont's head, carefully preserved in formaldehyde, land intact at Sir Walter's feet.

"This weapon belonged to him," Simon said, giving a cold smile to the vampires, who couldn't take their panic-stricken gaze from the jar on the ground. "I delighted in taking it from him, just as I'll revel in slaughtering every one of you."

A sharp cry interrupted his speech. Taking advantage of the momentary shock of his captors, Charles crushed the kneecap of the vampire to his right, grabbing up his sword when he fell to the ground. The other guard tried to hold on to his prisoner, but found himself lifted off the ground. Struggling and screaming in midair, the vampire couldn't prevent his body from flying to Simon's side where he was swiftly decapitated while Charles killed the still wounded vampire at his feet.

From there, everything happened quickly—so quickly Meghann barely had time to register the slaughter before her. Somehow she'd always thought battle was a long, drawn-out process; it never occurred to her that it could be done in the blink of an eye.

Sir Walter leaped at Simon but Charles quickly ran his sword through his back, neatly impaling him.

When one of the others tried to grab Charles, Meghann flung the ax in her hand, feeling a sense of grim satisfaction when it landed in the center of his head. Charles yanked the ax from the vampire's scalp and chopped his head off while Simon decapitated Sir Walter. Now only Paul remained, leaning over Charles with the ax he'd taken from him.

"Paul . . ." Charles stared up at his master, black eyes glistening with regret and sorrow.

"How could you do this?" Paul screamed, gesturing to the carnage all around them. "Slay your allies for this worthless—"

Paul let out a cry of frustration when an unseen force pulled Charles's body away from him. He ran after him, wielding the ax like a madman, but Simon blocked his path.

"No," Meghann whispered when Lee tried to run to Charles. "Stay here."

Meghann went over to her friend and almost cried when she saw how haggard Charles looked as he observed Paul thrashing about, desperately trying to break Simon's hold. Like an old man, he shuffled beside Meghann, walking in a stiff, slow manner as she led him to the car.

She locked eyes with Simon and he nodded at her silent plea. "Come on," she said to Charles. "We're leaving now."

"What? But Paul . . ." Then Charles understood— Lord Baldevar wouldn't kill Paul until they left. Perhaps Meghann was right after all . . . to those he singled out, Simon Baldevar was a powerful friend.

Charles turned to him, and ruthlessly shut all of Paul's pleas and accusations out of his mind. The creature that thrashed about in Lord Baldevar's grip was not the gentle vampire Charles had fallen in love with. Charles saw that years of loneliness and jealousy over the life Charles was able to form without him had warped Paul into something he'd never understand, something he was grateful to Simon for putting down, out of his misery.

Thank you, Charles said and Lord Baldevar tore his gaze from Meghann long enough to acknowledge Charles with a small nod.

"Meghann's with Lee," Charles said when Simon appeared in the living room. "He's examining her."

Simon nodded and sat down on the plush tan sofa, elegantly crossing his legs.

Charles eyed him uneasily; in a way the polite, constrained silence that hung between them was worse than enmity. At least then Charles knew what to say, how to react. Finally, all he could think to do was offer Lord Baldevar the bottle of absinthe cradled in his hands.

Simon shook his head and though his words were brusque, his tone was almost kindly when he spoke. "Intoxication is a sign of weakness, and vampires must, above all else, be strong."

"You mean in four hundred years you've never been drunk?"

Simon shook his head. "I did not care for liquor overmuch before I transformed and it's dangerous to be out of control. Besides," he said and gave Charles a flickering grin that made him see the charm Meghann always insisted Simon Baldevar possessed, "the stuff tastes like paint thinner. How do you force it down your throat?"

"After half a bottle, you don't taste much of anything." Still, Simon's lecture on weakness struck a cord—all the past month Charles had been drinking to excess. He closed the bottle and turned to Simon, feeling as if he were groping his way through a mine field as he tried to speak with this formidable being who was now a permanent part of Meghann's life—and his too. "Can I get you something else while we wait?"

"Perhaps you have some coffee of good quality?"

This was unreal, Charles thought, standing in the

center of Lee's homey, cheerful kitchen with its bright yellow wallpaper and curtains, chatting with Lord Baldevar. What would Alcuin think if he could see this? Then again, how would Alcuin feel about the behavior of the rest of his Council this evening?

While the coffee brewed, Charles turned to Simon. "Why did you help me tonight? Don't you want me dead? Meghann could have been killed when I went to San Francisco—Guy's attack was all my fault."

"You take too much upon yourself," Simon said mildly. "It is not your place to protect Meghann. Besides, like Meghann, you tend to forget your youth and inexperience. I am glad you were not there. Had you fought Guy and been killed, I am sure Meghann's grief could have caused a miscarriage."

"You're not angry with me?"

"You are a valiant friend to Meghann. The only way you can anger me is by hurting her."

"What about you?" Charles said, determined that he not take the easy way out and simply accept the compromise Lord Baldevar seemed to be offering. "I . . . I wouldn't stand by if you hurt Meghann."

"I would not expect you to." Simon accepted the steaming mug of coffee Charles gave him, drinking it black with two lumps of sugar. "But you must understand I will not tolerate any interference in my relationship with her—do you always put six spoons of sugar in your coffee?"

"Damn!" Charles emptied the mug into the stainless steel sink, and poured some more coffee into a fresh cup, keeping his eyes on the cream and sugar while he spoke. "Lord Baldevar, I think we should clear the air between us."

Simon nodded and poured himself a second cup of coffee. "Clear the air—you remind me of Meghann when you speak. I must admit, it was sheer brilliance on Alcuin's part to send you to my fete to speak with Meghann."

"What do you mean?"

Simon raised an eyebrow. "It was inevitable that you become such good friends. Your lover showed a shocking lack of sensitivity or even basic intelligence tonight if he could not understand the bond between you and Meghann. What a fool—thinking a man and woman can't have an enduring friendship without being lovers. I rather think you remind Meghann of her brothers. All her life she'd been surrounded by men. I'm sure your platonic friendship never struck her as odd. Why wouldn't you turn to each other? Two novice vampires with similar personalities, likes, and dislikes; and besides that, you're both outcasts—Meghann for being my consort and you for your predilections."

That was the first time Simon Baldevar alluded to his homosexuality without some kind of stinging insult. "You don't mind my friendship with Meghann?"

"It makes her happy," Simon responded.

"But I'm the one that convinced her to leave you."

Simon's face darkened but his voice was calm when he said, "That was at the behest of your pontiff, was it not? As I've told Meghann, there is no need to dwell on the past and its ugly memories."

Charles nodded, thinking perhaps all Lee had tried to drum into his head over the past month was true—if they couldn't kill Simon Baldevar, it was high time they made peace with him. "Just don't hurt her, that's all I ask."

"You have my word," Simon said and then cocked his head. "Do you sense blood in the air?"

Charles sniffed and then the coppery smell hit him hard. He followed his senses and heard a soft slurping sound—a vampire drinking blood. But if Lord Baldevar was in front of him, the only other vampire that could be drinking was Meghann!

He followed Simon to Lee's examining room and found Meghann on the examining table, dressed in a white hospital gown and drinking from one of the transfusion packs of blood.

"It's okay," she said to Simon when he came to her side. "I feel fine . . . better than fine . . . wonderful!"

"Meghann told me about how . . . hungry she's been," Lee explained. "That she was starting to want more than you could provide so I thought her rejection of foreign blood might simply be a disease of first-trimester pregnancy. Now that she's in the second trimester, she seems able to feed without any problems. Besides that, I have to say Meghann's in wonderful shape. Apart from the early sickness, she's having a model pregnancy—blood pressure is steady, weight gain in the acceptable range. We'll do an amniocentesis tomorrow night to check for congenital defects but I really don't expect to find any problems since you and Meghann are the closest blood relation. Tonight we'll do an ultrasound—I was going to invite you and Charles in here for it. I wanted to do it long before tonight but you needed to leave town because of your, um, enemies."

"We'll be able to see the baby," Meghann said to Simon, clutching his hand. She gave him a blinding grin and Charles had to swallow hard against the lump in his throat—he'd never seen Meghann this happy. He knew as well as she did all the atrocious things Lord Baldevar had done in his four hundred years but Charles thought there must be something good in the creature if he could cause the joy that radiated from Meghann's emerald eyes. Perhaps impending fatherhood was having a mellowing effect on Simon.

"Ready?" Lee asked and laid Meghann down on the table, pushing the hospital gown up to expose her abdomen, which he coated in a slick gel.

"Cold," Meghann complained while Charles started running the transducer over her stomach as Lee had taught him to do. Soon, blurry images appeared on the screen beside him.

"Stop," Lee ordered and frowned at the screen for a few moments before an expression of surprised delight appeared on his face. "Meghann, you're having twins!"

"Twins?" she gasped. "Are you sure?"

Lee pointed to two strange shapes and insisted they were the babies' heads. "And here . . . that's two placentas, thank God. The biggest danger in multiple pregnancies can come from two fetuses sharing the same placenta; one might be deprived of oxygen and nutrients. They're both developing at the same rate; see how one isn't significantly smaller than the other?"

"She's having twins?" Something flickered over Simon's face . . . to Charles, it almost seemed like fear.

"What's the matter?" Meghann asked. "Simon . . ."

"Nothing's wrong, little one," he said and gave her a quick smile. "I'm just a bit concerned. Don't twins carry a higher risk of premature labor and preeclampsia?"

"I intend to keep a close eye on Meghann," Lee said. "There are special tests to run on multiple pregnancies as the mother's due date approaches—"

"I'm sorry, Doctor. I must interrupt." Simon looked at Meghann and Charles. "You two understand that though I've destroyed the Council, there are still vampires that would slay you both? Meghann for carrying my heirs and you, Doctor Tarleton, for standing with me this evening. I think it would be provident to leave this area but I cannot ask Doctor Winslow to abandon his practice."

"I've already thought of that," Lee broke in. "Meghann's pregnancy is special and demands a high level of care—more so now that we know she's expecting twins. I'd already planned to bring another doctor in to handle my workload so I'd be free to concentrate on Meghann for the last twelve weeks of her pregnancy. I can be ready to leave here in a month."

"Wonderful," Simon replied. "The estate I've obtained—yes, Meghann, it's the house in Southampton, has a small guest cottage. You and Doctor Tarleton are welcome to reside there for the duration of Meghann's pregnancy."

"Of course," Lee said before Charles could answer but Charles simply nodded his agreement.

"Can you tell their sex?" Meghann asked while Lee finished the examination.

"Sorry." Lee grinned. "They're turned toward each other . . . my crystal ball is clouded. Anyway, how come you can't just 'read' what they are?"

"Probably because their brains aren't functioning at the level we need to intuit thoughts," Simon answered. "That's why we cannot read anyone suffering from profound retardation or mental illness."

"Do either one of you have a history of twins in your mortal family?" Lee asked.

Simon shook his head but Meghann said, "Two of my uncles on my father's side were fraternal twins. Simon, is this the first instance of a twin vampiric pregnancy?"

"As far as I know," he replied and kissed her cheek. "Trust you to do the unusual. I'll wait outside while you get dressed, little one." He stepped outside and Lee went with him, leaving Meghann and Charles alone for the first time that night.

Meghann pulled her green evening dress back on and turned her questioning eyes on Charles. "Is everything . . . okay between you and Simon?"

Charles shrugged and gave her a lopsided grin. "Politics make strange bedfellows. We're both agreed that we want the best for you—I told him the only way I'd take him on is if he hurts you. You would tell me if something happened, wouldn't you?"

"What do you think I am?" Meghann said scornfully. "I wouldn't stay with him if he tried to bully me like he used to do—even if he won't admit it, maybe he learned you can't use brute force to make someone love you. I told Simon the only way I'd be with him is if he didn't try and take away everyone I've come to care for in the past forty years."

"What about Jimmy Delacroix?" Charles asked quietly.

Meghann swallowed nervously and cut her eyes to the door. "I'm still working on him, Charles. What Simon did to him—it's despicable and unforgivable but I feel if I bring him back, it will make things better. And, Charles, he is better . . . wait till you see him! He's improved so much while I was gone . . . I think maybe all my chatter was holding him back or putting too much pressure on him. Maybe he needed to be left alone but when I got back . . . he grooms himself now! I lay out clothes and he puts them on, he eats on his own . . . he's even started showing some interest in picking out music."

"Is he vocalizing?"

"No," Meghann said. "Charles, I try to read him and it's like there's this wall up in his mind—I don't know if it's a defense mechanism to shut me out or he's hiding from himself. But I'm not too discouraged . . . he isn't even on Clozapine anymore! Charles, there's one thing I need to ask you. If Jimmy has a full recovery—well, he's not going to be very happy with me, and I· hardly blame him. But he'll need someone to guide him into our life—would you be his mentor?"

Charles thought Jimmy wouldn't be overly happy with him either—he'd ask why Charles hadn't done something to drag Meghann from Lord Baldevar. How could Jimmy Delacroix understand all that had happened when Charles didn't really understand himself? All he knew was Meghann finally seemed secure and happy, and on top of that, tonight had proven the only person who could really protect her was Lord Baldevar.

So Charles smiled at his best friend and nodded yes,

he'd help Jimmy Delacroix, swallowing all his misgivings and praying the little voice that whispered Meghann was making the biggest mistake of her life was wrong.

SEVENTEEN

Meghann started, then smiled at the blurry reflection fat black and goldfish swam through in the clear water of the large stone fountain. "I thought you were busy with all the wheeling and dealing you neglected during our honeymoon."

"I have other matters to attend to now," Simon said huskily and pulled her against him.

What a perfect spot for making love, Meghann thought, taking in the formal sculpture garden with its man-made streams, footbridges, and roses of every color perfuming the air. She looked up at Rodin's *The Kiss* and thought marble was one thing that couldn't possibly look as beautiful during the day as it did at night when the moonlight illuminated the polished, white surface.

"Now I know what it is," Meghann murmured breathlessly between kisses, twining her hands in the perfectly styled chestnut hair she'd longed to ruffle all night.

"What what is, my love?"

"What makes you so attractive," she said, giving Simon her best smile before licking the skin exposed in the half-open ruffled tuxedo shirt he wore. "Whenever I'm with you, the world has a glamour to it, enchantment."

"I believe it's called being in love, for I feel the same way with you." Simon smiled and pulled her off the fountain with him, one hand exploring her leg while they rolled around on the dewy grass.

"Strawberries and cream," Simon said as he pulled away the velvet laces on her dress and exposed her newly rounded breasts, now topped with bright red nipples. "I don't think I've ever seen you look more beautiful."

Meghann smiled at the compliment. When she'd first begun to show, she'd been shy about letting Simon see her thickening body until he convinced her, not with words, but with the ceaseless attention of his lips and hands to her fuller, rounded form that he truly did find her as attractive as ever.

"I love you," she cried when he entered her. What a curious intimacy this was, having Simon take her when his children were inside her. She'd never felt so possessed by anyone, felt herself on the brink of climax when a disturbing sound reached her ears—Louise Caraway angrily demanding that Vinny let her in the house. "Why is she here?"

"I invited her," Simon murmured, thrusting harder at Meghann's suspicious look. "Nothing untoward, little one—a minor business concern. I must meet with her."

"You're not going to stop now?" Meghann gasped.

"I value my life far more than that." He laughed at her horrified eyes. "But we must be quick, pet."

Meghann laughed throatily, and joined him in the never-changing rhythm that made them both scream out in delight.

Meghann found her gown at the feet of Michelangelo's *David* and tossed it on while Simon pulled his black pants and ruffled shirt on, the elegant dinner jacket hiding the grass stains on his shirt.

"Come along, my lady," Simon said to Meghann after a lengthy search for her shoes that somehow wound up under a privet hedge. "This visit provides me with a perfect opportunity to develop your gifts."

They entered the house through the back, hearing Louise continue to screech. "Get that asshole now!"

"I gather something happened after I left the party," Meghann commented and raised her eyebrows. "Can't leave you alone for a minute, can I?"

Simon gave an enigmatic shrug, and they entered the foyer together. He dismissed Vinny, and gave Louise/Louetta a mocking bow.

Meghann was shocked by the condition of the mortal in front of her. Even in her jealousy, she could admit Louise had an icy beauty, with her severely bobbed hair, flawless makeup, and tailored clothes. Now she tottered on her feet, her hair spiked wildly in every direction, and she'd obviously done some heavy drinking over the past several hours. What on earth had Simon done to her?

Apparently not nearly enough if she thinks she may show up on my doorstep screaming profanity.

"Louise," Simon said pleasantly. "Won't you introduce us to your friend?" He waved an elegant hand at the hulking mortal standing by Louise. He had to be at least six feet seven—a good three inches taller than Lord Baldevar. All his intimidating glare drew from Simon was the faintest hint of an amused smile.

"He's my boyfriend . . . I only screwed you because you forced me to but Tommy will make sure you don't put your hands on me again," Louise snarled and turned to Meghann. "You hear that, honey? Your husband told me he'd fire me if I didn't fuck him. But I'm suing him and Del Straker for sexual harassment."

Louise kept her gaze on Meghann, her smug vindictiveness changing to openmouthed shock when Meghann began giggling.

"Simon," Meghann gasped. "I don't believe it . . . oh, God, you su . . . su . . . sued for sexual harassment . . . ha, ha, ha, ha!"

"I am glad my legal troubles amuse you."

"But don't you see the irony?" Meghann giggled.

"It's almost as good as you getting syphilis! Oh, don't worry," she said to the pale Louise. "It was a long time ago . . . I'm sure you didn't catch anything."

"I know The Seraglio doesn't want the embarrassment of a trial," Louise said coyly, and Meghann wondered how the mortal could not feel the menace emanating from Simon's steely expression. "I'll settle with you right now if you give me my job back—with a twenty percent raise, of course."

"I could produce a dozen witnesses to testify in court about your calculating promiscuity," Simon said flatly. "Your frivolous lawsuit will be naught but an irritation."

"Don't you threaten her," the strapping bodyguard told Simon, stepping closer to him. "I'll mop the floor with you, you fucking perverted asshole."

"I rather doubt that," Simon replied and delivered a swift chop to the man's throat. He dropped to the floor, a wheezing sound coming from his ruined throat.

Simon gave Louise one withering glance. "Foolish woman, you should have been content with what you had, rather than try to rise above your station with blackmail threats. Now see what your actions have wrought, you white trash slattern."

Louise watched in stunned terror as Simon reached down and pulled Tommy upright with one hand. Her inertia broke and she started screaming hysterically when the majority shareholder for The Seraglio plunged his sharp fangs into Tommy's neck.

"Be quiet," Meghann snapped, and Louise's cries cut off abruptly. Poor Louise, Meghann thought; she thought power meant a position at the hotel—she had no idea what true power was. She'd never know the glory of holding others in your thrall against their will or know what it was to drain them dry and feel your victim die as you grew ever more powerful. . . .

A strangled whimper escaped her lips and Simon

looked up, smiling at the blood lust and naked craving that made her green eyes glow like a cat's.

He ignored the trembling Louise and spoke to Meghann. "Come feed, my pet."

When Meghann saw the blood trickling from Tommy's neck, all she could think was how badly she wanted it. Her concentration on Louise wavered, and the mortal started howling.

"Help me!" she screamed and made a wild dash for the door. "Somebody help me!"

Simon grabbed Louise by the hair and gave her an annoyed slap. "Stop that incessant noise at once."

With Louise once again silenced, he pointed to the bleeding mortal on the floor and Meghann felt her blood teeth rip through her gums. "Finish him, little one."

Meghann needed no further invitation. She threw herself on top of the mortal, and plunged her fangs into the wounds Simon had already made, sucking and tearing at her victim's flesh like a woman possessed. She felt an orgasmic rush go through her body when the blood started pouring down her throat.

No nausea attacked her while she devoured her host, hungrily sucking down all his nourishing, hot blood. She'd almost forgotten what it was to feed from a mortal, the heady sensation of life force and vitality invigorating her soul while the blood infused her body with dazzling strength.

Stop now, a voice reprimanded. It was Alcuin's training coming back—his exhortation that vampires take as little from their victims as possible. *He's going to die.*

You don't have to stop, Simon told her. *Drink until he lies dead at your feet. Remember the joy of having no constraint, of drinking until you are sated.*

Oh, how well she remembered those nights! Meghann pulled her prey into her arms; they almost looked like lovers except for his rolled-back eyes and the utter whiteness of his skin.

When she felt the man's body go slack in her arms, Meghann reluctantly tore her mouth from his neck, not hearing Louise's horrified shriek when she saw her blood teeth and the blood that covered her from her chin to the exposed swell of her breasts.

"I killed him," Meghann said, running her hand gingerly over his neck. It looked as if a lion had gotten at him! The left side of his neck was a gaping, savage mess of viciously lacerated tendon with small bits of skin clinging to the muscle.

He'll make your soul as bleak and shattered as his own.

Meghann didn't feel bleak—she felt supreme pleasure course through her and remembered from the past she'd remain this way all night. Her body would tingle with the strength she'd gained from her victim and she'd have a hyperawareness that would make the world seem to glow.

With an impatient gesture, Simon tore a strip from Louise's cerulean satin evening gown and handed it to Meghann. "Clean your face, sweet. Are you ready to learn how to use the blood rush?"

At Meghann's nod, Simon dragged Louise into the drawing room.

"Please let me go," Louise begged piteously. "I swear I won't tell . . ."

"I am not going to do anything," Simon told her and shoved her down on the silver and black chaise longue she'd sat in that night he used her to make Meghann jealous. "Meghann is."

"I am?" Meghann questioned numbly.

"Do you know why I torture my prey? The true source of a vampire's power is the ability to feed on pain, as well as blood." Simon stroked her cheek, and licked the blood on his hand. "I want you to destroy Louise . . . not by drinking her blood, but by controlling her mind. You're going to feed on her terror the same way you'd feed on her blood. Then, you can take her agony and transform it into strength. That is true magick, Meghann—the ability to derive power from mortal's torment."

"I don't understand," Meghann said.

"You will." Simon smiled. "You are now my apprentice and this is your first lesson." He gestured to Louise, still whimpering on the chaise longue but unable to move because of his iron grip on her psyche. "You agree we cannot let her leave here alive?"

Meghann nodded and Simon went on. "Then here is your task. We cannot mark her or kill her here . . . too many people know I amused myself with her. I do not care for the headache of diverting mortal authorities if they believe her death was homicide."

"So it has to look like suicide!" Meghann said.

"Close," Simon said. "It has to be suicide, Meghann. Make her commit suicide."

Now Meghann understood. She glanced at a plush black ottoman, and made it move across the floor until it was directly in front of Louise. Then she sat down, looking into the mortal's eyes and holding her hand— the tableau was a grotesque parody of the counseling sessions she used to have with mortal women.

He'll make your soul as bleak and shattered as his own.

"No!" Meghann cried and pulled her hands away from Louise. What was the matter with her? Killing to satisfy her blood lust was bad enough, but Simon was asking her to commit cold-blooded murder.

"Very well," Simon told her and gently shoved her out of the way so he sat across from Louise.

"You aren't mad?" Meghann asked, surprised that he'd let her off the hook so easily—maybe time really had mellowed Lord Baldevar.

"You found the blood lust tonight," Simon replied. "The rest will come in time. Now be silent and learn from what I do."

He gave Louise an open, disarming smile and spoke in soft, even tones—again Meghann was struck by the similarity to psychotherapy.

"You never came here tonight," Simon began. "Do you understand?"

Louise didn't respond like a person under hypnosis—her eyes were clear and focused, her voice steady. "Yes."

"Tell me about that man you came here with. Does he have family? Someone who will miss him?"

"He's just a degenerate gambler."

Simon grinned and in an aside to Meghann said, "That is why I adore this tacky whore of a city in the middle of the desert. There are so many transients, a vampire could feed for decades without arousing suspicion." He turned his attention back to Louise, and continued to mold her mind to suit his needs. "You were very upset at not getting that promotion. But you know that was not my fault. It is because you are incompetent."

"I am incompetent," Louise agreed in the same calm voice.

"You are very sad because you know your life will never be any better than it is tonight. So you have decided to end your life."

Simon smiled at Meghann's wide-eyed astonishment. "I am sorry the morals my uncle infested you with made this exercise impossible. It is a marvelous tool for sharpening your concentration."

He turned back to the mortal. "You will get into your car and drive directly home. Once in your house, you will write a note to your mother, saying *I just can't go on.* You'll sign it Louetta. After, you will go into the bathroom—do you shave your legs?"

Meghann almost laughed at what seemed like a non sequitur but Simon gestured for her to keep quiet.

"Yes," Louise said.

"Good. After you write your suicide letter . . . oh, before I forget, tell me the location of that videotape you blackmailed Del Straker with and where you're keeping the duplicates."

"I have a safe deposit box at my bank . . . 0927."

"Thank you. Once you've written your note, draw yourself a nice bubble bath. Let the warm water soothe you, relax you, then take your razor and draw it across your wrists. Stay in the tub afterward . . . do you understand?"

"Yes," Louise said without the slightest tremor in her voice. How was Simon doing this? Meghann wondered. Surely nothing could be stronger in the mortal mind than the will to live, the survival instinct.

"Powerful though the survival instinct is," Simon said to Meghann, "it is like flimsy gauze against the will of a vampire that knows how to use the power he gains from the blood rush. Now I must finish up."

Simon went through the commands again and Louise repeated his instructions verbatim when he asked her to. Afterward, without looking at Simon or Meghann, she stood up like an automaton, left the house, and got into her car.

Simon turned to Meghann. "This should only take a half hour or so but I must go to Louise's apartment—keep an eye on her. Suicides should never be left to chance; the survival instinct does make it a risky undertaking. Also, I must retrieve poor Del's tapes. Why don't you go upstairs and freshen up?"

Meghann nodded and Simon disappeared—drawing an envious sigh from her. She missed the astral plane, the ability to fly. Meghann headed for the master suite, looking forward to a long soak in the walnut-lined, claw-foot tub.

She discarded her blood-soaked gown, pinned her hair to the top of her head in a casual knot, and sank into the bath. Meghann leaned her head back, thinking that tonight was the first time in over forty years that she willfully killed a mortal when she fed.

She wasn't sure how she felt about it. On the one hand, she wasn't particularly conscience-stricken. But if she was discarding her values, why had she balked when Simon asked her to kill Louise?

Too, she wasn't sure she wanted to kill the next time she fed. But she couldn't tell herself tonight was simply a mistake; she'd taken far too much savage pleasure from the act of killing her host.

Am I going to become a killer again? Meghann wondered. She recoiled from that thought as she would from a physical blow. *I don't want to be evil,* Meghann thought desperately. *I don't want Alcuin to be right, I don't want to wake up some night and find I have no heart.*

Her hands flew to her stomach, caressing the hard mound. *Will I teach my children to kill? Raise them to regard mortals as nothing more than food? No, I'd never do that.*

Simon entered the room silently, admiring the way the dark wood of the tub enhanced Meghann's pale skin and flame-red hair. With the heat from the water turning her cheeks a becoming shade of pink, she'd be absolutely beautiful except for the crease between her eyes that marred her features.

"What troubles you, little one?"

Meghann's eyes flew open. "Louise is dead?" she asked. "What about that man?"

"Vinny has removed him for burial in the desert. As for Louise, she must have driven home in record time. Perhaps, in her—what is your phrase for the hidden mind?—subconscious she harbored a death wish." Simon took her hand. "Sweetheart, why do you frown? What bothers you about killing mortals?"

Meghann held his eyes. "I'm worried that feeling as you do . . . killing like you do would make me an unfit mother."

Simon eyed her for a few minutes and then posed a question. "Do you consider police unfit parents? Many of them kill regularly."

"That's self-defense," she pointed out.

"And you must drink blood to survive," Simon shot back. "Our children will crave that same sustenance.

Will you raise them to believe they're evil, that their need for blood is something shameful?"

"Of course not! But couldn't we teach them to leave their prey alive?"

"You can feed that way if that is your desire," Simon told her, careful to keep any impatience or derision out of his voice. Having Alcuin's tedious doctrine pour out of his consort's mouth was trying but it would be a fatal error to push Meghann. He was not going to repeat the mistakes of the past—this time he'd allow Meghann all the time she needed to develop her power, to understand mortals were no more than a source of food and occasionally amusement for vampires. "I will say one thing more and then the subject is closed. Tonight I saw you shine in a way you have not for decades. I would strongly urge you to put your foolish morals to the side, and revel in what you are—a predator without equal. May I join you, water nymph?"

Maggie!

Meghann went rigid and a sudden sense of wonder filled her pale face and unnaturally wide eyes.

Simon stared down at her, his mouth stretched into a grim, narrow line, but before he could speak Meghann said, "You felt it too?"

He took another look at her eyes, at the sweet, innocent joy radiating back at him, and asked, "Felt what?"

"They moved," Meghann told him, awe tingeing her voice.

"What?"

"The babies!" she shouted gleefully. "They moved inside me . . . I felt it!" She grabbed his hand, placing it on the center of her soaking wet abdomen.

Simon waited a few minutes, and then felt it . . . the smallest rippling across her flesh. His hand felt electrified by the brief contact with the new life inside Meghann.

Meghann leaned back in the tub, a dreamy smile

still on her face as she wrapped her hands protectively around the children in her womb. "Why did you look like that before—like something bit you?"

"I thought you were in pain," Simon said and Meghann accepted the explanation.

"Charles and Lee," she gasped, an even more dazzling smile lighting her features. "I have to call them . . . they'll be so thrilled when I tell them the babies moved!"

Maggie!

Meghann simply looked up at him, awaiting his response. Simon gazed hard into her wide, guileless green eyes. No, she could not deceive him like that— Meghann had not heard the low, despairing call.

"Simon?"

"Of course, little one," he said and smiled broadly. "Use the phone in my study. While you share this wonderful news with your friends, I'll attend to business and tell Del Straker he can have Louise's tapes as soon as I have the deed to his beach property."

Meghann rolled her eyes and pulled on a cinnamon silk bathrobe. "Have you ever used videotapes proving statutory rape to snatch an estate before?"

Simon laughed and ruffled her hair. He could not banter too long . . . that wretched voice might grow strong enough to reach Meghann if she remained nearby much longer. "I'll meet you downstairs, sweetheart."

A half hour later, Simon entered the study and found Meghann comfortably curled up on the large Chesterfield sofa while her dog sat at her feet, gnawing a rawhide bone with fierce concentration.

"Charles told me this was on—I couldn't resist watching for a little while," Meghann explained and cut her eyes to the large-screen television.

Simon settled down next to her. "What are you watching, little one?"

"*Horror of Dracula,*" she said, slapping him on the wrist when he rolled his eyes. "Don't be such a snob. How can you not like Christopher Lee?"

Simon observed the tall, black-caped figure with great, piercing dark eyes and conceded, "He does have a certain presence."

"Business settled?" Meghann asked absently, seeming captivated by a film Simon was certain she'd seen hundreds of times.

"Everything's taken care of," he replied, though he'd been startled for one of the few times in his immortal life when he heard Jimmy Delacroix call for the woman who, with her potions and "talking cure," was defying all precedent and bringing a vampire back from the insanity of transformation.

Or trying to, Simon amended. He was deeply grateful that his children chose such an opportune moment to announce their presence—otherwise Meghann might have heard that small voice calling to her.

Was she ever in love with the boy? Probably not. But Meghann was very much in love with the idea of independence, being her own mistress and answering to no one. That was the one thing Jimmy Delacroix could give her that would make her turn to him; he would never be able to subjugate her as Simon did.

So that left Simon with one alternative—reach into the boy's slowly healing mind and brutally crush the small spark of lucidity within him. Since he could not kill the boy until Meghann gave birth, he would simply monitor him carefully and undo Meghann's work should the need arise.

"What's wrong with you?"

"Hmmn?"

"You just looked so . . . so pensive."

"Merely puzzled, little one." Simon gestured to the

television screen. "This is based on Master Stoker's novel, is it not?"

"Slightly," Meghann admitted, her twitching lips indicating that she was trying not to giggle.

"So that means Castle Dracula is located in Transylvania?"

"Uh-huh," she said, eyes dancing at his mock confusion.

"But, little one, yon vampire has a British accent—not the Romanian one he should. Perhaps Dracula's parents sent him to Oxford in his formative years?"

"Fussbudget," Meghann said and stuck her tongue out.

"Wretched child, I must reprimand you for such disrespectful behavior toward your master." Simon reached out and pulled Meghann beneath him, delighting in the way she melted beneath him.

"Reprimand me again," Meghann murmured when he sat up.

"Watch your movie," Simon replied and pulled her into his lap, thinking it would be most enjoyable to tease her until the end of the film.

"How do you suppose that whole thing started?" Meghann asked at a shot of the vampire rising from his coffin, ready to commence his nighttime activities.

"It is not that difficult to comprehend," Simon said. "I think in reality vampires only wound up in coffins if their masters were careless with their transformation and let mortals see their changing body . . . you were quite ill the day before I completed your transformation. A hundred years before, without a stethoscope to detect your heartbeat, your family wouldn't have any way to tell you were still alive. So if I didn't reach you in time, into the coffin with you."

Meghann shuddered. "You mean that first night I could have woken up in a coffin?"

"In your time, it's more likely you'd have risen in a funeral parlor, being all made up for your viewing."

Simon took a dramatic pause. "But I awoke my first night as a vampire in a coffin."

"You were in a coffin?" Meghann gasped. "How? Why?"

"You know I stole my transformation blood," Simon said. "Two weeks I hovered between life and death . . . feverish, growing weaker with each day while Doctor Dee and Doctor Ahmed did all they could to help me."

"And then one day they thought you were dead!" Meghann cried.

"Not quite. Shall I tell you why I woke up in a coffin . . . how only a few short months after that shocking experience, I had my first battle with Alcuin?"

Meghann nodded, the vampire movie before her all but forgotten as she gave Simon her complete attention.

Simon started his story, smiling at Meghann's wide-eyed, eager stare . . . all traces of the hate and contempt he'd seen in her since Alcuin first contacted her vanished. She was once again the sweet, lively sprite he'd fallen in love with, and no insane vampire was going to take her from him. Simon knew Meghann's impatient nature well, knew she was frustrated by what appeared to be a lack of progress. Hopefully, she'd agree to kill him before she became aware he was recovering. Without Jimmy Delacroix to cling to, Meghann would be content to remain with her master.

EIGHTEEN

Yorkshire, England
June 3, 1592

   The unholy agony coursed through his body and wouldn't give him a moment's respite. It was like a thousand hot pincers stabbing him at once, making Simon finally plead with the God he'd turned his back on so long ago to please stop the pain. . . .

Simon's eyes snapped open and he gazed at the darkness surrounding him. Never had he seen such pitch-blackness—where was he? Why were his hands folded over his chest? He moved his hands out of the posture that made him deeply anxious for a reason he couldn't name and immediately brushed a hard surface directly above him.

Wood, Simon decided after he grazed his knuckles over the strange barrier. The wood (fresh-cut pine, he realized after breathing deeply) penned him in on all sides. If he moved his feet, he kicked the enclosure, and his hands—no matter where he moved his hands, they made contact with the pine.

Perhaps he was in a cabinet? Yes, if he was thinking clearly again (Simon shuddered when he remembered the raving savage he'd been reduced to after drinking the monster's blood), then he'd obviously survived transformation. That would mean his flesh was no longer safe from the sun during the day so his friends must have hidden him away.

"John?" he called out. "Khalid?" Deep silence greeted him . . . neither the astrologist nor the Moor physician answered his repeated calls. He'd have to find his own way out of the hiding place. If he was awake, Simon must assume it was night—Nicholas had only stirred during the day when they assaulted him. Simon raised his hand again, frowning when he saw jewels glittering in the darkness. Who would put rings on an invalid? He had no need of adornment on his sick bed. For that matter, why did silk and lace brush his face while he attacked the wood above him? Through his bafflement came one encouraging thought—if he could make out such details in this oppressive darkness, transformation must have made his eyes as sharp as a cat's.

Simon drew his foot as far back as he could and delivered a savage kick to the barrier at his feet. It shattered but instead of the air he fully expected to feel, a strange, cool substance with an earthy scent poured into his hiding spot.

Simon bent his knee, scratching his leg along the pine surface, until his hand grasped his calf. He grasped a handful of the slick, crumbling substance and brought it to his face, inhaling deeply . . . soil! Soil lurked outside the pine box . . .

Pine box and dirt . . . earth and wood . . . *a wood box surrounded by dirt . . .*

"No!" A horrified scream escaped his lips as the enormity of his situation hit him. Dear God . . . he hadn't been hidden, he'd been buried alive! The pine enclosure was no cabinet but a coffin!

Frantically, Simon clawed at the wood, feeling it splinter and crack under his panicked attack. One slat came free and Simon viciously tore it away, screaming when an avalanche of dirt poured onto his face.

"Get away!" Simon shouted irrationally at the soil and felt bemused shock when the dirt slid from him.

Of course, he thought. In his fright, he'd forgotten Nicholas's power . . . his power now. Simon shut his eyes, and forced himself to think calmly. Perhaps he didn't have to claw his way out of the grave . . . maybe he could move the dirt that threatened to suffocate him with his mind. He'd heard of such things.

Simon opened his eyes and glared at the packed soil. He imagined it flying off him, and in the next moment the dirt exploded upward, allowing Simon a glimpse of the waning moon far above him.

Without the weight of the soil over the coffin, Simon was able to batter away the lid and stand up in the grave. Easily, he jumped and cleared the gaping hole, staring down in horror at the destroyed coffin. Why had his friends allowed this to happen? They'd seen Nicholas—they knew no matter how he looked, he wasn't dead.

John Dee and Dr. Ahmed hadn't done this, Simon decided swiftly. He cast his mind over the past few days and realized his ears had sharpened much as his eyesight was now keener. Even in his delirium, he'd heard the servants gathering in the hallway, whispering in awed, hushed voices about their master's strange condition. Might they have thrown him in that cheap box?

It made sense. Certainly it explained why he hadn't lain in state . . . though that could also be explained by the unusually hot summer. Earl or no, if Simon had been dead, it would have been necessary to dispose of his remains quickly. Obviously the servants (those ignorant wretches that were so damned loyal to the memory of his father and brother) overpowered Simon's two protectors and buried him hastily.

Simon fell to his knees, feeling a resurgence of the pain he thought was gone for good. No, he thought, focusing on the sensation. This wasn't pain at all. It was more like a deep hunger . . . a . . . a . . .

Need, Simon realized. What was this strange yearning that made his body tremble and set his teeth on edge?

A soft whimper shattered his concentration and Simon spun around, seeing a young woman with filthy, gnarled hair, dressed in a coarse woolen gown.

"Dead," the girl cried and pointed a shaking finger at him. With one strangled cry, she spun on her heel and attempted to run away.

Easily, Simon caught up with her, taking a running tackle and pinning the peasant beneath him.

"Why do you come to such a lonely spot by yourself?" he demanded and then his eyes widened in shock when he heard an answer though the girl's lips never moved—*a bit of the dirt from the warlock's grave would give me such power* . . .

"Witch!" Simon accused, finding the need in him soothed by the girl's bulging eyes and heaving chest. Her fear was good; it restored him, as did the lovely thumping vein in her neck. What drew him to that bluish line on her pale skin? What was that delightful sound . . . something like a river flowing throughout her body? And the smell . . . a delicious aroma of copper and iron . . .

The girl screamed and Simon winced at the sudden sharp pain in his lower lip. Puzzled, he watched two bright droplets of blood fall on the girl's dress and realized he'd cut himself somehow.

Of course! Simon ran his tongue over his lower lip and felt the new teeth cutting into his flesh. He'd developed fangs like Nicholas . . . fangs that had emerged when he'd leaned closer to the girl. Now he knew what he'd heard . . . it was blood flowing through the girl's body. A voice deeper than instinct whispered that her blood would heal him, give him power he'd never before imagined.

Simon gave his victim a smile that made her eyes roll back until only the whites showed. He was grateful for her terror; it made it so much easier to hold her still as he sank his new teeth into the soft, pliant skin of her neck.

Simon discovered heaven when her rich, healthy blood poured into his mouth and down his throat. Nothing . . . not lovemaking, not gold, not even the power the spirits gave him could compare to the bliss he felt as he drank. Something that had tasted foul while he was human was now more delectable than the finest wine; not even the best whiskey could provide the warmth that filled his body.

Even better though, Simon felt his strength increasing with each mouthful of the coppery elixir. The blood gave him unbelievable vigor; he felt he had the stamina of seven bulls! He could rip the venerable oak tree behind him out by the roots with one hand, and his mind—merciful God, what the blood did for his mind! How could this peasant's blood increase his cleverness, make him feel more self-assured than he ever had before? It was absolutely wonderful what the blood did for him. Simon wanted to drink forever. . . .

The hot stream became a mere trickle and Simon felt the body under him lose its rigidity. Reluctantly, he raised his mouth and stared down at the girl. Dead, he observed coolly when he stared at the dull, pasty skin and sightless, staring eyes.

Simon picked the corpse up and threw it into his grave, again using the mind trick to make the soil fold over her so the grave looked untouched before setting off to find his friends.

Hearing footsteps, Simon spun around, only to discover the sounds were not directly behind him but at the foot of the isolated hill he'd been buried on. Glaring down from his vantage point, he was able to see Dr. Dee and Dr. Ahmed.

"My lord!" John Dee cried in joy and then took a step back, seeming revolted by his friend's appearance.

"Why do you stare at me like that?" Simon de-

manded and then a series of thoughts assaulted him—
*his hair hangs to his shoulders, his nails are claws better
suited to some daemon creature, he's covered in blood, soil
clings to his clothing, he's paler than the moon above him* . . .

Simon fell to his knees, hands cradling his head.
Nicholas had been right—to hear every passing
thought would drive you mad. But how did he keep
the noise from entering his mind?

Dimly, Simon remembered some of the tricks Father
Bain had taught him to keep daemons from entering
his mind . . . surely they might work at expelling foreign thoughts. Simon conjured up an image of a steel
shield and imagined it deflecting thoughts instead of
blows. Soon, the chaos in his mind vanished and he
was able to stand again.

"Why did I awaken inside a cheap box? Did you
believe I was deceased . . . even after witnessing Master
Aermville's strange daytime condition?" He frowned
at his friends while keeping the shield image sharp
and ready.

"My lord," Dr. Ahmed began, "there are things you
are unaware of. At dawn this morning, your fever
broke. You ceased raving and fell back upon your bed,
utterly still. It is unfortunate that your wife was in the
room—"

"Isabelle?" Simon frowned—after Michael died, Isabelle had attempted to take her own life by throwing
herself from the roof of the estate. Unfortunately, the
rosebushes surrounding the house cushioned her fall
and instead of her dying, her back was merely broken.
She was unable to walk and spent most of her time in
bed, alternately weeping wildly or staring without
speaking for hours on end.

"She was having a lucid period," Dr. Ahmed said to
his unasked question, and Simon nodded, pleased that
the physician's thoughts weren't penetrating his shield.

"I believe the thought of your imminent death restored her," John Dee put in, and Simon laughed

grimly at the observation he agreed with wholeheartedly.

"When you fell back," Dr. Ahmed continued, "Lady Isabelle brought a small mirror she had around her waist to your nose. She screamed because your image was naught but a blur in the mirror. The priest at her side told her not to worry over whatever you'd become—since there was no sign of breath, it was obvious you were dead and the servants could remove your unholy remains from the bedchamber."

"Our most pressing concern," John told him, "was to keep you safe from daylight. The draperies in your bedchamber were drawn but you'd be exposed to full sunlight if the servants took you into the hallway. Quickly, I presumed on our association and asked your . . . wife . . . if Doctor Ahmed and I might have her permission to prepare your body for burial. We agreed to the shoddy coffin your wife wanted to put your remains in because we felt you'd be able to tear it apart when you awoke . . . if you awoke before Khalid and I arrived at your grave.

"We assumed you'd be interred in the family cemetery and it would be a simple matter to free you at sunset, but Lady Isabelle decreed you could not be set in hallowed ground. She had the guards chase myself and Doctor Ahmed as well as your personal guard from the estate while her men-at-arms buried you in a secret location. My lord, we would have arrived earlier but the men returned but an hour an ago from burying you. Then, your guards had to threaten the information from the fools and we spent the past hour walking to this distant place. You have my deepest apologies for the shock and terror you must have felt at regaining your senses to find yourself buried alive."

Simon held his hand up. "You need not apologize to me. Now, come along with me—don't you want to see my wife's face when she lays eyes on her resurrected husband?"

Simon turned from the mound of soil he never wanted to lay eyes on again and descended the sharp incline. At the foot of the hill, he gave a brief nod to his personal guard of black mutes. He was not surprised Isabelle had attempted to drive them away. He knew their dark skin and silent stares frightened her almost as much their stalwart devotion to their master did. Simon laughed when he saw the mutes regarding him with the same mixture of loyalty and gratitude as always. He reflected that even serving a monster returned from the dead was a far better fate than what Simon had rescued them from in Algiers—being galley slaves chained to an oar for the rest of their miserable lives.

"My lord," John said, interrupting his thoughts. The astrologist held out a hooded black velvet cloak. "Do you wish to hide your face until you are . . ."

"Presentable?" Simon laughed and waved away the cloak. "I far prefer to put the fear of the devil in my cowardly servants."

Simon flung open the heavy oak door to the house, ignoring the horrified gasps and stares of the servants as he stalked toward the great hall.

Some of the servants tried to rush him, but Simon shook his head when the mutes attempted to surround him so their master wouldn't be assaulted. Easily, he shoved those foolish enough to approach out of his path, the slight pressure making them fly through the air.

"What?" Simon snarled, deliberately making his voice harsh and raspy to further terrorize the shivering wretches before him. "No word of welcome for your master freshly returned from hell?"

Simon stalked past some whimpering servants and stood at the head of the table, glaring at the pale, moaning assembly before him. "I want every one of

you, with the exception of Adelaide, my personal
guards, and Yusef the cook gone from this estate immediately. Speak a word to anyone of what you have
witnessed and I swear I shall pay you a visit in the
blackest part of night. Now be gone!"

Simon turned around, a grim smile on his face as
he heard the hasty press to the front door. The servants were running over each other in their haste to
escape the house. Now, for Isabelle. He'd go to her
bedroom . . .

No sooner had the thought formed in his mind than
he found himself standing at Isabelle's bedside. He
had a vague impression of flying through a cold, dark
place in the seconds it took for him to travel from the
great hall to Isabelle's suite.

Magus that he was, Simon quickly realized he'd been
on the astral plane. Of course he'd gone there before
but he'd never brought his body with him—just his
soul. He remembered Nicholas telling him vampires
could disappear and reappear at any spot they chose
within a thirty-mile radius but apparently the young
minstrel hadn't known the journey took place on the
astral plane.

Simon had no time to wonder at yet another benefit
of his new existence—Isabelle and the wretched old
priest she'd brought over from France were screaming
prayers at him.

"Good evening, wife," Simon said, giving the emaciated, sore-covered woman on the bed a cold grin.
"Did you truly think you could rid yourself of me by
throwing my body into a cheap box and chasing my
friends from my home?"

He felt liquid land on his cheek and whirled around
to glare at the wizened prelate, clutching a stone phil-
ter of holy water.

"*Revenez, diable!*" the priest thundered. "*Au nom d'un
Dieu, revenez a votre tombe!*"

"*Soyez silencieux!*" Simon retorted when the priest ordered him back to his grave. The priest's eyes widened when his exorcism was cut off as abruptly as though Simon had gagged him.

Was there no end to what he could do now? Simon wondered, circling around the old priest.

"Raise your hand," he ordered, still speaking French because the ignorant priest spoke not a word of English even after living nearly a decade on English soil. Obediently, the priest raised his right hand.

"Sit," Simon said and the priest sank to the ground.

"What have you done to him?" Isabelle screamed from her bed. "How have you bewitched a man of the cloth?"

Feeling as mischievous as a young lad, Simon gave the dying woman on the bed a smile filled with such villainy he was sure Master Shakespeare would have agreed to let him play Iago if he could just see it.

"I died a man this morning and return to earth tonight as the Prince of Darkness," Simon whispered, forcing himself not to smile at the ridiculous speech.

Isabelle went several shades paler and her hands flew to the onyx and ivory carved rosary at her neck.

"Those foolish relics cannot repulse me!" Simon yanked the rosary off her neck, and watched the small beads roll across the stone floor.

He grasped his wife's chin between his fingers, feeling utter delight course through him when he saw the terror in her large, purple eyes. Beautiful eyes, Simon thought with some regret as he remembered the lush, red-haired beauty Isabelle had been when he had first met her. Now, as disease ravaged her, there was more fiery hair on her pillow than her scalp, and her body was nothing but a pile of bones covered with ashy, rotting skin. If only the woman had not been such a pious, cold fool—perhaps if she'd borne his son, they could have had the same cordial peace he'd observed in the marriages of most of his friends at court.

But no, Isabelle not only miscarried his heir, she

killed the nephew he'd grown to love like a son with her superstition and distrust of him. Her slow death from the pox wasn't enough, Simon thought viciously. He meant to break her, leave her with no hope or dignity—only then would he feel she'd paid adequately for all she'd done.

"That priest," Simon said slowly, pointing to the man still sitting docilely on the floor. "He's been with you since your childhood, has he not?"

"Yes," Isabelle whispered. "Harm one hair on his head and you'll spend eternity in hell, devil!"

"You fool, I shall never see heaven or hell! That"— Simon gestured to the open window and star-studded sky outside—"is where I shall reside for all eternity—in the night. You, on the other hand, can only be a few months from death. But before you go, don't you think you should repay yon priest for all his kindness toward you?"

He gave a cruel smile at her puzzled but still hate-filled eyes and turned to the priest. "Arise, old man, and come to the bed."

The priest obeyed him instantly.

"Remove all your clothing."

"Pere Villiere," Isabelle cried when the priest pulled off his robe to reveal his wrinkled old form. "Stop, I implore you! Fight this devil's hold upon your soul!"

"No mere mortal can fight me, wife," Simon said and reached over to tear the ragged, colorless shift from her body.

"Stop!" Isabelle cried. "What are you doing?"

"Climb on top of her, good Father," Simon said and watched the old priest straddle his wife.

"That's right," Simon said when the priest's hand started to roam over Isabelle's form. His wife was too weak to struggle much, but she wept mightily as her childhood priest obeyed all of Simon's commands— stroking her breasts, planting kisses on her protesting lips, and finally entering her.

"Would you say evil has triumphed this night, Isabelle?" Simon whispered into her ear as the priest raped her. Watching the helpless old cleric obey his commands, Simon felt his own erection begin—not because the sight of his wife's gaunt form enticed him but because he was filled with the same sense of power he had when he drank the peasant girl's blood. Somehow he had not thought of this aspect of immortality—when Nicholas made his offer, all Simon could think of was that he'd escape an early death from the pox.

But now he realized he had abilities he'd never even guessed at. No longer did he need his grimoires and herbs, the incantations he'd devoted his youth to learning. Now he could make people obey his will . . . even fly the astral plane with no effort at all!

Simon frowned at the wheezing, gasping sound coming from the elderly priest. Apparently sex was too much for his heart, Simon observed as the priest collapsed on top of Isabelle.

"Pity there's no one to give him the last rites," Simon said mockingly as he tossed the dead priest to the floor and leaped on top of Isabelle. The thought of raping this weeping skeleton made his stomach turn but watching the priest obey him . . . the delightful feeling of control made Simon's blood craving return; he felt the blood teeth rip out of his gums again.

At the sight of his fangs, Isabelle simply fainted and Simon lunged greedily at her neck, eager for the blood until the substance filled his mouth and he found himself by the side of her bed, gagging and using all his will to keep from vomiting.

After a few moments, Simon felt a soft hand on his hair and glared up to see Adelaide. His old nurse simply smiled down at him, seeming not at all frightened by the fangs that hadn't receded yet or his fresh-from-the-grave appearance.

"Lovey," she said, "yer drinking blood now to survive . . . yer nice friend explained it all to me. Has it not occurred to ye that if ye drink from someone as ill as yer wife, her bad humors might enter ye and make ye as sick as she is?"

Simon frowned, realizing Adelaide was probably right, but if he was immortal, as Nicholas had promised, surely any illness he contracted was only a fleeting problem. Already his equilibrium had been restored to him and he rose off the floor without Adelaide's assistance.

"Shall I prepare yer bath or were ye planning to remain like that?" she inquired archly, taking in the blood on his face and soil from the grave clinging to his body.

Simon laughed and followed her to the Turkish bath he'd had installed in the house after Roger died, allowing his thoughts to wander while Adelaide used the silver scraper he'd brought back from Istanbul to scrape him free of sweat and dirt and pared his hair and fingernails back to an acceptable length.

"Don't get too puffed up with yer new power, laddie," Adelaide cautioned.

"Is something wrong?" he asked, alert to the note of warning in her voice.

"I'll leave it to yer friends to tell ye—ye'll need to form a plan. Just remember, yer not the first to have this power . . . didn't that boy-lover tell ye there were others?"

"As always, you're right, Adelaide. I'd hate to think I'd no longer have your counsel once death claims you."

"Why, laddie." Adelaide reached up to stroke his cheek, her normally hard green eyes misty and soft. "Are ye offering me yer new state?"

"Who else would I give it to?" Simon laughed and followed her to his bedchamber. How could he withhold transformation from Adelaide—the only mother he'd ever known? Who knew what might have hap-

pened to him without Adelaide encouraging him to
believe he could have more from life than the pitiful
existence fate and his father had tried to force on him?

He dressed quickly and joined Dr. Ahmed and Dr.
Dee in the great hall. Ravenous, Simon attacked the
buffet the cook had laid out while he had bathed.

When he'd eaten his fill (more than three times
what he usually ate), he turned to his friends. "Adelaide hinted there might be some trouble I should
know about."

John Dee nodded. "The last few days, you've had
periods of respite—not rest, precisely, but you did become a bit calmer. I used that time to search through
Master Aermville's belongings. Most of it was mere
clothes and his instruments but I trust these will interest you." He placed an intricately carved jade box in
Simon's hands.

Simon opened it and pulled out a sheaf of letters—
some yellowed and crumbling with age, others new but
written on waterproof parchment. He leaned back in
his chair and glanced at the letters, starting with the
oldest and working his way to the more recent ones.

Again, his new gifts surprised him as he found himself reading the letters, composed in a code that cun-
ningly used Latin and Greek, in a matter of minutes.
From what Simon gathered, the letters represented a
period of time going back to the year 1494. Apparently
that was when Nicholas Aermville made the acquaintance of a creature named Alcuin.

This Alcuin must have been the mentor Nicholas
spoke of, Simon mused as he read, for the letters were
mainly advice from Alcuin to Nicholas. A couple of
times the letters referred to great gatherings, leading
Simon to believe these creatures were a sizable population and they apparently congregated together. That
gave him pause—needing blood as they did, how could
more than a few be in the same place? They must live
near large cities, Simon decided, a place where there

was a surplus population so a few missing people wouldn't be remarked upon.

In the next letter (from 1505), Simon discovered he was wrong. These creatures apparently lived in rural seclusion but they didn't attract unwanted attention because they made a point of denying their blood lust, as Alcuin termed it. Letter after letter urged Nicholas to suppress his desire, go without feeding as long as he could. When he felt the craving, the young vampire was supposed to pray for guidance.

Simon's lips curled in disgust—who would want to spend eternity in a life of prayer and denial? Simon's answer to why the annoyingly pious creature chose to spend immortality in a state of abstinence came in the next letter when Alcuin made a fleeting reference to a mortal career as a bishop.

Idly Simon wondered how a priest came to be a vampire, for it was plain this mewling, sanctimonious man was no magus cleverly disguising himself with a church career as Father Bain had been . . . this Alcuin obviously believed all the self-righteous prattle in his letters.

Bored with page after page of lectures about helping mortals and praying for God's aid in overcoming the devil-tinge in their blood (*if you dislike it so much, why not greet the sun?* Simon thought in contempt), he started skipping through the letters—stopping cold when he saw his name mentioned in the last one.

16 April, 1592
Nicholas,
  How glad I am now that you chose not to accompany us to the New World—I fear the utter misery of the people would shock your gentle spirit though I have no doubt your lute would bring them some cheer. Remember what I told you; God did not give you the gift of music just to entertain the nobility. You should also use your talents to raise the spirits of those with little happiness in their lives.

In your last post, you asked me to describe the New World. In many ways, I am reminded of Ireland—again there is the nightmare of being surrounded by the despondent spirits of a conquered people while living in a land of unsurpassed physical beauty. The Spanish colonists work the natives (women and children too, I'm afraid) to death while they rape the land of all its fertile resources.

As you know, I've set up a small mission here. We provide medicine for the ill, food, shelter, and Extreme Unction to any that request it but the only people we attempt to convert are the priests who offer no comfort to these poor souls but rather tell them they deserve to suffer because they are not baptized Christians. I remind these mortal priests of Our Dear Lord Jesus Christ who embraced the indigent, lived among the lepers and outcasts.

I wish I could stay here for a longer period of time, but I must return to Europe. In my absence, a great many transformations are being performed despite my warnings that our strange existence is not suitable to most. Only the strongest will and purest heart can resist the temptations blood lust places before us.

Nicholas, I fear your Lord Baldevar is not of that special mien, that rather than resist temptation he might very well wallow in it. From what little you write, I fear this is a man with a dark spirit. You tell me the English court buzzes with rumor that he is a sorcerer and you yourself know he is perverting the science of alchemy to chase down immortality. When men wish to live forever, it is usually because they rightfully fear damnation in the afterlife. I know you believe he has a soft side, but I fear this may be an illusion. My young friend, has it never occurred to you that in your loneliness you are endowing Lord Baldevar with attributes he does not possess? I beg of you—do not offer him transformation. I know you've

*been bereft since Alec chose to greet the sun, but better
no lover than one that might destroy you.*

*Please, Nicholas, do not speak to this man of immor-
tality until I come home. Bring him to me that I might
see what is truly in his heart.*

May the blessings of Christ be upon you.
Alcuin

Stunned, Simon looked up at his friends. "This creature knows who I am! When he cannot find Nicholas,
how long will it take him to search for me?"

"That letter was written close to three months ago,"
Dr. Ahmed said. "With favorable tides, he'll arrive in
Europe by summer's end."

"That gives us but a few weeks to prepare for his
arrival," Simon said, and his friends nodded their
agreement.

This Alcuin patronized Nicholas Aermville, Simon
thought. Surely the creature (who'd obviously lived a
long, long life) would avenge his friend's death. Simon's first craven thought was that he should flee England and take up a new identity but he soon dismissed
such a cowardly notion. Even if he got away successfully, Alcuin might be able to track him down . . .
sense him in some unknown way. The only thing to
do was face down the creature and whatever followers
he had. Followers . . .

"I should really replace my servants," Simon said
with a wicked grin. "I can turn this estate into a vampire colony. This house needs roughly fifty servants to
maintain it properly . . . fifty soldiers to battle this Alcuin and whatever disciples he brings along."

"How will you feed all of them?" John demanded.

Simon shrugged. "There's the village and York's but
a few miles away. With the ability to fly, they can also
raid the lowlands for prey."

"I think it makes perfect sense," Khalid interjected.
"We are badly outmatched because this Alcuin has

lived longer than all of our ages combined. But we've all read the missives he wrote to Nicholas Aermville. When he mentions followers, he never mentions a high number—certainly not the kind of army Lord Baldevar will amass. Numerical superiority will be our only advantage."

"Not just numbers," Simon interrupted, the wolfish smile still on his face. "My followers will be harder than his. After all, what if all his flock is like Nicholas—soft-minded and defenseless? I'm not going to transform ordinary souls. I want highwaymen, murderers, renegades, sorcerers like myself if we can find them . . . mortals that already have larceny in their blood!"

"Mortals without conscience," John nodded. "I think your plan sound but for one thing, my lord. Do not transform another magus . . . he might attempt to wrest control from you."

"Agreed," Simon said. "Hard mortals but not overly intelligent or ambitious ones . . . mortals so thankful for what I give they'll never think to challenge me. But, John, how can you tell me not to transform another magus? Did I not promise you my new power in exchange for your aid?"

The astrologist sighed and gazed moodily into his silver chalice. "I would be most grateful but after watching your torment . . . my lord, I am in my old age. I do not believe my frail body could withstand the process. With your permission, I wish to stay with you and offer what services I can but I believe your blood would kill me."

Simon nodded—he'd had the same thought but he'd offered transformation anyway, feeling it was Dr. Dee's decision to make. He turned to his physician. "Khalid?"

For the first time in twelve years, Simon saw a smile on the Moor's round, solemn face. "I am but a few years your senior, Lord Baldevar. I shall gladly partake

of your blood . . . who knows what medicine I'll be
capable of in a few hundred years?"

"Wonderful," Simon said and lifted his chalice high.
"To life eternal and vanquished foes!"

NINETEEN

Six months later
December 25, 1592

Simon awoke and felt an odd tension in the air. Another one of his kind was nearby, a being that emanated a great sense of power as well as an intense anger and heavy sorrow. The anger, Simon knew, was directed at him . . . this must be Alcuin, arrived at last. What caused the creature's sadness Simon neither knew nor cared—he had to prepare for the confrontation ahead.

Simon threw back the ermine coverlet and arose from the feather-stuffed mattress lying in the center of the large cave that had served as his sanctuary for the past few months. He dressed hastily, preparing himself for the battle he instinctively felt would settle the war that had been raging on his estate for over two months now. He buckled his great-grandfather's jewel-encrusted broadsword around his waist. Like most of his peers, he far preferred the sleek, elegant rapier to this heavy relic of another time. Unfortunately, that thin whippet of steel was nothing compared to the broadsword his enemies favored. Simon often wondered if they preferred the broadsword because they felt it a better tool for decapitation or perhaps they'd simply formed an attachment to the ungainly weapon during their mortal lifetimes. It had taken Simon a few nights to adjust to the weight of the broadsword but he was now capable of using it with the same light, swift touch he'd had with his rapier.

Simon stepped out of the cave and gave an uncontrollable shiver at the bleak silence that greeted him. At first when he'd arise the sounds from the village a few miles from his cave reached his ears. Now all the vampires he'd needed to create had bled the village dry. An eerie stillness hung over the area, making it seem haunted, desolate.

A good thing he'd kill Alcuin this evening, Simon thought and started his stealthy, silent walk back to the estate. He was worried about the things he'd transformed—they had no restraint, they killed in such large numbers that Simon knew a Crown inquiry was only a matter of time. Already the residents of York barricaded their houses at night; many gathered in churches for extra protection. Soon Elizabeth would have to send troops up here to see who or what was killing off so many of her people, and then what? What if her soldiers found some of the vampires during the day and watched in horror as their bodies burned when they were exposed to sunlight?

Simon knew he had to dispose of the rogue killers that wouldn't learn discretion, were incapable of learning much of anything. With few exceptions, they were as low and stupid in their new life as in their old. They were incapable of flying the astral plane, could master only the simplest tricks, like moving about small objects with the force of their minds and keeping their prey still while they fed. For the most part, Simon regretted their existence and was almost glad his enemies were killing a great many of them. The fifty he'd started with had been no more than ten at dawn. But his slain army had carried quite a few of Alcuin's acolytes to hell with them so their purpose was served.

Still, all this death and slaughter had done something to the once beautiful area. Simon remembered as a small boy he'd thought the howling wind of the winter months a daemon that meant to carry him off to hell. That had merely been childish nonsense but now something dark and evil had definitely settled over the land. Not only couldn't he hear mortals anymore, it seemed the beasts had fled too . . . no sheep, no horses, not even the owls made a sound this night. He was eager to achieve a victory and leave this chilling, cursed place.

Since he was only a quarter mile from the estate now, Simon stopped and glared up at the starless sky and quarter moon. *"Metatron, Melekh, Beroth, Noth, obtestor te Deo viventi ut virtute verbarum harum me invisibilem faceres."*

He kept walking, knowing his presence was now somewhat cloaked. Simon had discovered that although his incantation made him completely invisible to his own young apprentices it only offered him a few moments of protection before his enemies sensed him. Still, those precious moments had allowed him to sneak up on several of them and decapitate them swiftly.

Simon smiled briefly, thinking the incantation for invisibility would have required a waxen figure back when he was human to have any chance of success, that he'd have to be careful to perform the ritual during the right month, the right phase of the moon. Now his ability was so sharp he had only to say the words and receive what he wanted. Daemons he could summon easily; he did not even need the magick circle to protect him.

Simon sighed ruefully, remembering the only thing he needed protection from was vampires that wanted him dead. He had not yet arrived at a spell or weapon to satisfactorily rid himself of them. He strode the dark, unlit path with confidence, steadfastly refusing to acknowledge any trepidation at the evening ahead.

Along the path he discovered the decapitated

corpses of two more of his progeny and one vampire he didn't recognize—an enemy, then. Simon knew he could leave them where they were; the sunlight would incinerate any evidence of their existence.

A chilling scream shattered the thick silence and Simon jumped, his heart racing for a few moments before he gained control over himself and continued walking. He should be used to the sound by now—it was the shriek of a vampire receiving a stake through its heart.

When his enemies arrived, Simon quickly learned that decapitation was a merciful fate compared to the hell a vampire went through if any heavy weapon punctured its heart. The impaled vampire could only squirm around miserably, its wonderful strength and ability to deflect blows vanished. Once again, it could and did suffer pain . . . the pain of the weapon lodged in its chest and the torture it was put through when the interrogators made a vain attempt to elicit information on the mysterious Lord Baldevar's whereabouts.

Of course, the torture that rivaled anything Simon had ever heard of in London Tower gained his enemies nothing. Simon told no one—not even Khalid or Dr. Dee—where he slept during the day. Fighting his enemies on the family estate gave Simon a definite advantage; only someone born to the Yorkshire Dales would know how to search the complex network of limestone caves and sea caverns.

Then again, this Alcuin . . . how sharp were his abilities? Simon paused, concentrating on the atmosphere around him. He realized he no longer felt hunted, focused on. The creature had other matters on its mind now—that sadness overwhelmed it. Was Alcuin upset because so many of his followers were dead? Perhaps, while he was distracted, Simon could take him by surprise.

Another piteous scream reached his ears and Simon

thought under their simpering piety, his enemies enjoyed the power they gained from inflicting misery as much as he was learning to. In a way, feeding on emotion provided almost as much sustenance as drinking blood.

Of course these vampires would have no more opportunity to torture their helpless quarry. Whether he cared for his spawn or no, Simon was their master and as such he owed them protection. It was his place and his alone to end their existence if he felt the action was warranted. But he knew from experience this was the perfect moment to attack and kill a few more of his foes; they were too involved in the torture to keep their senses peeled for the presence of another vampire.

Simon leaped through the air soundlessly, grasping the heavy limb of the tree above him. He slithered along on his stomach until he was poised directly above the clearing where three vampires stood clustered around a long wooden stake that imprisoned another vampire. The unfortunate's head was down, a sword hilt bulging from his chest.

"Look at this," Simon heard a deep voice rumble. "We've caught ourselves a Moor tonight . . . heretic in mortal life and unholy abomination now. Where's your master, filth?"

Khalid, Simon thought, his heart thumping so loudly he thought his enemies would surely hear its furious beat—they had Khalid! Simon forced himself to calm down; he'd do his friend no good if his ill temper led him to rash action. No matter that he simply wanted to leap to the stake and cut his friend down, he must proceed calmly.

While Simon planned his attack, Khalid gave his interrogator a disdainful reply, halting and labored though it was. "I call no one master and as for filth, it is not I who smell like I spent the day lying in a pile of horse dung."

"All you infidels are so proud of your bathing—another sign of your vanity," the vampire sneered, but Simon thought the stung growl in his voice proved Khalid's jab had found its mark. "I rid the great land of Spain of your kind while I worked beside Torquemada and I shall be pleased to send you to hell along with your brethren in the name of God."

This thing had been an Inquisitor? That explained the overzealous tone that was the mark of the true fanatic. Simon withdrew two small daggers from his belt and pulled himself into a crouch on the tree limb, poised for attack.

Before he could leap from his perch, the Inquisitor vampire raised his great sword and decapitated Khalid. Simon saw the smallest ghost of surprise enter his friend's eyes before the sharp blade sent his head to the ground.

Simon took advantage of his enemies' self-congratulations and jumped from the tree, bringing two of the vampires down to the ground with him. While they sprawled, unable to adjust to the unexpected attack, Simon planted his daggers in their backs, severing their hearts from behind.

With a roar of outrage, the other vampire hurled himself at Simon and they both rolled along the ground. All Simon's furious struggles were for naught—he could not extract himself from the steely grip of his foe. Never had he encountered such brute physical strength . . . no wonder this thing had overpowered Khalid.

When the vampire loosened his grip to grab his sword, Simon was able to shove him hard and crawl a scant inch away. He reached for his own sword but it was kicked from his hand with a blow that shattered his wrist. Simon yelped in pain while rolling to the side to evade the broadsword that almost took his head from his shoulders.

"Devil's spawn," the hulking vampire hissed at Simon as he stood over him.

His hand already healed, Simon battered his head against his adversary's kneecap, feeling grim pleasure when a sharp crack shattered the silence around them and the giant fell to the ground beside Simon.

With the vampire prone and temporarily immobilized by pain, Simon was able to throw himself on top of it and attach himself to its neck like a leech. The outraged vampire tried to throw him off but Simon sank his blood teeth in as far as they would go and his hands gained such a firm purchase on his enemy's back that Simon could feel his short, sharp nails ripping through the vampire's muscles all the way to the bone beneath.

Bloodletting was his only chance for survival. Simon knew in a swordfight this immense, vastly experienced creature would tear him to shreds. Thank God, Simon thought as the potent vampire blood poured into him, he'd made the lifesaving discovery that a bled vampire had no more strength than a mortal. That trick he'd learned a few months before when one of his spawn drained a girl Simon had claimed for his own. He'd meant to savor her beauty a few nights before drinking her blood. Outraged when he saw the husk she'd been reduced to, Simon grabbed the miserable thing that had killed her and tore its neck apart. Immediately he'd seen that a starved or drained vampire lost a great deal of its power though it was restored once the creature fed again.

Now Simon felt the thrashing body beneath him start to weaken, and raised his mouth. He didn't want to kill this creature—if his enemies could gain information through torture, so could he.

"You are not so far gone you cannot comprehend me," Simon said flatly. "Answer my questions truthfully or before I end your worthless existence I shall sacrifice your soul to my dark gods."

The small, boarlike eyes opened and the vampire glared feebly.

Simon yanked him to his feet and kept a rough hand beneath his elbow so his enemy wouldn't collapse.

"Take me to Alcuin," Simon ordered.

"I am Alcuin," the vampire said, and Simon snorted in derision.

"Do you forget I am of the nobility? I know well the difference between master and servant. You're but a lackey."

"I am no lackey," the thing thundered. "I serve at my master's right hand! It is I who plan our battles . . ."

"So if I torture you, I'll gain valuable information," Simon said dryly and watched a dull flush show up on the vampire's coarse-featured face. "Pickings must be scant among our number that my enemy relies on such a lack-wit. Perhaps you thought my threat an idle one but I assure you I'll send your soul to hell within a minute if you don't tell me where Alcuin is."

The thing glared in hostile, arrogant silence until Simon began to chant and the already frigid temperature plummeted further while a foul odor started to permeate the air.

A look of terror entered the vampire's eyes and he cried hastily, "In your wife's chambers, you fiend! The poor woman approaches death and my master is giving her the last rites."

Simon roared and gave his prisoner a scornful glance as he dragged him to the manor house. "Yon leader has closeted himself with Isabelle? What kind of sentimental fool is this creature that he pauses in the midst of battle to give benediction to some worthless mortal bitch? Walk faster, imbecile. I am most eager to face down your equally feebleminded master."

"He'll kill you," the vampire snarled and received a sharp rap to his head.

"Not while I hold you hostage," Simon returned calmly. "If Alcuin frets over some dying female he's never met before, he'll not take one step toward me while I hold a sword to your neck. How is it he's survived all this time with such a soft heart?"

"We've never encountered one like you before," the vampire said and quickly clamped his mouth into a grim line when he realized Simon had again gotten him to admit more than he should have.

So he unsettled Alcuin as much as the old bishop bothered him, Simon mused while he strode through the ajar front door and headed for the stairs. He wanted to use the astral plane but he hadn't yet figured out a way to hold another soul in his grasp throughout flight. His prisoner made no attempt to inform his master of their approach and Simon almost laughed at himself for this lapse into mortal thinking. Alcuin would not need a shout or noise to know they drew near—no doubt his senses were already at full alert.

Simon drew his sword and put the blade to his enemy's neck, dragging him toward Isabelle's chambers by the hair. As they came closer, the sonorous Latin chant of the last rites reached his sharp ears . . . so Isabelle was finally dying. Simon felt nothing at her death, but the anguish in Alcuin's sobbing voice intrigued him. Why did he feel such grief for a woman he didn't know?

Entering the bedchamber, Simon saw the room was bathed in thick darkness. No candles flickered and the thick velvet draperies Isabelle favored were drawn tightly shut so no moonlight could illuminate the chamber. Even with his new, keen sight, Simon could only see a cloaked figure clutching Isabelle's bony white hand.

"Go now and join your son and husband," the cloaked figure whispered, and Simon clenched his jaw to keep from shivering. Even though Alcuin spoke gently, there was nothing weak about his voice or the aura of impenetrable strength that surrounded him. "Go and forget the pain that wretched, vicious fiend caused you."

"Do you feel any sorrow at what you've done to this gentlewoman?" Simon started at this direct indication that Alcuin was aware of his presence. Though the creature didn't take its eyes from Isabelle's corpse or raise his voice, Simon could not have felt more disconcerted if Alcuin had glared and shouted loudly enough to shatter glass. Usually he was the one that kept his opponents off balance with a countenance of self-possession and calm that was more terrifying than outright fury. It was most unsettling to meet someone whose air of intimidating nonchalance surpassed his own.

"What do you know of her character?" Simon sneered back, keeping his own voice calm. At all costs, he must not allow Alcuin to see that he'd never before felt so uneasy. Throughout this battle, he'd never been frightened but now Simon knew he was up against something almost as powerful as the spirits he summoned to do his bidding. "And why do you trespass on my estate?"

Your estate. Simon thought there might be the smallest touch of irony to the creature's tone. "Is this not the property of the father and brother you slaughtered—to say nothing of the innocent child you destroyed?"

"Judge not lest ye be judged," Simon returned.

"Never twist the Word of the Lord to suit your own needs in my presence, nephew." Now the vampire raised his eyes from Isabelle's form, and Simon gasped to see his own gold eyes reflecting back at him with fury and anguish.

Alcuin nodded. "Aye, you are my kinsman, seven generations removed. Though it shames me to see such a venal creature as a descendant of my mortal bloodline, it is our common blood that makes it my responsibility to see that your unchecked evil shall not continue any longer."

"Why is it the men in my family always seek to destroy me, uncle?" Simon laughed harshly and then gestured to the struggling vampire beneath his sword. "Step toward me and your worthless disciple dies."

From the folds of his woolen black monk's robes, Alcuin drew forth his own sword and advanced on Simon. "Unlike you, this good Christian has no reason to fear death. If I cannot protect him from your blade, he is assured a place in paradise."

Simon's lips curled and his blade cut into Guy's flesh, a scarlet pool of blood forming on the Toledo steel blade. "Good Christian? Do you expect me to believe you've spent hundreds of years upon this earth and still believe in some simple concept that is no more than a clever way to keep the peasants from revolt?"

"I believe there is something twisted and rotten inside you, nephew. I believe you've never been touched by concern for your fellow man or love. For that I truly pity you for you will never know the rewards of loving and being loved in return."

"I don't need your pity," Simon snarled, enraged by the way this thing looked down on him. "But answer me this before I slaughter you, priest. Why bother yourself with this battle? Had you simply kept to your corner of the world, I should have been content to remain in mine. I don't wish to wrest control from you; I simply want to be left alone."

Alcuin glanced at Guy and Simon felt a force, almost like one of the gales he'd encountered at sea, try to pull his hostage from his grip. Simon bit down on his lip and concentrated all his strength on holding on to his prisoner but it was no use . . . he simply could not battle the unseen power that tore Guy out from under his sword.

Guy's body flew across the chamber and Alcuin

swiftly closed the gap between himself and Simon, sword aimed at his head.

The priest had backed him into a corner almost before he knew what was happening. Desperately, Simon glanced at a ponderous dark wood cabinet and the thing flew at Alcuin, knocking his sword from his hand and pinning him to the ground under its heavy weight.

The cabinet flew off Alcuin's body before Simon could even take a step toward him and Simon felt that same mysterious force take hold of him, shoving him against the wall, keeping him there while Alcuin drew closer.

The vampire's hood had fallen off and Simon's eyes widened when he saw Alcuin's strangely shiny, translucent skin that allowed all his veins a hideous prominence and rotted blood teeth that hung well past his chin.

"Monster," Simon spat. "What happened in your transformation to give you such a revolting appearance?"

"My face disturbs you?" Alcuin said calmly, and Simon could see he was well used to being greeted with revulsion. "I may have been cursed with a gruesome visage but I far prefer my skin-deep deformity to your sickness, Simon Baldevar. God may have blessed you with outer beauty but your soul . . . the ugliness inside you would crack any looking glass. Your heart is empty . . . you kill and cause pain with no remorse whatsoever. As a mortal, you were vile but what you've become since you transformed is an unholy abomination. Your wicked life must end now."

"Never!" Simon screamed out when Alcuin raised his sword. Swiftly, he yelled the darkest incantation he knew to stop the priest from killing him. "*Obtestor te, simulacrum malum ac seditiosum, quod in profundo tenebrarum habitiat!*"

The priest did not even look frightened when Simon was released from the unseen grip while a strange buzzing cloud came toward Alcuin. He simply stared into the dark mist and clutched the plain wood cross at his hip, the gentle whisper of his voice somehow cutting into the chaotic scream of the power Simon had summoned.

"I adjure you, ancient serpent, by the judge of the living and the dead, by Him who has the power to consign you back to hell, to depart forthwith in fear from me, a servant of God.

"Depart," Alcuin continued, but the ancient power, enraged when it could not overtake him, turned its fury on the creature that dared summon it and then gave nothing in return.

Simon saw the cloud coming at him and realized it was no single daemon but an entire nest of evil things eager to possess him as fitting payment for being summoned from their dank abode. His instincts screamed at him to flee, and he blindly sought the astral plane, knowing the spirit realm offered his only hope for escape.

Damn! By the soft pink cord floating behind him, Simon knew he hadn't been successful in bringing his body with him; only his soul was on the astral plane. That meant his body was vulnerable to the machinations of those loathsome things he'd called upon.

Simon rushed through the various realms, seeking out a place he'd never been to but heard of from Father Bain. Hidden deep in the astral plane was the domain of souls that had not yet walked the earth. A clever magus could tap into their vast energy and draw their untouched essence into himself. Simon needed the potency he'd gain from draining them to battle Alcuin and the monsters he'd invoked.

Come into me, Simon thought, trying to lure the souls to him.

He felt something come near and for a moment felt awe at the purity that enveloped him. This wasn't the simpering holiness of Isabelle chanting her rosary and glaring her eyes while he took her but genuine innocence combined with a vital exuberance that charmed him.

Who are you? Simon tried to ask, and the spirit pulled away, seeming frightened by his intensity.

Come back, he screamed without words. *Don't fear me.* Simon had all but forgotten his original intent . . . it would be obscene to drain this divinity, steal her (the emanation was most certainly feminine) energy so she could never be born on earth. He wasn't going to harm the spirit; he simply wanted it to remain with him. With sudden certainty, Simon knew this was the soul of the *soror mystica* that John Dee had prophesized.

The spirit came closer, intrigued but somehow cautious. Simon knew it was drawn to him, felt that pull between them, yet at the same time there was a deep reluctance . . . the spirit seemed afraid of him.

Come to me, Simon said. *Be the bride my friend has foreseen.*

Be ye banished from this pure soul—you destroy everything you touch, a cold voice responded. That wasn't the spirit speaking . . . it was the voice of that treacherous cleric, Alcuin.

"Damn you!" Simon bellowed and felt himself plummet with a sickening, dizzy speed. He spiraled away from the peaceful, misty haven and felt a cold wind against his cheek, a harsh rod cutting into his back.

What was wrong with him? Simon had never felt so weak in his life. Even transformation hadn't left his limbs feeling so heavy and fatigued that he didn't have the strength to move so much as his finger. His mind even felt exhausted, to the point where his head ached abominably from the simple effort of thinking. It was as if his mind and body had been used terribly.

The daemons, Simon realized tiredly. He was suffering the aftereffects of possession . . . symptoms few people ever had because most either died or lost their minds if a daemon overtook them.

Why were they gone? His desperate flight to the astral plane couldn't have saved him. If anything, the monsters should have been overjoyed to find they need not battle for his soul. Instead, they had unquestioned dominion over an immortal body. They could put the body through all manner of contortions and it would not sicken and die as a human body would.

"Why did you put yourself at risk for that scum, master?" Simon heard a wheedling yet deep voice inquire. "What do you care if Lord Baldevar's devils claimed him now or when he got to hell?"

"It was not Lord Baldevar I saved but the world he inhabits—a world that shelters us as well as the mortals we've sworn to protect," a patient voice responded. "We could not leave a vampire in the throes of possession. Would you care to let something like that walk the earth for all eternity? I had to perform an exorcism."

"I could have beheaded him."

Simon choked back a laugh at such idiocy—he wasn't about to let his enemies know he was aware. Let them continue to discuss him as though he had no more intelligence than the wood piled at his feet.

Wood piled at his feet? Damn these smug priests—they meant to burn him at the stake like some village hag accused of witchcraft! Simon kept his head low but concentrated on trying to draw some strength back into himself.

"Your sword would work against a possessed mortal—assuming you'd decided his soul was not worth battling the devil for," Alcuin responded with the same patience as before. "But a possessed vampire? You could not get near the thing! If the daemons did not kill you straightaway, they might well have decided to inhabit your body in addition to Lord Baldevar's. Though the daemons are gone, what remains is just as evil. Go and behead Lord Baldevar so we may end this foul night."

Simon heard the footsteps rapidly approaching and managed to raise his head and scream, "No!"

"Priest," Simon said conversationally to Alcuin when Guy took an uneasy step back. "My thanks for your aid in ridding my body of that undesired presence but you're a fool if you think your simpleton apprentice can destroy me."

Alcuin simply ignored his speech and Guy lifted his sword again, giving a dismayed grunt when he somersaulted in the air, landing in an undignified heap by Alcuin while the sword he hadn't been able to cling to flew behind Simon and began cutting through the ropes that bound him to the stake.

"Halt," Alcuin intoned and though the sword clattered noisily to the floor, it had already done its work well and Simon was able to begin freeing his wrists from the intricate knots that bound him to the stake.

Guy pulled himself up, his entire body quivering with insane hatred and outraged humiliation when he glared into Simon's mocking eyes.

"Go and seek your daytime shelter, Guy," Alcuin said quietly. The giant started to protest his master's quiet directive but something in Alcuin's stare made him drop his sword and turn his back without another word.

"A more incompetent man-at-arms I've ne'er encountered," Simon quipped, howling with derisive laughter when the vampire stopped, growled something incomprehensible, and then continued walking, reluctance to leave the scene apparent in every line of his trembling, enraged body.

"How well you've trained him," Simon remarked to Alcuin, using the steely whisper that always put his enemies off balance. He didn't expect such a simple trick to faze this creature but he did intend to see if the priest could be goaded into rash action by his words.

As he anticipated, Alcuin refused to acknowledge him but Simon felt the priest's intense concentration and knew Alcuin was gauging his reaction to Guy's departure.

"Think you I'll waste myself on some fool beneath my contempt?" Simon questioned, careful to keep his hands behind his back and not reveal that he was free of the stake. "No doubt you intend for me to chase after your apprentice and attack while I am preoccupied. I'll not fall for such a simple tactic—you've wasted your pawn, uncle."

Now Alcuin turned to him and for the first time there was some emotion in his fathomless gold eyes. "I do not treat people as pawns to be moved about without a care for their well-being, nephew."

"No?" Simon questioned, keeping his eyes on Alcuin's grotesque hand clutching the broadsword at his side. The priest made no move toward him and Simon knew Alcuin was well aware his hands were free of their restraints. He and Alcuin were at an uneasy standstill, each waiting for the other to make the offensive strike.

"Did you send that fool away because you fear my power, Uncle, and know I can dispatch him easily?" Simon taunted. "What a noble gesture, though I can easily accuse you of playing favorites, you sanctimonious fraud. You spare Torquemada's minion but what of all the vampires I've rendered to dust this long winter season? How many that you swore to protect will you allow to die in an effort to put me in the ground?"

The priest said nothing, seeming as mesmerized by Simon's words as a cobra unwillingly dancing to a snake charmer's pipes. Here was the path to Alcuin's destruction. No incantation or physical warfare was necessary . . . Simon need only prey upon the reproach Alcuin felt in his heart for all the vampires killed in this battle. Simon could bring the pompous cleric to his knees by using his guilt and grief to weaken him.

At the gleam of victory in Simon's eyes, the fog lifted from Alcuin's expression and he struck so quickly his sword lashed through Simon's throat before he knew what was happening.

The blade made easy work of his jugular but a swift chop at Alcuin's stomach made the priest bend over in pain and Simon spun away, using the long wooden stake to deflect the blows Alcuin rained upon him.

Simon felt blood soaking through his shirt, though the wound was already closing. Helplessly, Simon watched the priest's sword cut through his pathetic wooden weapon and knew his demise was at hand. Naturally, Guy and Alcuin had stripped him of all his weapons before they'd tied him to the stake. He was still too weak to use sorcery and he had no weapon to battle Alcuin. His only hope was to get the sword out of Alcuin's hands.

Remembering lessons from an old sword master, Simon lunged at Alcuin's wrists but he could not wrest the weapon away from him. The priest threw off his frenzied attack, seeming to expand no more effort than he would use to brush a fly from his robe.

Soon, Alcuin backed Simon against an oak tree, his wooden stake hacked to little more than a block of wood the length of his arm. The priest towered above him, his broadsword glittering obscenely in the fading moonlight.

Puzzled, Simon watched his enemy raise the sword high above his head and then lower it abruptly, seeming dazed and weak. What was wrong with the bishop—why didn't he simply lop off Simon's head?

"Your time for demanding that the hawks bow down to the rabbit mortals is done," Simon hissed, knowing such a speech when his own death seemed imminent was a ridiculous boast. His words were no more than an attempt to distract the priest and snatch the sword from his hands. "I'll seek out every vampire that lives in fear of your wrath and tell them they need skulk about no more! From here on, we enjoy the night in any manner we please.

"And that spirit you tore me from?" Simon taunted, knowing he'd found the chink in his foe's armor by the way Alcuin's lips twisted into a frightening grimace of outraged horror. "She's meant to be my *soror mystica* and give me what you'll never have—a son."

"Never!" Alcuin cried and raised his sword. He lowered it in a clumsy, heavy-handed arc that Simon was easily able to avoid by moving his head slightly. What was the matter with Alcuin? Had the exorcism he performed weakened him? Simon made a move for his sword but Alcuin stepped away and glared down at him.

"I'll not have you corrupting another woman with your unwholesome ways as you did to Isabelle! I vow you'll never break that soul . . . if I could not protect Isabelle from you, at least I can prevent you from ever ruining that unborn spirit!"

Simon raised an eyebrow, circling Alcuin warily. "Isabelle, is it? Chaste cleric, what kind of affection did you harbor in your breast for that dead pile of bones? Do you despise me because her blood was too sick to feast upon . . . her body too decayed for you to . . ."

"Enough!" Alcuin roared, and Simon fell back, biting down on his lip to keep the cries of pain from escaping his mouth. All of a sudden, he rolled about on the ground, an excruciating torment coursing through him. What was this agony that seeped into his bones and made him feel every part of him was afire with pain?

"Sunrise," Alcuin whispered, and Simon forced his eyes open, seeing that the priest, though still upright, was hunched over, apparently in the grip of the same suffering that afflicted Simon.

"I cannot put my sword through you because the coming day has weakened me but I can still get away and seek my resting place. You, though, are too young to escape. God has spoken, Simon Baldevar. The sunlight shall send you to the hell you belong in."

"I think not," Simon hissed and he saw the uneasy speculation in Alcuin's gaze. The priest started to speak and then clutched at his chest, moaning in pain.

"Go on, Uncle," Simon gasped out. "Get you gone before the sun rises and deprives me of the pleasure of killing you when next we meet." Gathering up all his strength, Simon threw back his head and screamed, "John!"

Alcuin opened his mouth to speak again, no doubt to demand to know whom Simon could call now that his vampire army lay dead around him, but a weak ray of sunlight appeared on his chest, and the skin over his heart burst into flames. Hastily, the priest stamped it out and then disappeared but not before giving Simon a bitter, helpless glance.

Come on, John, Simon thought desperately. *Appear, damn it, before this wretched sun destroys me.* Frantically, Simon started pawing through the dirt . . . maybe he could dig a grave to shelter him from the sun. He'd made no more than a few scratches when sunlight began to pour over the earth.

It wasn't one flame that attacked him, more like fire bolts rained down on his body, indiscriminately consuming whatever flesh they touched. Simon could do nothing to save himself from the monstrous fire that enveloped him, blistering his skin and devouring his internal organs.

Then darkness descended and for a moment Simon thought he was mercifully losing awareness but then he felt a pummeling sensation, something beating every inch of his body before rough hands yanked him up and tossed him into a blessedly dark shelter.

"My lord, you cannot rest yet!" a voice hissed urgently into his ear. "You must drink and be replenished else you may spend eternity little more than a blackened monstrosity."

Simon came back to a miserable state of half awareness at the coppery taste on his lips, the liquid being
poured down his throat. Gradually, the agony receded
and he was able to open his eyes, see the blood-filled
wine cask that was pressed to his mouth.

Simon drank thirstily, watching in bemused amazement as the hideous burns over his body faded, leaving
his skin pale and flawless. His vision returned, and he
saw that he was in the special windowless carriage he'd
commissioned shortly after he transformed. Seated beside him and holding the cask that had saved his life
was John Dee.

"Thank you, John." Simon heard the slurred quality
to his speech and knew that though the blood had
healed him, the sun was nearly completely raised and
it was time for him to sleep. But he had to stay awake
just a few more moments . . .

"Why do you thank me, my lord? 'Twas your new
skill that cloaked my presence and that of the coach-
man from your enemies. A good plan, that . . . to keep
us hidden in case you needed to flee the estate during
the day."

"Not just my ability," Simon gasped out. "Your own
magick kept you hidden those moments my concentration was taxed in dealing with my enemies. Now we
must . . . must make plans before the weariness over-
takes me. Tell the driver to head toward Leith. I'll
board a ship this evening . . . have to leave England . . . Alcuin too strong . . ."

Simon stopped and managed, in spite of his exhaustion, to smile briefly. "Priest hopes sun rendered me
to dust . . . but knows Lord Baldevar might not be
dead . . . must hide . . . build my strength . . . next
time I challenge him . . . kill him . . ."

He felt John Dee grasp his shoulder. "There shall
be no more communication between us."

"No," Simon agreed, acutely feeling the loss of his
esteemed friend. The entire court knew he patronized

Dr. Dee; no doubt Alcuin was well aware of their friendship. If they corresponded, the priest or one of his minions might discover him before Simon was ready to attack again. For that matter, Simon would also have to abandon his estate and his trading company. From this night forward he'd have precious little but the clothes on his back.

But what did that matter to a vampire? He could easily reach into mortals' minds and make them hand over their entire fortune with one command . . . within a fortnight he'd be comfortable once more. And as long as he was discreet, he could develop his ability without the threat of Alcuin hanging over him like some noxious storm cloud.

"John," Simon muttered. "You saved my life this day and I only wish you were not too frail to accept the one boon I have to repay you. Since I cannot . . . cannot . . . transform you, I bequeath to you the contents of my hidden temple. All the man . . . manuscripts are yours and there are several trunks filled with nutmeg and cloves—they'll give you an income. Take all that and any of my writings you wish credit for with my blessing and I would ask but two more favors."

"Anything, my friend."

Simon took a deep breath and then spoke in a rush, trying to beat out the vampire slumber that usually claimed him long before this hour. "One year from this date, you'll receive a letter from an Italian nobleman interested in purchasing some of your library collection. Write back to me only when our Gloriana lies dying—I would see her once more before she passes from this life."

"Of course. And the other favor?"

"Isabelle," Simon said and his features twisted into an enraged mask that made his friend shudder beside him. "That blasted cleric is going to bury her, I'm sure. Try and find her corpse . . . I want the emerald ring."

"The one Bess gave you at your wedding? Why?"

"I must give it to my *soror mystica*," Simon said and finally dropped into the near-death trance that ruled his daylight hours now. As he drifted off, his final thought wasn't of his humiliation at Alcuin's hands or even the revenge he'd have one night for all the pontiff had taken from him. All the horror and violence of the night faded when Simon thought of that enchanting spirit destined to become his bride.

TWENTY

Southampton, New York
December 30, 1998

Meghann felt an icy hand brush her cheek, and opened her eyes, smiling up at the intrusion to her dreams.

"Forgive me, sweetheart," Simon said and leaned down to kiss her, his lips still carrying the chill of the frigid winter night. "You looked so sweet I couldn't resist waking you."

"It's okay," Meghann said drowsily and accepted his help to get into a sitting position. "Tired of sleeping during the night. Where did Charles and Lee go?"

"They retired to their cottage for a late dinner, and speaking of which . . ." Simon presented her with a silver tray laden with cheeseburgers, fries, and the thick vanilla shake she'd expressed a craving for.

"Want some?" Meghann asked after he balanced the tray over her knees.

Simon selected one thick french fry but instead of eating it he fed it to her. "When you finish your third meal of the night, I have a surprise for you, little glutton."

"I'm eating for three," Meghann said primly and devoured the second rare burger. "What's the surprise?"

"A belated Christmas present." Simon smiled and

handed her a large square box wrapped in cheerful red paper embossed with poinsettias.

"Monopoly!" she squealed in happy surprise after she tore the wrappings. "The 1935 version . . . Simon, did you get this just because I went on about my father buying it the first year it came out?"

"Didn't you say this game engrossed you and your siblings during various illnesses and vacations? I thought it might provide some diversion since you've become bored with your novels and psychology journals, watching movies, and you dislike chess so much."

"I like chess just fine—as long as I'm not playing against you," Meghann said and stuck out her tongue. "What fun is a game where you're defeated in five minutes?"

"Did it take me that long to trounce you?" Simon questioned and ducked the pillow launched at his head. "Of course, I'm aware that with this particular game, it may be a few hours before my superior skill does you in."

"I think you know where you can put your superior skill," she said sweetly and as they began playing, Meghann reflected that no one but Simon could have made the past five weeks of enforced bed rest not only bearable but also actually enjoyable.

An icy tentacle of fear still wrapped around her heart when she remembered that night five weeks before when she had gotten out of bed and felt a warm gush of blood run down her legs. Only Simon's unruffled calm had kept her from complete hysteria while he hurriedly summoned Lee.

An ultrasound had revealed placenta previa . . . a condition of pregnancy where the placenta attached itself to the lower half of the uterus, partially or entirely covering the cervix. Lee had explained that placenta previa could cause hemorrhaging and usually necessitated a caesarian delivery. He had gone on to explain that any bleeding during the pregnancy could irritate the uterus to the point of contractions, thus bringing on premature labor.

Fortunately, Meghann had experienced no contractions and the bleeding had stopped as inexplicably as it started. Lee had said the ultrasound revealed the placenta was only partially, as opposed to completely, covering the mouth of the uterus, which was good news. Since there hadn't been any sign of fetal distress, it was decided Meghann's pregnancy could continue but Lee had ordered complete bed rest.

Since the disturbing show of blood, Meghann's pregnancy had progressed uneventfully, though she was often tired and had started catnapping throughout the night. When she was awake, she felt restless and bored, though Simon, Charles, and Lee did all they could to bolster her spirits.

"Thank God it's only three more weeks," Meghann said, triumphantly placing a hotel on Boardwalk. In three weeks, she'd reach the thirty-seventh week of pregnancy. According to Lee, that was the perfect time for a C-section. He'd explained that natural childbirth was dangerous because contractions could cause severe bleeding, endangering Meghann's life as well as the twins if she hemorrhaged. In anticipation of premature delivery, Lee flooded her system with beta methizone to develop the twins' lungs. Fortunately, they didn't appear to have a vampire's immunity to drugs and the latest ultrasound showed their lungs were so mature they might be able to breathe on their own even if they were born now.

"Will you concede defeat?" Simon taunted after Meghann had a disastrous turn, landing on one of his hotel properties for the third time in a row.

Grimly, Meghann mortgaged most of her property and came up with the necessary money to pay her debt without going bankrupt.

At the next throw of the dice, Simon seemed about to breeze past Boardwalk but one die mysteriously

turned over from a three to a two . . . landing him
smack on Meghann's hotel.

"Pay up!"

Simon reached across the board and yanked her
into his lap. "Using your power to cheat at a game . . .
you must pay a forfeit."

Meghann wrapped her arms around him, kissing
him hungrily and cursing the damned placenta previa
that barred sexual intercourse.

A sudden thump made all the pieces on the board
scatter as Max jumped up on the bed.

"Game called on account of dog walk," Meghann
said when Max handed Simon the leash carefully balanced in his mouth.

He cuffed the setter affectionately and attached his
leash. "I know . . . you have no desire to walk alone
since that foolish hunter mistook you for a deer. Aren't
you fortunate he merely grazed your hind leg?"

"Have fun," Meghann called as they left the room.
She knew the hunter's body had landed in the ocean
after Simon had fed on the idiot that almost killed her
dog. She returned the game to its box and made a
few notes on a yellow legal pad concerning Jimmy Delacroix's care. Since she'd become bedridden, Charles
had taken over his therapy with the assistance of
Meghann's directives. He too was puzzled by Jimmy's
condition. Though he drank blood docilely and
groomed himself, Jimmy made no attempt at communication. Meghann refused to speculate that perhaps
this zombielike state was a full recovery, that Jimmy
would make no further progress. If that were so, she'd
have to consider beheading him rather than let him
spend immortality as a vegetable and she simply
couldn't bring herself to do that, not when she was so
sure she could reach past that inexplicable blankness
and bring him back to complete awareness. . . .

Maggie, help me! Please help me!

The desperate howl went through her head like a

knife. As she put a hand to her aching temple, Meghann's eyes flew open—frowning when she saw no one in the room with her. Could that scream really have reverberated only in her mind? It was so loud she would swear it was audible and not mental . . .

Maggie!

"Jimmy," she whispered, feeling joy in spite of the pain in her invaded mind. Without another thought, she got off the bed and sprinted, as much as her bulk would allow her to, toward Jimmy's room, grateful that he was installed on the same floor so she wouldn't have to attempt the stairs.

Maggie, don't let him hurt me!

It's okay, Jimmy, she tried to tell him, unsure if he heard her or not. Poor Jimmy . . . why hadn't she foreseen this? Imagine coming out of a catatonic state and waking up in a strange room . . . he must be terrified. And his last memory was probably of Simon transforming him . . . no wonder Jimmy was begging her not to let her hurt him.

Maggie!

Meghann staggered into the wall, the force of Jimmy's terrified plea striking her like a physical blow.

I'm coming, Jimmy, she thought back and felt the panicked presence boring down on her recede slightly. No one, not even Simon, had ever invaded her mind like this. Then again, Simon had never called out to her in a state of hysteria, with no idea what the raw power of a vampiric scream could do to its receiver. For all she knew, Jimmy might not even know yet that he was a vampire . . . what was that little surprise going to do to his newfound sanity? She'd have to break the news of his immortality very gently.

Meghann straightened up and hurried toward Jimmy, startled when she saw that the door to his room was ajar. He was stuck in that room until Simon released him—maybe his howls made the door swing open? She ran down the hall and stopped dead in the doorway, shocked by the tableau before her.

Simon stood over Jimmy, curled up in the fetal position. Jimmy's eyes were still unfocused and his lips were trembling like he was trying to speak but couldn't quite remember how.

"What are you doing to him?" Meghann cried. She clung to the heavy brass doorknob to stay upright, overwhelmed by the malevolent force that emanated from Simon. She looked down at Jimmy and knew that her abrupt appearance was the only reason Jimmy's mind wasn't obliterated . . . Simon was focusing all his power on destroying Jimmy; that's why he hadn't been aware of her presence.

Meghann thought of the past few months . . . of that mysterious block in Jimmy's mind that prevented recovery. Not so mysterious now that she saw Simon towering over Jimmy . . . he'd been coming in here and undoing all her work, suppressing Jimmy's mind with the power of his own. All Simon's vows to leave Jimmy in peace were lies . . . treacherous lies. With a sudden sense of foreboding, Meghann wondered what else he'd lied to her about.

After a long moment, Simon raised his eyes from Jimmy and looked Meghann over coolly, not at all perturbed by the aghast fury in her eyes.

"Get back into bed this instant," Simon said in greeting, his tone brooking no refusal.

"Bed?" she repeated before she remembered her condition. No matter what Simon had been up to with Jimmy, he was right about the need for her to get off her feet. Never moving her eyes from Simon, Meghann inched over to Jimmy's twin bed and gingerly eased herself down.

Simon sat down next to her, giving her a rueful smile. When she tried to spring away from him, one hand lashed out to imprison her wrists in an iron grip.

"I'd hoped this could wait until you'd delivered,"

he said and gestured to Jimmy, still curled up on the floor.

"What did you hope could wait? Jimmy's been getting better, hasn't he? You despicable bastard," she said, her voice full of the old revulsion and anger that hadn't colored her conversations with Simon for months. "How long have you been undermining Jimmy's progress . . . creeping in here and holding him down?"

"Meghann—"

"Goddamn you, how long?" she screamed and bit at the hand clamping down on hers with her blood teeth.

In one fluid movement, Simon wrapped his free hand around her neck and forced her head back against the headboard. He loomed over her, gold eyes blazing with the air of simmering menace that always made her quake and back down.

"Don't you look at me like that!" she shouted, working furiously to suppress her tears. What was the matter with her—wanting to cry like a child because the dreamlike sweetness of the past few months had vanished the moment she saw Simon leaning over Jimmy and she realized every honeyed word out of Lord Baldevar's mouth had been part of a calculated plan to make her drop her guard and trust him?

Nothing had changed, Meghann realized. With a sinking heart, Meghann asked herself how she could put her heart in the hands of a creature with no love inside him, just a sick desire to dominate and hurt everyone around him.

"Don't be melodramatic. I have no intention of harming you. I'm simply restraining you until you're capable of discussing this matter calmly and not biting me like some savage, untrained dog."

"There's nothing to discuss," she said shakily, trying without success to move away from the hand locking her head into place. "I asked one thing of you—"

"You asked a great deal of me—including that I shelter your friend, a friend that caused our needless separation. But I did that gladly, just as I forgave your stake and running off to my enemy forty years ago. I was even willing to overlook your cheap promiscuous ways all the years we were apart. But I must draw the line when you have the gall to expect that I'd stand by and allow you that wretch on the floor."

"Allow?" Meghann questioned and burst into bitter, slightly hysterical laughter. "How could I forget . . . I'm not allowed to have anything the lord and master doesn't approve of, am I? Like a family and people to love! You took all of that away from me the night you forced this damned cursed existence on me . . . never letting me contact my family, forbidding me to have any friends. Goddamn you, Simon Baldevar—you're not going to take Jimmy away from me!"

"I did not think I'd have to," Simon said, giving her the overpleasant, sardonic grin that made her skin crawl. "You did a rather good job of removing yourself from Mr. Delacroix's life. Or will you not admit that you neglected your patient shamefully once you rediscovered the joys of my bed?"

"No!" Meghann shouted, hardening her eyes. She wouldn't let the bastard see how his words cut into her, that he was right about her ignoring Jimmy over the past five months. Meghann sagged into the bed, and squeezed her eyes shut. A hellish vision floated into her mind, not the appalling picture of Simon leaning over Jimmy but over another man . . . Johnny Devlin.

Johnny, her childhood sweetheart, wartime fiancé . . . and her first victim. Meghann saw herself, deathly ill from transformation and frenzied with the desperate need for blood. Oh, she'd been desperate but not desperate enough to do as Simon ordered and kill her terrified, half-conscious fiancé. It was only after Simon dragged her to him, keeping her head firmly positioned over his jugular, while he kept pressuring her to drink, drink, drink, that she finally sank her blood teeth into Johnny's neck and drained him of life.

Meghann had never forgiven herself for Johnny but her one weak consolation was that if she had a second chance, she'd have found a way to refuse the hideous choice Simon put before her. Now even that pathetic straw was gone. Once again, Simon Baldevar got her to betray a man she professed to love.

But what happened to Jimmy Delacroix was far worse than Johnny. How could she have done this . . . seen the pathetic shell Simon had reduced Jimmy to and still fallen back under his spell?

Because it was easy, Meghann told herself with loathing. So much easier to fuck Simon than fight him, easy to stop struggling and put her faith in him . . . faith he'd just ripped out of her, along with her heart.

"There's no need for weeping, little one," she heard him whisper. Now that she lay broken and sobbing on the bed, the overbearing brute was gone . . . now Simon would offer his silly little doll some more of his false soothing.

"Leave me alone," she sobbed, moving away from the arms that tried to pull her against him.

"You're being foolish," Simon said softly, though he did remove his hands. "Why castigate yourself for making a wise choice? Really, sweetheart, only a complete featherhead would continue to battle me. Naturally you chose to accept love and all the comfort I wished to bestow upon you in place of that futile resistance. Why should you have held yourself chaste and bitter, slaving in behalf of a witless creature, instead of embracing me and all I can give you?"

"I don't want anything from you!" Meghann screamed and slapped him across the face with all her strength, wondering if he'd dare strike her back while she was pregnant.

Simon only smiled, rubbing his wounded cheek. "I'd heard breeding women have black moods and unpredictable behavior. You need to rest, little one. I'll take you back to our room so you can calm down and stop endangering our children's health with all this aggravation—"

"Get your filthy hands off me before I bite them off!"

"Stop behaving like a wayward brat," Simon said, ignoring her furious struggles when he tried to gather her up to carry her away from Jimmy's room.

"Put me down, damn you! Put me down!"

Roughly, Simon grabbed her, giving her a small shake about the shoulders. "Cease that caterwauling and fighting immediately. Do you wish to bring on premature labor?"

"Leave me alone . . ." she started to say, and Simon simply clamped his hand over her mouth, all her frenzied attempts to pull away from him having as much affect as a fly against his impenetrable strength.

"Get off her, motherfucker."

Meghann felt Simon's arms slacken as they both turned stunned eyes to the figure standing by the door—Jimmy Delacroix, looking more than a bit bewildered but ready for battle with the leg he'd ripped from the solitary wood chair in his room serving as a makeshift stake.

"Jimmy?" Meghann said hesitantly, peering at him from her position behind Simon. She couldn't believe that her eyes weren't deceiving her, that Jimmy Delacroix was really standing and talking, the hateful blank stare replaced by a guarded expression that made Meghann smile in spite of her misery.

"Don't worry, Maggie," he said brusquely, not moving his eyes from Simon or his appraising amber gaze. "I'm not gonna let this freak hurt you anymore."

"Jimmy!" she said joyously and took advantage of

Simon's momentary shock, leaping past him to fly toward Jimmy, her arms open to embrace him.

But Jimmy took a step back, looking at her body with bewilderment. "What the hell happened to you?"

"Huh?" she said and then realized what a shock her swollen figure must be to him. She stopped cold, her arms falling limply to her sides while her face suffused with a blush of deep humiliation.

But Jimmy didn't seem upset. Shaking off his momentary disconcertment, he swept her off her feet and planted a huge kiss on her surprised lips.

"What the hell's been happening, Maggie?" Jimmy said gleefully and kissed her again. "Have I been sick? I mean, Jesus, when did you get so pregnant?"

"What?" she asked, acutely disturbed by Simon's continued silence.

"Have I been sick?" Jimmy repeated and then he glanced at her in perplexed confusion. "Maggie, something's the matter with me . . . I feel different."

"Oh, honey," she whispered, feeling an aching wave of pity for the man still cradling her to him. "You . . . you're a vampire now, have been for nearly eight months."

"Eight months?" Jimmy echoed and sank to the floor, Meghann petting his long hair consolingly. "No, it's not possible, it . . ."

But he broke off and Meghann saw that he knew it was true. Besides being in her bloodline, Jimmy was far too young a vampire and too distressed for his thoughts not to reach her. She saw his bewilderment at the odd strength that coursed through him, the suddenly keen hearing that made him hear the tide of the ocean as clearly as though he stood on the shore though he was in this homely room he'd never seen before. And worse, there was a need . . . a sudden craving . . .

"No!" Jimmy howled. It was on him, a desire for

blood a thousand times stronger than the worst time he'd ever needed a drink.

Meghann left him momentarily, reaching into the small refrigerator in a corner of the room. She returned to him with a transfusion pack of blood that Jimmy looked at for a split second with a mortal's loathing before he snatched it from her grasp and drank thirstily.

"It's okay," Maggie whispered to him while he devoured the blood. God, how she knew what he was going through, knew what it was to hate yourself for enjoying the taste of copper and iron, for feeling a sudden sense of well-being and power.

Do you see now? Meghann said and felt a brief moment of amusement at Jimmy's shock to hear her unspoken words. Most likely, Simon would hear every word but she had to try and bar him from these words she meant only for Jimmy.

This is the blood lust? Jimmy questioned back, looking like a shaky toddler just learning to walk when he answered her back telepathically.

Meghann nodded and stroked his long hair comfortingly. *This is why I never wanted to transform you, Jimmy. Maybe we do gain longevity and some powers I'll teach you but there's always the blood lust. That's the curse of a vampire's existence. It's bad enough fighting it myself . . . I never wanted to see you struggle with it too.*

But what changed your mind? Why did you transform me?

Oh, Jimmy . . .

"Wait," Jimmy said and tossed the empty plastic bag away. At the unwanted memory, the ability to speak telepathically abandoned him and his agonized shriek filled the room. "You didn't transform me . . . it was . . . oh, God, no!"

"It doesn't matter," Meghann said and glared at Simon, lounging on the bed and looking more like a hawk than ever with his tawny eyes focused on her and

Jimmy . . . a hunter ready to swoop down on his prey but holding back, savoring their terror before making the kill.

Finally, Meghann looked away, turning her attention back to her shattered lover. Over and over she crooned that it didn't matter who transformed him, he was still capable of finding peace within his new existence. She and Charles would help him tame the blood lust and he'd never have to do anything that shamed him or made him feel he was some unholy monster.

"Jimmy," she said, forcing him to look at her. *God*, she prayed, *don't let this shock make him slip back into the catatonia.* "When that fiend transformed you, he deliberately made it difficult . . . he wanted you to fall into the insanity that makes so many transformations a failure. And you did—Jimmy, you were out of your head, completely mindless and unable to focus on anything but your need for blood. But I kept talking to you, pleading with you to come back, and you heard me . . . you got your mind back! No vampire has ever recovered his sanity after a bad transformation—only you! That proves how strong you are, that you're capable of anything, anything at all . . ."

Slowly, Jimmy raised his head from her tear-drenched shoulder and took a sniffling breath. "Yeah," he agreed and gave Meghann a timid, hopeful smile. "I kind of remember hearing you. It was like I was at the bottom of a well and your voice was coming at me. I wanted so much to tell you I heard you but he held me back." From Meghann's protective embrace, Jimmy threw Simon, still eerily quiet, a ferocious look.

"You're right, Maggie," Jimmy said firmly and stood up, helping Meghann to her feet. He clutched her shoulders and gazed lovingly at her bloated body, causing Meghann to give him another puzzled glance.

"Wow," he said and his hands grazed her abdomen

gingerly. Then, he raised his eyes again and gave her a reprimanding glance.

"You shouldn't have done this, you know," he said reproachfully and indicated Simon. "Don't think I'm not grateful that you saved me from whatever hell he had me living through but Jesus Christ, Maggie! You didn't just risk your own neck this time . . . what if he hurt our baby?"

"Our baby?" she repeated numbly and then heard the malicious laugh behind her. Turning, she saw Simon rise off the bed and make his leisurely way toward her.

Before she could move, he came behind her, putting one hand around her stomach while the other shoved Jimmy away when he moved to protect her.

"Get the fuck away from her!" Jimmy growled and Simon laughed again, keeping a firm hold on Meghann, squirming and clawing at the arms encircling her.

"You may rest assured I will not harm her." Simon ran his hand over Meghann's cheek, purring out, "Mr. Delacroix seems confused as to the paternity of your child, little one. Shouldn't you enlighten him or may I have that delightful task?"

"Maggie, what the hell is he talking about?" Jimmy questioned uneasily, and Meghann saw the appalling knowledge bloom in his eyes as Simon's hands caressed her distended stomach with familiar, loving hands. He knew Simon Baldevar wouldn't touch her that way if she were pregnant with another man's child.

"Maggie, no!" he screamed, eyes and voice pleading for her to refute the hideous truth Lord Baldevar put before him.

Meghann brought her foot down with all her strength, feeling grim satisfaction when she heard Simon's big toe crack under the assault. He loosened his grip and she ran to Jimmy.

"It's true," Meghann said quietly and took a deep

breath, determined that her confession not be the victory Simon wanted. "But he raped me . . . that night he killed Alcuin and kidnapped me . . ."

"I know, Maggie. When I went to the house to rescue you, I saw what he did to you. Fucking rapist," Jimmy snarled and hurled the chair leg at Simon's heart.

Easily, Simon sidestepped the missile and stalked toward Jimmy but Meghann placed herself between them. At the amused scorn in Simon's gaze, something cracked inside her. Meghann was past anger, past any sane emotion, her only desire to make Simon hurt as badly as she did.

"It used to make me sick, knowing I was carrying the child of a bastard like you," she said coldly. "But I love my children enough to overlook the unfortunate accident of who their father is. And I'm going to spare them that knowledge—these children will never know you, never! Alcuin was right—you destroy everything you touch. I don't know why the hell I didn't listen when he begged me to see through all your phony love. Kill me or let me leave this room with Jimmy, Lord Baldevar. Those are your only two choices because I'd die before I let you be a part of my children's life."

Abruptly, Jimmy shoved her behind him. "Maggie, get the hell out of here before he kills you!" he screamed.

Simon gave Jimmy a brief look of annoyance before lifting him off the ground with one hand and flinging him halfway through the brick wall of the fireplace behind him. Stunned by a blow that would have killed him if he were mortal, Jimmy could only watch helplessly as Simon grasped Meghann's chin.

"Mr. Delacroix," the vampire said calmly, and Meghann felt more than a little panic at the flat glint in his eyes, his bone-white skin and lips stretched into a narrow, grim line. "Even if I believed Meghann's words, I would not kill her now. I'd wait until she served some purpose and gave me my heir." Visibly dismissing Jimmy, he turned back to Meghann and favored her with a faint grin. "Words are cheap, pet. What say you to backing that little speech with action, Lady Baldevar?"

Crossing her arms over her chest, Meghann nodded and Simon sank to his knees before her, laughing at her perplexed look.

"You claim to regret not heeding my uncle's warning to spurn my love. As I recall, he did not simply caution but offered you a way to rid yourself of me once and for all. Remember? You must call out to the great Alcuin and allow him to possess your body so he may slaughter me. Summon my old enemy . . . you know I shall make no attempt to strike you now. Even a fiend such as myself would not kill a woman bearing his son. With me destroyed, you and your lover can live happily ever after . . . perhaps he'll even be good-natured enough to play father to our child. Come now, Meghann, achieve your heart's desire with one word—*Alcuin.*"

Meghann raised her hands, and her mouth opened but no sound came forth . . . she could push nothing past the lump in her throat. *Alcuin,* she tried to say but a bittersweet kaleidoscope of memories flashed before her. The small bedroom faded into the vastness of the Nevada desert, where she had nearly lost her life and clung to Simon, begging him not to leave her alone while he had held her close and assured her no one would hurt her again. Then she saw Simon crush her to him when she shyly offered him her father's ring after he had asked her to marry him. Unbidden, she felt herself back in the rustic little wedding chapel softly lit with dozens of candles that blurred and became indistinct when she had blinked back tears of joy as she placed the ring on Simon's finger.

"Something wrong?" Simon inquired silkily and

gave her an arch grin that made her curl her fist and land a staggering blow on his chest.

"I hate you!" she screamed and hit at him blindly, wanting to kill him when she heard his triumphant peal of laughter. "It's not true, it's not! You . . . you've spelled me somehow, warped my mind!"

"If I had you under any spell, you'd be far more amiable, I assure you. Come now, sweetheart—enough of this foolishness. We both know your cruel words had no substance behind them. You still love me, no matter how piqued you are by my treatment of that nonentity." Simon swung her into his lap, pinning her arms to her chest to keep her still. "Can't you see I had to keep him unaware so you would not be burdened with the upheaval of his reemergence? Look how upset you are and I admit I am to blame for part of that, but I did not shatter our bargain. I was willing to give him his freedom after you gave birth. I still might allow him to live . . . if you fulfill your part of our deal."

"Do you think I'm stupid enough to believe you tortured Jimmy out of concern for my health or that you had any intention of letting him go?" Meghann snapped, glowering at the condescending gold eyes. "You just don't want any competition, you . . . you insecure prick! And what deal are you talking about?"

"You'll have to curb your tongue around our children—I'll not have my heirs exposed to such sordid language. I'm sure you don't recall our deal . . . you have no desire to at present. But I shall refresh your selective memory. You agreed that once Mr. Delacroix regained his faculties, you would tell him all that has happened between us . . . or I would. Shall I start with this?" Simon held up his hand so the plain gold wedding band was reflected prominently in the overhead light.

Though Jimmy was a few feet from them, his vampire eyes gave him the ability to make out of every detail of the gold ring . . . a ring he'd seen a thousand times before around Meghann's neck.

"Your father's ring?" Jimmy said incredulously, and Meghann resisted an impulse to hide her head in her hands so she wouldn't have to see the hurt disillusionment in his eyes. "Why the hell is that thing wearing your father's ring?"

"Because I gave it to him," she said tiredly. She sighed and glanced at the floor, unable to meet Jimmy's eyes when she told him everything that had happened while he was insensible.

Meghann spared herself nothing, suppressed no truth Simon could later use against her. She started at the beginning, telling Jimmy she'd barely had time to grieve over Simon's kidnapping him when she discovered she was pregnant. She explained why she needed to drink Lord Baldevar's blood, their bargain that she could work on healing Jimmy in exchange for carrying Simon's child willingly.

She told him about the friendship that sprang up between her and the fiend, how it deepened when she clung to Simon in terror after Guy Balmont's surprise attack. There was no joy, only shame in her voice when she said she'd not only been Lord Baldevar's lover the past five months, but his wife.

"There's no excuse for what I've done . . . none at all. I'm so sorry, Jimmy," she said through her bitter sobbing. "You were my best friend, next to Charles, and I never wanted you to be hurt. Believe me, I'd never have taken a lover if I knew Lord Baldevar was alive. The fiend will kill anyone I try to love. Now that I'm pregnant, I'm stuck with him—if I want to be in my babies' lives, that is. And it's more than that . . . in some twisted way, I do love him—almost as much as I hate him. Leave, Jimmy, please. Just forget me."

"Maggie, no! It's a joke, right?" Jimmy pleaded. "Like before—you're tricking him and you'll kill him when the moment's right. Maggie, there's no way you can love this asshole."

"I'm sorry," she began but Simon put a finger over her lips, pressing down so she couldn't open her mouth to bite him.

"You do not owe him remorse. Never apologize to those beneath you, little one. Mr. Delacroix has his wits, what little there were to begin with, as well as the gift of immortality. If he hungers for you, that is his dilemma." Simon placed his chin over Meghann's head and gave Jimmy a grin full of mock compassion. "I truly sympathize with you, Mr. Delacroix. Of course you fell in love with Meghann . . . I cannot fault your taste, but this extraordinary creature was never meant for such as you. Go and find some bland little sparrow to share your nights with and never cross my path again if you wish to remain alive."

"Meghann?" Charles and Lee stood in the doorway, their eyes darting between the couple by the bed and the man that stood a few feet from them, brick dust clinging to his hair while he slumped and blinked back tears.

"She's simply absorbing the shock of Mr. Delacroix's startling recovery," Simon said and glanced at Charles, waving his hand in a dismissive gesture at Jimmy. "Do with him as you will. I'm taking Meghann back to bed so she can relax. Doctor Winslow, come with me . . . I'd like you to make sure this distress hasn't aggravated her condition."

"No!" Jimmy yelled and yanked his arm away from Charles. "I'm not going anywhere . . . especially not with you! Maggie thinks she loves this psycho . . . why the hell didn't you get her away from him when he first started to fuck with her head?"

"She needed his blood," Lee started to explain.

"Who the hell are you?" Jimmy demanded but turned his fury on Meghann before Lee could reply. "And you! You used to have a mind of your own—

wouldn't give a creep like this the time of day. After all you told me he did to you, if you stay with him you're nothing more than a damned stupid bitch!"

"What did you call me?" Meghann said incredulously, and Simon deposited her on the bed.

"Do you see now why I tell you all your altruistic efforts are for naught . . . that they will not be appreciated?" Simon scolded. "Look at this cur . . . you salvaged his mind and in place of thanks, you receive insults. Doctor Tarleton, please escort Meghann to her room while I deal with this worthless specimen that thinks he can address my consort in such a manner."

"Fuck you! She's not your consort and she never will be!" Jimmy screamed. "You've done something to Maggie, twisted her somehow. Come on, motherfucker . . . Maggie may not be able to kill you, but I won't have any problem with it. When you're gone, she'll be herself again."

"Simon, no!" Meghann yelled when he stepped toward Jimmy, and all four men flinched at the high-pitched shriek that cracked the window behind her.

"Please," she said and clutched at his hands. "What do you care what he says or calls you? I said I love you . . . isn't that enough? Please don't hurt him!"

"Maggie, shut up!" Jimmy snarled. "Let me hear you say you love him one more time and—"

"And what?" Simon inquired icily, throwing off Meghann's hands and stalking toward Jimmy.

Jimmy took an uneasy step back . . . where the hell had that unreasoning anger come from? Was this part of the blood lust too, that rage that made him want to wrap his hands around Maggie's throat and take all of that *I love you* talk out of her by force? And why was he yelling at Maggie, calling her names when none of this was her fault, when the cause of all the hell of the past year was standing right in front of him, those damned yellow eyes daring Jimmy to come closer?

"I'm not gonna back down," Jimmy said, so furious

he wasn't even afraid of the homicidal rage brewing in Simon's gaze. "I'll die before I stand by and let Maggie stay with you . . . she doesn't know what she's doing."

"You wish to lay down your life for a woman you mean naught to? Very well, such an imbecile has no business being a vampire anyway." He spared a brief glance at Charles, unable to do anything so far except stare in shock at the two enraged vampires before him. "Take Meghann from this room now."

"No!" Meghann screamed before Charles could move toward her. "Simon, please listen . . ." she started to say but Jimmy flew at Simon, a frenzied desperate attack as he pummeled and clawed, trying to get him down on the floor.

For one moment, his hate actually lent him enough strength to surprise Simon and a ragged line of scratches appeared on one cheek but Simon soon regained his equilibrium and flung Jimmy from him with an outraged roar.

Now he stood over the prone vampire but didn't continue the physical assault. Instead, he lifted his hands far above him and began a low, even chant that made a strange dark light illuminate his hands.

"Jimmy, get away!" Meghann screamed and broke away from Charles. She knew what Simon was doing . . . had done it herself to kill a vampire when she had no stake or weapon to aid her. He was using a Druidic ritual, appealing to an ancient Celtic goddess to give his hands the strength to plunge past Jimmy's breastplate and remove his heart. If she could stop the chant, she could prevent Simon from gaining the power he needed and maybe distract him long enough for Jimmy to escape.

Jimmy heard her terror and broke the paralysis Simon's words already held him in. He managed to get one foot up and slam it through his enemy's groin, making him fly off his feet.

"No!" Charles screamed when Simon flew at Meghann, scrambling toward the two creatures fighting over her. Though Simon swiftly regained his balance, he wasn't able to stop himself from crashing into her.

Meghann didn't simply fall to the floor; she slammed through it, a choked cry of pain issuing from her.

"Meghann!" Simon turned her over gently, his face turning an unnatural shade of white when he saw the crimson stain spreading over her nightgown.

"Help me," she panted, barely able to speak through the monstrous pain ripping through her.

Lee ran to her and pushed the nightgown up. "It looks like placental abruption and she's hemorrhaging—must be disseminated intravascular coagulation for her to bleed like this." Simon and Charles both blanched at the prognosis as well as the river of bright red blood pouring down Meghann's legs. "She's lost the ability to clot. Pick her up easy, I've got to do a caesarian stat . . . may even have to do a hysterectomy to save her."

Simon picked her up, flinching when Meghann moaned and clutched at her abdomen. Swiftly, he followed Lee out of the room, not even seeming to notice Jimmy backed against the wall.

"Get out of here, Jimmy," Charles said when they left the room.

"I didn't mean it!" Jimmy burst out, eyes beseeching Charles to understand. "I didn't see her behind him! Jesus, I'd let him kill me before I hurt her like that."

Charles nodded briefly, some of the panic leaving his expression as he turned to Jimmy. "It was just a terrible accident but that doesn't matter. You're lucky Lord Baldevar really does love Meghann. If he weren't so concerned with saving her life, you'd be dead by now. But whatever happens, he's going to hunt you down. Here," Charles said and withdrew a fat wad of bills from his wallet. "Get to the house in Rockaway. Under Max's doghouse, Meghann put the address of your sister . . . she moved your family after Simon transformed you, to keep them safe."

Jimmy flinched at that information, that even if Maggie had done something he really didn't want to think about with Simon Baldevar, she'd still cared enough to look after him and his sister.

"I can't leave . . . I have to help Maggie. . . ." Jimmy didn't care if Simon hurt him. He had to go to Maggie and do whatever he could to save her.

"You can't do anything for her now," Charles said but softened his tone at Jimmy's shattered expression. "Look, you know I'll do everything I can for her, and the other man is Lee . . . the most gifted obstetrician I know. I'll let you know what happened . . . send a letter care of your sister. Please, Jimmy, get away from here before Simon destroys all her hard work to bring you back by slaughtering you."

Jimmy nodded and stepped into the hallway with Charles, feeling something start to block him but then ease away.

"One thing," Jimmy said and put his hand on Charles's shoulder. "Please tell Maggie I didn't mean to hurt her. Tell her that I love her."

"Of course," Charles said and without another thought for Jimmy Delacroix, flew the astral plane, his destination the large ballroom that had been transformed into a surgery and state-of-the-art neonatal ICU for the twins, should they need it.

Charles arrived and saw Simon and Lee already scrubbed and masked, Meghann prepped for surgery on the operating table.

"Let me," Charles said to Simon after he scrubbed up and inserted the feeding tube in Simon's hands through Meghann's nose. He attached it to one of the packs of Simon's blood, prepared weeks before at Lee's suggestion. "You concentrate on keeping her calm."

Simon nodded and wiped a cold cloth across Meghann's clammy brow, holding the hand that gripped his with bone-crushing intensity.

"Promise me," she gasped, fighting to speak through the agony that gripped her.

"Anything, little one."

"Don't . . . don't forget me. . . ."

"Don't you dare talk that way," Simon said fiercely, meeting her pain-glazed eyes. "I won't forget you because you're going to be at my side, raising our children."

"I hope so," Meghann said and smiled through her tears. No matter how angry she was over what he'd done to Jimmy, this might be the last time she talked to him and she didn't want it to be a conversation of remonstration or hate. "But if I'm not . . . please, you raise these children like I want . . . you be soft and tender . . . like you are with me. Don't . . . please say it wasn't an act, that you really can live like that—"

"Hush," Simon said. "I'll be everything you want in a father for your children and if I'm not, you'll be here to nag and carp."

"One more—ow, Jesus! Lee, what's going on?"

Over his surgical mask, Meghann saw the fear in Lee's eyes and felt grateful when he didn't try to lie. "There's some fetal distress. Are you ready for the caesarian?"

Meghann swallowed back her apprehension, knowing the pain she was in would only get worse when Lee cut into her, and nodded. "Just one . . . Simon, don't hurt Jimmy Delacroix. He didn't want this to happen . . . promise me you won't go after him."

A narrow slash of red appeared in his cheeks but Simon only said, "Anything you want, Meghann. Now relax and think only of the wonderful little babies you're going to see soon."

* * *

Dimly, Meghann heard the fetal heart monitor and knew that one of the babies was in trouble, or maybe both. The heartbeat was too slow . . . their only hope was delivery. *Please,* she prayed to anyone that might be listening, *let Lee complete the caesarian before they die.*

The pain was hideous, worse than anything she'd ever felt before . . . worse than transformation even. She knew she was in shock, knew it by the horrible shaking cold that gripped her. She felt the sweat pouring off her clammy skin and the nausea that gripped her through the pain.

"Gonna be sick," she slurred and felt someone, Simon or Charles, grab her by the shoulders and pull her up so she wouldn't choke on the vomit.

"Help me," she whispered, not sure whom she was addressing. She felt a hand grip hers and managed to open her eyes, gazing into Simon's eyes. His eyes were narrowed and his jaw clenched as though he were in pain too and then Meghann understood . . . he was taking some of her agony into himself, trying to lessen it for her. In that moment, she felt any remaining anger fall away. All that mattered was that this was the father of the children she wanted so badly to live.

"Thank you," she tried to say but in that moment she suddenly found herself standing over her supine body.

Charles stood guard by the machines that monitored her vital signs and frowned. "She's passed out from the shock."

"Might be the best thing," Lee murmured and made a neat, vertical incision from her navel to the pubic bone, spreading the abdominal muscles apart before making another vertical incision through the wall of her uterus. "Good thing she can't feel the pain, doesn't know what's going on."

But I do know, Meghann tried to say. Why couldn't they hear her? She glanced at Simon, frowning down at her bloodless, still face.

Simon, don't you hear me?

Abruptly, his head jerked up and when their eyes met, Meghann saw something in his eyes she'd never seen before—terror.

Meghann, don't you drift away, he said and she moved toward his outstretched hands, finding herself back in her body, almost welcoming the fierce pain. Let her feel pain as long as she remained here, didn't die.

"Don't let me die," she whispered, her voice so weak that only Simon, positioned right by her mouth, could hear her. "I . . . I have to know the babies are okay."

"You won't die," Simon promised and leaned down to kiss her, pulling back in shock at her ice-cold flesh. He turned to Lee, a hard-driving edge in his voice. "Hurry!"

"What is it?" Charles demanded.

"She's dying," Simon told him, looking almost as pale as the semiconscious woman on the operating table.

"Damn . . . I can't stop the hemorrhaging! Charles, I need your help!" Lee said, handing Simon two incredibly tiny, bloodied figures that Meghann knew were her children. She wanted so much to hold them but she felt herself fading away again.

Was that really her—that still figure with a mop of fiery red hair framing a face that resembled white dough? Look at those deep creases around her eyes and mouth, she thought with an odd sense of detachment from the dying body on the operating table.

Just a little more time, Meghann pleaded with an unseen force but it kept dragging her away from the nightmarish scene of seeing her body die, watching the life drain from her as blood spurted up from the sickly green sheet covering her and drenched Lee's surgical gown. The blood kept coming despite all Lee's frantic efforts to save her, and Meghann was hurtling away, drifting toward some strange place. . . .

Come back, Meghann!

Take care of my children, she tried to say to Simon, and her last emotion before the peaceful blackness claimed her was a soft pity when she saw Simon clinging to the empty shell that was her body and pleading with her not to die.

TWENTY-ONE

Southampton, New York
Six weeks later

"What's it say?" Maggie's father asked, squinting at the sign going up on the scoreboard. "I left my glasses back at home."

Maggie put her hand up to shield her eyes from the flat glare of the afternoon sun, praying this was the news she and all the other Dodgers fans were hoping for. The Dodgers had this game well in hand, shutting the Braves out 6–0. If they won today and the St. Louis Cardinals lost, the Dodgers would clinch the National League Pennant and go to the World Series. "It's the final score for Cards game. Three to one . . . oh, my God . . . three to one! The Cardinals lost, they're out of the race!"

"The Cardinals lost—we're gonna win the pennant, we're gonna win the pennant!" Bridie, Maggie's best friend, screamed and linked her hands with Maggie's while they jumped up and down.

"Isn't this the greatest?" Maggie shouted, and Bridie started to nod her head in enthusiastic agreement but Maggie yanked her hands away, staring at her best friend with large, frightened eyes.

"Maggie?"

Maggie squeezed her eyes shut so she wouldn't have to see the wizened scarecrow that had taken Bridie's place, her face a sad network of wrinkles and liver spots with a brow per-

manently creased in pain. The crone clung to Maggie's hand and asked her why she'd disappeared so long ago, why she'd run off with . . .

"Maggie, come on," she heard Bridie implore. "What the heck is wrong with you? You look like you just saw a ghost."

Maggie opened her eyes a cautious slit and then uttered a short, nervous laugh of relief. Her mind was playing tricks on her . . . there was nothing wrong with Bridie. There was no strange old woman, just her pretty blond friend wearing a pink sundress.

"I just felt funny for a second," Maggie said and sank back into her seat.

"It's no wonder you feel funny," her father grumbled at her. "It's not bad enough you forgot to put on your hat this morning so you picked up the sunburn of your life . . . then you have two beers on top of it at the game. You're probably dehydrated. Go get yourself a drink of water and splash your face before I have to carry you out of here."

"But, Daddy," Maggie argued, "I wanna see Wyatt finish the inning and clinch the pennant. . . ."

"There's only one out so far. Now go find a water fountain and don't argue with your father if you know what's good for you, Meghann Katherine."

Don't argue with me, Meghann. Maggie frowned, pushing her way past some spectators as she searched for a ladies' room. It seemed she could remember someone besides her father calling her by her hated full name. Some man with a fancy, know-it-all way of talking and a deep, whispery voice she didn't dare disobey. . . .

"No!" Maggie said out loud, startling the only other woman in the rest room. Maggie simply shrugged at the woman's inquisitive look and splashed her face with the icy water from the sink, scowling at the bedraggled girl that stared back at her in the mirror.

What difference did it make who called her Meghann? That didn't matter . . . what mattered was that Maggie was an absolute mess. Her wispy red hair had escaped the black net snood at the nape of her neck and now flew around in every direction, making her look as if she'd just been in the electric chair. Worse, her face was a freckled, sunburned horror . . . she looked like a rotting tomato!

Maggie wet her hands and slicked her hair down, forcing the errant strands back into the snood. There wasn't much she could do for her face except dab a little powder on to conceal the worst of the damage. Maggie took out her compact and pressed the puff down into powder before bringing it up to her face but what she saw when she looked in the mirror again made her pull back with a shriek of horror.

Her reflection was gone . . . in its place was a freakish half-there image of a woman with waist-length red hair and sad, sad green eyes.

Why can't I see my reflection anymore, Simon?

Don't let it cause you sadness. What you see in the mirror is undeniable proof that you are a supernatural creature with unquestioned dominion over the night, freedom from death and disease.

"No!" Maggie howled and ran blindly from the room. She had to get back to the stands, to Bridie and her father. This horrible, unspeakable thing wouldn't be true if she could just get back where she belonged. . . .

"No!" she screamed again at the plainly dressed balding man who leaned against a cement post, his kind brown eyes filled with pity as he met her defiant gaze.

"You're not real!" she yelled at him, tears streaming down her face. *"You're not, you're not! You're a dream . . . an awful, nasty dream, and I want to wake up now! I want to be Maggie again."*

"Banrion," Alcuin whispered sadly and engulfed her in his arms while she wept. *"I've never known anyone as hurt by immortality as my lost young queen. I'd do anything to turn the clock and bring you back to this safe, good world of yours."*

"This really happened," she sniffled. *"My father . . . he took all of us kids out of school, even let my friend Bridie come along, so we could watch the Dodgers win the pennant. It was just like I remembered except I didn't see anything out*

of the ordinary when I looked at Bridie. How could I . . . I had no idea one night I'd stand over her deathbed and use my vampiric power to end her suffering."

Even with Alcuin holding her, that didn't seem real at all. Maggie O'Neill a vampire, consort to a strange, brutal creature that made her call him master? No, how could that have happened when she stood here in Braves Field, hearing the exultant shouts of Dodger fans as their beloved team came one out closer to the pennant? It was much more likely this bishop turned vampire would vanish and then Maggie and her family would take the train back to New York, chattering the entire way about the Dodgers' chances against the formidable Yankees. Then, privately, she and Bridie would discuss an issue of even more importance . . . whether Maggie's cousin Mickey would make good on his promise and call Bridie for a date over the Thanksgiving vacation.

"This all feels so real," she said wistfully. This wasn't at all like a dream, where the world was all shadows with no true substance. Couldn't she feel the firmness of the cement beneath her feet, the sunburn stinging her cheeks? She'd never had a dream like this.

"It isn't precisely a dream, Banrion."

"Then what is it? Am I dead?"

"Not quite," Alcuin answered. "But you are gravely ill. I've come to tell you that you may stay here if that is your desire and no one will disturb you—not even Simon Baldevar."

"Simon." Meghann (she knew she had to acknowledge that she hadn't been that innocent young girl Maggie for a very long time) sighed and her eyes darkened. Impulsively, she clutched at Alcuin's hands, searching his eyes for the reproach and hurt she was sure would be there . . . they'd parted so horribly the last time. "Please don't hate me for what I said. I'm so sorry—"

"Banrion," Alcuin interrupted, raising one hand to still her speech. "Don't apologize. If anything, I must beg your pardon. My behavior was reprehensible . . . advocating bloodshed instead of peace. It took that rage and hurt in your eyes for me to see what my battle with Simon has turned me into. To think that I'd be willing to forsake the love of a girl I consider my daughter rather than cease my war with him. For four hundred years, I've been consumed with hatred . . . not just because of what my nephew does to mortals but I've also wanted revenge ever since I saw what he did to Isabelle."

"Simon thinks you were in love with Isabelle."

"Perhaps I was. Even lying on her deathbed, with her body rotting away and her mind deteriorating, Isabelle Baldevar was possessed of a quiet grace and brave dignity I've never encountered in another being. When I saw that sweet young woman dying and I thought of all Simon took from her—"

"Simon didn't take anything from her!" Meghann interrupted hotly. "It was he who had everything taken from him by that rotten family of his. They treated him like dirt, gave him nothing, but he still managed to build up his own fortune and then that greedy Roger tried to take that away too. It's his own fault Simon killed him and married Isabelle. Simon was just protecting what he'd worked so hard to build. If Isabelle hadn't been so stupid and superstitious, she wouldn't have lost her son. When Michael got sick, she should have let Simon's doctor look after him . . ."

Alcuin seemed bemused by Meghann's impassioned speech and she broke off abruptly, thinking she was probably the first person in four hundred years to defend Simon Baldevar's character. Even here, where she could see and feel the sunlight Simon had taken from her with his poisoned blood and talk to the family he'd insisted she break off contact with . . . even here she loved him enough to champion him.

"Banrion," Alcuin was saying, and she looked up, concentrating on his words. "Only Simon and Isabelle will ever know the full truth of what happened during their marriage. I am still amazed that my nephew confided in you, felt the need to justify his life to anyone. He must love you deeply."

"Didn't you say Simon is incapable of love?"

"He was," Alcuin said with a sad smile. "For four hundred years, he reveled in the blood lust and thrived on causing pain. He still does, I fear, but now there's another side to

Lord Baldevar . . . the soft, tender facet of his personality he displays when he's with you. It doesn't surprise me that you love him . . . he's worked very hard to win your heart.

"Banrion, I know you're confused and I wish I had time to talk to you but the longer you remain here, the harder it will be to go back . . . if that's your desire."

"Of course I want to go back . . . I have to, my children need me. They did survive, didn't they? Alcuin, tell me they're all right!"

Alcuin just smiled and placed a shiny, intricately carved silver cross around her neck. "I gave this to my sister the day I performed her marriage ceremony, some seven centuries ago. Please pass it on to your daughter . . . yes, Banrion, you have a little girl. I already sense in her that bright-eyed exuberance I prayed the burdens of immortality wouldn't steal from you. Strange how I always thought Simon wanted to twist that unique fire in your soul . . . break you like he did Isabelle. Now I find it's why he made you his soror mystica; the only woman he considered fit to bear his child. Perhaps there is some small spark of goodness within Lord Baldevar if he has the sense to love you."

"Alcuin, I know I told you I love him. But I love you too and I believe in what you taught me, how you think a vampire should live. I may love him but I don't want to be like Simon, I don't."

"Banrion," Alcuin said firmly, putting his hands on both sides of her face. "You could never be like Simon Baldevar. I wish I could soothe you and say your love will triumph over the darkness in Lord Baldevar's soul but it takes a great deal of time for water to wear away stone. I am not sure you want to take on such an enormous and possibly futile task but perhaps you must . . . for your children's sake. Now, much as I enjoy seeing you, it's time to go, Banrion."

Meghann nodded, standing on tiptoe to kiss Alcuin's cheek in farewell.

"I love you, Father," she said, knowing Alcuin was as much a parent to her as Jack O'Neill had been. What would

*have become of her without this kindly creature to guide her
through immortality?*

*"I love you too, Banrion . . . you and Charles, for carry-
ing on my creed after my death while the others succumbed
to their need for power. Tell him how very proud I am of you
both and tell Simon Baldevar I only hope he realizes what he
has in you. Now just listen, Banrion . . . listen."*

*Listen? Meghann frowned—what was she supposed to lis-
ten to? She heard nothing now, not the remembered cheers at
Braves Field or Alcuin's quiet, diffident tones. She heard nothing and then there was something very faint. Yes, there was
something in the fog around her, a desperate mewling sound.
Why, that must be . . .*

"A baby crying!" Meghann exclaimed and found
herself on a queen-size bed with crisp lilac sheets and
a violet quilt. Looking around the plainly furnished
room with cream stucco walls, she realized this was one
of the many unused rooms in the Southampton house.
She must have been brought in here to recover from
the birth. Yes, she'd definitely given birth, Meghann
thought, running her hands over her now flat abdomen. But what had happened to the twins?

Meghann became aware of an uncomfortable twinge
in her nose and brought her hand up, feeling the
stomach tube. She ripped the thing out, wondering
how long she'd lain unconscious and needed to be fed
that way. And if she was so sick she had to drink blood
through a tube, why wasn't someone watching over
her—Charles or Lee? The last thing Meghann expected was that she'd wake up alone, in an unfamiliar
room. Why wasn't someone here to tell her what had
happened to her children?

Her children . . . Meghann strained her ears, praying to hear that soft cry that woke her up. But the
house around her was utterly still; she was beginning
to wonder if there was anyone in the house at all when

a raspy, muted sound disturbed the thick silence around her.

It was the sound of someone crying . . . not a baby but a man. A man who'd lost all hope and wept in despair but muffled the noise so no one would hear him.

Meghann jumped out of bed, grabbing the walnut bedpost when the world spun around briefly. Apparently she wasn't fully recovered yet. But she couldn't get back into bed; she had to hurry toward that terrible sobbing, find out what was causing it.

The weeping led her to the large, cheerful room on the third floor she and Simon had chosen for the twins' nursery. Meghann hesitated before the closed door, afraid to take the final step and find out if her babies had survived that hellish delivery. As she faltered, the masculine sobs grew stronger and Meghann forced herself to open the door.

The sight that greeted her was one she could never have prepared herself for. In place of Charles or Lee, it was Simon hunched over a cradle while his shoulders shook from the force of his tears. Meghann felt shaken to her core, stunned and embarrassed for Simon; she knew he wouldn't want anyone to see him like this.

She should say something, let him know she was in the room, but she could push nothing past her own grief at seeing that solitary cradle decorated in the bright rose bunting she'd bought months before. Where was the other cradle, the one draped in Victorian lace? The other baby must have died and now this child was dying too . . . what else could make Simon Baldevar cry but the death of the child he'd wanted for so long?

"I'm so very sorry," she heard him whisper and she sobbed out loud, hating herself for the accident that had led to this catastrophe. If only she hadn't placed herself in the middle of that awful fight, her children wouldn't be dead before they'd even had a chance to live. This was all her fault. . . .

Simon straightened and spun around, his amber eyes first betraying shock, then filling with a hope that stunned her almost as much as his appearance.

"Meghann?" he said and sounded almost as surprised as she felt.

She could only nod; she'd never seen Simon look like this. His eyes were sunken beneath deep purple hollows and his skin had the sickly cast of a blood-starved vampire.

"Meghann," he said again and the savage joy in his eyes dimmed when he saw the tears coursing down her face. "Sweetheart, why on earth are you crying?"

"The baby," she choked out and pointed a shaking finger at the silent bundle he clutched to his chest. "The baby is dying. . . ."

"No, Meghann," Simon said and his calm assurance cut through her grief. "Where would you get such a notion? There's nothing wrong with our daughter."

"Daughter?" Meghann gasped, her entire being focused on the bundle Simon held out to her.

"Would you like to hold Elizabeth?" Simon asked with a broad grin, and Meghann felt an answering grin form on her lips.

"God, yes," Meghann said and rushed forward, stumbling when dizziness claimed her again.

"Easy," Simon told her and put one hand under her elbow while he tucked the infant against him with his other hand.

"You've had a trying ordeal," Simon said and guided her to the padded rocking chair by the bay window.

Meghann eased into the chair and Simon's grin deepened at her outstretched hands and eager expression. Gingerly, he gave the child to Meghann and she wrapped her arms around her daughter. Startled by the transfer from her father's familiar embrace to strange hands, the baby opened her eyes to gaze at her mother. Meghann had only a second to admire her daughter's spring-green eyes before the child let out a fretful wail.

"Don't look so stricken," Simon whispered at Meghann's wounded expression. "Elizabeth is only telling you that she's hungry."

"Hungry?" Meghann frowned and then felt a warm, moist gush against her nightgown. "Why . . . that's my milk! Can I feed her?"

"Who else do you think has fed her these past six weeks?"

"I've been unconscious for six weeks?" Meghann asked disbelievingly as her daughter's cries escalated into outraged howls. She seemed to be saying, could Meghann please hold off on her questions until one very hungry baby had been fed?

"I . . . Simon, I'm not sure of how to do this."

"Don't worry," he said and pulled on the laces of her nightgown. "Elizabeth knows what to do."

Simon was right. No sooner did Meghann guide the small head toward her breast than the baby honed in on the familiar nipple and began to suck vigorously.

"Oh," Meghann breathed at the pulling sensation on her nipple as the baby nursed. In a way, feeding the baby was a bit like being bled, but having Simon sink his fangs into her and drink her blood never made her feel this good. This was good and right in a way that bloodletting would never be. It didn't feel draining at all to feed Elizabeth; instead, feeding the baby made the hot, heavy ache in her breasts fade as her daughter ate greedily.

Meghann put her hand on the child's head, stroking the silky cap of bright chestnut curls while she transferred the baby to her other breast. The baby didn't even look up, so intent was she on feeding.

Meghann felt tears prick her eyelids again when she noticed one tiny, perfect hand perched on her chest. She'd never seen anything as beautiful as that little fist, the delicate ivory whiteness of her skin, the pearly miniature fingernails, and the surprising strength in the infant's grip when Meghann slipped her thumb into her daughter's hand.

"I love you," Meghann whispered and the baby merely looked at her before letting out a loud, watery belch. Meghann laughed and settled back in the rocking chair, undoing the blanket so she could inspect her daughter.

Meghann had heard that infants usually went to sleep after eating but Elizabeth remained awake, returning her mother's curious gaze with one of her own. She lay docile and quiet while Meghann examined the plump little body and then focused her attention on her daughter's face, finding herself and Simon in the little girl's features.

She has my eyes, Meghann thought, smiling at the bright green, almond-shaped eyes with their fringe of long brown lashes. *But she has her father's hair . . . that bright shade of chestnut with hints of red, thick and wavy like his instead of straight like mine. And his nose is straight and narrow like that. But those are my lips . . . and look at that; she's going to have Simon's cheekbones . . . high and elegant.*

"Isn't she beautiful?" Meghann whispered but there was no response. She frowned and looked up only to see that she and Elizabeth were alone in the room. She'd been so engrossed in Elizabeth she never heard Simon leave.

Meghann started rocking back and forth in the chair, bringing a little smile to Elizabeth's face. Her breath caught at the slanting grin so like Simon's and she covered the little face in kisses. Her own child smiling at her, her and Simon Baldevar's child.

Meghann cuddled the sleeping baby closer and continued to rock. In that dream or wherever her soul had gone, Meghann had felt such regret for what she lost when she became a vampire. Now, looking down at her daughter's face, she knew she'd do it all over again . . . do anything for the end result of holding this wonderful child.

Where had Simon vanished to? Meghann wanted him to come back; she wanted to share their daughter with him and tell him . . .

Tell him what? Meghann sighed, making Elizabeth whimper softly in her sleep. Tell him she wasn't angry; all was forgiven? Should she forgive Simon—again? How could she overlook what he'd done to Jimmy Delacroix, when his actions so clearly showed his astonishing capacity for ruthlessness? Meghann shivered, her mind presenting her with the image of Simon leaning over Jimmy, his features twisted into an evil mask of malice and hate that made her heart tighten with fear. How could she expose Elizabeth to a creature like that?

"He'd never be like that with her," Meghann said aloud and knew that was the truth. Elizabeth would never see her father's worst side. The proof of his intentions toward his daughter was all around her—from her daughter's well-cared-for, clean little body to the fantasy of a room he'd created for her.

The pinched, anxious look left her eyes as she took in the nursery. Meghann might have picked out the furniture but it was Simon's talent and imagination that had transformed the room into a perfect place for a child to grow up with the murals he'd painted on the walls and ceiling.

They were whimsical, painstakingly drawn scenes of fairy tales. The handsome prince placing the glass slipper on Cinderella's foot, the pig gazing up adoringly at the wonderfully drawn spider with the grouchy rat Wilbur looking on . . . that was from *Charlotte's Web*, one of Meghann's favorite stories. All of the murals were so carefully drawn, meticulous attention paid to the smallest detail—the lacy design of the spiderweb, the sunlight flittering through the slats in the barn, the shimmering, translucent glass of Cinderella's slipper.

It was impossible to hate Simon in this beautiful room he'd created for their child, hard to despise him when she looked down at the little girl that was the result of their reunion. Meghann closed her eyes and rocked, lulled into a semihypnotic state by the creak of the rocking chair and her daughter's perfect, even breathing.

Startled by the sudden odor of blood in the air, Meghann opened her eyes and saw Simon at her side, holding out a silver goblet and cask. She reached up for the blood, nearly doubled over with hunger and need.

"I'll take the baby while you feed."

With some regret, Meghann allowed Simon to take the baby and watched him stretch out against the green-and-white-striped window seat, holding Elizabeth up so she could see the ocean.

"That's going to be your view, princess," Simon murmured while Meghann gulped down the blood he'd brought her. Warm, she thought, not from a transfusion pack and not a vampire's blood. Simon must have gone out on a quick hunt while she nursed Elizabeth.

He must have fed during his absence too, she thought, noticing how much better he looked. The sunken eyes and sickly skin had vanished, replaced with his usual creamy color and alert gold eyes.

"It wasn't the blood that restored me, Meghann . . . it was you. I truly thought I'd lost you, sweetheart. When you came in before and heard my apology . . . I'd give my daughter anything, and the one thing she needed above all else—her mother—I could not provide."

Simon offered the baby one finger, smiling as the infant grasped it with all her strength. "You see she has your eyes? Last night, they hadn't completely changed yet from infant blue. It killed me to look at her and see you . . . think our daughter's eyes were all I'd have to remember you. We managed to stop your bleeding . . . or rather I should say, Doctor Winslow's skill stopped your bleeding. But it seemed you'd already lost too much . . . you wouldn't wake up no matter how much blood we pumped into you. We tried not to say it, but it seemed your mind and soul had moved on even though your vampire body wouldn't die and set you free." Simon's eyes narrowed and he leaned over, careful not to disturb Elizabeth, as he fingered the silver cross around Meghann's neck. "I have not seen that before."

"Alcuin gave it to me," Meghann replied, staring down with some shock at the gift that had managed to make it into the physical world with her. Simon showed no surprise when she explained the crucifix's provenance, though his mouth curved down in displeasure. "He wants me to give it to Elizabeth."

"The great saint of the vampires wishes to pass on a relic to my child?"

"My child too," Meghann said pointedly. "And I think you should know I wouldn't be here if it wasn't for Alcuin. I'm not sure where I was but it . . . I was Maggie again, with no memory whatsoever of you or transformation. I would have died and stayed in that place but Alcuin came and told me if I wanted to come back here, he'd help me do it."

Simon raised an eyebrow. "Alcuin sent you back to me? Has death turned the cleric daft?"

"He helped me back because I asked him to—nothing would keep me from my baby," Meghann said quietly. "He said nothing about you except . . . he said he hoped you realized what you had in me."

For a moment something dark passed over Simon's face and then it was gone. He stood up and smiled at Meghann as he sat down in the rocking chair. "I know Alcuin considers me evil . . . I was not aware he questioned my intelligence. Let's not discuss my uncle's ramblings right now. I'd like to hold both my girls, little one. Will you come sit with us?"

Any lingering uncertainty faded at the protective hands wrapped around Elizabeth, the soft, hopeful look in Simon's eyes as he smiled up at her. Meghann couldn't shatter this moment with harsh words and re-criminations. Smiling back at him, she perched on his lap, one hand wrapped around his neck while the other rested on top of their daughter's head.

The baby turned toward her hand and made a soft murmur of contentment. Simon smiled at the sound and whispered so the infant wouldn't wake up. "You were wrong, Meghann."

"Hmmn?" she said disinterestedly, taking the baby from his arms so she could cuddle the warm little bundle.

"When you screamed that I wanted to take every-thing worth living for away from you. I do want you to have a family to love."

Meghann flushed, remembering all the insults and barbs she'd flung at him in her rage when she found out what he'd been doing to Jimmy. She'd told him that she hated him, that she'd never allow him near their child. Yet here she was, nestling on his lap, taking comfort in the heat of his body that she felt through his thick linen shirt. No doubt he thought her the stu-pid bitch Jimmy Delacroix called her.

"Capricious, perhaps." Simon smiled at her. "Cer-tainly not stupid . . . merely possessed of a ferocious Irish temper you make little effort to restrain. I did not bring that up to reproach you, Meghann, or be-cause I'm fishing for an apology I know will be never be forthcoming—"

"Apology!" Meghann said heatedly and immediately lowered her voice at Elizabeth's wide-open, startled eyes. She continued on in a sarcastic whisper. "You want me to beg your pardon for catching you red-handed, you arrogant devil. . . ."

Simon threw back his head and laughed, drawing an enthusiastic gurgle from Elizabeth. "Sometimes it's amusing to be on the rough side of your tongue, little one. No, I neither expect nor crave an apology. I merely meant to ask if you could be content with what I give you."

Meghann didn't have to ask what he meant. Simon wanted to know if she could accept him as he was . . . both the gentle lover and father he'd be with her and Elizabeth, as well as the brutal creature that dealt so mercilessly with anyone he considered his enemy—like Jimmy Delacroix. But he didn't have to hate anyone to hurt them, Meghann knew. Simon didn't hate the mortals he fed from . . . he simply considered them insignificant beings to use as the spirit moved him and would never understand Meghann's guilt at satisfying the blood lust.

Nor would he even try to reform himself in an effort to please her. If Meghann couldn't reconcile herself to what Lord Baldevar was, their lives together would be nothing but misery as she reacted with bitter disappointment every time he did something that went against her scruples.

Too, what kind of life would it be for Elizabeth . . . watching her parents tear into each other with hateful, cutting words? Through her practice, Meghann had seen the end result of disastrous marriages . . . the bleak-eyed children that broke her heart when she saw that they had no belief at all in love because they'd never been given any or never seen their parents give each other anything but grief and pain. She'd never allow that to happen to Elizabeth.

That left her with two alternatives—leave Lord Baldevar but allow him to be part of Elizabeth's life or accept him completely, swallowing her fear and disgust at the worst part of his soul. If she did that, though, what would happen to her soul . . . and Elizabeth's?

"Little one," Simon said after a prolonged silence, "why isn't it enough that I care for you and Elizabeth as I've never cared for anyone else? Are you truly going to toss what we could have away for a world of strangers that will never even appreciate your actions?"

Meghann flinched at Simon's harsh tone, at his bitter but somehow accepting expression. It was almost as though he knew she was going to leave him and he'd resigned himself to losing her. Would Simon really let her walk away? Meghann thought, trying to remember when she'd ever seen him look like this, and then it came to her. He'd worn this probing, intense expression the first night they met—when he was trying to decide whether to kill her or transform her.

"That was no decision at all." Simon laughed and attached his lips to the hollow of her throat. She felt a small stab of desire go through her and barely heard the rest of his words. "It only took one kiss for me to know I was never going to let you go. One kiss, Meghann, and I fell in love with you."

"No one ever kissed me like you did," she murmured shyly and felt his hand on the back of her neck, guiding her lips to his. Apparently he wasn't planning to let her go at all—though he seemed to have decided that talking was pointless. They had one moment of delicious contact before a high-pitched squeal made Meghann pull away. Looking down, she saw that she'd squished the baby when she pressed herself against Simon. The infant shifted and then opened her green eyes to give her thoughtless parents a sleepy glare.

Meghann and Simon looked down at the perturbed little face and laughed together.

"Prickly little thing, isn't she?" Meghann giggled, feeling the tension in the room dissipate as they smiled at the scowling baby.

"My daughter has the temperament of an angel,"

Simon sniffed and gave her a flickering grin. "Unless someone denies her or causes her trouble . . . then she screams like a banshee until all her wishes are satisfied."

"I wonder where she got that from?" Meghann said wryly while she set the baby down in her antique mahogany Empire cradle. Simon stood on the other side, and together they rocked Elizabeth to sleep, gazing at each other all the time with hungry, eager eyes.

"Good night, precious," Meghann whispered and leaned down to kiss the downy forehead.

"She'll be awake soon enough," Simon said. "She eats every three hours. Speaking of which, I must feed you now, little mother. You still look somewhat drawn and you're nursing Elizabeth—you must eat to keep up your strength. And afterward . . . well, who's to say what we'll do with the time we have together before Elizabeth needs to eat again?"

Meghann smiled and allowed him to sweep her up, returning his passionate kiss with one of her own before they left the nursery. Maybe he was evil and maybe in the future he'd commit some heinous act that would make her hate him all over again. But right now Meghann wanted to take the love he was so eager to give her, to share his joy in the child they'd brought into the world. She'd think of all he was and all he was capable of later . . . much, much later.

TWENTY-TWO

"Is something wrong, Simon?"

"What on earth could be wrong?" Simon asked rhetorically. "You survived your ordeal, we have a beautiful daughter, and you're no longer behaving like a shrew."

Meghann swallowed various retorts on what had caused her shrewish state and speared a piece of filet mignon. The glib speech did nothing to assuage her suspicions—something was wrong with Simon; she just couldn't put her finger on it.

Meghann's ruminations were interrupted by the soft click of the front door opening. Her heart leaped when she recognized the presence entering the house and she started toward it but was only a few feet from her chair when Charles Tarleton appeared at the threshold to the dining room, Lee by his side. Both of them looked at Meghann as if they couldn't really believe she was there.

"Meghann!" Charles finally shouted, rushing toward her and spinning her around, planting a firm kiss on her cheek. "Meghann, I can't believe . . ."

"I've been getting a lot of that tonight." She smiled through the tears that matched the streaks on her friend's face.

"Get away from her," Lee ordered with an earsplitting grin. "Let me say hello."

"When? How?" Charles said, not to Meghann but to Simon.

"She awoke earlier this evening," Simon explained. "Apparently Elizabeth's cries brought her back to us."

Though Simon's expression didn't change and his tone remained calm, Meghann knew he sent some implicit message to Charles, for her friend's eyes widened slightly before he regained his composure. What was going on here? Meghann wondered. Since when were Charles and Simon chummy enough to speak to each other telepathically? More important, what where they saying to each other that they didn't want her to hear?

But Meghann was too happy at seeing her friends to ask questions. She simply took her seat by Simon while Lee and Charles helped themselves to the sumptuous buffet at the rosewood sideboard.

Ravenous after a diet that Charles informed her had involved no more than blood and an IV drip for six weeks, Meghann devoured a sixteen-ounce filet mignon, along with several thick slices of duck, stuffing, roast potatoes, and various vegetables. Simon, Charles, and Lee attacked their plates with equal fervor, and the meal became quite cheerful, with several toasts of the Chateau Y'Quem that Simon produced drunk to Meghann's recovery and Elizabeth's birth.

"Meghann." Charles sobered briefly and took her hand. "I'm so sorry that you woke up by yourself—you must have been terribly frightened and confused. I wish Lee or I had been with you but we really thought we'd be saying good-bye tonight. We thought it only right that Lord, uh, Simon have some time alone with you."

Meghann thought of Simon's ghastly appearance when she first woke up, and felt a rush of tenderness toward Charles and Lee. How kind of them to respect Simon's feelings and stay away so they wouldn't bear witness to that terrible grief that drove him to weep.

Of course . . . why hadn't she seen it before? The new friendship between Charles and Simon was forged during that long, awful vigil when they didn't know whether she'd live or die. Meghann thought again of the hideous dark circles under Simon's eyes, the starved, pale quality of his skin, and knew he must have stayed by her side practically the whole time she lay unconscious. It was his devotion toward her that finally made Charles drop his guard and trust Lord Baldevar.

Meghann started to tell all three men what their loyalty and care meant to her when an imperious wail shattered the festive atmosphere.

"At least we don't need one of those baby monitors." Meghann sighed and stood up. "Is it the sharpened hearing of a vampire or is she just an exceptionally loud baby?"

"Don't malign my daughter, madam—there's nothing wrong with a strong set of lungs. I must say though, she's about to get a pleasant surprise," Simon commented with a wry grin. "You'll probably have Elizabeth in her cups from all the wine you've drunk."

Meghann poked her tongue out and beckoned for Charles to accompany her to the nursery. They flew up and in a matter of seconds Meghann scooped the red-faced, squalling bundle out of the cradle. Rapidly, she undid the top three buttons on her button-down moss-green dress and exchanged a breast for peace as Elizabeth began to feed with the same hungry voracity she'd displayed earlier.

"You can fly again?"

Meghann nodded and leaned back in the rocking chair. "I finally feel myself for the first time in months. All those months of not being able to fly the plane—it was like being mortal! Speaking of which, why is Lee still mortal?"

"What?"

Meghann was startled at how discomfited Charles looked. "I thought you were going to transform him after I gave birth." Lee had refused transformation earlier, saying there wasn't any proof Meghann's labor wouldn't continue throughout the day, and he thought someone should be able to stay by her side during the day in case of an emergency.

"Meghann," Charles began and then stopped. He sat down heavily in the window seat, his face an unhappy mix of distress, sorrow, and a little pity.

"Meghann," he said again and stretched his hand over to finger Elizabeth's rose-petal-soft cheek, smiling at the little girl. "Have you noticed anything strange about Elizabeth?"

"Strange?" Meghann frowned. "Why, no—not at all. She's seems perfectly normal."

"Right," Charles said and sighed. "She is perfectly normal. Meghann, your daughter is mortal."

"What?" Astonished, she sat ramrod straight, making her nipple fall out of Elizabeth's mouth. At the baby's irritated whimper, Meghann guided her head back to her breast. "Mortal? But how? Simon and I are—"

"Whatever you are, you were once human. Apparently we never lose the mortal genetic code completely . . . it's just buried within our DNA. My guess is that Elizabeth's mortality is caused by the same factor that causes blue eyes—recessive genes."

"Yes." Meghann spoke slowly, trying to absorb the shock. She looked down at the cherubic little face, the *human* face of her child, and tried to marshal her thoughts into a coherent line. "But how can you be sure she's mortal? If it's that she tolerates daylight, why, that's the whole promise of the philosophers' stone. . . ."

At those words Charles flinched as though she'd struck him. "No, Meghann. Elizabeth is not a realization of the philosophers' stone. She's simply a mortal child born of immortal parents. How do we know? Our first sign was that she rejected blood, would digest nothing but your milk. If that wasn't enough, we ran some blood tests, scraped her ileum . . . Meghann, there's nothing of the vampire in your daughter."

"You're not a vampire," Meghann said to the dozing child in her arms. At the news, Meghann felt shocked, for she'd never once imagined this when she fretted about how her child would turn out. She'd been so worried, despite her and Simon being of the same bloodline, that Elizabeth would be deformed somehow or stillborn like all the other vampire children.

"Oh, Charles," Meghann said, thinking her friend looked even more upset when she smiled. "Why do you look so sad? This is wonderful! Elizabeth can go to school with other children, play outside, and enjoy the sun—the sun! Charles, who's going to take care of Elizabeth while I sleep?"

"That's why Lee hasn't transformed. He watches over Elizabeth during the day and he'll continue to do so until she's capable of taking care of herself. Meghann, don't look like that—it's no imposition. As far as immortality goes, Lee's only in his forties and exceptionally healthy . . . he should be able to transform with no difficulties once Elizabeth's an adult. Neither of us would pass up this chance to raise a child and we love your daughter as though she were our flesh and blood. I can't tell you how grateful, how proud we were when Simon asked Lee to formally adopt Elizabeth."

"He what?"

Charles smiled at her astonishment. "Simon said Elizabeth needs a daytime protector and there was no one he thought more deserving than the doctor who brought her into the world safely. It doesn't seem to bother him at all that Lee's homosexual. No doubt all Lord Baldevar's vile remarks about sodomites were just a way to get under my skin."

Meghann kept silent but she knew the chance to unsettle Charles by attacking the homosexuality he'd been so ashamed of as a mortal man was far from the only reason Simon reacted with such rancor to her friend. Four centuries had passed but he still despised homosexuals after the humiliating encounter with Nicholas Aermville. How much Simon must respect Lee to overlook those deep-seated resentments and turn to Lee as the only person fit to guard his daughter during the day!

"Of course, it'll be much easier now that you're well," Charles continued, taking Meghann's silence for nothing more than deep surprise. "Think of how much the world has changed since you and I were young, Meghann. No one will think twice about a gay man and a heterosexual woman raising a child together. Simon also said . . . he said he thought if you did die, you'd at least be comforted by the thought that Lee and I were raising Elizabeth."

Meghann blinked rapidly, thinking perhaps Alcuin was wrong and it wouldn't take that long for water to wear away stone after all. But she didn't think it was going to be her love that changed Lord Baldevar . . . it would be the love he had for his daughter that might erode the darkness inside him. That would be an unselfish love, that had nothing of the obsession and dark desire that drove Simon to slay anyone that threatened his relationship with Meghann, like Jimmy Delacroix . . .

"Jimmy!" she cried and shut her mouth abruptly—it would never do for Simon to hear her inquire about him. She gave Charles a questioning tremulous glance . . . was Jimmy still alive?

Charles saw her trepidation and nodded. *He's safe, Meghann. Simon's honored his promise to you and left him alone. I'll help him adjust to immortality . . . don't worry about Jimmy anymore.*

Meghann nodded and turned her attention back to Elizabeth. She knew she'd miss Jimmy, her best friend next to Charles, but she thought it best if they didn't see each other. With her out of his life and Charles guiding him through the confusion of immortality, maybe Jimmy could find his way and build a new life for himself.

"Charles," she said suddenly, forgetting Jimmy as her friend's words sank in and their meaning disturbed her. "Why did you say Simon wants you and Lee to raise Elizabeth? You made it sound like he won't be here."

Again, Charles gave her that complex glance of pity, pain, and reticence. She knew Charles wanted to tell her what caused his sadness but something was holding him back. "Meghann, I . . . it's Simon's place to tell you."

"Tell me what?" she demanded and at that moment, she heard an utterly alien cry unlike anything she'd ever heard before. It was like sharp nails raked slowly against a chalkboard with an overlying whine of need. The sounds made her break out in gooseflesh, and Elizabeth woke up, crying frightened, agitated tears.

Meghann held the baby close and put her hands over the little girl's ears to try and block out the noise. "Hush, honey, hush. Charles, what on earth is that?" She forced herself to listen and thought if you took away the strangeness, then it was just like . . .

A baby crying!

"The other twin," Meghann said slowly and stared at Charles, bafflement plain on her face. "But I . . . I thought the other baby must have died . . ."

Her voice trailed off, both because it was impossible to speak over the escalating screech and because she'd just realized how strange it was that she hadn't thought about her presumably dead child at all. It was as though she'd only been expecting one child . . . she'd literally forgotten she'd been carrying twins. No, not forgotten—now she felt the slight block in her mind and knew there was only one being powerful enough to put it there.

"But why?" she puzzled out loud. "I don't understand—why would Simon hide my own baby from me, make me not even think about it?" Alarm made her voice scale up and almost but not quite drown out the relentless cry that made her teeth clench.

"Meghann—" Charles began but Meghann thrust Elizabeth at him and flew out of the room, directing herself toward the source of the noise. She had to see her other baby, the one she feared she'd lost.

She found herself in a room without any light, so dark even her vampire eyes had trouble making out details. The shutters were pulled tightly to drown out any illumination from the moon and she could see that the bulb had even been removed from the overhead socket.

In the center of the room stood an ormolu mahogany cradle . . . the twin to Elizabeth's. Why was Simon separating the children, sequestering a baby in this drab cave of a room with no toys, no furniture, nothing but the one cradle?

Meghann moved toward the howling occupant of the cradle, finding her eardrums nearly pierced by the high-pitched, indescribable wail.

"Don't cry," she started to croon but pulled back in shock, stuffing her fingers into her mouth to keep from screaming when she saw the shimmering, translucent skin, the grotesque red and blue veins identical to the ones that used to cover Alcuin's face. The baby had a short, sharp pair of blood teeth that had cut through his colorless lips. Far worse than his skin though were the child's eyes. There were only black pupils surrounded by a blank iris with no color whatsoever.

Feeble choking sounds emerged from Meghann as her breath went out of her in a sickly burst. She blinked her eyes rapidly and kept her fingers firmly lodged between her teeth, fearing that if she took them out she'd start to scream and never stop. *He's suffering enough,* she thought blindly. *How can I, his mother, make it worse by screaming at the sight of him?*

Dear God, why was this baby so deformed while Elizabeth was perfect? Meghann felt hot, salty tears run down her face and land on the hands clenched to her mouth.

Poor baby, she thought, looking down with pity and revulsion at the thing shrieking madly. Just like those others . . . the spawn of two vampires resulting in hideously deformed offspring, freaks.

Strong hands grabbed her shoulders and Meghann did scream, an unrestrained sound full of fear and desolation and a touch of madness.

"No, no." Simon rocked her from behind, holding her tightly. "It's all right, Meghann . . . not as bad as it looks. I wanted to wait until you recovered your strength a bit and then I'd explain . . .

"Damn you!" he thundered at Charles, dragging a shuffling mortal toward the cradle. "You should have fed him while Meghann nursed Elizabeth."

"You know he has no set feeding schedule," Charles explained hurriedly. "He hasn't needed to feed in two nights."

"Don't bother me with explanations—just feed him so Meghann can put her mind at ease. Sweetheart, look . . . look, I tell you!"

Ruthlessly, Simon held Meghann's head in place, forcing her to watch as Charles lifted the baby out of his crib and placed him at the mortal's neck.

Meghann saw the vicious punctures dotting the man's neck and wrists and knew the mortal had already been bled heavily, must be spelled to be this docile. This must be where Simon got the blood he fed her before.

He's a child molester, Charles said to Meghann while he held the man in place. *Don't pity him—if there were any justice in the world, he'd suffer far worse than being slowly bled to death by a vampire baby.*

The baby stopped crying when his lips made contact with the mortal's flesh—must smell his blood, Meghann thought irreverently. The small, sharp fangs settled in the mortal's jugular and the baby drank the blood as thirstily as Elizabeth had drunk milk from Meghann's breast.

As he fed, a startling metamorphosis occurred. The translucent skin that displayed knotted veins disappeared, its place taken by skin of a pale, milky shade. Meghann shook off Simon's grasp and put a cautious hand on the infant's face, lifting up one eyelid. Yes, the blood had even given color to his eyes, transforming them to a peculiar but arresting shade of silvery gray.

At her touch, the baby pulled away from her fingers and hissed . . . a genuine hiss no different from the sound a snake might make. Meghann pulled away, chilled at this fresh evidence of how alien her child was.

"No," she choked out. How could a baby glare like that, fix her with a stare of hatred, and spit in that sibilant hiss unlike anything she'd ever heard before? What was wrong with him?

He's evil, a voice whispered slyly. *He's the abomination Guy tried to spare the world by killing you. Maybe it would have been better—*

"No!" she screamed again and turned on her heel, running from the room as fast as she could. *She* was the abomination—what else would you call a mother that couldn't stand the sight of her own flesh and blood? She had to get out of that room, had to think and get herself together. She had to try and accept what she'd just seen, had to find a way to be a mother to that poor, monstrous . . .

"Meghann!"

"Let her go," she heard Simon say as she hurried out into the freezing night.

* * *

She had no idea how long she walked until the sub-zero temperature and frigid wind blowing in from the sea penetrated her misery as well as her normal resistance to cold. Shivering, Meghann glanced around and saw no familiar landmarks, only an endless stretch of white sand and the dark outline of palatial mansions she thought out of place amidst the wild beauty of the Hamptons.

She sat down at the edge of the shore, the icy water of the tide almost touching her feet, and curled up into a ball, her knees drawn up to her chest in an effort to keep warm. Of course, she could fly back to the house but she wasn't ready to go back yet.

Meghann put her chin on her knees and glared moodily at the black sea and horizon, not really seeing it—not seeing anything but her son's face. It wasn't the grotesqueries of his prefeeding state that tormented her, that made her flee the house . . . it was that snarl he gave her when she touched him. Was it that he sensed her horror and rejected her before she could reject him?

Meghann sobbed, hating herself for not loving her son as she'd loved her daughter from the moment Simon put her in her arms. Where was that warm surge of feeling that welled up inside her when she thought of Elizabeth, of those innocent green eyes reflecting back at her, her sweet face scrunched up in sleep? Was she so shallow, so loathsome that her love for Elizabeth was based only on her daughter's comeliness? Was she only capable of loving a pretty child? As she sat chilled by more than the winter cold, fresh sobs burst from her and she wished God would strike her down. . . .

"Stop that this instant."

Meghann was too heartsick to be startled and allowed Simon to wrap her in a sable-lined cloak, forgetting her usual protestations of animal rights and the cruelty of fur coats. Nor did she pull away from the strong arms that wrapped around her.

"I won't have you tearing yourself apart this way. Of course you're disturbed . . . do you think I wasn't shocked when Doctor Winslow pulled Mikal out of you?"

Mikal—Meghann nodded at the name she and Simon had agreed upon for their son. Mikal John Khalid Baldevar. John for Dr. Dee and Meghann's father, Khalid for Simon's slain friend, and Mikal as a variation on Michael, the name of Simon's beloved nephew.

"Oh, Simon . . ." she started to say but she was still crying too hard for speech. Finally, she looked up and beseeched, *What's wrong with him?*

The arms holding her close became like iron and the line of his jaw hardened before Simon answered tightly, "There is nothing wrong with our son, Meghann."

"Nothing wrong!" she exclaimed, shocked out of her tears by his matter-of-fact denial. "How can you say that? Didn't you see . . ."

Meghann broke off because she already knew the answer—Simon didn't see, would never see anything wrong with the son he'd wanted for so long, his heir and his hope of seeing daylight again.

"Didn't you see?" Simon demanded and hauled her roughly to her feet. "Didn't you see the blood replenish him, make him whole? I know what you're thinking, Meghann . . . you worry that our son will always have to hide his face . . ."

Meghann nodded, more tears escaping her when she thought of explaining to a small child why he couldn't be seen, must be kept hidden like some guilty secret.

"No, Meghann," Simon said and shook her slightly. "He isn't like Alcuin. Did the priest's skin change because he fed? Once Mikal drinks, his deformities fade away. . . ."

"For how long?" Meghann demanded. "What will

we do if we . . . if we take him outside and he suddenly changes . . ."

"He'll grow out of it . . . just as Elizabeth will change from a chubby infant to a beautiful young woman someday. Don't look at me like that, Meghann. I do not speak from fervent delusion but fact. When Mikal was newborn, the blood only healed him for a few hours. But each night his periods of remission grow longer; now he remains well for two nights after drinking. That's why I believe the deformities will fade altogether as he grows older."

"He hates me," Meghann said in a small voice and squeezed her eyes shut.

"He's naught but a senseless babe, incapable of hating anyone. I should have warned you not to touch him while he fed—his reaction was no more than an animal protecting his food, warning you off. He thought you were going to take his blood."

Meghann nodded and felt some small relief at Simon's explanation but there were other things about her son that disturbed her. "If there's nothing wrong with him, then why are you keeping him shut up in that miserable dark room like a leper? Why isn't he in the nursery with Elizabeth?"

"His cries disturb her. As for the room, Mikal is a vampire. He has our abilities but none of our intelligence yet. He moves things around with no thought to his safety. It was necessary to keep him in a room with no objects that he might fling around and harm himself with should they hit him. As for the dark, his eyes are extremely sensitive to light. Even candlelight causes severe discomfort—Doctor Winslow thinks prolonged exposure to any kind of light might result in blindness."

Appalled, Meghann could only gape at him . . . this was the worst news yet! "You mean he has to live in pitch-black for the rest of his life? Simon, my God! How can you say nothing's wrong . . . would you like to live like a bat? You thought the offspring of two vampires would live in sunlight and now it turns out we have better tolerance to light than Mikal does!"

"Mikal is not even a year old," Simon said, and she detected a cutting edge to his even tone. "I never thought he'd be born with the promise of the philosophers' stone. I thought he'd grow into it, realize his full potential when he grew to manhood. His eyes will strengthen just as his limbs will grow and soon he'll enjoy the day just as Elizabeth does."

"What if his eyes don't improve? What if he never adapts?"

Simon raised an eyebrow. "What do you suggest, Meghann? Shall I kill him?"

"Of course not!" she cried. "It's just . . . it's just if he's forced to live in shadows, it'll be him to pay and suffer, not us! And we're the ones who deserve it because we brought him into the world, he didn't ask to be born . . ."

"My love," Simon said softly and stroked her face with his fingertips. "How can you despise yourself and think you're an unnatural mother? If you don't love your son as much as Elizabeth, then why do you weep so at the thought of his pain? Dry your eyes, sweet. I don't wish to see you weeping when I say good-bye."

"Good-bye?" Meghann repeated, dumbfounded. She looked up and the meaning of the cashmere overcoat Simon wore finally penetrated her senses. He wouldn't put that on just to find her.

"Yes, good-bye," Simon said and took her hands. "There isn't much time to explain . . . Mikal and I are due at the airport in an hour."

"Mikal? What about Elizabeth?" *What about me?*

"Elizabeth remains with you."

"You're leaving her—leaving me? Goddamn you, Simon!" Meghann screamed and yanked her hands away, green eyes blazing with fury and hurt. "What is it—you don't need me now that you have your precious son? And Elizabeth . . . you snake, I thought you loved her! How can you just leave your daughter? Is it because she's mortal so she serves no purpose?"

"Isn't that what everyone will think?" Simon asked with a bitter smirk. "What a fiend Lord Baldevar is—he abandoned Meghann when she presented him with a puny mortal girl instead of the philosophers' stone. There's no need to attack her or her daughter. Lord Baldevar's issue is no threat to anyone. Meghann, the fools will never even think we had two children. They won't harm Elizabeth and I can go into hiding with Mikal."

"Was this what you planned all along?" Meghann demanded. "Was all your talk of us raising our child together lies to soothe me? Did you always intend to take my baby from me? How can you take Mikal from me and give up Elizabeth without a second thought? Why are you doing this? Don't you want me and Elizabeth?"

"Meghann, you talk as though we'll never see each other again . . . as though I'll never see my daughter. How can you think I don't want you—after all I've done to keep you by my side? I love you . . . love you so much I won't refuse if you insist on coming with Mikal and me. But Elizabeth remains here with your friends."

"No!" Meghann cried. "No, no! I'll never leave my daughter. I love her." Meghann thought of the tiny white fist curled up on her breast, of her daughter's innocent trusting gaze when she looked at her mother, and knew she could never bear to be parted from her. But what about Mikal? How could she allow Simon to whisk him off to God knows where?

"I know you love Elizabeth. Do you think I do not?" Simon took her hands again, kneeling before her on the cold sand. "Haven't you told me a thousand times what you want for your child? To grow up well loved and cared for, to have the school days and friends and fun any child is entitled to? Meghann, Elizabeth can have all that with Doctor Winslow looking after her during the day. And she can have something I didn't dare hope to give her until tonight . . . her mother. I cannot ask you to give up the child you've wanted for so long."

"Mikal is my child too. Why do you want them raised separately? Why can't Elizabeth and I come with you?"

Simon's hands tightened over hers until Meghann cried out but his grip didn't relax. "Meghann, don't you see how different our children are? I was not deluding you all these months I said we'd never be separated again. I fully expected one child that we would raise together. Then, when we learned you were having twins, I had the first inkling this could happen but I never said anything because there was no point in upsetting you with idle speculation. But now . . . Meghann, Mikal will have to be raised in absolute secrecy. The faintest whisper of his existence and there isn't a vampire in the world that wouldn't try to slaughter him out of fear of what he'll become. I'll not have my son grow up feeling like a hunted animal . . . I'll take him somewhere remote, away from crowds and prying eyes. It will be a lonely existence but he'll never have anything to compare it to. But, darling, there is no reason to force Elizabeth to live that way too and I know a life in obscurity is the last thing you want for her. Mikal might not develop the ability to walk in daylight until he's well into his teens . . . do you think he won't grow to hate and resent his twin, envy her freedom to roam about during the day, to be accepted by society? For even if he adapts to the sun earlier, I still won't be able to chance him being seen until he's capable of defending himself from our enemies. Can't you see how Mikal will grow to despise the mortal sister that won't have to hide, as he will? Just as she will envy him the powers she won't possess, the powers that might endanger her if he should attempt to harm her in a fit of rage? The children must be raised separately, Meghann. First, because our enemies must see you with Elizabeth, must believe she's the only child of our union until Mikal is strong enough to withstand any attack. Also, once she and Mikal are adults . . . he with the ability to enjoy daylight as she does and she transformed so she is no defenseless mortal . . . then, we can all reunite with no fear of our enemies or worry that the twins will hate each other."

Elizabeth transformed? Someday see blood lust shining in her daughter's eyes? Meghann shivered and put the unpleasant image from her mind. She need not think about that for years, and anyway, it would be Elizabeth's place to decide whether she wanted to remain mortal or become a vampire. No one would force immortality on her—Meghann would make sure of that.

But as to the rest of what Simon said . . . Meghann understood now. She saw how the children would grow to hate each other—Mikal wanting Elizabeth's freedom to enjoy life and the sun with no fear of discovery, Elizabeth wanting what any child would see as glamorous magical powers. Only as adults would they be able to see past resentment and perhaps come to love each other.

"Yes," Meghann said and nodded at Simon. She knelt down next to him, pushing an errant lock of chestnut hair off his forehead. "But you can't raise an infant alone. Who'll watch him when you feed? Simon, it's too much . . . you'll need help. But what other vampire can we trust besides Charles?"

"I won't be alone, little one." Simon grinned at her puzzled frown and went on. "Mikal and I are traveling to Adelaide."

"Adelaide?" Thunderstruck, Meghann could only gape while Simon laughed gently.

"Yes, Meghann—Adelaide. Who else could I entrust my son's care to but my own good nurse?"

"But . . . but . . . you mean you transformed her? But I thought she died, that everyone you loved died in that first battle with Alcuin."

"Everyone at my side certainly did die. I sent Adelaide away long before Alcuin arrived at the estate. Women, even vampire women, have no place on a battlefield. Since the massacre, Adelaide's existence has been a secret—her true identity known only to her and me. It was she who gave me shelter all those years I wanted the world to believe I was dead. And it's she who'll help me raise my son."

And it's she who Mikal will come to think of as his mother, Meghann thought, envying a woman she didn't know. But it was wrong to think that way and Meghann knew it. She should be thankful Mikal would have a mother figure in his life, glad Simon wouldn't have to raise their son all by himself.

"I'll be able to leave him in Adelaide's care and make secret visits every now and again, Meghann . . . to visit you and our daughter. Too, I'll want to appear in public so our enemies do not forget my existence. I am not overly concerned that anyone will attempt to attack you now—particularly since they won't perceive Elizabeth as a threat. Besides, with your strength back and Doctor Tarleton at your side, I believe the two of you can repel any attack."

Meghann smiled at the compliment and tried to hold back her tears. What had happened to her? Years before, even in those heated minutes after she found out what Simon had done to Jimmy, she'd have been glad to be free of him, would feel nothing but a sense of relief at his departure. But now . . . now it was only the thought of leaving her daughter that kept Meghann from throwing herself into Simon's arms and insisting he take her with him.

"Ah, Meghann," Simon whispered and bent her back gently, lowering her to the ground with the sable coat serving as a blanket. "Don't look so sad, little one, or I won't be able to leave. What are the few years it will take for Mikal to grow to manhood compared to the forty years we were without each other? And I'll see you and Elizabeth, just as you can come visit Mikal. Don't cry, my sweet, don't think this is the end. A few short years from now and we'll be together forever. Come on, sweetheart. Send me off with love and not tears."

With the soft fur coat beneath her and Simon's warm, hard body covering hers, Meghann didn't feel the cold, didn't think of her heartbreak as his hands and mouth roved over her body. It felt like Simon was committing her flesh to memory with each caress, just as her eager hands sought him out for sensory memories after he left. Each touch, each mouthful of blood she swallowed after he guided her head to his neck, this was what she'd hold in her heart after he left her.

Perhaps because she was so newly recovered, Simon didn't feed from her but instead attached his mouth to her breast, just as their daughter had done earlier. But instead of the warm gentleness she felt when she fed Elizabeth, Meghann felt an electric jolt go through her that intensified when Simon kissed her again and she tasted her milk on his tongue.

Afterward, Meghann dressed slowly, her heart galloping and her hands shaking so hard it seemed like hours before she finally got every button on her dress. The lovemaking had banished all her sadness; now Meghann felt she could part with Simon and Mikal without tears. But there was one thing she'd do for her son before she allowed Simon to take him away from her.

"Listen to me," Meghann said urgently and grabbed Simon's hands in a grip almost as strong as the one he'd used on her earlier. "Before I gave birth, I made you promise to raise our children the way you knew I wanted—with love and sensitivity. You swear to me you won't raise Mikal to hate and think he's superior to those he feeds from. You just remember that if you make him think mortals are nothing, you'll be raising him to think his own sister is nothing."

"You think I would rear my son with no sense of love or obligation toward his own kin? He shall feel the same love and reverence toward Elizabeth that I do . . . she is my daughter, not some insignificant mortal like the rest of the human race. Hush," Simon said and put his hand over her mouth when she started to speak again. "I know very well what you want. I give you my word that Mikal will not be raised to be no more than a killer with no sensitivity."

Meghann accepted his promise with a nod and started back toward the house but Simon grabbed her to him and she thought she felt him tremble slightly. That's when she realized the effort behind his leaving her with Elizabeth. This was the first truly unselfish thing Simon Baldevar had ever done. After all, he could have hidden Elizabeth from her, or taken her and Elizabeth with him when he went into hiding with Mikal. But he hadn't done that . . . he wanted his daughter to have the best life she could and if he had to sacrifice his consort to give Elizabeth her mother, he'd do it.

He's changed, Meghann thought. Not completely—the jealous lover and ruthless vampire were still there but they were no longer the only parts of his heart and soul. Now there was something else in Simon and she had to help him develop it.

"I know what I'll have to say in public," she said softly. "I'll have to tell the world Lord Baldevar is nothing but a low-life fiend—abandoning his daughter just because she's human. But when Elizabeth is old enough to ask questions, I'll tell her that her father . . . my husband . . . is a good man, one she should be proud to call Father."

There was no higher compliment she could bestow upon him and Simon knew it. He grabbed her close, hugging her tightly against him. He said nothing in reply, simply held her for a while with bone-crushing intensity until his grip finally relaxed and they started walking back to the house, arm in arm.

She hadn't wandered that far from the house, Meghann realized, only a few miles. Of course, they could have flown back to the house but Meghann didn't think Simon was any more eager to begin their separation than she was. This silent walk was the last time they might have alone together for a very long time.

When they rounded the curve to the house, Meghann saw Charles and Lee waiting at the end of driveway, next to the enormous Bentley. Lee had a small blue bundle in his arms.

"Elizabeth?" Meghann asked Charles briefly.

"Sleeping inside. I didn't think you'd want her out here in the cold."

Meghann nodded and stretched her hands out to Lee—she had to hold her son at least once before he and Simon left.

Without his disfigurements and horrible crying, Meghann was able to examine her son and saw he was a nice-looking little boy. He lacked the promise of beauty Elizabeth already had but she saw things to make her smile . . . most particularly those pure silver eyes, unique and quite beautiful in their own right.

"My father had black hair," Meghann said in a thick voice as she ran her hands over the small thatch of inky black hair on Mikal's forehead. "But, Simon . . . why is he so thin? He must be at least three pounds lighter than Elizabeth."

"It's his intestinal lining," Simon explained. "He cannot digest anything but blood. Don't look so alarmed, little one. Would you feed Elizabeth anything but milk in this stage of her development? I'm sure as he grows older, he'll develop tolerance to food."

So far, all of Simon's hopes seemed pinned on Mikal's improving as he grew older. *Please, God*, Meghann prayed. *Let it happen the way Simon thinks it will—let my son get some enjoyment out of life, let him feel the sun warming him, let him have an appetite for something besides human blood.* Suddenly Meghann was glad her children would be raised separately, glad Elizabeth would never see her small brother clinging to a human host and drinking his blood. What would that sight do to her daughter, seeing her vampire brother feed night after night and then trying to go out and fit into the mortal world, knowing all the while what lurked in her house?

Elizabeth must never see us feed, Meghann said, and Charles nodded. She saw Simon's eyes narrow briefly but if he'd heard her he said nothing, merely held out his arms for her to give him Mikal.

As Meghann handed him the baby, something monstrous passed before her eyes, a premonition of such evil she cried out in fear and staggered against Charles.

"Meghann?" Charles said in alarm while Simon stared at her anxiously, Mikal cradled against him.

"I'm okay," she managed. "Still a little woozy, I guess." She saw that Simon plainly didn't believe her but what could she tell him? For one of the few times in her vampire life, the Sight had failed her. Normally Meghann's visions were very clear but this . . . this was no more than a brief flash of fear before it vanished. Meghann had no idea what, if anything, she'd been warned against. Later, after Simon left, she'd try to clarify the vision through meditation.

Simon strapped Mikal into a car seat and shut the car door, shaking hands with Charles and Lee before he turned to Meghann. Their good-bye had been said on the beach; she knew there'd be no impassioned parting with Charles and Lee standing there.

Simon's lips barely grazed hers as he leaned down to her. *I love you, Meghann.*

"Be careful," Meghann whispered fiercely into his ear, the premonition still disturbing her.

She felt his hands twine in her hair, then jerk a handful of hair to make her look up and blink nervously at the hard light shining in his gold eyes. *What is it?*

You're mine, Meghann. I'd be most displeasured if you forgot that during the time we're apart. With that silent directive, Simon spun away her from her and got into the car, not even turning around to give her another glance.

The hell with you, Meghann thought in outrage as she watched the car lumber away. *I'm not property to be called yours!* Who did Simon Baldevar think he was? And to think she'd been all but ready to canonize him a few minutes ago! Why, he hadn't changed at all.

No, that wasn't true—Simon had changed. He'd changed a great deal if he'd give up the woman he'd fought and schemed for with all his power simply to make his mortal daughter happy. And he'd entrusted her care to Charles as well as Lee . . . and Charles was one of his bitterest enemies only a few months ago.

What a complex mix of pure tenderness and absolute malevolence Simon was, Meghann thought as she watched the car carrying him and her son disappear from sight. A year ago she hadn't understood that, hadn't seen anything but the malice that allowed him to kill Alcuin and try to destroy Jimmy so easily. Now, though, Meghann knew however strong the evil inside him was, it was tempered by the love he had for her and their children.

But she worried about that evil for it was just as strong a part of him as any softness he might feel toward those he chose to love. Maybe it was a good thing he'd left, a good thing Elizabeth would never be tainted by the darkness in her father's soul. She and Charles might be vampires, but they didn't glory in causing death and pain the way Simon did.

Meghann shuddered when she thought of what Mikal might become with Simon raising him but could think of nothing to do to help her son. Nothing short of death would separate Simon from his son, and even if she did get Mikal away from him, Meghann didn't think she was strong enough to protect her son from all those that would try to harm him. Nor did she wish to go into hiding and have poor Elizabeth raised like some hermit just because Mikal couldn't be seen. No, it was better to let Simon take Mikal. She just had to pray Simon would honor his vow to her and bring Mikal up to be more than a bloodthirsty soulless killer.

Meghann heard a faint whimper inside the house and knew Elizabeth was waking up, ready to be fed again. As she started toward the house, she thought she had far more than she'd dared to dream of last year when she found out Simon was alive. She may have lost Alcuin and Jimmy but she had a beautiful daughter, her dearest friends at her side to help her raise Elizabeth, and the knowledge that Mikal would be safe with his father. She also had years to decide whether she wanted to be Simon Baldevar's consort, despite all she knew about him.

I have all I can hope for, Meghann thought and turned to smile at her friends. "Come on . . . I hear Elizabeth crying."

ABOUT THE AUTHOR

Trisha Baker makes her home in New York and New Orleans. She is currently working on the third novel in the CRIMSON trilogy. She loves hearing from her readers; you may write to her c/o Pinnacle Books. Please include a self-addressed, stamped envelope if you wish to receive a response. You can also visit her Web site at www.crimsonkiss.com.

Scare Up One of These Pinnacle Horrors

__**Haunted**
  by Tamara Thorne   0-7860-1090-8   **$5.99**US/**$7.99**CAI

__**Thirst**
  by Michael Cecilione   0-7860-1091-6   **$5.99**US/**$7.99**CAI

__**The Haunting**
  by Ruby Jean Jensen   0-7860-1095-9   **$5.99**US/**$7.99**CAI

__**The Summoning**
  by Bentley Little   0-7860-1480-6   **$6.99**US/**$8.99**CAI

Call toll free **1-888-345-BOOK** to order by phone or use this coupo
to order by mail.

Name_____

Address_____

City_____ State_____ Zip_____

Please send me the books that I checked above.

I am enclosing	$_____
Plus postage and handling*	$_____
Sales tax (in NY, TN, and DC)	$_____
Total amount enclosed	$_____

*Add $2.50 for the first book and $.50 for each additional book.

Send check or money order (no cash or CODs) to: **Kensington Publishin
Corp., Dept. C.O., 850 Third Avenue, 16th Floor, New York, NY 10022**

Prices and numbers subject to change without notice.

All orders subject to availability.

Visit our website at **www.kensingtonbooks.com**.